"I didn't come here to gloat.

"I came," Garth continued, "because I thought you might need someone to talk to…because I was concerned."

"Concerned for whom, Garth?" Claudia froze. "Certainly not for me, the woman, the wife, you betrayed so easily."

"Claudia, for God's sake…I came here to talk to you about Tara."

"But we are talking about her, aren't we?" she said softly.

Across the silence that divided them, their eyes met and it was Garth's that fell first.

"Claudia," he began rawly, but she shook her head. One look at her face told Garth that he would be wasting his time trying to reason with her. He had handled things badly.

As he let himself out of the house, he reminded himself that there was that school of belief that said the greater the love, the greater the hatred following any form of betrayal, but his betrayal…

There were always two sides to every story, and she hadn't ever been prepared to listen while he told her his.

Penny Jordan's novels "…touch every emotion."
—*Romantic Times*

PENNY JORDAN
TO LOVE, HONOR AND BETRAY

MIRA

ISBN 1-55166-444-5

TO LOVE, HONOR AND BETRAY

Printed in U.S.A.

TO LOVE, HONOR AND BETRAY

1

——➤ ◂——

Lying across her mother's bed, long legs dangling over the side, one hand propping up her chin, the other pushing aside the thick, dark heaviness of her long, curly hair, and waiting while her mother put the final touches to her make-up, Tara started to read from the local newspaper she had stopped off to buy as she drove through town.

'"Town Honours Prominent Local Businesswoman,"' she read aloud, telling her mother unnecessarily, 'that's you,' before continuing, '"Last Saturday evening, a celebratory dinner was held in the town's twelfth-century Knights Hospitallers' Hall to mark a decade of fundraising by the Upper Charfont Beneficiary Trust and to honour one of its founder members and, more recently, its chairperson, Mrs Claudia Wallace."'

'Sounds good, Ma,' Tara told Claudia in the soft, husky voice whose intonations and idiosyncrasies were so exactly those of her mother that when Tara was at home, callers often confused the two of them. She turned back to the article.

'"Over the past decade, Mrs Wallace has worked tirelessly and successfully to promote the interests and activities of the Trust and it is thanks to her that it has seen donations rise so spectacularly. Not only has Mrs Wallace worked selflessly to raise funds for charity, she has, in addition, privately given her time and her skills as a trained probation officer and the senior partner in a successful local private counselling and advisory practice to train and, where necessary, give her own services to help with the charity's work.

'"In recognition of her committed involvement with the community, the Town Council has proposed that the new day care and recreation centre for physically disadvantaged residents be named after her...."'

Tara looked away from the newspaper and studied her mother's reflection in the mirror.

'You don't look forty-five,' she told her judiciously. 'In fact...have you *ever* thought of remarrying, Ma?' she asked her mother curiously. 'I mean, it's over ten years now since you and Dad divorced and...'

Very carefully, Claudia put down her mascara and turned to face her daughter. At twenty-three, Tara might now, in the eyes of the world, be very much an adult young woman but to her she was still her daughter, her little girl, the most precious gift that life had given her, and as such, Claudia had every mother's need to protect and guard her.

'After all, it's not as though there aren't at least a dozen men that *I* know of who'd love to marry you, given half the chance.'

Claudia gave her a wry look and suggested, 'I think that's rather an exaggeration, don't you?'

'Well, there's Charles Weatherall and Paul Avery and then there's John Fellows and, of course, there's Luke,' she slipped in.

'Luke is a client, that's all,' Claudia told her calmly, but she still turned her head away just in case that small flutter of sensation she could feel inside should somehow or other reveal itself outwardly. Not that there was any reason why the mention of Luke's name *should* cause that disturbing slight palpitation of her heartbeat, she reminded herself severely. For a start, he was at least seven years her junior.

'Mmm... So you *haven't* considered remarrying, then,' Tara repeated. Claudia studied her daughter thoughtfully.

Despite all her attempts to sound and look light-hearted, Claudia could sense Tara's tension.

'I haven't, no,' she conceded, and then waited.

'Mmm... Have you seen anything of Dad recently?' Claudia's stomach muscles knotted. Now it was her turn to hide the quick, fierce stab of tension that struck through her at Tara's carefully casual mention of Garth, and instinctively Claudia looked away from her, letting the smooth, silky bell of her blonde bob swing forward to conceal her face as she responded, 'No. No, I haven't. Is there any reason why I should have done?'

'No, none at all. It's just that... well, Dad's been seeing quite a lot of Rachel Bedlington, that's the new account executive who joined the company just after Christmas. She's in her early thirties. Dad head-hunted her from Faversham Bayliss. She specialises in women-focused ads. You know the type. New woman drives the car while wimpish boyfriend looks on.'

'Yes, I know the type,' Claudia agreed calmly, and it wasn't just the advertisements she was referring to. She could see Garth's new account executive already—elegant, intelligent, witty, young... She would be besotted with him, of course. What young woman in her position wouldn't be? And, in all fairness, Claudia had to admit that her ex-husband might be fifty, but he was still physically an outstandingly good-looking and a very masculine man—even more so now perhaps in his maturity than he had been when he had been young.

'I don't think it's anything serious,' Tara hastened to add, but Claudia could see from her expression, hear in her voice that, on the contrary, she thought it was extremely serious. Taking a deep breath, she turned her head to look smilingly at her daughter—*their* daughter—hers and Garth's.

'It's all right, darling,' she told her equably. 'Your father is, after all, perfectly free to have a relationship with someone else. We are divorced and have been for ten years.'

'I know.'

As she watched the expressions chase one another across Tara's face, Claudia acknowledged that physically no one would ever guess that they were mother and daughter.

For a start, Tara was a good eight inches taller than she was herself, but then that seemed to be the usual way of things these days. She didn't think she had a single friend whose daughter didn't tower inches above them.

Tara also had completely different colouring from her mother's. Where Claudia had a pale, delicate, English-rose complexion and the soft blonde hair to go with it, Tara's skin tone was much, much warmer, her eyes darker and her hair a rich dark brown tumbling past her shoulders in heavy, lustrous curls. Her deep green eyes were Garth's, and like her, his hair, too, was very dark, but unlike Tara's, Garth's was straight.

'Dad said that you were going to be nominated for the Businesswoman of the Year award,' Tara announced abruptly.

Now Claudia couldn't conceal her reaction.

How on earth had *Garth* known that? *She* had only been told of the nomination a matter of days ago herself.

'He's very proud of you, Ma,' Tara asserted. 'We both are. Everyone thinks you're wonderful,' she added, 'and you are.'

'The last time you flattered me like this, I seem to remember it had something to do with the fact that you'd completely burned out one of my best pans,' Claudia reminded her dryly.

'Boiling eggs, which I forgot,' Tara agreed laughing, and then suddenly the laughter died.

'Ryland is going back to Boston at the end of the month,' she told Claudia quietly. 'He's asked me to go with him.'

'For a holiday?' Claudia asked lightly even while she *knew*, guessed, sensed what was coming, felt it in every doom-laden wave of panic that struck her body.

'No…well, at first, perhaps. Ry…'

Ryland Johnson was Tara's American boyfriend, seven years her senior. Tara had brought him home to meet Claudia at Christmas, and she had liked him immediately and immensely. It was obvious to Claudia even then that the two of them were head over heels in love.

'He only planned to stay over here for a year and… He wants me to meet his family and his friends. He wants…'

Tara bit her lip.

'I know what you're thinking,' she told her mother, adding pleadingly, 'Please don't be unhappy. America isn't so very far away, not these days, and you… I love him so much, Ma,' she confessed helplessly, flinging herself bodily into Claudia's arms as the tears filled her eyes. 'I *know* how you must be feeling and *I* wish, too, that I could have fallen in love with someone from home…that we could have lived here close to you and… I'm going to miss you so much.'

Claudia closed her eyes, not to suppress her own tears but to suppress the sick feeling of dread that was surging over her.

'Does…have you told your father yet?' she managed to ask through dry lips.

Tara shook her head.

'No. I wanted to tell you first. Dad just thinks I'm going for a holiday. Well, officially, that's all it is, but…I'm not, and it will be much easier for me to get a visa that way. I don't know which I'm dreading the most,' she added with a shaky smile, 'the vetting I'm going to get from the US government or the one Ryland says I'll get from his aunt. If anything, I suspect his aunt's will be worse. Apparently, she's fantastically wealthy and very WASP about whom Ryland marries. Ryland says she's a terrifying combination of old New England blood and equally old New England money.'

Tara giggled as she released Claudia and stepped back. 'I'm dreading having to meet her,' she announced indifferently. 'According to Ry, she's going to want to know everything there is to know about my background. Not that I *ve* any worries in that department. After all, your family and Dad's go back for ever, don't they?

'Ma…what is it? Please don't look like that,' Tara begged shakily as she saw her mother's expression.

Claudia had gone white, the bone structure of her pretty heart-shaped face suddenly standing out so sharply that Tara had an unnerving and distressing image of how her mother might look in twenty years' time. Her normal warm and loving soft blue eyes looked so bleak and filled with despair that Tara had to fight to control her own emotions.

'Ma, I *know* how you must feel,' she repeated

huskily, 'but there'll be visits, holidays…and who knows, perhaps Ryland will change his mind once he gets me over there and decide that he doesn't want to marry me after all,' she finished lightly. But Claudia knew that she didn't mean it…didn't *want* to mean it.

'Have you applied for your visa yet?' she managed to ask as she fought to control her reactions to the blow Tara had just unwittingly dealt her.

'I've applied but I haven't got it as yet,' Tara told her cheerfully. 'Not that there should be too much of a problem getting a visitor's visa. It's when Ry and I get married and I need to apply for citizenship that we might have some difficulties. Ryland keeps teasing me that if I can pass his aunt's inspection of my antecedents, then I won't have any problems with the US government and everyone knows how strict they are and how thoroughly they go into a person's background.

'Ma…what is it…what's wrong?' Tara demanded anxiously as her mother gave a small strangled gasp and then covered her mouth with her hand.

'Nothing,' Claudia lied. 'I just don't…I think I may have eaten something that disagreed with me. I just feel a little bit nauseous.'

'If you feel sick, do you think you should be going out this evening, then?' Tara cautioned with maternal solicitude that, at any other time, would have brought Claudia to touched laughter. In that respect, in her nature, her upbringing, her reactions and responses to others, Tara was totally and completely *her* child, even if her swift intelligence and her equally swift assimilation of information were her father's inheritance to her.

'I...I...I *have* to go out,' Claudia told her truthfully. 'I'm giving a talk to the Townswomen's Guild and I can't let them down.'

'You could, but you won't,' Tara corrected her lovingly. 'I'm sorry if I've given you a shock. I...' She dipped her head in the same protectively defensive gesture Claudia herself had adopted earlier. 'I... Ryland asked me to go back to Boston with him several weeks ago, but I couldn't get down to see you before now and I didn't want... I wanted to tell you *myself*...to be *here*. I love him so much, Ma. He's everything I've ever wanted in a man. You *do* like him, don't you?'

'Yes. I do like him,' Claudia agreed truthfully.

'I know how you must be feeling,' Tara had told her when she announced her plans. But could she? How could anyone?

Perhaps she *ought* to have been prepared...to have known...guessed... She had, after all, seen at Christmas how much Tara and Ryland were in love, but she had somehow assumed—because she had wanted, needed, to assume, no doubt—that Ryland had decided to make his future in Britain. Still, even if she had known, what could she have done? How could she have prevented the catastrophe now staring her in the face?

How *could* she prevent it? There was no way. She could only hope and pray, beg God, fate, call it what you would that ruled one's life, to help her.

'I came down specially to tell you,' she heard Tara saying softly. 'I wish I could stay longer, Ma, but I can't. I've got a client meeting in the morning and then I've got to break the news to Dad that it isn't just a few weeks' holiday that I want.' Tara reached out and hugged her mother tightly.

'Please tell me that you'll be happy for me,' she begged in a hoarse little pain-filled whisper.

'I'll be happy for you,' Claudia repeated dutifully, and as she said it she gave up a silent prayer that it would be true and that she *would* be able to be happy for her daughter instead of…

'I'd better let you get to that meeting,' Tara told her mother gruffly as she hugged her a second time even more fiercely than the first. 'I promise we'll both come and see you before we go, and once we're over there I'll want you to come and stay. I want to show you off to Ryland's family so that they can see how lucky I am to have such a special, wonderful mother. You *are* special and wonderful and I do love you very, very much…and I think I'm just so lucky to have you for my mother, to have you and Dad as my parents.'

The subject of Claudia's talk to the members of the Townswomen's Guild had originally been spurred by her awareness that many of her closest friends had recently had to readapt to a married life where their children had flown the nest and, so far as nature was concerned, they themselves were in many ways now redundant.

'It's a matter of what you actually *do* with your time,' one friend had commented woefully to Claudia, adding self-critically, 'I never thought I'd ever be the kind of mother who couldn't wait for her own children to produce their children so that she could be a grandmother but…'

'We aren't old in the same way that our mothers and their mothers before them were old at our age,' another friend had told her. 'After all, in terms of life expectancy, fifty is nothing these days, but it's what you *do* with those years…how you *fill* them…the fact that you feel a need to fill them when, for virtually the whole of your adult life, what you've been struggling to do is to *make* time, not fill it.'

But after the bombshell Tara had dropped on her, Claudia knew that she couldn't follow through with her original plans without being in danger of betraying her own emotions. So instead, and to their bemusement, she rather suspected, she gave the women an abbreviated talk on the problems that could face new, first-time fathers.

After the meeting, several people wanted to talk to her, to congratulate her in the main on the article that had appeared in the local paper and that Tara had read out to her earlier. Just listening to them brought back such a sharp mental image of Tara lying on her bed that she could hardly bear to have them speak.

It was a relief to escape and finally be on her own; it was even a relief to know that she was going to *be* alone once she got home. At least, it was a relief to know that Tara wouldn't be there, that she could finally relax her guard a little and allow herself to show some real emotion.

The intensity of her own sense of foreboding and doom, her own fear and despair had shaken her. Why had she not guessed…realised… prepared herself for something like this? Why had she allowed herself to become so complacent, to think…

'Claudia.' She stopped, forcing herself to smile as one of her closest friends approached her. 'I saw Tara driving through town earlier. You *are* lucky to have a daughter and to have such a close relationship with her,' she commented enviously, before adding, 'Not that you don't deserve it. You and Tara are both lucky,' she amended firmly. 'My boys…' She paused. 'Do you know, if you weren't so…so *you*…there are times when I could almost hate you. You've got everything right.'

'Not everything,' Claudia felt bound to point out to her quietly, reminding her when she gave her a surprised look, 'Garth and I are no longer married, Chris.'

'You're divorced. Yes, I know, but even your divorce has been a model of what a divorce should be. Neither of you has ever been heard to utter a word of criticism against the other. Despite the trauma you were going through at the time, I can remember how determined both you and Garth were that Tara shouldn't suffer. It was all done so…so quietly and discreetly, with

Garth moving out of Ivy House and buying himself that new place on the other side of town.

'But it isn't just the *way* the two of you handled your divorce. It's everything even before then. While the rest of us were all complaining about having to manage our careers and bring up our children, you and Garth moved here from London. You gave up your job as a probation officer to be at home with Tara when she was a baby. Then when you and Garth divorced, you set up your own business and worked from home until you were well enough established to branch out and take on office premises.

'I *know* how hard you work—what long hours—and you've always managed to find time for your friends and your charity work. So far as I know, neither you nor Garth has ever missed even one of Tara's school events. You're a wonderful cook—'

'I'm an *adequate* cook,' Claudia interrupted her dryly.

Chris overrode her, insisting, 'You're a wonderful cook, *and* you still look stunning and sexy, as my darling husband frequently reminds me.' She continued firmly, 'I doubt that there's a single one of your friends whose husband, whose partner, hasn't compared her to you at some stage or another and found her wanting.'

'I sincerely hope not,' Claudia declared truthfully.

'Well, it's true,' Chris persisted. 'But more than that, what I envy you most of all for, Claudia, is that you are just such a nice person. You're generous, warm, witty...and honest...so totally honest in everything you do. Claudia, what is it?' she demanded uncertainly as she saw the sudden quick tears fill her friend's eyes. 'I didn't mean to embarrass you...I was just—'

'It's all right,' Claudia assured her hastily. 'I'm just...I'm just a little bit tired. I... Too many late nights,' she fibbed, 'which is why I've promised myself an early one tonight.'

'Yes, I'd better go, as well,' Chris agreed, taking her hint. 'I'll see you on Thursday...it's our week for lunch,' she reminded Claudia.

'I'll be there,' Claudia agreed.

It was still light as Claudia turned off the road and in through the arched gateway in the brick wall that surrounded her home.

She and Garth had first seen Ivy House on a cold snowy day when the branches of the tree had been bare and the ivy clothing the house itself and the brick wall around it frosted white against the mellow backdrop of the Cotswold stone.

The house had originally been built in the eighteenth century as a dower home attached to the estate of the then Sir Vernon Cupshaw. The main house had fallen into disrepair after the Great War, when all three sons of the family had been killed, and the estate had eventually been broken up. Claudia and Garth had bought the house and learned of its history from the last surviving spinster aunt of the original family. Claudia could still remember how the old lady had looked from her to the small bundle that was Tara, whom she had been holding, as she told them, 'This house needs love and I can see that you have it. It also needs children...just as *our* family needed children.' Claudia hadn't been able to tell her what she already knew, which was that Tara would be an *only* child.

They had had to do a great deal of work to turn the house into the comfortable home it now was and, after the breakdown of their marriage, one of the hardest things Claudia had had to prepare herself for was the prospect of losing Ivy House, but Garth had insisted that she was to keep it.

'It's Tara's *home*,' he had reminded her quietly when she had pointed out to him with fierce, bitter passion that she didn't want his charity...that she didn't, in fact, want anything of him. But even then...even then that had not been entirely true and they had both known it. But Garth, whether out of guilt or compassion, had refrained from telling her so.

To discover that the man she had loved, trusted, put her faith, her whole self in, had betrayed her, had been almost more than Claudia could bear. To know that he had slept with another woman, touched her, embraced her, physically known and shared with her the intimacy that Claudia had believed was hers alone had almost destroyed her and it had certainly destroyed their marriage. How could it not have done so?

But Chris was right about one thing. She and Garth had made a pact to remember that, whatever their own differences, whatever their own pain, they would not allow the death of their love for one another to touch Tara, their precious and much loved daughter, all the more loved because for Claudia she would always be her only child. The doctors had told her that after…

'You are so lucky,' Chris had commented enviously and Claudia was remembering those words as she stopped her car and climbed out.

The ivy still clothed the front of the house but now it had been joined by the wisteria she and Garth had planted the year after they moved in. It had finished flowering now, and its silvery green tendrils rustled softly in the evening air as Claudia inserted her key in the lock.

Upper Charfont was the kind of vintage small English town where up until very recently back doors were frequently left unlocked and neighbours knew all of one another's business. Claudia had been a little wary at first about moving into that kind of environment, but Garth had gently reassured her, pointing out the advantages of a semi-rural upbringing for Tara and the fact that the town was less than an hour's drive away from the small Cotswold village to which her parents had recently retired.

Her father was an army man, Brigadier Peter Fulshaw, and it had been through him that she had originally met Garth, who had been one of his young officers. The peripatetic nature of her childhood, moving from one army base to another, had meant that Claudia had a very strong yearning to give her own child the kind of settled existence she herself had never experienced, the chance to develop friendships that would be with her all her life, and Garth had agreed with her. On that, as well as on so many other subjects, they had thought exactly alike, but even then he…

Claudia tried to shake aside her memories as she let herself into the house and locked the door behind her. But tonight for some reason, success in burying thoughts of the past eluded her. Everywhere she looked there were reminders of Garth and the life they had shared. The wall lights in the hallway, which she had just switched on, had been a find they had made in an antique shop in Brighton, pounced on with great glee and borne triumphantly home where Garth had carried them off to his workroom above the garage to clean and polish them.

He had left the army by then, working initially for the PR firm run by an old school friend of his father's and then later setting up his own rival business.

Like her own, Garth's parents were still alive, living just outside York in the constituency that Garth's father had represented as a Member of Parliament before his retirement.

Claudia still saw them regularly and loved them dearly. Just like her own parents, they adored Tara and spoiled her dreadfully. She was, after all, for both of them, their only grandchild since she and Garth were themselves only children.

'I'm so sorry that there can't be any more little

ones, darling,' her mother had tried to comfort her after she had broken the news to her that Tara would be her only child. 'But sometimes… Are you sure?'

'I'm sure, Mummy,' Claudia had told her, her voice raw with pain.

'But at least you have Tara, and she's such a beautiful, healthy baby. You'd never know that she'd been born prematurely. You can't imagine how your father and I felt when we got Garth's telephone call. I wanted to come home straight away, but of course we couldn't get flights, and with Garth's parents being away at the same time… I must say I was surprised that the hospital allowed you home with her so soon.'

'They knew we were planning to move,' Claudia had reminded her mother quickly before adding, 'Anyway, that's all behind us now. I do wish you wouldn't keep harping on about it. I'm sorry, Mummy,' she had apologised when she saw her mother's expression. 'It's just that I don't like being reminded…' She bit her lip.

'It's all right, darling, I *do* understand,' her mother had assured her, patting her hand. 'I know how dreadful it must have been for you, especially when… Well, after losing your first baby and then to nearly lose our darling, precious Tara, as well…'

'Yes,' Claudia had agreed. Even nearly eighteen months after the event, she had still hated being reminded of the early miscarriage she had suffered with the baby she had been carrying before Tara's arrival. Friends had told her then that it was a relatively common occurrence and that the best thing she could do was to get pregnant again just as quickly as she could.

She had still been working at that time, of course, with Garth still in the army, and it had seemed to make sense for her to continue with her probationary work, a very newly qualified and raw probation officer, she reminded herself bleakly now, remembering the interview she had had with her supervisor at the end of her initial training period.

'Idealism and concern for others are all very praiseworthy, my dear,' the older woman had told her, 'but in this job you *have* to learn to achieve a certain amount of detachment. It's essential if one is to do one's job properly.'

In those days, twenty-odd years ago, the problems and pitfalls in the field of social work she had chosen weren't as widely recognised as they were now, Claudia acknowledged as she opened the door into the drawing room and walked in. The traumas and trials, accusations of negligence and lack of expertise, of pointless meddling in other people's lives had still lain ahead, but she had known that the older woman was right and that she *was* too sensitive, too much in danger of becoming overinvolved with the problems of her clients to be truly effective on their behalf.

She had been sensitive, too, to the unspoken criticism of her colleagues, suspicious of her prosperous and, to them, protected upper-middle-class background and upbringing. What could *she* possibly know of the difficulties and dangers that beset the people *they* were dealing with and their poverty-trapped, inner-city lives? In the end, her conscience had coerced her into accepting that no matter how much she cared, no matter how passionately she *wanted* to help, no matter how praiseworthy her commitment to the job and excellent her qualifications for it, she was simply not the best person, the right person, to help those she was supposed to be helping.

The drawing room was Claudia's second favourite room in the house. Elegantly proportioned, it faced south and always seemed to be flooded with light. It still had the same soft yellow colour scheme Claudia had chosen for it when she and Garth had first moved in. The Knoll sofas that faced one another across the fireplace had been a gift from her and Garth's parents and, if anything, Claudia loved them even more now over twenty years later than she had done then, their heavy damask dull gold covers softened and gentled with age. Mellow and lived-in, the whole room had the kind of ambience about it, the kind of feel, that made newcomers comment on how welcoming it was.

Above the fireplace was a portrait of her father in his full regimentals. It had been presented to him on his retirement and her mother had insisted that she had spent enough of her life looking at him in his uniform and that Claudia and Garth should have it.

On the stairs, Claudia had a further collection of family portraits, some simple pencil sketches, others more detailed, along with the totally unrecognisable 'picture' that Tara had drawn of her parents in her first term at school.

On the opposite wall from the fireplace above the pretty antique side table that Garth's mother had inherited from her own family and passed on to Claudia hung a portrait of another man in regimentals.

Instinctively, she walked over to it, switched on the picture light above it and studied it sombrely.

Garth had been twenty-seven when it had been painted and it had been a wedding gift from the regiment to them—a *surprise* wedding gift as the artist had painted the portrait from photographs. It was still a good likeness, though, with Garth's face turned slightly to the left so that the clear thrust of his jaw could be seen along with the aquiline profile of his nose.

Put Garth in a Roman centurion's outfit and he would immediately fulfil every Hollywood mogul's ideal of what a sexy man in uniform should look like, a friend had once commented to Claudia, and it was true. Garth's predecessors had originally come from Pembrokeshire in Wales and there was a joke in the family that it wasn't merely driftwood washed up from the shipwrecks of the fleeing remnants of the Spanish Armada that his ancestors had salvaged from the Pembroke beaches.

Clearly, Garth's skin tone and thick dark hair suggested that he could have Latin blood somewhere in his veins, and those who knew the family history had been very quick to point out that

Tara's lustrous dark curls could also be a part of that inheritance.

Fact or fiction, what was true was that Garth was a stunningly handsome man, an outrageously sexy man, so Claudia had been told enviously at their wedding, but oddly enough, it wasn't Garth's strongly sensual physical appeal that had initially attracted her.

Perhaps because of his career and his knowledge of the more base and raw instincts of the male sex, her father in particular had always been very protective of her, over-protective perhaps in some ways. Certainly it had taken a good deal of persuasion and coaxing on both her own part and that of her mother to gain his approval when she had wanted to go to university.

Garth, as one of her father's junior officers, had been deputised to escort her to a regimental ball. He had called to collect her in the shiny, bright red Morgan sports car that had been his parents' twenty-first birthday present to him and Claudia remembered that she had found both the car and the man rather too over the top, too stereotypical and obvious in many ways for her own taste.

It had been a warm June night and still light as they set out for the ball. They had had the country lane that led from her parents' house to the main road to themselves, and typically, or so she had decided, Garth had insisted on driving his car rather fast if admittedly very dexterously. Then, just as they had straightened out of a sharp bend, Claudia had seen a hedgehog crossing the road. Her immediate instinct was to call out in protest as she anticipated the animal's fateful demise, but to her astonishment as he, too, spotted the small creature, Garth had immediately taken evasive action, braking and turning the front of the car away from the road and plunging it instead nose first through a muddy ditch and up a bank into a thorny hedge.

Neither the hedgehog nor Claudia and Garth themselves suffered any physical damage but the same could not be said for the car. Along with the mud spattering its immaculate paintwork, Claudia had also been able to see the long and quite deep scratches the sharp thorns of the hedge had inflicted. But it wasn't the state of his precious car and its paintwork that had Garth virtually leaping out of the car the moment he had it back on the road. No, it was the still dazed and obviously petrified little animal that he ran to rescue from its plight. He carefully picked it up and, opening a nearby farm gate, carried it to a much safer environment.

It had been then that she had fallen in love with him, Claudia remembered. Not because of his astounding good looks, nor even because of the way he apologised to her for the fact that they would now be rather late arriving at the ball, but because of the completely natural and instinctive way he had put the hedgehog's safety above the value of his clearly very personally precious car, and it had been an honest and automatic reaction, Claudia had known, not something showy and false done simply to impress *her*. And she had loved him for it…for the personality, the warmth, the genuine caring and concern she had felt it revealed. The same love and caring he had always shown to Tara.

There was a telephone on the small coffee-table next to the fire. She walked over to it and, before she could change her mind, quickly dialled the number of Garth's London pent-house. After their divorce, he had bought a small property on the other side of the town but during the week he stayed in London in order to be close to his work.

The phone rang five times and then the receiver at the other end was lifted and an attractively husky female voice that Claudia didn't recognise said hello.

Without responding, Claudia replaced the receiver. Her hand was trembling and for some ridiculous reason she could feel the aching sensation at the back of her throat that presaged tears.

Why on *earth* should she cry just because a *woman* answered Garth's phone? They had been divorced for years and she, after all, had been the one to agitate for the divorce. She knew that there had been other women in Garth's life since they went their separate ways and she knew, too, that...

Straightening her spine, she readjusted several stems of the lilies she had already perfectly arranged earlier in the day. She was at a very vulnerable age, she reminded herself, that certain age where, while physically her looks might say that she was still a very attractive and sexually valuable woman, her hormones were beginning to tell her a different story. How many times lately had she heard other women of around the same age or slightly older bemoaning the fact that it wasn't just in their almost-adult off-springs' lives that they now felt redundant but in their partners' beds, as well? 'I still want sex,' one had complained frankly to her only the other day. 'But somehow these days I feel that *it* doesn't want me very much any more.'

Claudia sympathised. She didn't have a man, a lover, in her life. She had had offers, of course, approaches…men who had hovered on the edge of her life during the years of her marriage to Garth, moving a little closer, making their intentions, their desires, a little bit plainer, some of them married, some of them not. No, she certainly needn't have gone short of sex and perhaps even love if she had wanted it…them. But she had been too busy with other and more important concerns. Tara for one…and then there had been her business, her charity work, her friends.

'Don't you miss it?' someone had asked her curiously in the early years after the divorce. 'The sex. The having someone to snuggle up to in bed, the comfort of having someone there to hold you. You must get—'

'Frustrated,' Claudia had supplied calmly for her before shaking her head and denying, 'No, not really…I don't have the time.'

And it had been true, and besides…besides… Her sex drive had always been inextricably linked to her emotions, *driven* by them almost;

love for her was even more important, more driving, than lust.

And after Garth—well, after Garth it wasn't just that she couldn't ever *imagine* wanting another man, loving another man the way she had loved and wanted him, she had actively not wanted to become so emotionally involved with anyone else again.

The devastation upon discovering that Garth had been unfaithful to her had quite simply been so complete, so overwhelming, that she had never wanted to allow anyone else close enough to risk it again. Her love for Garth might have died, been destroyed, annihilated, by her discovery of his infidelity and the fact that, for so many years, she had been living a lie, a myth—believing in their marriage, in him—but her fear of the pain it had caused her had certainly not died.

She *did* have men friends, yes, and she went out on dates with them; but she had certainly never come anywhere near close to wanting to share anything more than friendship with them. Or at least she hadn't until she met Luke Palliser.

Was that further confirmation of the fact that she had reached the treacherous choppy waters of middle age, the fact that she was physically attracted to a younger man?

As she left the drawing room and turned to go upstairs, Claudia paused by Tara's picture of her parents. Neither of them was, of course, remotely recognisable if you discounted the colour of their hair—hers yellow, Garth's black and straight.

Tara!

Claudia bit her lip as she felt the familiar surge of love thinking about Tara always brought flooding through her, but this time it wasn't just love she felt. This time there was fear and dread, as well. And guilt, too. Oh, yes, there was guilt.

2

'I thought I heard the phone ring,' Garth Wallace commented as he walked into the sitting room of his London apartment carrying the papers he had been to retrieve from the briefcase in his bedroom.

'You did,' Estelle Frensham agreed. She had been working for the firm as a temp, filling in for Garth's personal assistant who was on maternity leave. 'But whoever it was rang off without speaking. I did a check on the number, though. This is it.' Silently, Garth studied the piece of paper she had given him. Apart from his eyebrows snapping together in a frown, his expression gave nothing away to Estelle as she watched him. He had recognised the number right away. How could he not do when for over ten years it had been his own? There was only one person who was likely to ring him from Ivy House, and so far as he knew, Tara, his daughter, was presently in London.

Tara. *His* daughter. *Their* daughter, his and Claudia's. Despite the fact that physically she resembled him much more than she did Claudia, Tara was in every other imaginable way so much more Claudia's child. Every mannerism, every mere inflection of her voice to him were copies of Claudia's, and sometimes watching her, he wasn't sure if those similarities made him hate himself more or loathe himself less. One thing was sure; they certainly didn't alter his love for Tara herself, nor change the way he felt about her mother.

If Tara was in London and Claudia *had* rung him, it could only be because her need to talk to him was desperately important. Claudia would never ring otherwise.

He glanced at his watch and then announced, 'Look, Estelle, I've changed my mind. We'll leave it for this evening, I think. I want to spend a little more time on this one. I'll ring the client in the morning and put off my meeting until later in the week.'

Estelle gave him an assessing look. They had been working all out at the agency to get some kind of campaign down on paper for the new client who had approached them to take on his business, which was why she was working here this evening instead of working out at the gym. Not that she minded—Garth's company was preferable any day of the week, any time of the day or night, to going to the gym, even if all he had in mind was work. At least for now.

From the moment he had first interviewed her for the temporary vacancy at the agency eight weeks ago, Estelle had decided that just as soon as she could arrange it, she and Garth were going to be lovers. Just the thought of it, of the pleasure she had promised herself that lay in store for her, made her start to ache deep down inside, the kind of ache she knew from long experience could only be soothed by the release of a full orgasm.

She wondered what Garth's reaction would be if she came right out with it now and told him how she felt, what she needed. Some men liked women who were totally up front and unashamed of admitting their sexual needs, but Garth, she suspected, was not one of them. And so far he had certainly neither said nor done anything to suggest that he *was* sexually attracted to her. Still, there was no other permanent woman in his life, apart from occasional dates with one of the agency's account executives—a woman in her thirties who Estelle knew would be no competition for her! She had managed to ascertain that much and she had checked, as well, that he was as heterosexual as he looked—no doubts there, either.

So far, it appeared he hadn't recognised her deliberate sexual come-ons to him or he had recognised them but was ignoring them—and of the two Estelle knew which one she preferred. And tonight she had hoped...but obviously tonight was not going to be the night. Estelle was no fool and she calmly gathered up the papers she had spread out on the workmanlike desk-cum-table that dominated his large square sitting room. All right, so things might not be ending as she had hoped and planned, but if she couldn't have Garth then there was always Blade. Oh, yes, there was always Blade. Blade who would happily provide her with *whatever* kind of sex she wanted, Blade with whom her relationship was not so much one of love and hate, as mutual dislike and contempt and mutual need and lust, as well. As she collected her belongings, she was already planning how she would spend the rest of the evening.

Watching her, Garth wondered what she was thinking. She had made it clear right from their first interview that she found him sexually attractive, but Garth was used to women coming on to him, and if necessary he could always tell the agency who had supplied her to find the firm an alternative.

She wouldn't be the first young and not-so-young female employee they had taken on who had made it plain she was attracted to him, but over the years he had learned to recognise all the warning signs and to deflect potential pitfalls in plenty of time to negotiate a way around them.

'I'll call you a cab,' he told her crisply, reaching out to pick up the phone.

That was one thing about Garth, Estelle recognised. He was quite definitely very much the old-fashioned sort when it came to the way he took what he saw as his responsibility towards his female employees. Very protective, very gentlemanly, in the very best senses of both words. Unfortunately.

As she bent down to retrieve an errant piece of paper, she deliberately allowed the long wrap skirt she was wearing to part, showing him the slender gym-honed full length of her thigh and revealing, if he should be interested, the fact that what she was wearing underneath it was either extremely brief or totally non-existent. But as she glanced towards Garth, Estelle saw that he was looking the other way, his mind plainly on other things. Never mind, she promised herself as her taxi arrived, there would always be another time, and for now her growing frustration and need called out for Blade.

Garth waited until he had seen Estelle stepping safely into the taxi he had called—the same reliable firm the business always used. Garth had heard too many scary stories of women being abused by unauthorised cab drivers to take any risks with the safety of his employees. Then he reached out to pick up the telephone a second time, punching in the number Estelle had written down for him.

After she had undressed and showered, Claudia opened the drawer of her dressing-room cupboard, pausing as she stared down at the small bottle of sleeping tablets she kept there. Her doctor had prescribed them in the early weeks after she asked Garth to leave. She rarely used them now, but at the same time she was never without a bottle. Just occasionally there were nights, a week or more of them at times, when something would happen, trigger her memory, and she would know that sleep was going to be impossible…unwanted even, because if she *did* sleep, she would be haunted by her nightmares, her fears, her guilt, and then and only then did she resort to the awful and frighteningly empty oblivion of drug-induced sleep as an escape.

The last time she had taken them had been towards the end of last year. Garth's birthday…his fiftieth.

Tara had thrown a party for him. She had begged Claudia to go, but as she had quietly explained to Tara at the time, Garth was hardly likely to want her to be there.

'But we're still family,' Tara had protested stubbornly while Claudia had shaken her head.

'You and Garth are still family, Tara. You and I are still family, but the three of us…'

'You were both there for my twenty-first and for my graduation,' Tara had reminded her mother, 'and everyone said then that both of you…' She stopped.

What everyone had said at the time was that it was a shame that her parents had split up and even more of a shame that they couldn't get back together, but Tara knew that to say as much to either her father or her mother was to court one of their rare displays of anger—a defensive anger in her mother's case and a protective one in her father's.

'Gramps and Nan will be there and so will the Brig and Nannie,' she had coaxed, referring not only to her paternal grandparents but her maternal ones, as well, but still Claudia had refused.

She had known perfectly well, of course, having been told by her mother, that they had accepted Tara's invitation to celebrate their ex-son-in-law's fiftieth birthday.

'We could hardly refuse, darling, and in fact, your father simply wouldn't have heard of it. You know how much he thinks of Garth.'

'Yes, I know, and there's certainly no reason why you shouldn't both go,' Claudia had assured her mother quietly.

'It will seem so odd without _you_ being there....'

'It won't seem odd at all, at least not to me or to Garth,' Claudia had had to point out to her mother as she reminded her gently, 'We _are_ divorced and have been for a full decade now.'

'Yes, I realise that,' her mother had fretted, 'although I've never really understood why.'

'I told you at the time. Garth had...there was—'

'Garth was a little bit naughty, I know that, darling, but men are sometimes like that,' her mother had interrupted her. 'That's just the way they are. Even your father...not that he ever...not that there was...but Garth is such a very handsome and charming man that—'

'I'm not going,' Claudia had told her mother firmly and she hadn't done so.

Instead, she had gone to bed early with her sleeping tablet and her unwanted memories. On that occasion, the tablet hadn't worked, but her memories had. Perhaps tonight she ought to take two instead of her usual one.

When the telephone rang an hour later, Claudia was deeply asleep.

Frowning, Garth replaced the receiver and

then dialled the number of his daughter's London flat.

'Daddy,' Tara exclaimed, her voice full of love and warmth as she recognised his voice. 'I'm glad you rang.'

'Oh, have you been trying to get in touch with me?'

'No, it's not that. It's just that I drove over to see Ma this afternoon. There was something I wanted to tell her. She's had the most fabulous write-up in the local rag. Have you seen it?'

'Yes, I have,' Garth agreed curtly.

He had seen, as well, the photographs accompanying the article. In one of them, a man was standing close to his ex-wife's side, his expression as he looked at her both predatory and betrayingly indulgent.

Garth knew him by reputation. He had downsized his business interests, moving out of the city and back to his roots where he was apparently intending to run his computer-based business from his old home town. Claudia, if what he had heard on the grapevine was true, had been approached by him for her views and advice on the type of problems likely to be faced by potential home computer workers he might employ. Garth had his own ideas about why Luke Palliser might be interested in his ex-wife, and they had nothing whatsoever to do with her professional expertise.

'Whatever you wanted to say to your mother must have been important if it necessitated driving all the way to Gloucestershire and then back again without staying overnight,' Garth commented as he switched his thoughts back from his ex-wife to his daughter.

'Well, yes, it was, but I couldn't have stayed anyway. There wouldn't have been any point. Ma was going out for the evening. Daddy…'

Garth waited. He knew of old *that* particular note in his daughter's voice. It had accompanied every minor and sometimes not-so-minor mishap in Tara's life, from the collision that had bent the front wheel of her first proper bike to the less dire but far more expensive bump that had damaged the small car he had given her for her eighteenth birthday.

'You know I told you that I needed to take all my holiday allowance because I was planning to spend time in Boston with Ry?'

'Yes…'

'Well, I didn't want to say anything to you at the time—not until I'd told Ma—but Ry and I…it could be *more* than just a few weeks I'll be spending in America.' She paused, allowing her words to sink in, but Garth wasn't in need of any extra time to assimilate what she was telling him. He had known…guessed…sensed already, his guesswork keeping pace with her carefully delivered words.

As his hand gripped the telephone receiver, he could feel his palm starting to sweat. At the same time, a cold shock of nausea was gripping his stomach. *Now* he knew why Claudia had been trying to get in touch with him.

'Daddy, are you still there?' he heard Tara demanding uncertainly.

'Yes, I'm still here,' he told her, praying that his voice sounded far calmer than he felt.

'Can you talk to Ma for me?' Tara was asking him. 'I *know* she's upset and the *last* thing I want to do is to hurt her, but I love Ry so much.... I just wish there was some way we could all be together, but it's a bit like it was when you and Ma told me that you were going to divorce, isn't it? Sometimes you just *can't* have all the people you love with you.

'Ryland's family, his *work*, are in Boston. He's always known that it's expected that he'll go back to take his place in the family firm and it's what he wants to do. You and Ma will be able to come over for holidays. I've already told Ma that...and we'll be able to come over here, and besides, nothing is settled yet. I've still got to go through the grilling process,' Tara went on mock-humorously. 'And according to Ry, a full investigation by the FBI is nothing to what his aunt is going to put me through. She's going to want to see family trees, proof of a clean bill of health and a total lack of any inherited disruptive genes before she'll even call me by my first name, never mind accept that Ry wants to marry me, according to him. Not that Ry cares whether or not she does approve, but he says that won't matter to her. Once she realises how we feel about one another, she'll set the full investigative process into motion whether we agree to it or not.

'She's the main shareholder in the family business—her late husband, Ry's father's brother, was the elder son. When Ry's uncle died, naturally his controlling share of the business passed on to her. Ry's father has some shares and like Ry he works for the business. From what Ry has told me about her, she's terribly starchy. Apparently she's going to want to know all about my own family background. Not that I'm worried, really. It will be easy peasy. Gramps and Nan go way back and the Brig knows the name and address and how many fillings every single member of the clan has ever had. Daddy, are you still there?'

'Yes, I'm still here,' Garth confirmed quietly.

'You *will* speak to Ma for me, won't you?' Tara coaxed. 'I know that secretly she was hoping I'd marry a nice local boy and settle down within pram walking distance of Ivy House and I'd have liked that, too, but...I really do love Ry.'

'Have you applied for your visa yet?' Tara heard her father asking her sombrely.

'I've filled in the forms, but Ry says there won't be any problems putting down that this is a holiday and we can sort the rest out over there. That's funny. Ma asked me exactly the same question.'

After he had finished speaking with Tara, Garth tried Claudia's number again even though it was almost midnight.

Once more there was no reply. Where was she? Tara had told him she was going out. Out where and with whom? The man in the newspaper, Luke Palliser, whose expression and body language had made it so plain that he wanted far more than a mere business relationship? Was she even now in his arms...in his bed? Stop it, Garth warned himself as he paced the floor. What the hell was happening to him? Surely he knew Claudia better than that. The last thing that would be on her mind right now would be sex, as he ought to know. The *only* thing, the only *person*, on her mind right now would be Tara. Even when Tara was a baby, he had once half-jokingly told Claudia he felt she loved her more than she had ever loved him or could ever love him.

'Yes, I think I do,' Claudia had agreed seriously, 'but it's a very different kind of love. The love that perhaps only a woman who has already lost one child can know. It doesn't take away from my love for you, Garth. It's simply different...very different.'

After the taxi had dropped her off outside her apartment block, Estelle made sure it was well out of sight before punching a number into her mobile phone. Perhaps she *was* being overcautious but she had made it a rule never to mix her private and public personae, and Blade was very much part of the intensely private side of her life.

'But that's close to incest,' a friend had gasped in shock when as a young teenager Estelle had boasted in lavish detail about just what kind of relationship she actually enjoyed with her stepbrother. The other girl had been shocked, but Estelle enjoyed knowing that what she and Blade did together would have been forbidden by their parents. It was all the more exciting and exhilarating knowing what secrecy and deceit they had to employ.

When she had told Blade what she had boasted to a friend, they had had an argument during which he had hit her once very hard across the mouth before forcing her to go down on him thirstily with her mouth as he swore at her and not stopping until he had finally come, his semen spilling from her mouth and running down over her naked body.

Estelle had found it one of the most thrilling, erotic things they had ever done and had her own orgasms without his even touching her, long before he had come himself. She had been thirteen then and Blade had been eighteen. They had continued their sexual relationship all through Blade's years at university as well as her own—frantic, heated, obsessively driven sado-masochistic sex sessions interspersed with long time periods when they neither spoke nor even saw one another.

Estelle could remember one particular occasion when they hadn't seen one another from the time Blade had returned to university at the end of the summer until his arrival at home just before Christmas. She had been out with friends when he arrived—a deliberate ploy—knowing how infuriated he would be when she wasn't there waiting for him. But the party she had gone to had turned out to be rather wilder than she had expected. The school friend who was giving it had an older brother who had turned up with his friends.

Estelle hadn't had sex with them; she had grown wary and wiser since the days when she had enjoyed confiding all her secrets to her friends. The outside world knew and saw one Estelle; she and Blade knew quite another. But she had enjoyed some pretty heavy snogging sessions and when she arrived home at one o'clock in the morning, very much on a sexually driven high, fuelled in reality far more by the knowledge of what potentially lay ahead of her with Blade than what had already happened, the thrill that had shot through her body as Blade unlocked the front door to her was almost orgasmic in itself.

He didn't speak; neither of them did. Instead, he simply stood at the bottom of the stairs watching her while she walked up. By the time she reached the top, her nipples ached as though they were already raw, she felt wetter than she had ever felt in her whole life and her clitoris felt so swollen she could hardly walk.

Her bedroom with its own *en suite* bathroom was at the opposite end of the house from that of her mother and father. Her mother was fond of saying that she believed that teenage girls needed their privacy, but what Estelle knew she meant in reality was that she simply didn't want to be bothered with her.

Estelle had learned long ago that her mother neither liked nor loved her—and she certainly hadn't wanted her. It was no secret to Estelle that her conception had been an accident since her mother had never wanted children.

'I'll kill myself,' Estelle had once threatened dramatically as a girl. 'You just want to get rid of me!'

As she turned away from her, Estelle had heard her mother saying grimly, 'Isn't that the truth!' But it had been another few years before Lorraine had bluntly told her that she had tried to abort Estelle in the early days of her pregnancy.

'I believe a girl Estelle's age is old enough to be trusted to make her own rules,' Lorraine responded with a dismissive toss of her head when people commented on the amount of freedom she allowed Estelle. As if one difficult child weren't enough, Ethian Morton, her second husband and Blade's father, had been less than pleased when his first wife's partner had declared that Blade was beyond their control thanks to the poor quality of the fathering he had received during his parents' marriage and that they were passing the responsibility for the boy back to his natural father.

Despite being expelled from three boarding schools for inappropriate behaviour, much to Ethian's relief Blade had managed to scrape through enough A levels to get into an admittedly second-rate university. Both parents were also relieved when neither of their offspring had wanted to join them on the skiing holiday they were due to take, starting just as soon after the Christmas festivities had ended as they had decently been able to arrange it, which meant, in fact, that they were flying out to Colorado on Boxing Day.

'You're leaving Blade and Estelle at home on their own?' one neighbour had asked, unable to conceal her feelings.

'Blade's an adult,' Lorraine had reminded her, affronted, 'and he and Estelle get on wonderfully well together. In point of fact, they're closer in many ways than if they were actually brother and sister. He's very protective of her. It's quite sweet, really.

'Nosy cow,' she had said angrily to Ethian later. 'Just because *she* runs around those noisy brats of hers all day long and enjoys playing earth mother and martyr.'

Estelle's bathroom was mirrored all along one wall. Blade's suggestion and her fifteenth-birthday present from her parents. When she walked into it, she didn't bother closing the door. She tugged off the skimpy dress she had been wearing, let it fall to the floor and then stood in front of the mirror staring at her reflection. Her mouth was swollen, the bright red lipstick she favoured smeared. She was tall and slim, her breasts firm and high enough for her not to need to bother wearing a bra, and besides, she liked the feel of her nipples rubbing against the fabric of her clothes and she liked even more the looks she got from men when they saw their taut outline.

Eyes half-closed, she licked the swollen flesh

of her mouth, sliding her hand inside her knickers so that she could feel her own wetness. A familiar clutching sensation seized her lower belly. Closing her eyes, she wriggled out of her knickers.

She heard the bathroom door close and slowly opened her eyes, one hand still on her body, teasing the quivering piece of flesh her clitoris had become, the other still holding her wet knickers, her gaze locking with Blade's as she returned his silently intense scrutiny.

'What have you been doing?' he demanded expressionlessly as he came towards her, the question almost a mild, uncritical whisper, but Estelle knew better. Her heart started to pound as she felt the onset of a familiar feverish excitement and fear.

'Smell,' she taunted, holding out her knickers to him. As she knew he would, he took them, smoothing them out very gently before inhaling the scent of her sex from them. *Her* sex and no one else's.

'Come here,' he ordered, still using the same soft, gentle voice, but Estelle wasn't deceived. Trembling from head to foot with the sensation that to her was almost more pleasurable than the release from it that lay ahead, she did as he instructed.

As she approached him, Blade unzipped his jeans, and as she had expected, he wasn't wearing anything underneath them. His penis was stiff and rigidly erect, rising from its bed of thick, coarse, tangled dark hair. In the early days of their intimacy, his sexual organ had fascinated her and as a punishment for her 'transgressions' he had ordered her to wash his penis for him, sometimes by lapping it with her tongue, sometimes with soap and water.

Walking past her now, he lay down on the floor and commanded, 'Come here.' Estelle's whole body convulsed, quivering with sexual urgency. 'Sit on it,' he demanded, drawing her towards his erect penis.

Willingly she complied, straddling him and lowering herself eagerly onto him. As she did so, he started to thrust upwards so forcefully that the sensation of him inside her was almost more pain than pleasure and at the same time he reached down between her legs and used his fingers on her clitoris.

It was too much for her self-control. Within seconds she had started to climax.

They spent what was left of the night in her bathroom and after he had finally spent himself and had his orgasm, Estelle knew that she was going to be sore, but she didn't care. She had loved every moment with Blade, *every* moment.

The memory of that high still had the power to make her smile and to make her wet, very, very wet indeed. She was smiling now, her hand automatically reaching between her legs, her body turned into the protection of Blade's doorway as she heard him answer her phone call.

'Blade, it's me, Estelle,' she told him softly. 'Are you in?' That question was their private code and meant 'I want sex.'

She could almost feel the dark, triumphant smile slicing his face as he told her softly, 'No, I'm afraid I'm not. It's all right, darling,' she heard him saying as he half covered the receiver. 'It's only my sister.' Then his voice dropped to a whiplash sting of mocking sound as he told her, 'If you're really desperate for it, Estelle, I could always talk you through it. You've always enjoyed that, haven't you? Or, of course, you could come round and watch…even join in.'

Furious, Estelle cut the connection. She was more than well aware of Blade's predilection for voyeurism and three in a bed, but right now she wasn't in the mood for playing games or sharing. Right now she wanted him to herself. All to herself.

Angrily, she turned on her heel and started to walk towards her own apartment building. There was a man standing on the pavement several feet away from her, waiting to cross the road.

Hungrily, Estelle studied him, her eyes gleaming with predatory sexual urgency. He wasn't her type, though, thin and pallid-looking, his body stance limp and docile, and no doubt his sex was the same.

Glaring at him in disgust, Estelle mentally cursed Blade, knowing how much he would be enjoying having the woman who was with him right now, all the more so because he knew Estelle was going hungry…wanting him, needing him.

3

Uneasily, Garth glanced at his watch as he replaced the receiver following yet another unanswered call to Claudia.

It was now gone one o'clock in the morning. Claudia might have been going out but… At this time of the night, with the roads almost empty, it would take him less than two hours to drive to Upper Charfont. He was sorely tempted to do so, but he knew perfectly well how Claudia would react to his unheralded arrival at *that* time of night. And someone who knew them both was almost bound to see his car there—Upper Charfont was that kind of town. Not that *he* minded, but he knew that Claudia would.

He would ring her first thing in the morning, he promised himself—if indeed she was there to be rung and not…not what?

Not with Luke Palliser.

Irritably, Garth stretched his now-tense body, wincing as he heard the tell-tale crack of his neck. Without being vain, he knew he was in damn good shape for his age. He looked after himself, ate well and sensibly, exercised moderately, regularly counted his blessings amongst which Tara had to be close to the top of the list of the

most valued and precious of all the good things
that life had given him. The price of having her in
his life had come so high, though, that there had
been times when to his own shame he had almost wished she had never come into being and
times, too, when he had been acutely and ridiculously jealous of the intensity and immensity of
Claudia's love for her, but then he suspected he
had always been far more passionately in love
with Claudia than she had been with him.

He could still remember the sense of dismay
he had experienced when his then commanding
officer, Claudia's father, had announced that he
wished Garth to escort his daughter to the regimental ball. He had known only that the brigadier had a daughter and that she was away at
university and he wasn't quite sure what he had
expected.

What he had *known* was that he would much
rather his partner had been the long-legged
'model' he had been introduced to at a London
party and whom he had been discreetly pursuing for the previous six weeks. Not so much, he
had to admit, because of her good looks and
'model' status—Garth had always preferred his
women curvaceous rather than bone thin and the
'model' had had a hectic, frenzied air about her,
which, coupled with the slight gauntness of her
body, had even in those relatively innocent pre-
anorexia-and-bulimia days hinted that the soft
drugs then fashionably in vogue amongst
London's trendy young set might be more than a
mere fashion appendage for her—but, if he was

honest, because of the hints the acquaintance who had introduced them had dropped about her sexual availability.

For Garth, a single young man with a healthy sex drive, the opportunity to escort to the ball a young woman he was pretty sure he had a strong chance of ending up in bed with afterwards was far more appealing than the prospect of an evening spent dutifully making polite conversation with the brigadier's no doubt plain and dull daughter.

Only Claudia hadn't been plain and she had certainly been far from dull, and when he went to pick her up he had realised at once that she was as pleased at the prospect of an evening spent with him as he had been with her.

Petite and blonde, with the kind of curvy feminine figure that made Garth instinctively want to wrap his hands around her waist just to test his belief that it was small enough for them to encompass it, physically she was enough and more to make him drool with longing. But there was a lot more to Claudia than her delicate physical beauty as he had quickly discovered, and by the end of the evening he had known that she was the girl he wanted to be his wife.

Claudia herself had taken rather more persuading. Not because she didn't share his feeling as she had told him seriously the first time he proposed to her—she did—but because she had seen too many army marriages founder on the rocks of misunderstanding and conflicting pressures to want to entrust the future of her children, *their* children, to a marriage that might not last.

Even then, her priority had been the security of the family she so much wanted to have, the children she so much wanted to bear.

'How can you say you love me?' she had raged at him when she found out what had happened. 'How *can* you claim that you love me when you've slept with someone else?'

He had tried to explain, make her understand, tell her that it had been a mistake…an accident almost, but she had refused to believe him, refused virtually to listen.

He had always known that beneath her outer softness and apparent vulnerability, she had unsuspected strength, but he had never imagined that that strength could be turned against him. He had tried to get her to change her mind, but she had refused to listen, and in the end he had had to accept the fact that their marriage was over, that her pride would not allow her to understand or forgive what he had done.

In the first couple of years after the divorce, he had done what all men in his position did, trying to disperse the pain and sense of loss in the arms and beds of other women.

It hadn't worked, but then he hadn't really expected it to, and at least being single and determined to stay free of any new emotional entanglements had meant that he was able during the lean years of the economic crisis to concentrate all his time and attention on his business. It had come through the recession relatively unscathed and they were, in fact, now rather unexpectedly very much to the forefront of their field.

Like Claudia, he had met and known about Tara's involvement with Ryland but like her he had been caught off guard by Tara's announcement that she and Ryland planned to marry.

An hour later, still unable to sleep, Garth looked at the luminous dial of his wrist-watch. Two-fifteen a.m. He *could* try Claudia again and he was sorely tempted to do so, but if she still hadn't returned home, if she was *still* perhaps with Luke Palliser, he knew he didn't want to know.

It was ten years now since they had separated and while Claudia wasn't and never had been the type of woman to want a merely sexual relationship, nor to publicly flaunt an emotional one, she was very much a woman whom men automatically found attractive and wanted to get closer to—wanted to protect, if that wasn't too politically incorrect and chauvinistic a thing to profess.

During their marriage, he had seen the admiring looks other men had given her and the envious ones they had sent him too often not to know that if Claudia was still on her own it was because that was her choice.

'Get involved with someone else...marry again? No, never,' she had told him quietly when he made the mistake of venting his bitterness on her shortly after their divorce had been finalised. 'I loved *you*, Garth,' she had told him. 'I loved you and I trusted you, I believed in you…in us, but you betrayed me.' With quiet, dignified sorrow, she had gone on to ask, 'If I can't trust you, what man can I trust?' Answering her own question, she had added, 'I can't and I don't intend to try.'

'You mean you don't *want* to try, just as you don't *want* to try to understand, to accept,' Garth had returned hotly, still half-unable to believe that she had gone through with it and that they were actually divorced. 'You've got all the emotional commitment you want, Claudia, all the emotional commitment *you* can give. You've got Tara. I wonder what would have happened if during the early days of our marriage we'd discovered that *I* couldn't father children. How strong would your adherence to our marriage and your marriage vows have been then?'

He had told himself in the bitterness of his loss that the pain he had seen burning in her eyes as she listened quietly to his angry outburst—a pain he had caused—was justified and that so were his accusations.

'You're not divorcing me because I've slept with someone else,' he had told her angrily during one of their pre-separation quarrels. 'You're doing it because I'm simply surplus to requirements, because you don't *want* me any more, because all you want, the only one you want is Tara.'

'That's not true,' Claudia had denied vehemently.

'Isn't it?' he had challenged her. 'How come,

then, that we haven't had sex since Christmas, three months before you found out—'

'I tried,' Claudia had parried defensively, 'but you were away so much, working late so often—'

'And sex is something we can only have late at night in the dark? What happened to Sunday morning, Saturday afternoon, rainy evenings…?'

'Tara was younger then. Now she's older, she might—'

'She might what? Realise that her parents have a natural, normal, loving sexual relationship? Only they don't…didn't…did we, Claudia? There's nothing natural about the kind of sex *we* have these days, nothing warm or loving, not with you lying there practically willing me to get it over and done with.'

'You're wrong. It isn't…' Claudia had begun and then stopped.

Of course it hadn't been the lack of sex in their marriage that had infuriated and hurt him, Garth admitted to himself now. It had been his fear that he was losing Claudia's love, that she no longer needed or wanted him, that she and Tara formed their own perfect charm circle in which there was no place for him. That he was in his wife's life, if not his daughter's, superfluous to requirements.

But he had been wrong to accuse Claudia as he had done then of being sexually cold and unloving. When they had first been lovers, first been married, she had thrilled and touched him with her gentle sensuality, her total and complete giving of herself to him and to their mutual desire.

She had been a virgin when they met but had

kept that fact from him, so totally ardent and responsive in his arms the first time they had made love that it was not until he had felt the unexpected resistance and tightness of her inexperienced body that he had realised the truth.

That, if anything, had made him love her even more than he did already, setting the seal on what to him had been her absolute and total perfection, not because no other man had known her so intimately but because she had loved *him* enough to give herself to him so totally and completely.

He glanced again at his alarm clock. No, he couldn't ring her now. He would have to wait until the morning.

He could well imagine how she had reacted to Tara's news and how she must be feeling. And how much it would have hurt her pride to have to get in touch with him.

'Easy peasy,' Tara had said, and he had heard the pride in her voice as she laughed off Ry's aunt's inquisition into her family background.

Easy peasy. If only that were the truth.

Estelle opened her eyes, the luminous numbers on her clock radio showing that it was quarter to three. Frowning, she wondered sleepily what had woken her and then she heard it—the soft creak of a door opening within her apartment.

She knew who it was, of course. Only one person besides herself had a key to her home and she was sitting up in bed waiting for him when he turned the handle of the door and walked in, soft-footed as a mountain cat, feral eyes gleaming in the half-light as he brought into the room with him the raw, pulsing intensity of his sexually driven persona and with it the scent of sex that clung to his skin—another woman's sex, Estelle acknowledged as she felt the familiar excitement leap and crackle between them like an unseen charge of electricity.

It had always been like this with him, right from that first time when she had still been a child and he had been the older stepbrother. She had adored him from the start. She was his, he had told her. She would always be his.

'Open your legs,' she heard him demanding softly as he approached her bed.

Smiling luxuriously, she did so. The girl or girls whom he had had earlier had plainly not satisfied him, but she was not surprised, and although he might at times like to torment her by denying it and denying her, she was as essential to *him* as he was to her.

As she lay there on the bed, she could feel the anticipation and urgency pulsing through her; just watching him watching her was all it took. He had started to undress, but his gaze never moved from her open legs, not even when he dropped his trousers and she couldn't stop herself from giving a small, sharp moan at the sight of his erect penis.

The myth that you could tell the size of a man's sexual equipment from the size of his feet and hands was in Blade's case just that—a myth.

Short and stocky, he had almost femininely small hands and feet, but his sex...

A sharp thrill of sexual energy trembled through her as she studied it. Thick, much thicker than that of any other man she had known, hard, too, and so voracious in its appetite for the deep plunging thrusting she loved. Indeed, loved so much that sometimes even when she couldn't satisfy it or him, she knew that no other man could ever make her feel the way Blade did.

'Mmm, that feels good,' Blade told her, his voice a soft, lulling coo of warmth. He stroked her with expert fingers, kneeling between her parted legs. 'So wet, so warm...so hungry, so...empty...'

Estelle wriggled in mute ecstasy as he inserted his fingers into her—just enough to make her aware of their presence, to make her feel tight and hot and achingly eager for the thick, hot shaft of flesh he was starting to rub with his free hand.

Estelle thrust her hips up, trying to draw his fingers deeper inside her, but he kept on teasing her by withdrawing them each time she surged upwards, leaving her empty and aching, her frustration turning her earlier smile to an angry glower as she tried and failed to trap his fingers inside her.

Laughing at her, he stroked the hard length of his penis, holding her off as she tried to reach for him and then forcing her hands away as she made to satisfy her frustrated need by herself. He pinned down one of her arms with his knee and held the other in a painful grip, laughing tauntingly down at her, his thick red lips drawn back against his teeth so that he did look almost dangerously vulpine as he reached out and thrust into her with his fingers again, telling her softly, 'That's right, babe, go ahead and fuck yourself on my fingers,' laughing when he heard the small explosive sound she made and demanding, 'What is it you want? More…? How much more…? This much?'

She ought to have been prepared for it. After all, he had done it to her before, yet the sharp, thrilling bite of pain he was causing her made her cry out and brought as he had known it would the first frantic convulsions of her orgasm. But he didn't let her have it, removing his hand from her body and taunting her excitedly as she reached for his erection.

'Oh, no, not yet, you can't have it yet. First you've got to stroke him a little…suck him, show him how much you want him,' he mocked as her hand and then her mouth closed hungrily over his body and she started to rock herself rhythmically to and fro, her eyes closed as she did so, still sucking deeply on him.

He waited until he was almost ready to come before removing himself from her mouth and thrusting deeply and urgently into the eagerly open wetness of her body, automatically reaching out for a pillow to hold over her mouth to silence her screams of pleasure as she climaxed, even though the days were now long gone when he had to prevent their parents from hearing the noise she made.

Estelle had never had a flatmate because she liked her privacy, and one of the earliest lessons she had learned was to distrust her own sex.

Gloatingly, just before dawn, Blade surveyed Estelle's naked body. The whole room smelled of sex and he breathed in the scent of it, of himself, with luxurious, satiated enjoyment. Then, after gathering up his clothes, he dressed and headed for the door.

He and Estelle never slept together. They didn't have that kind of relationship, and besides, the two girls he had left curled up on his bed would still be there waiting for him, or rather, waiting for the money he had promised to pay them.

'What's wrong?' Lovingly, Ryland reached out an arm and drew Tara closer against his body.

'How did you know I was awake?' she asked him, sidestepping the question.

'I knew,' Ryland told her and then prodded gently, 'You're worrying about your Mom, aren't you?'

Tara turned her head and pressed her face into his chest.

'She didn't say anything to me about our going to Boston, but I could see in her face…her eyes… I know.' She gulped back a small choking sob. 'I feel so guilty about leaving her, Ry, but I know, I just know that I couldn't bear not to be with you.'

'There's no way you are *going* to be without me

even if I have to kidnap you and drag you bodily onto the plane with me,' Ryland assured her, adding more seriously, 'If there was any way I could change things, stay over here, I would, but I can't. I'm the only male of my generation. My uncle was twelve years older than my father—if he and my aunt had had a son, perhaps things might have been different. As it is, it's always been kinda understood that when my aunt retires, I'll be taking over from her and running the business.'

'Doesn't your cousin—' Tara began, referring to his aunt's and late uncle's only child, a daughter, but Ryland shook his head before she could finish explaining.

'Margot isn't interested in the business. She never has been. She isn't that kind of woman.'

'What do you mean?' Tara asked him, wrinkling her forehead. All she knew about his cousin was that she was nearly seven years Ryland's senior and unmarried.

'Margot works in the business, yes,' Ryland agreed. 'She works in the archive department where we house all the originals of everything we've published. But she has no wish to take over and run the company.'

'But she could marry and have children,' Tara pointed out.

'No,' Ryland returned, shaking his head, 'no, she won't.'

'How can you be so sure?' Tara half teased him. 'I know she's not so young any more but...'

'Margot will never marry because it's impossible for her to marry the man she wants,' Ryland told her bluntly, explaining when he saw her puzzled expression, 'Margot loves Lloyd—her mother's brother's son. They're first cousins. It's against the law in the state of Massachusetts and a number of others for them to marry and my aunt would never have condoned their getting married even in another state. Margot fell in love with him when she was fifteen and since then... It isn't something that's discussed in the family.'

'Does he...Lloyd...love her?' Tara interrupted him, her eyes full of tender compassion.

'I...Lloyd has been married and has two step-children. He doesn't have Margot's in-tense...well, she's a very driven sort of person. Lloyd lives in California. My aunt decided to set up a branch of the business out there, printing pretty much the same sort of stuff for the campus at UCLA as we do for Yale and Harvard. She put Lloyd in charge of that end of things.'

'She sent him away from Margot, you mean,' Tara said in a low voice.

'It's impossible—illegal—for them to be to-gether,' Ryland reminded her quietly. 'She did it for the best. Except when Lloyd met someone else out there and decided to get married, well, Margot had a bit of a breakdown. They meet every summer at the island. There's an island my great-grandfather bought, just off the coast—'

'An island, your family owns an island...?' Tara began, but Ryland shook his head dismiss-ively.

'It's nothing,' he told her, 'just an exposed

piece of rocky headland, really, but...' He paused. 'It's there Margot and Lloyd see each other. Not that it's ever mentioned.'

Tara shivered and wrapped her arms tightly around her body, trying to imagine how it must feel to love a man you could never really be with, to want a man you could never truly have.

In their early days together when he had been telling her about his family background, Ryland had played down the role he knew he was ultimately going to have in the family business.

He had told Tara he had come to England to study British publishing and he had then gone on to explain to her the nature of his family's business, telling her that his great-grandfather had started a small company to publish textbooks and papers written by his friends at Yale and Harvard.

The business had grown and become extremely profitable, still maintaining its close links with the university.

After his uncle's untimely death in a sailing accident—his hobby had been racing ocean-going yachts—his wife, Ryland's aunt, had stepped into his shoes and run the business as its chief executive. Ryland's father continued with his own work, bringing in new manuscripts for them to publish and sell. Under his aunt's aegis, the company had gone from strength to strength. She had an extremely sharp financial brain and Boston's money men had a great deal of respect for her—as did Ryland himself.

Any one of Boston's first families would have

been highly delighted to see their daughter marrying Martha Adams's nephew, Ryland suspected, but marriage hadn't been something he had been remotely interested in—until he had seen Tara. Within days, within hours of meeting her, he had known that she was the one—the only one.

Perhaps he was more like his cousin Margot than he had previously imagined, he acknowledged ruefully.

There was something in Tara's make-up, a streak of idealism, the result perhaps of having always and only ever known the loving, tender protection of those around her and of having known, as well, just how much she was cherished and valued, that somehow set her apart and made her special, made him love her.

'I do understand you have to return,' Tara assured him, adding, 'I just wish that Boston wasn't so far away.'

'It isn't,' Ryland murmured, tilting her face up towards his own so that he could look down into her eyes as he whispered softly a second time, 'It isn't.'

As he bent to kiss her, Tara shook her head. 'Not to us, perhaps, but it is to Ma. I could see it in her eyes. She looked almost…almost frightened…as though… I've never seen her look like that before. Not even when she and Dad… I hated it when they divorced. I don't want anything like that to ever happen to us, Ry.'

'It won't,' he reassured her gently. 'It won't.

Your mother probably just needs a little time to get used to the idea of our living in Boston,' he added comfortingly. 'After all, she's got her own life. She's still a very active and attractive woman...a very, very attractive woman,' he noted appreciatively, causing Tara to give him an indignant pinch. 'Perhaps we could give ourselves a week or so to settle in and then get her to come over for a visit,' Ryland suggested as he removed Tara's fingers from his arm and then bent his head to slowly suck them one by one.

'Mmm...' Tara moaned responsively.

'Mmm...' Ryland agreed as he eased her down against the bed and transferred the moist heat of his mouth from her fingers to her nipple.

Tara closed her eyes and gave herself up voluptuously to the pleasure of his lovemaking.

Ryland had teased her shortly after they had revealed their love for one another and celebrated that revelation with a romantic and very sensual weekend away at a discreet country hotel in a bedroom complete with a four-poster, a huge open fire and, even better, a bed-sized open space in front of it that there was a delicious wantonness, a wildness almost, about the way she lost herself in their lovemaking that was intriguingly at odds with the mild-mannered and restrained day-to-day image she presented to the outside world.

'That's because I'm in love with you,' Tara had told him seriously and meant it, because it was true.

Her emotions had always been close to the sur-

face, easily stirred and fired, and it had taken the
gentle influence of her mother to help her learn
how to harness the impetuous, impulsive side of
her nature and to look beyond its immediacy to
the eventual consequences. Tara felt privileged
that in her the passionate intensity she felt, an inheritance from her father's side of the family,
was tempered and strengthened by the quiet
wisdom that was her mother's. Passion and sen-
sitivity—they could, for someone without the
loving parenting she had received, have been uncomfortable bedfellows, but Tara loved and valued both sides of her personality because they
were her emotional inheritance from her parents.

She *liked* knowing that in her individuality she
was still a part of them, just as the children she
and Ryland produced would be a part of them.
Like her, she hoped that they, too, would one day
listen with the same rapt attention as she had
while their grandparents told them stories of
their own youth and that they, as she had done,
would absorb from those stories a sense of family
and continuity, a sense of security and safety, of
warmth and belonging.

It still sometimes brought quick emotional
tears to her eyes to visit her grandparents and to
see the love and pride in their eyes, to see and
touch the familiar things that she had known
from babyhood: the Sèvres dinner service that a
member of her mother's mother's family had
brought back from France; the medals her maternal grandfather had received on the death of his
uncle, a veteran of the Somme; the linen sheets

both of her grandmothers had been presented with on their respective marriages and that both of them had ruefully admitted they never used, much preferring the easier laundering of modern bedclothes.

Despite her totally modern outlook on life, Tara was a girl who was very much in touch with, very much in *tune* with, her family's past. Ryland, who had already recognised that about her, hoped it might incline his aunt to look favourably on Tara and approve of their marriage.

He might neither need nor particularly want that approval and the inheritance that would ultimately go with it, but as he had already told Tara, he felt it was his duty to accept the role in the family business for which he had been groomed. There were certain things about his family and that role that he had not as yet told Tara, but they did not affect his love for her, and who knew, if his cousin Margot changed her mind about remaining single…

He smiled in the darkness as Tara fell asleep in his arms. How could his family *not* love her? How could they possibly find fault with a person as instantly lovable and totally adorable, so perfect in every way, as his Tara?

'Ryland's coming home and he's bringing a girl with him.'

'A girl? Who?'

Lloyd propped himself up on one elbow as he looked down into the face of his lover—and cousin.

Margot shrugged dismissively. 'I don't know, some English girl.'

'Is it serious?'

'No relationships are allowed to be serious in this family until mother's sanctioned it. You know that.'

The expression on her face echoed the bitterness and resentment in her voice as she sat up in bed and reached for the packet of cigarettes on the bedside table, lighting one and drawing fiercely on it.

In the clear light of the island morning, the sharp angularity of the bones both of her body and her face was almost cruelly revealed. What had, on the girl, been extreme slimness had become, on the woman she was now, an almost bony thinness, the outward expression of her inner frustration and bitterness, as though these deep-rooted feelings that had distorted her life had eaten away at her flesh as thoroughly and destructively as any bodily illness.

'My God, if only things were different,' she burst out intensely, her dark eyes flashing as she turned to look at the man lying beside her.

Three years separated them in age—three thousand miles in distance, apart from the brief days and hours they occasionally managed to snatch together, those and the six weeks they shared annually here on the island that belonged to Margot's mother and his aunt.

Every summer for over twenty years, both of them had come here to be together, away from prying eyes. As first cousins, certain states considered their blood relationship too close for them to marry and legalise their love for each other as Margot so passionately wished they might. Margot wasn't sure which was the stronger feeling she had for these weeks in the summer—hatred or longing. Longing when they were apart from one another and hatred when she was here because being here meant being aware of the fact that she could never ever have her heart's desire; that she could never be with Lloyd as she ached and wanted to be with him. As they both wanted her to be with him, she amended hastily. After all, he suffered just as much as she did, yearned just as much as she did…ached, needed, wanted, loved just as much as she did.

They had both known, of course, even before they had fallen in love that such a love was forbidden.

'But what will happen if I get pregnant?' Margot had asked Lloyd tremulously the first time they had made love, lying uncomfortably together in the sandy earth amongst the trees, hidden out of sight of the house.

'You won't,' Lloyd had assured her, showing her the condom he had bought.

That had been the beginning of it, the beginning of what to her was a continuous rack of pain from which there was no relief, no cessation, no, not even sometimes in his arms, because always at the back of her mind was the knowledge that their togetherness was only temporary, that ultimately they would have to part and go back to their separate lives.

'Stay with me,' she had begged frantically one summer a number of years ago.

'I can't. You know that,' he had told her. 'I think Carole-Ann might be beginning to suspect something. In fact, I think we might have to—'

'No!' Margot had burst out explosively before he could finish. 'If she *does* suspect, then we'll just have to find some way of... She can't stop us being together, Lloyd. She has you all the time. Does she know how lucky she is to be your wife?' she had demanded passionately. 'How much I wish...'

Lloyd had turned and taken her in his arms. 'You know that can't be,' he told her.

'Oh, Lloyd,' she cried. 'God, *why* does it have to be like this? *Why* can't we be together? Go away somewhere—abroad?'

'You know we can't do that. How would we live? Both of us are dependent on the business.'

'The summer's passing quickly.' Margot shivered now. 'Another three weeks and you'll be going back. Oh, Lloyd, I don't know how I can bear it.'

Helplessly, she started to cry.

Tiredly, Lloyd closed his eyes. They weren't young any more. The UCLA branch of their business, which his aunt had originally set up as much to put some distance between him and Margot as anything else, had proved to be extremely profitable and certainly no sinecure. He loved Margot, of course he did, and he always would, but sometimes the intensity of her passion for him, her need, her *dependency* on him, wore him down.

These six weeks he spent on the island every summer, technically updating his aunt on everything that had been happening with his side of the business, were, for Margot, the pivot of her whole existence.

'If we didn't have this, there'd be no point in my going on living,' she had told him more than once. Increasingly, though, he was guiltily aware that while Margot was so emotionally dependent on him, *he* was not free to live his own life.

It had been different when they were young. Then he had shared her passion, been as overwhelmed by his feelings for her as she was by hers for him. But now!

He was approaching forty and what did he have to show for it?

In material terms and so far as others were concerned, no doubt he seemed as though he was doing all right. He had a good job, money in the bank, a nice apartment, a new car.

But what about in other terms? What about those aspects of his life that could not be assessed in dollars or possessions?

He was divorced now with two stepdaughters whom he rarely saw, a few friends and Margot....

'Lloyd, tell me everything's going to be all

right, that we'll always be together,' Margot was demanding passionately.

Tiredly, he reassured her but he knew his voice lacked conviction.

4

What was that noise? Groggily, Claudia tried to focus on the high-pitched ringing sound that had broken into her heavy drugged sleep, the doubled effect of the two pills she had taken so deadening that it was several seconds before she realised that the noise was the telephone and another several more before she came to enough to reach for the receiver.

'Claudia, it's Maxine,' she heard her assistant announcing herself. 'Is everything OK? I was a bit concerned when you didn't arrive this morning.'

Guiltily, Claudia started to open her eyes and then widened them quickly in disbelief as she caught sight of her alarm clock. It was gone eleven in the morning. No wonder Maxine had been concerned.

'Er...I'm sorry, Maxine,' she apologised hastily. 'I...I meant to ring you last night to warn you that I'd decided to work at home this morning. I've got some paperwork here I need to catch up on.'

It wasn't completely untrue; she *did* have paperwork to attend to, Claudia comforted herself several minutes later after she had replaced the receiver.

Paperwork to *do*, maybe, but she certainly wasn't in any fit state to accomplish very much, she admitted wearily.

She had slept so deeply that if she had had any bad dreams she certainly couldn't remember them, but even so, the drugged oblivion of her night's sleep was just as exhausting as though she *had* lain sleepless and tormented. The numbing lethargy that still gripped her made her feel both guilty and angry. Quickly, she got out of bed, collected fresh underwear and headed for the shower.

But as she stood beneath its stinging, reviving spray, she acknowledged that at least her sleeping tablets had been able to keep last night's nightmares at bay.

She stopped soaping herself and stood motionless beneath the water, shuddering as she recalled the eager happiness in Tara's voice when she told her excitedly about her plans. And she, what had *she* done to prepare and protect her precious, much-loved daughter from what she now feared and dreaded lay ahead of her?

Slow, painful tears seeped from beneath her closed eyelids as Claudia acknowledged what she had done, or rather, not done. When faced with a crisis, the need to be strong and independent, to take control and confront the danger facing her, she had retreated to the security of the kind of behaviour more appropriate to her mother's generation by asking, 'Have you told your father yet?'

And then she had compounded her irresponsibility by escaping into a drug-induced sleep that had achieved nothing other than to worry her loyal and hard-working assistant.

But what could she do, what could she say? Maybe, after all, she was over-reacting, over-worrying.

If only. If only.

As she stepped out of the shower and reached for a towel, Claudia caught sight of her reflection in the bathroom mirror. The anguish she was feeling was clearly revealed in the drawn, drained tension of her expression. The last time she had seen that particular look on her face had been during the early days when she and Garth had agreed to divorce.

Garth...

It had been foolish of her to react so emotionally last night and try to ring him. She knew from Tara that he had been dating on a casual basis for the past few months. Tara had complained to her that she didn't think the thirty-odd-year-old woman he had apparently been seeing was good enough for her father.

Like her, Garth hadn't had anyone serious in his life since their marriage had ended, but hardly for the same reasons. Garth was an extremely attractive and very sensual man, the kind of man who, in the early days of their marriage, had been so emotionally as well as openly physically loving with her in public that her friends had often commented enviously to her on the depth and intensity of his love for her.

Perhaps unusually so for a man of his generation and upbringing, Garth was a highly tactile man, both as a lover and a father, and Tara was like him in that respect. She, too, was very much given to loving hugs and kisses while Claudia, as she was the first to acknowledge, tended to wait for the other person to make the first move, to hold herself back a little.

Even now, she disliked being reminded of how much she had missed Garth's physical warmth in the early days after she had found out the truth, how often she had woken from the wretchedness of her merciless dreams and turned instinctively towards his side of the bed expecting him to be there to reach out for her and hold her close, only to remember that the emotional agony of her waking hours was even greater than that of her nightmares.

She was over that now, of course. Well over it, and as a woman of forty-five, the mother of a grown-up daughter, as well, she did not think it appropriate to allow herself to yearn helplessly like some lovesick teenager for the physical and emotional contact, the closeness of a lover, a someone of her own that her life now denied her. Divorcing Garth had been the right decision, the only decision she could have made in the circumstances. He had, after all, betrayed her and betrayed her in such a way, deceiving her, lying to her so comprehensively and for so long, that there had been no way the damage he had done to their relationship could ever be repaired. So yesterday, why had she turned, yearning so instinctively, to him for help?

Because he was Tara's *father*. *That* was why and that was the *only* reason why, she assured herself sternly as she went back to her bedroom, securing the towel around her still-damp body, then reaching for the hair-dryer.

Since the break-up of her marriage, she had become fiercely protective, even defensive, about her independence and her ability to face the world alone, to manage whatever problems she might have alone. She had no need of anyone, any man, to lean on, to provide her with emotional support; she had proved that.

Last night, she had panicked, over-reacted unthinkingly with that silly and fortunately unanswered telephone call to Garth. This morning, she thankfully was much more in control of herself...much more herself, she decided firmly.

The hand holding the hair-dryer had started to tremble. Slowly, Claudia put the dryer down and took a deep breath, purposefully counting silently as she released it.

Now, she commanded herself sternly, let's start again. Today is Thursday. It is nearly twelve noon. You have wasted a whole morning, so what are you going to do with the rest of your day?

Mentally, she reviewed her commitments.

She had an informal arrangement for lunch, following which she had a planning meeting at three and then, finally, her treat for the day, which was her first discussion with the man who she was hoping would design her garden for her. She had first heard about him earlier in the year when she had attended the Chelsea Flower Show as the guest of one of her corporate clients and had immediately fallen in love with his work, only to discover that he was extremely selective about whom he accepted as a client and that, in addition, he had a waiting list of people wanting to consult him over a yard long. Eventually, however, her determination had paid off and it was planned that she should have initial talks then meet with him in the very near future.

Her thoughts on the garden, she walked over to the bedroom window that looked out over it. The house had had a large rear garden when they bought it, to which they had added a couple of good-sized paddocks. When they first moved in, this garden had consisted of a shabby lawn framed by overgrown herbaceous borders and separated from the kitchen garden and green-house that lay beyond it by an unruly hedge.

Just before Tara's sixth birthday, a space had been cleared on the lawn for the pretty chalet-style Wendy house they had bought as a birthday present. Claudia had spent the whole of the previous month sewing pretty gingham curtains for it, complete with tie-backs and matching ap-pliquéd gingham cushions for the child-sized furniture.

In time, at Tara's insistence, a small 'garden' area had been fenced off around her 'house', tak-ing the place of the slide and swing whose scuff marks had made bald patches in the lawn over the years. They had planted a rambling rose against the house, Garth insisting that she hold the rose straight while he dug and then filled in the hole he had made for it. It now virtually covered the small wooden building, but Tara had steadfastly refused to allow her to do anything to change her now-outgrown childhood retreat until last Christmas when she had suddenly announced that she was going to 'clear her stuff' out of the Wendy house and that it was high time that it was passed on to someone who could enjoy it.

Perhaps she should have guessed then, Claudia reflected. Perhaps that instinct that all mothers had, were supposed to possess and that she had believed she did possess, should have told her that it wasn't just the Wendy house that Tara had now outgrown and was ready to leave behind, but it hadn't fully sunk in. Perhaps she had been too engrossed with the adrenalin-spiked sense of urgency that Christmas, with its unique blend of planning and chaos, always brought her or it could be that she simply hadn't wanted to face the truth. And even if she had, what could she have done? Prevented Tara from seeing Ryland, stopped her from loving him?

The garden, she reminded herself fiercely. Think about the garden. You were so excited about it…remember?

Remember! Of course she did. After all, for the past few months, she had spent virtually every spare moment she had poring over gardening books, her mouth watering as she studied the temptation of their photographs depicting formal yew hedges—the perfect green backdrop for a profusion of artlessly and deliciously blowsy massed plantings of cottage garden–type flowers, their softness relieving the architectural sternness of their supporting hedges—pergolaed walkways dripping with wisteria and soft pink roses, the picturesque tranquillity of a formal pond... She wanted them all like a child let loose in a sweet shop.

Yes, far better to think about her garden than to allow herself to fall back into the quicksand of panic and fear that recalling Tara's visit brought, she decided quickly.

A friend had warned her against introducing koi carp to her as yet non-existent pond.

'They might be beautiful, but they are also the most dreadful scavengers. I've watched them push my poor lilies from one end of our pond to the other,' she had complained, 'and then they've got the cheek to come up to the surface demanding food every time I walk past.'

Claudia pictured a pond, a double row of neatly clipped yew hedges bisecting her immaculate new lawn and framing the kind of borders that would be filled with a profusion of traditional perennials like delphiniums, poppies, alliums and lupins. A path would lead through them to a small, secluded, secret inner garden, perhaps with a weeping pear and a bed of pure white flowers, she decided frantically, attempting to visualise the garden plan she was hastily trying to construct but that kept on being obscured by the far clearer image of her daughter and the news she had brought her last night.

Sharply, Claudia warned herself not to give in to her panic. What good would it do? She looked away from the window, pushing her fingers into her hair.

She needed time. Time to think, time to...

5

Garth had left London later than he had planned due to an urgent phone call from a client. To compound things, he had been caught up in a series of roadworks that had delayed him by over another hour, so that it was gone eleven o'clock before he finally drove into Upper Charfont.

His own three-storey town house with its long narrow garden and neat Georgian sash windows backed onto the river and was part of a civic conservation area. The architect and the builder who had been responsible for the renovation and rebuilding of the original neglected Georgian terrace and its surrounding environs were both clients, and a little bit of old-style country bargaining had led to Garth's getting the house at a very advantageous price.

In recent years he hadn't spent as much time in it as he would have liked. During the recession the business had demanded his full attention, which had necessitated his living in London virtually full time, though he had always made sure that he could work from Upper Charfont during Tara's school holidays.

As in everything else appertaining to their divorce, Claudia had been meticulous about ensuring that Tara was encouraged to spend time with him; there had been no set-down and rigidly enforced 'visiting rights'.

'Tara is, after all, your daughter,' Claudia had told him, her back stiff, her face averted from him, her voice low and so calm that if he hadn't known better, he would never have guessed that while she spoke to him she was crying, 'and she loves and needs you in her life *as* her father.'

For once, the weather had lived up to its early-morning promise with clear blue skies and sunshine. It was market day and the town was thronged with sightseers and locals alike, dressed casually in shorts and T-shirts. This was one of the times when he regretted the uncharacteristic impulse that had led to his following the Prince of Wales's example by driving a highly visible and highly enviable Aston Martin, he acknowledged as he saw the looks not just of envy but also of recognition greeting him as he drove through the town.

As he found a parking space close to the offices from which Claudia ran her business, he reflected wryly that knowing the town and its people, news of his arrival would probably reach her office before he did. Although he knew she would have argued to the contrary, pointing out with that chilly, distancing manner she almost always adopted towards him these days that since she was no longer a part of his life, nor he of hers, there was no reason or purpose to have him hold any views about anything she did, he was quite extraordinarily proud of her and all that she had achieved, not just in establishing her business and turning it into such a successful venture, but he was proud of her and for her in many other ways, as well.

She was a kind counsellor, a good friend, a loving daughter and daughter-in-law, and as a mother...

A female tourist in the town watching him as he climbed out of his car would have wondered who or what it was that could have brought such a pensive look of pain, mingled with compassion, to the face of so sexy a man. Whoever or whatever it was, she didn't doubt for one moment that there would be plenty of female volunteers to help him banish it.

Maxine Jarvis, Claudia's assistant, was in the reception area of the offices when he walked in. Recognising him, she told him quickly, 'I'm afraid Claudia isn't here. She's working at home today.'

'That's no problem,' Garth assured her, but Maxine noticed that he was frowning as he turned to leave.

After he had gone, she wondered if she ought to ring Claudia and warn her that her ex-husband had been in looking for her, and then, remembering the shuttered look with which Claudia tended to react to any comments about her ex-husband or her marriage, she decided that she might be better off simply saying and doing nothing.

Like everyone else who knew Claudia, Maxine

admired the way she had handled her divorce, which, if the rumours that had gone round the town at the time were to be believed, had been brought on by Garth's infidelity, and the way she had refused to allow her own feelings to damage Tara's relationship with her father.

Not many women would be so altruistic, so determined to control their own feelings no matter what the personal cost, and to put those of their child first, but then, Claudia had always been a wonderfully devoted mother. Demanding though her work might be, there had never been a single occasion that Maxine could remember in all the years she had worked for her when Claudia had not put Tara's needs first, even if that had meant risking losing an important contract by putting a client second to her daughter. In Maxine's view, the friend who had suggested once when Claudia was out of earshot that if Claudia had more often put Garth's needs ahead of those of his daughter or even given them parity to hers, then he and Claudia might still be married, in Maxine's view, was no friend at all.

Garth frowned again as he turned into Ivy House's driveway. After parking his car, he got out and started to walk towards the front door, and then, on impulse, he changed his mind and turned on his heel to walk round to the rear of the house towards the conservatory—the conservatory they had added to celebrate their tenth wedding anniversary.

Appraisingly, he studied it. The heavy bronze

frog he and Tara had chosen together as a pre-birthday present for Claudia that same year was still there standing guard to the left of the door. Quickly, he bent down and felt beneath it, his fingers curling over the familiar shape of the key he found there.

He and Claudia had not had the kind of divorce that had necessitated anything so aggressive or traumatic as changing the house's locks. And some habits, it seemed, lasted longer than others. Quietly, he unlocked the conservatory door and walked in.

It wasn't that he feared that Claudia would refuse to let him into the house; the relationship they presently shared was civil enough if coolly distant. It was just…

Just what? That he wanted to surprise her—to catch her off guard, to *see* her face before she had time to hide behind the barrier he knew she would throw up against him?

'Why?' he had asked her passionately in the early years after their divorce. 'Why the *hell* do you have to treat me with this ridiculous blanket of cold civility, Claudia, after all we've—'

'Why? Because I *have* to,' she had flung back at him bitingly. 'I *have* to because if I don't, I might start letting you see how I really feel about you, Garth, and for Tara's sake, I can't afford to do that.'

'Do you really hate me that much?' he had asked her emotively.

'Yes,' she had told him. 'Yes, I do.'

'Well, you know what they say,' he had returned. 'Hate and love are merely different sides of the same coin, and where there's hate, there must also be love.'

'Where there was love, there is now hate,' Claudia had corrected him. 'Hate for you and hate even more for myself that I was ever fool enough to love you…to trust you.'

Maxine had said that Claudia was working from home, but there was no sound of any kind of activity coming from the room where he knew she worked, and a sharp prickle of atavistic emotion jarred up his spine.

The mere fact that Claudia had actually telephoned him last night was a clear indication of just how distraught she must have been, not that he had needed any telephone call to warn him of the devastating effect Tara's news would have on her.

The house felt alien and alarmingly silent, a house he remembered being filled with the sounds of Tara's childhood. Suddenly impelled by a sharp sense of urgency, he started to take the stairs two at a time, calling her name as he did so.

Later, Claudia told herself that her instinctive automatic response to the sound of Garth's voice—a response that had her racing to her bedroom door and flinging it open, ignoring the fact that she was still only wearing the towel she had wrapped around her naked body after her shower—was simply a reflex action and nothing more. Just in time, she realised what she was doing, and as Garth reached the landing, Claudia took a deep breath and stepped through the doorway.

'Garth, what are you doing here?' she demanded unsteadily, an uncomfortable colour flooding her face and then slowly spreading to her body as she recognised how betraying her presence here at home and still not being dressed must be—especially to someone who had once known her as well as Garth did.

The relief Garth had felt when he first saw her evaporated as he saw the way she was reacting to his presence, her obvious discomfort, the way her face and body had coloured, the way she was looking almost furtively back into the bedroom, as though...

'Why didn't you go into work this morning?' he demanded suspiciously.

Claudia stared at him.

'That's none of your business,' she told him crisply, turning on her heel dismissively and walking back into her bedroom.

Garth followed her.

'Isn't it?' he demanded, and then stopped. The bed was made up, no sign of an alien male presence to sully its immaculate neatness. Claudia's hair-dryer lay on a chair on top of the clean underwear she had obviously put out to wear.

'Garth, what are you doing...what are you looking for?' Claudia demanded sharply as she quickly checked the bedside table, thankful to see that there was no sign of the bottle of sleeping tablets—not that it was any business of Garth's what she did, not any more, but she knew him and knew he would fuss if he thought…

'I'm not looking for anyone…anything,' Garth denied quickly, catching himself up as he realised how much he had betrayed himself and the reason for his male aggression and hostility. Had he really expected to find someone else in Claudia's bed?

Logically, perhaps not, but emotionally, even after so many years apart, he wasn't ready for that, for another man in Claudia's life.

'You rang me last night,' he told Claudia as he felt his blood pressure and his heartbeat start to return to normal.

Claudia avoided meeting his eyes, giving a small, oddly girlish shrug as she responded, 'Did I? I…'

'Claudia, don't play games with me,' Garth warned her. 'I'm not asking you a question. I'm making a statement. *You* rang me *and* I know why. Tara's told you that she's going to marry Ryland.'

'She has told me, yes,' Claudia agreed, still refusing to look at him, 'and yes, I did ring you, but why on earth that should bring you rushing down here behaving like some character out of a bad play, I really don't know.'

'You're lying, Claudia. For God's sake, I *know* you rang *and* I know why. It's nothing to be ashamed of. If you needed—'

'I need nothing and no one, but most of all, I do *not* need *you*,' Claudia interrupted him with a fierce passion. 'I would never let myself need a man I can't trust, a man who—'

'*Let* yourself need,' Garth broke in. 'Hell, Claudia, there's no shame in being afraid...in being vulnerable...human...in turning to someone else for help.'

'I want you to leave, Garth. I want you to leave right now,' Claudia told him, then walked away from him and went to stand in front of the window. Dear God, she couldn't bear this. She simply didn't have the emotional reserves to cope with it, not right now, not after last night. She could feel her heart starting to beat furiously fast. She tried to swallow and found that she couldn't. Her palms felt damp and she knew that any minute now she was going to start to visibly betray what she was feeling—the panic, the fear, the despair—and the last person she wanted to see her doing that was Garth, the *very* last.

Didn't he *know*, couldn't he understand, that superimposed over every memory she had of him was the image she had created out of the darkest depths of her imagination of him with *her*, of him loving *her*, of his face contorted with passion and need as he possessed *her*, and that image was like a sickness buried deep inside her that surfaced through all the smothering layers of rigid self-control she had placed over it to reduce her to a pulsing, aching, dying thing of burning acid jealousy and bitterness?

'Claudia, look, I know how you must be feeling.'

Instead of leaving, he had walked up behind

her, and Claudia tensed as she felt his breath against her hair.

'No, you do *not* know how I'm feeling, Garth,' she snapped. 'How can you? How can anyone know?'

Claudia could hear hysteria edging up under her voice. Damn Garth. Why had he had to do this, come here like this and undermine her previous self-control?

'Tara is my daughter, too, and I'm going to miss her as well—'

'Miss her? It isn't because I'm going to *miss* her that...' Gulping in air, Claudia shook her head, unable to go on any further. 'I don't know what brought you here, Garth,' she continued when she had finally regained control of herself. 'I've got a very busy day ahead of me and right now I'd like to get dressed.'

'Why did you ring me last night?'

Somehow or other, Claudia found the strength to turn round and face him. 'That was a *mistake*,' she told him quietly. 'I...I—'

'Dialled the wrong number?' Garth suggested harshly.

Claudia shook her head. He knew perfectly well she hadn't done that; they both did.

'It was a mistake, Garth,' she repeated.

'No, it wasn't,' Garth contradicted her. 'You rang *me* because for once your emotions, your *real* emotions got the better of you. You rang me because you were afraid, because *you needed* me.'

'No,' Claudia denied. 'I *don't* need you, Garth. I stopped needing you a long time ago, and—'

'You needed me as Tara's father,' Garth continued as though she hadn't spoken, as though she hadn't uttered those passionate words of denial and fury. 'Clo...'

The unexpected use of his old pet name for her was like a sawtooth file being used on an oversensitive raw nerve ending, and Claudia flinched, visibly unable to suppress the tears that suddenly filled her eyes. Garth reached out and caught hold of her, drawing her close.

She still smelled the same as she had always done, of vanilla and soft clean skin and something that was and always would be essentially her. She still felt the same, too, feminine, womanly, all the woman he had ever really wanted although he knew that she would never believe that.

'Clo, it's all right, it's all right,' he told her huskily. Unexpectedly, uncontrollably, he was transported back to another place, another time, another life, when he had had the right to hold her, to touch her. 'Claudia...'

Memory...instinct...could be a dangerously powerful and unmerciful force. Her eyes closed, her body taut with anger and rejection, Claudia's senses registered the tone of his voice, recognised its hunger, and like Garth, she was transported back to a time when all that it had taken to arouse her had been that particular note in his voice, that special touch of his hands caressing her body.

As he felt her body relax, Garth automatically

closed the gap between them, bending his head to cover her quiescent mouth with his own.

She felt so good, so right…so *Claudia*. As his hands sensuously kneaded the warm flesh of her arms, he started to circle her lips with the tip of his tongue, waiting for her lips to part in their private sexual signal, their special shorthand message passed from him to her and back again that very soon the hungry, urgent thrust of his tongue within her mouth would be echoed by the even more hungry, urgent thrust of his body within hers.

Outside in the street, a car door slammed abruptly, bringing Claudia back to reality. Hot-faced, she tried to thrust Garth away.

She was forty-five, damn it, and even if she hadn't, even if she wasn't…even if they *didn't*…there was no way she considered the kind of openly sexual way Garth was behaving acceptable in a relationship between people of their age. It just wasn't…it just didn't…

'Let me go,' she demanded freezingly, pushing him back more defiantly. 'Let go of me, Garth! I can't bear your touching me…I loathe your touching me,' she told him vehemently, the flustered colour burning even more hotly in her face.

'No,' Garth challenged her furiously. He knew that he was deliberately feeding his own anger and using it to mask very different, far more complex emotions.

It had shaken him badly to discover just how frighteningly easy it had been to allow his emotions to work that time trick on him, that subtle but volatile and dangerous mirage that exchanged reality for fiction.

'Yes,' Claudia insisted icily.

Freezing her feelings, numbing herself, had been the only way she had of denying her pain, of escaping from it all those years ago when...

'I can't bear it when you touch me, Garth,' she reiterated quietly. 'I can't bear it because every time you do, I see *her*. I see you touching *her* and I feel sick...I am sick,' she told him expressionlessly.

'I'm sick, too,' Garth retorted bitterly. 'Sick of being treated like a leper, sick of being made to feel that I'm some kind of lowlife who doesn't... I've tried to tell you. It wasn't *like* that, Claudia. It just wasn't like that. I thought... I can't even remember touching her, never mind—'

'Really...you can't *remember*?' Claudia could hear her voice rising, cracking under the strain of trying to maintain her self-control. 'You can't remember making love to her in our home...our bed? You can't remember that you...'

She was screaming the words at him, Claudia recognised in horror, shouting them, as out of control now as she had been all those years ago when she had first realised, first acknowledged the truth.

'Claudia...' Garth protested, swearing under his breath with male impotence in the face of so much female fury.

'Get out,' Claudia demanded. 'Just go, Garth. You may have come here to gloat, to—'

'To what? Just what the hell do you think I am?' Garth demanded. 'Claudia, I didn't—'

'To remind me that you warned me that something like this might happen. How that must please you, Garth. How happy it must make you—'

'Claudia. I didn't come here to gloat. I came because I thought you might need someone to talk to…because I was concerned.'

'Concerned.' Claudia froze. 'Concerned,' she repeated, her voice metallic and sharp with disbelief. 'Concerned for whom, Garth? Certainly not for me, the woman, the wife, you betrayed so easily. Did you talk about me when you were in bed with her? Did you discuss your *concern* for me with her? Ah, but I was forgetting. If you can't remember making love to her, then you certainly won't be able to remember discussing me, will you?'

'Claudia, for God's sake… I came here to talk to you about Tara, about her…' Garth held his breath, waiting for her to retaliate, and when she didn't, he started to release it very slowly.

'But we *are* talking about her, aren't we?' she said softly now.

Across the silence that divided them, their eyes met and it was Garth's that fell first.

'Claudia,' he began rawly, but she shook her head, the tempest of the emotions that had driven her so close to the edge of her self-control safely harnessed now, and she wasn't going to allow Garth to provoke her into another demeaning outburst.

'I've got to get ready to go out, Garth, I'm already running late,' she told him crisply.

One look at her face told Garth that he would be wasting his time trying to talk to her, to reason with her. Shaking his head, he turned round and headed for the open doorway, cursing himself as he did so. He had handled things badly. Beneath her outwardly calm, gentle demeanour, Claudia had a very strong skein of the same stubborn pride and indomitable spirit that had made her father, the brigadier, the respected warrior that he was.

In Claudia, though, its inflexibility was normally tempered by her woman's awareness that life came in varying shades of grey, rather than two opposing colours of black and white—apart from where he was concerned.

As he let himself out of the house and headed for his car, he reminded himself that there was that school of belief that said the greater the love, the greater the hatred following any form of betrayal, but his betrayal...

There were always two sides to every story and she hadn't ever been prepared to listen while he told her his.

After the miscarriage of their first child, Claudia had become so depressed and withdrawn, so caught up in her own grief and sense of loss, that she had not realised that he was grieving, too, that he needed...wanted... As he started the engine, Garth shook his head. What was the point in thinking about that now? It was over. They were over; the only thing they had in common any more was their love for Tara.

Tara...

As the big car purred out of the drive, Garth realised that something was obscuring his vision. He switched on the windscreen wipers and then frowned, grimacing to himself, blinking fiercely. Men weren't supposed to cry, were they? He could remember saying that to Claudia the night she had silently put Tara into his arms for the first time. She had been pathetically small, and he had ached with the overwhelming need to protect her and to keep her safe.

Tara. She was an adult now, not a child, and he could no longer guarantee to make the world, or life, safe and secure for her.

Claudia blinked as she focused vaguely on the flashing light on the telephone, her heart beating unsteadily. She felt...she felt... She was afraid, she acknowledged as she tried to analyse her feelings. How long had she been standing here staring into space? How long was it since Garth had gone?

She felt empty, hollow, disembodied and yet so heavy. So weighed down with the burden of her pain that her feet felt leaden, unable to move.

The telephone had stopped ringing. No doubt her caller would ring back. She was, she discovered, still wrapped only in the towel she had pulled on after her shower. She started to shiver. Beyond the bedroom window, the garden still basked in the warmth of the sun, but Claudia no longer saw it with the zest of a pioneer and adventurer bent on transforming it into her own private vision of paradise. In fact, it wasn't the garden she saw at all.

She had always hated rows, arguments. They left her feeling sick, disorientated, weakened physically and emotionally, and the unexpectedness of this one with Garth had doubled its traumatic effect on her nervous system.

Like a sleepwalker, she started to get dressed, keeping her eyes focused on her dressing-table and its collection of silver-framed photographs, all of them of Tara—Tara as a baby, as a little girl, a teenager, a graduate. Her car keys lay on the dressing-table in front of one of the photographs, the one of Tara in her christening robe. Numbly, Claudia picked them up. She was dressed now, although she couldn't have said what she had on…couldn't have said and didn't care.

Tara… The agonising ache inside her became a racking physical pain.

As she walked slowly downstairs, she could hear a sharp, anxious voice inside her head scolding her, telling her that there were things she had to do, people she had to see, but she ignored it, blotting it out.

There was something else she had to do, somewhere she had to be that was far more important.

The phone on his desk was ringing. Automatically, Lloyd reached out and picked it up.

'Lloyd, Lloyd, when are you coming back to the island?' His heart sank as he recognised

Margot's voice. He could tell from the sound of it that she was crying. Unwillingly, he pictured her.

She would be lying on her bed, her dark eyes burning with intensity, her thin frame curled protectively into a foetus-like ball.

Her body had developed a hard, angular edge to it and she had about her a hungry, voracious look. But as he of all people had good reason to know, her hunger wasn't for food.

'The summer is our time,' she was protesting tearfully now. 'My time with you. It's the only time we have together. Oh, Lloyd, I can't bear it here without you.'

The words made a sound like a long, tormented wail, assaulting his eardrums with their pain.

'I had to come back, Margot, but I should be through here by the weekend.'

'The weekend... That means we'll have missed a full week together. Ring me tonight, won't you? I'll be... thinking of you.'

As he replaced the receiver, Lloyd stared unseeingly across his desk. He normally closed his office during the summer vacation—after all, with the campus practically deserted, there was no need for him to keep it open. Their business in California, like that in Boston, came from the universities' professors and students whose work they published, but his assistant had sounded so excited over the telephone about the manuscript he had received in Lloyd's absence that Lloyd

had agreed to fly home to meet with the author
and read the manuscript.

Margot had protested, of course, pleading
with him not to go.

'We have so little time together,' she had reminded him, and of course it was the truth, but
these past few summers he had somehow or
other found that when he was with her, the intensity of her love, her need, made him feel uncomfortably claustrophobic. It wasn't that he
loved her any the less, he hastily reassured himself. How could he? She had given up so much
for him, for their love, even to the extent of...

Pushing away his chair, he got up and walked
across to the window.

He lived on the coast, and his apartment had
wonderful views of the ocean. Whenever he had
time, he enjoyed walking along the beach. When
they were younger, the girls had enjoyed going
with him, but they were almost grown up now,
students at UCLA and with far better things to
do with their time than visiting their ex-
stepfather—he hadn't had any children with
Carole-Ann. When the girls were younger, he
had often thought that he would enjoy being a
birth father. He liked children, but during the
few years he had been married, he had felt that it
would almost be tantamount to being unfaithful
to Margot to have a sexual relationship with
Carole-Ann, even though she was his wife. After
all, their marriage had been more or less a business arrangement anyway. He had thought that
the presence of a wife and two children in his

background added the necessary *gravitas* to his professional status, and she, after a bad divorce and two failed live-in relationships, had told him quite bluntly what she wanted. It wasn't for sex so much as security, financial security and stability, for her and her daughters. And so they had married.

Margot had hated his marrying Carole-Ann; she had refused point-blank to attend the wedding or to meet with Carole-Ann and the girls.

Carole-Ann had known all about Margot. Impossible for him not to have told her.

'I love her,' he had told her quietly, 'but we can't marry and—'

'Not in some states maybe, but you could go away together, abroad…'

'No. To live apart from family and friends, in a kind of exile, that isn't what either of us wants. Margot is inclined to be a little highly strung.' He had paused, wondering how much he should tell Carole-Ann and then decided that it wasn't necessary to explain to her that the pressure of their love for one another had already brought Margot close to the edge of a nervous breakdown.

'I can't give Lloyd up…I can't. Please don't make me,' she had cried hysterically when her mother had intervened in their teenage love affair to remind them that they were by law prohibited from sharing their lives. 'If you try to make us part, I shall kill myself,' she had threatened, and both Lloyd and her mother had known that there was a very real possibility that she would do exactly that.

Then, he had loved her just as much as she loved him. But there had always been room for other things in his life; he had played sports in those days, enjoyed sailing and socialising. But Margot had become so upset about the time they spent apart, the activities that kept them apart, that he had unwillingly dropped them to please her.

Uncharacteristically, it had originally been her idea that he should marry. Family pressure had been brought to bear on them both to make him agree to move to California, but following his departure, Margot had immediately stopped eating and made herself so ill that her mother had been forced to give in and agree that Lloyd should return to Boston and to the island every summer.

'You want me to marry, but why?' Lloyd had questioned Margot in astonishment when she had first raised the subject with him.

'Because, don't you see,' she had demanded passionately, 'that way, no one will be able to object.'

'What about my wife?'

'You're not to call her that,' Margot had immediately flashed furiously at him. 'She is not to be your wife...only I can ever really be that. She is simply to be married to you. It will be a marriage of convenience, that's all.'

Lloyd had laughed at her indulgently at the time. He had felt very indulgent towards her in those days. Since his move to UCLA and his taking on full responsibility for their business there, he felt that he had become immeasurably more mature, a man of the world, whereas Margot was still very much a cherished and protected girl.

But then he had met Carole-Ann, and Margot's suggestion had suddenly seemed to make good sense. There was a part of Lloyd that enjoyed playing the archetypal Bostonian gentleman's role…of rescuing a woman in distress. And at first Margot had seemed pleased. It was only later, after he had proposed and Carole-Ann had accepted, that she had started asking questions, telephoning him at all hours of the day and night—a habit that she had continued even after he and Carole-Ann were married.

'Look, I don't give a shit if she disturbs your sleep,' Carole-Ann had yelled at him once in the middle of a row, 'but I won't have the crazy bitch disturbing me, and waking up the kids.'

'She loves me—' Lloyd had started to protest.

But Carole-Ann had cut him short, telling him in angry disgust, 'She's mad, obsessed, possessed by what she feels for you, but as for love… I don't think she's capable of knowing what that means. If she really loved you, she'd want you to have a proper life of your own….'

That had been one of the worst summers, the worst years, of his life.

Six weeks after his return home from the island, he had received a hysterical telephone call from Margot.

'But you can't be pregnant,' he had protested in shock, his hand tightening sweatily around the receiver, his heart pounding sickly and heavily.

'I'm five weeks late,' Margot had screamed. 'Five weeks! Oh, God, Lloyd, what are we going to do?'

In the end, it had turned out to be a false alarm, but it had been after that that Margot had announced to him her decision to be sterilised.

'Margot, no,' he had protested instinctively, telling himself that the tight sensation he could feel in his throat was the anguish of his love for her rather than that of any psychological sense of a noose tightening around his neck. 'You could meet someone else, marry, have children with him...'

'No,' she had howled, the sound a primal protest. 'I shall never marry, never. The only man I want to marry is you, the only child I want is yours. You're just saying that because you don't love me any more,' she had accused him. 'You don't care. You—'

'Of course I love you,' Lloyd had protested.

At the end of the year, Carole-Ann informed him that she was filing for divorce. She had met someone else, she told him, shrugging aside his shock.

He had kept in touch with the girls although he had said nothing to Margot about doing so. She had, after his divorce, begun cross-questioning him about the places he went and the people, the women, he met. His was a lonely life; he had friends, of course, but his relationship with Margot had to be kept a secret from them. She at least had her family, their family, around her.

He glanced at his watch. Two o'clock. His meeting with Dr Jamie Friedland was at two-fifteen. Danny, his assistant, had made all the arrangements. Since the professor was apparently still looking for an apartment, having spent his first term at UCLA in someone else's spare room, it made sense for their meeting to take place at Lloyd's apartment. Normally, he preferred to see potential authors away from his own home, but Danny had been so thoroughly excited about the professor's manuscript that Lloyd hadn't had the heart to remind him of that.

Certainly his work made very interesting reading—what Lloyd could understand of it, which wasn't very much. But according to Danny, who could, it was a definitive work on its subject, breaking new ground and raising questions about established procedures other academics were going to find hard to answer.

Out of the corner of his eye, Lloyd saw a car turning into his driveway, a small European convertible sports model, driven by a redhead, her long hair mussed by the wind.

Frowning, Lloyd watched as she parked the car and got out. Tall and fashionably voluptuous, she moved with a confidence, an inherent liking of herself, that momentarily took his breath away. He couldn't remember the last time he had seen a woman so completely at peace with herself. She was, he decided, the complete antithesis of Margot. His frown deepened as he saw her look up at his window before heading for the entrance to his apartment. Ten seconds later as his intercom buzzed, he heard her announcing her arrival.

Dr Jamie Friedland to see Lloyd Kennet.

As he activated the automatic lock and let her in, Lloyd had the oddest sensation of being on the brink of something so fateful and portentous that for a moment, he almost felt half-afraid to meet her.

Irritably, he pushed it away. So he had made a mistake assuming that she was a man. Why should that matter?

6

——►◄——

No one paid any attention to the fashionably dressed, elegant woman parking her car on the sunny residential London street. Why should they? The BMW might have been a more expensive, more up-market model than the others of its breed parked outside their owners' smartly painted front gates, but it fitted neatly alongside the wide variety of chunky four-wheel-drive vehicles that had become the nineties' version of the more traditional Volvo estate as the favourite vehicle for the school-and-shopping run.

The large double-fronted house close to which she had parked had recently been converted into a small hotel—the kind patronised by ladies of a certain age up from the country to spend a few days shopping and catching up with old friends. It might not have the éclat or the convenience of its Knightsbridge sisters but, 'My dear, one gets…feels…so comfortable there—and safe….' and its prices were, of course, so much cheaper.

But it wasn't the hotel that was Claudia's destination even though she spent several minutes staring at it.

The street, her surroundings, once so familiar to her, had changed dramatically from the days when she and Garth had rented a flat in one of the shabby and rather run-down terraced houses that had lined it. Since then, they had been smartened up and gentrified out of all recognition, their gleaming paintwork and shiny, clean, linen-draped windows confusing and bewildering her.

The flat she and Garth had rented had been at number twelve on the top floor—or rather in the attic—up a flight of rickety stairs covered by a piece of dust-filled, ancient, dark red patterned carpet—or at least they assumed it had once been dark red.

They had found it at the end of a long week of scouring the city for somewhere suitable to live that they could afford, and with Garth having only hours of his leave left before he was due to return to his regiment, they had pounced in relief on the opportunity to rent a place that was within their budget.

'At least we'll have our own bathroom and kitchen,' Claudia had murmured when Garth shook his head over the grimy shabbiness of the small rooms, 'and decorating it will give me something to do while you're away.'

'You'll be working,' Garth had reminded her before adding protectively, 'and besides, I don't like the idea of your climbing about on ladders when I'm not here.'

They had still been very much at the honeymoon stage of their marriage then, still very protective of their love and their privacy, and Claudia had been adoringly proud of the way

Garth had refused both his and her own parents' offer of financial assistance towards providing them with a better home.

'No, we must start as we mean to go on,' Garth had told her firmly while they were discussing the subject. All the protests she had been about to make melted beneath his kisses, just as her body did, when he added, whispering the words against her mouth, 'I want to look after you myself, sweet. I want to take care of you.'

It might have been the seventies, she might have had her own newly burgeoning career, but Claudia had been brought up in a household by parents who adhered to the old-fashioned values of *their* own parents, and while she would have hated Garth to be domineering or bossy, to expect her to treat him as some kind of superior simply because he was a man, she made no bones about the fact that she enjoyed being pampered by him, being shown that he loved and cared about her; that he wanted to protect her and look after her. It was, after all, exactly the way her father treated her mother, and her parents had been happily married now for over twenty-five years.

They had moved into the flat one rainy weekend, good-humouredly assisted by some of Garth's friends from the regiment, who had helped carry the sturdy pieces of furniture, given to Claudia and Garth by their parents, up to their new home.

'But, darling, why waste your money buying furniture when Daddy and I have so much,' her mother had protested when Claudia tried to object. 'This table was your great-grandmother's,' she'd added softly after she and Claudia had gone up into the attic to sort through the furniture that was stored there.

And even though the solid furnishings looked slightly incongruous in the rather down-at-heel surroundings of their new home, it was comforting to have things around them that came from both their families, Claudia had told Garth lovingly.

Only their bed was new—at Garth's masterful insistence—and Claudia had blushed slightly when they had gone to buy it and the salesman had insisted that they try it out.

'We find that many couples these days are going for the larger king-sized bed,' the salesman had told them, obviously scenting a better commission from the larger sale.

Garth had shaken his head and whispered teasingly to Claudia, 'No way. I want you just as close to me as I can get you, in bed and out of it. I don't want there to be *any* space, *any* distance, *anything* or *anyone* between us, Claudia,' he had emphasised later when they had been alone in his car. He had parked down a quiet, overgrown country track, then pulled her into his arms and kissed her passionately to reinforce the intensity of his words.

Claudia had responded to him equally passionately, if a little shyly. She might not any longer be a virgin but she was still a little hesitant, a little unsure, even a little afraid of her own sexuality. She had been startled by her physical hunger for him and wondered how uninhibited it was permissible for a woman to be.

After Garth and his friends had finished carrying the furniture up the four flights of stairs to their attic home, Claudia had cooked them all a huge meal of spaghetti Bolognese cooked on the Baby Belling stove that was part of the fitments of the flat and that Claudia and her mother had spent hours cleaning with hundreds of packs of Brillo pads.

Afterwards, they had all gone to the local pub, where the short army haircuts of the men had marked them out quite clearly as what they were among the other young men there with floppy, often shoulder-length hair.

The air in the pub had been thick with cigarette smoke and the sweet, cloying smell of hash, and Claudia had been glad when it eventually came time to leave.

She and Garth had walked home, arms around one another, and in the shadows on the corner of the street, Garth had stopped and pulled her quickly into his arms, kissing her with fierce passion.

'God, I want you, Claudia,' he told her thickly. 'Tonight, watching you...' He stopped, shaking his head, not totally sure just how she would react if he told her about the almost savage spurt of lust and love he had felt earlier on in the evening, watching her as she leaned over the sink to reach something on its far side, the action drawing the fabric of her jeans tightly across the rounded peachiness of her behind.

The temptation to walk up behind her and reach around her to caress the warm weight of her breasts while he... Perhaps it was just as well that they *hadn't* been alone and that the others had still been there at the time, he reflected wryly as he studied her face in the moonlight. She was so soft and gentle, so sweetly responsive, that he couldn't quite bring himself to demand more of her, to show her the more forceful and sensual side of his sexuality. There was something about Claudia—a combination perhaps of her own innate gentleness and her upbringing—that set her apart from her more robust peers, which was one of the reasons he had fallen in love with her in the first place, Garth freely acknowledged.

It was late, gone midnight, when they eventually let themselves into the dark and silent house. The single, low-watt bulbs that were supposed to illuminate the stairs and each landing of the flats obviously needed replacing. Dark, shadowed landings were all very well when *he* was with Claudia, but he didn't want her having to walk the four flights to their flat on her own when he *wasn't* there with her, Garth decided, making a mental note to replace the light-bulbs in the morning and to speak to their landlord about them.

He was due back with the regiment tomorrow, and later as they lay in bed together, he could hear Claudia sigh.

'What is it?' he asked her softly, reaching for her in the darkness.

'Nothing, really. I just wish you didn't have to go back tomorrow.'

'I know, but it won't be for long. I've got some real leave coming up at the end of the month,' he reminded her comfortingly.

In the darkness, Claudia bit her lip. Some real leave, yes, followed by a tour of duty in Northern Ireland. She was not an army daughter for nothing.

'Dad was saying that they're talking about making cuts in any new intake and of amalgamating some of the smaller regiments,' she commented.

'Mmm...I know,' Garth agreed. His new father-in-law had already warned him about the rumours he'd heard that promotions were going to be hard to come by in the future. At the end of the year, Garth's present contract would expire and he had not yet made his mind up whether or not he would sign on for another term. When he had originally decided on a career in the army, he had not been thinking about how it would affect a wife and children, but he had recently seen several of his peers' marriages break down under the pressure of the separations that an army wife inevitably suffered.

As Garth bent his head in the darkness to find her mouth with his own, Claudia knew that it wasn't just the thought of his departure tomorrow that was bothering her.

On Monday morning, she started her new job

working as a probation officer for one of the London borough councils.

Technically, she was well qualified for the job but she had felt at her interview that her supervisor seemed, for some reason, antagonistic towards her. Nothing she could actually put her finger on, just one or two slightly acid remarks about her background and a sense of the other woman's rather challenging attitude, although, to be fair, she had to admit that the inner-city conditions in which she would be working *were* going to be tough.

'The army life I've been brought up in isn't a totally protected environment,' Claudia had responded as calmly as she could to Janice Long's sharp probing. 'There can be problems with drink and drugs, marital breakdowns and, of course, the trauma of men being badly injured and killed.'

'Men...' the other woman had responded, 'but here in *this* borough, we often have to deal with children who have been abused...beaten... starved, subjected to every kind of emotional and physical as well as sexual degradation. They are so vulnerable it's easy for them to go off the rails.' She had added, 'How well do you think you are equipped to deal with them?'

'I'm not,' Claudia had replied honestly. 'I doubt that anyone is. I can't imagine that it's *ever* possible to totally ignore one's feelings under such circumstances, but with time and training I hope and believe that one can put aside one's own personal response in order to help those we're there to help.'

She had got the job but she suspected that she had not really convinced Janice Long that she was the right candidate for it.

'Mmm…' Garth murmured as he nibbled at her lips. 'You taste good… You taste good all over, Clo,' he added huskily as he lowered his head and started nibbling gently at the tender flesh of her throat.

Claudia's whole body quivered. She knew what *that* particular note in Garth's voice meant.

The first time he had told her that he wanted to kiss her, taste her all over, she had been more shocked than aroused, and even now there was still a part of her that felt faintly awkward, uncertain, about the intimacy of what he was doing. Although the sensation of his mouth…

She shuddered more deeply as his warm, moist tongue started to circle her nipple, then she closed her eyes and deliberately willed herself to stop thinking about tomorrow and to enjoy instead the delicious sensation of sensual pleasure and sexual excitement that was building up inside her body.

As Garth felt her body begin to relax, he started to draw her nipple deeper into his mouth, alternately teasing it with delicate flicks of his tongue then with a much deeper, hungrier, fullmouthed suckling that made Claudia tense her muscles and arch her back as her whole body responded to the rhythmic pressure of his mouth.

Garth loved Claudia's breasts. He loved *all* of

her, of course, but her breasts were just perfect,
filling the palms of his hands when he cupped
them, soft and warm and satin skinned, her nipples a warm coral pink discreetly demure when
she was not aroused but very erotically hard and
swollen in response to his lovemaking. Her
breasts were, in fact, a reflection of Claudia herself, modest and quiescent publicly, but *privately*,
delicious and erotic and unexpectedly very sensually responsive.

In the darkness, Claudia felt Garth's hand
stroking her breasts, then moving to her waist
and lower. Automatically, she moved with him,
parting her legs, quivering slightly with the onset of her need to feel him within her.

His index finger circled her navel and teased a
little bit farther down. In response, Claudia bit
reprimandingly on his ear in a mingling of feminine urgency and warning.

Recognising this wordless signal of her need,
Garth tugged passionately on her nipple, using
his body weight to keep her pinned to the bed beneath him as he felt the reactive shudders of responsive pleasure galvanising her body.

The last thing on Claudia's mind now was
work. The *only* thoughts she wanted or needed to
have were those of Garth and how he was making her feel; of how he *would* soon be making her
feel when the full, strong, pulsating length of
him was sheathed hotly inside her own body.

Behind her closed eyelids, she was already
visualising the coming together of their bodies,
his proud and hard, the skin stretched tight over

the passion-filled, dark-veined surge of his manhood, the glands totally and, to her mind, oddly vulnerably exposed, the skin hot and silky to her touch, thirsty for the tender moistness that lay within her own body, which she pictured as a soft, wet, life-giving protective place where he would be kept safe. Here in this secret and private garden of Eden, his body could take its fill of pleasure in perfect safety until with all the sternness of the sleeping Earth Mother once worshipped and feared by the ancient Greeks, she reminded him of his duty, his purpose, the soft muscles that had held him so tenderly now tightening around him, making him, making *both* of them, obey the laws of nature as they drew from him the spark of life.

It might not technically be necessary to have an orgasm in order to become pregnant, but Claudia was secretly convinced that there was something about the deep, convulsive movement that rendered her womb particularly responsive and receptive to the act of procreation, the creation of a new life.

If that was not the case, then why had Mother Nature specifically designed a woman so that she should experience this need to have her man penetrate her so deeply, completely, that she should feel as she did right now, Claudia asked herself dizzily…and why also would a man *want* to do so?

If the clitoris was a woman's prime source of pleasure, then why *should she* have this need, this urgency, this wanton, aching, screaming compulsion to urge Garth ever deeper inside her, to feel the hot, wet explosion of his release just as close to her womb as he could possibly get?

Very slowly, Garth released Claudia's nipple, kissing his way down over her flat belly, her skin damp and softly sheeny with sexual arousal, but she still covered her sex with her hand.

Circling her navel with his tongue, Garth placed his hand over hers, lacing his fingers down through hers as he slowly and deliberately stroked the crisp dark curls that covered her pubic mound and then slipped one finger deeper, parting the demurely closed outer lips of her sex to explore the moist sensuality they were concealing.

The sensation of her own hand pressed hard against her pubic bone while Garth's finger stroked her made Claudia moan a small, shocked protest. There had been times, rather shockingly frequent occasions, in fact, during their engagement when Garth had not been there, when she had lain alone on her bed touching herself, exploring herself, initially simply idly, wondering how she might feel to Garth. But then, as her newly aroused female senses caught fire, her touch had been more deliberate, more purposeful and urgent. She had *never* discussed these acts with Garth, nor had he previously indicated that he knew that they took place.

Now, instinctively, she realised that he did, an awareness that was confirmed when he whispered rawly against her stomach, 'I want you to think of me like this when I'm not here, Clo. I want you to remember how good it feels. It does feel good, doesn't it...?'

Unable to stop herself from shuddering as his fingertip gently rotated the small, throbbing, almost too sensitive nub of her clitoris, Claudia could only moan a choked response. Automatically, her legs were opening, her hips moving in a hungry, grinding motion as she locked the fingers of her free hand in Garth's hair and tugged protestingly, at the same time trying to free her other hand.

Amazingly, Garth let it go, his own hands reaching for her hips. Claudia expelled her breath in a relief-cracked groan, eagerly anticipating the slow thrust of him within her achingly responsive and ready body, but instead of penetrating her, Garth lowered his head and manoeuvred her so that her body opened easily and eagerly for him as he ran the tip of his tongue from her clitoris right down the length of her most private region and then back up again, firmly repeating the caress over and over again until the whole of her sex felt swollen and wet, tingling, aching, with the heat of a sexual urgency so intense that had she been able, Claudia knew that she would have taken the initiative herself.

Even so, it shocked her when Garth seemed to read her mind, taking hold of her and rolling down onto the bed on his back while he lifted her over his body, over it and down onto it, down onto *him*.

'You want me...take me,' he whispered rawly to her. 'Show me how hungry you are for me,

Clo…show me how much you want me. Yes, that's it,' he told her thickly as she moved on top of him, lifting her hips, then lifting herself as she slowly and uncertainly at first started to ride him. The look on his face told her all she needed to know, giving her the courage and encouragement to take control of her own sexuality and of *him*. She heard him groan as she deliberately compressed her muscles and held him still.

Hungrily, he reached for her breasts. Claudia leaned forward, moving oh so slowly and deliberately up and down the thick, hot moistness of his shaft, slowly at first then faster while Garth groaned and kneaded her breast and then reached down between her legs to tug on her now erotically engorged clitoris.

The combined sensation of Garth touching her while his penis filled her was almost too much for Claudia to bear. She was aware of a sensation of hurtling towards a barrier and knew that once through it she would have absolutely no control. Everything was rushing over her too fast for her to stop and she heard herself cry out Garth's name. Then she screamed as her body exploded in a climax so intense that she was still shuddering with the aftershock of it minutes later when she lay wrapped in Garth's arms, the tears of release lying damply on his chest.

'*That's* how I want you to remember me… *us*…when I'm not here,' Garth whispered roughly to her as he kissed her damp eyelids and then her mouth. 'That's how I'm going to make love to you the night we conceive our child.'

They had already talked about the family they planned to have, not for a while yet, but neither of them wanted to wait too long. Claudia wanted four children, two boys and two girls, but Garth had demurred that maybe they should stop at two.

'Four will be expensive to educate, especially if I stay on in the army,' he had warned her.

That was another subject they had discussed at great length. Claudia was well aware of what it meant to be an army wife, and the last thing she would ever do would be to want to come between Garth and a career he loved, but Garth himself, as she knew, was now having second thoughts about his own commitment to the army.

'I wish you weren't going back tomorrow,' Claudia repeated drowsily to him as she started to slide towards sleep.

Garth groaned. 'So do I. Oh, God, Clo, but that was good...*you* were good....'

Slowly and lovingly, he ran his hands over her orgasm-relaxed body. He didn't consider himself to be a man who was in any way oversexed and he hoped he wasn't a selfish lover, but he was, he acknowledged, quite highly sexed and Claudia aroused him as no other woman had ever done or would ever do. If they woke up early enough in the morning, he would be able to make love to her again before he had to leave. As he eased her body down against his own, he wondered how she would react if he asked her to forgo wearing any underwear the next time he came home. Just the thought of her sweet, warm body being covered only by a dress or skirt made him start to ache and tingle.

Stop that, he warned his slowly engorging penis sternly. You're going to have to wait until morning.

Claudia listened intently as Janice Long started to outline the details of one of the cases Claudia would be working on.

'She's eighteen now,' she told Claudia, watching her reaction to the identity photograph inside the file depicting a ravishingly pretty dark-haired girl. 'She's also a heroin addict,' her supervisor continued grimly. 'She first came to our notice three years ago when the police picked her up for soliciting. She told us then that she was seventeen and that she'd run away from home because her stepfather was abusing her. It's a common enough story,' she added when she heard Claudia's quickly indrawn breath of pity.

'Yes, I know,' Claudia agreed, 'but that doesn't make it any the less appalling.'

'Mmm…I dare say it wouldn't if it happened to be true. Katriona, though, unfortunately happens to be an extremely skilled and habitual liar. Most of these girls are. They live in a fantasy world half the time. That's part of their problem. Ours is trying to separate the fantasy from the reality.'

Although she didn't say so, Claudia thought the older woman was being unduly hard. The girl was, after all, just that, and it made Claudia's compassionate heart ache for her to think of how frightened she must have been to find herself on the streets, alone and vulnerable.

As Janice Long watched her, she sighed under her breath. Here was another one, wet behind the ears and dewy-eyed, running over with the milk of human kindness for the rest of mankind. Well, she'd soon learn, just as she'd had to do herself.

The people they were dealing with might be victims and in need of their help but that didn't stop them from possessing their fair share of human vices, being manipulative and crafty, underhanded, deceitful, dishonest and sometimes downright dangerous.

Katriona, for all her stunning good looks and her comparative youth, was no angel. Unlike many others of her ilk, her drug habit had not been forced on her by a manipulative pimp intent on keeping her 'on the game' so that he could live off the money she made him. Katriona didn't *have* a pimp—she didn't need one as she had more than once boasted to Janice. *She* was the one who used men, not the other way around.

She had told Janice that she started using drugs simply because she wanted to see how it felt and she had laughed when the young trainee with Janice at the time was unable to conceal her shocked reaction at this information.

Privately, Janice suspected that Katriona paid for her addiction by selling drugs to some of the other youngsters who shared the squat with her, but neither she nor the police had ever been able to prove it.

'You can't pin anything on me,' Katriona had announced smugly the last time the police had picked her up and Janice had known that she was pleased by their inability to do anything.

One thing Janice did know, or rather thought she knew, was that, despite all her denials, at some stage in her life Katriona had been abused in some way by a man, if not sexually then certainly emotionally and physically. Her hatred and bitter contempt of them were classic signs even if Katriona herself would never admit it.

The whole of her past was, in fact, shrouded in mystery, but again that was not so unusual with these youngsters. Boys as well as girls arrived in London, sleeping rough and disappearing into the teeming underworld of youthful vice and squalor until they were picked up by the police and passed on to the social services. By that time, they had generally invented a new past for themselves.

Sometimes, unfortunately all too rarely, fate was kind and a much loved youngster was reunited with his or her distraught parents, but more often than not...

Janice frowned as she studied Claudia's downbent head. They always proved to be more trouble than they were worth, these upper-middleclass, overidealistic young graduates who hadn't a clue what life was really all about and who still described their parents as 'Mummy' and 'Daddy' while working with...

Mummy and Daddy. God, Katriona would laugh in her face. Either that or scream a torrent of vile abuse at her the moment she heard Claudia's 'Queen's' English accent. But it was not her job to protect the likes of the Claudias of this world from reality. No one had forced her to take the job—a job for which she was completely and culturally unfit so far as Janice was concerned.

She herself had grown up on a vast council estate in the north of England. The only reason she had ever been allowed to take up the place she had won to the local grammar school had been because the headmaster of her junior school had stepped in and persuaded her parents to allow her to go.

Even then, there had been the indignity of having to wear a second-hand uniform, of there never being enough money to pay for her school dinners—and as for any school trips…

She had soon learned to adopt an attitude of indifference to shield herself from the taunts of her schoolmates. At university, when she hadn't been studying for her degree, she had been working to support herself and keeping out of the way of the bosses.

Bar work during term time and the back-breaking slog of fruit picking during the summer. Those summer jobs had been the worst. You always got some man who thought you owed him a favour for letting you have the job—and the kind of favour he wanted meant lying on your back with your legs wide open for him.

Well, not Janice. She had seen too much of what that brought you.

'But who are her parents? Where has she come from?' she heard Claudia asking her frowningly as she studied the file Janice had given her.

Janice gave a small shrug. 'Who knows? Maybe not even her. With her looks, she could have Gypsy or Italian blood but...' Janice gave another shrug.

'But hasn't anyone ever asked her, talked to her?' Claudia protested.

Janice raised her eyebrows. '*Talked* to her? We're dealing with an out and out heroin addict here. You don't talk to them...you talk *at* them and if you're lucky something might just about get through.'

'You sound as though...as though she's some-one to be written off.'

'She's already written herself off,' Janice told her brutally. 'She'll be dead before she's twenty-one.'

'But surely something can be done,' Claudia persisted, unable to conceal her shock. 'A rehab clinic...or...'

Janice shook her head. 'You'd be wasting your time and the taxpayers' money,' she countered grimly. 'She'd never agree to go into rehab and even if she did... One of the first things you have to understand is that...' She paused and shook her head.

What was the point in telling her? Let the girl find out for herself. Young trainees. Why the hell did she always have to be landed with them?

* * *

Determinedly, Claudia refused to allow her feelings of revulsion to show as she followed Janice up the cold, damp concrete stairwell littered with rubbish, its air heavy with the fetid stench of urine and vomit. The huge tower block, like its neighbours, was a rabbit warren of crumbling concrete, of decaying lives. Its very existence, Claudia reflected, was an indictment, a testimony, of man's inhumanity to man.

'Two more flights,' Janice puffed. 'By the way, don't ever be tempted to risk the lifts in these places,' she warned Claudia. 'They're notorious for breaking down—one of our team forgot and ended up being trapped inside one for almost forty-eight hours.'

Claudia shuddered.

'Here we are,' Janice announced. 'It's this way.'

Numbly, Claudia followed her supervisor as she hurried down the walkway that overlooked the dismal rectangle of land enclosed by the tower blocks. Down below them on the ground, a group of teenagers kicked aimlessly at the rubbish that had fallen from a skip, their shoulders hunched defensively, defeatedly, Claudia recognised.

'It's this one,' Janice told her, stopping outside a flat that looked more like a heavily fortified prison than a home, its windows blank and barred, its original wooden door replaced by one of heavy metal.

Janice rapped briskly and then waited. Claudia could hear the sounds of bolts being withdrawn on the other side of the door and her stomach muscles started to clench. A sharp sense that she was somehow standing at the portal of a potentially fateful event suddenly swept through her, banishing logic and reason.

As a panel was pushed to one side to reveal a spy hole, Claudia fought the temptation to give in to the inner voice urging her to flee, to leave, before it was too late.

'What do you want?' she heard a male voice demanding truculently from inside the flat.

'I want to see Katriona Spencer,' Janice responded crisply.

'Well, she don't want to see you,' the voice responded. 'She's busy doing a bit of business. Know what I mean?' he added with a leering laugh.

'Tell her no visit, no giro payment,' Janice told him unperturbedly. There was a few minutes' wait, then just when Claudia thought they were going to have to leave, she could hear the sound of further heavy bolts being drawn back and the door swung open.

If she had thought the stench on the stairs hardly bearable, it was nothing compared to the appalling smell from inside the flat. It made her gag and want to retch as she followed Janice inside. It was, she acknowledged, the stench of degradation and pollution, of human beings who had descended into something dark and obscene.

As Claudia followed Janice through the claustrophobic hallway and into the room that lay beyond it, a thin bearded youth, his torso bare, his jeans pulled down to reveal his flat, thin buttocks, stood up and slowly started to pull them up. Behind him on a filthy mattress a girl lay naked. Hastily, Claudia averted her eyes, but Janice far more hardily demanded, 'Where's Katriona, Lucy?'

'She's upstairs,' the girl responded listlessly, ignoring her nudity and her spread-legged pose as she reached across the grubby mattress for the needle that Claudia could now see glinting in the thin light coming into the room.

As she moved, Claudia could see the existing needle tracks in her arms, and her emotions switched from shocked revulsion to compassionate pity.

'Save it,' Janice advised her, correctly reading her thoughts as she indicated that they were to go upstairs. 'Like Katriona, Lucy services her habit through prostitution,' she informed Claudia as they walked back into the hallway. 'Unlike Katriona, though—at least as yet—Lucy has one prison sentence behind her and another all too likely.'

'What for?' Claudia asked her, expecting to hear that the girl had stolen goods to pay for her habit or perhaps sold them to the other users.

Instead, to her shock, Janice told her bluntly, 'She murdered her own child—oh, it's not uncommon,' she warned Claudia when she saw her expression. 'It wasn't deliberate, of course. It never is. She just lost her temper with the poor little sod one night when the punters hadn't paid her enough for her fix. She lost her temper and lashed out at him when he didn't get out of the way in time. She picked him up and threw him against the wall. He was five years old and a tough little tyke but not tough enough—she broke his skull. Luckily for him he died in hospital three days later without recovering consciousness.'

'Luckily!' Claudia protested, too shocked to hide her feelings.

'If he'd lived, he'd have been brain damaged and if Lucy wasn't prepared to look after him properly, to love and protect him as a healthy, undamaged child, just what chance do you think he would have had with the handicap she inflicted on him?'

Claudia made no answer. What answer was there to make?

'In here,' Janice instructed as they reached the landing. She pushed open one of the bedroom doors.

After the filth and squalor of the downstairs flat, combined with the horror of the story she had just been told, the sight of the young woman seated on the bed studying her reflection in the dressing-table mirror as she slowly brushed her lustrous, long black hair was so incongruous, so normal, that Claudia could only stare at her.

Unlike the girl they had just seen below, this one was clear-eyed and intelligent-looking, her green eyes sharply intent in her small triangular face. She was very pretty, more than pretty, Claudia acknowledged, round about her own build but taller, dressed in a long-sleeved, unexpectedly clean-looking T-shirt and a pair of jeans.

'Who's this?' the girl demanded of Janice, jerking her head in Claudia's direction.

'Claudia has just joined us,' Janice explained smoothly.

The other girl gave Claudia a contemptuous look.

'A trainee, eh. Jesus, just look at her,' she mocked. 'I'll bet she's never even opened her legs for a man, never mind…'

Claudia battened down her instinctive sense of outrage and revulsion, her anger at the way the girl was unwittingly intruding on the privacy of her lovemaking with Garth, defiling it almost, her training coming to the fore as she calmly ignored what the girl was saying.

'Never mind that, Katriona,' Janice challenged her, reaching out before the girl could stop her and holding her wrist firmly with one hand while with the other she pushed up the fabric of her shirt to reveal a heartbreakingly fragile arm and its even more heartbreaking evidence of her drug use. 'She certainly doesn't use,' she told the girl sharply, 'and neither would you if you had any brains.'

'No?' the girl derided, tossing back the thick, heavy weight of her glossy, curly hair. 'Well, I've certainly got enough sense not to fall for that old line. What do you want?'

'You're on probation for soliciting,' Janice reminded her. 'It's a condition of your probation that we see you.'

'So, you've seen me.' Katriona shrugged dismissively, then reached out to the dressing-table for a lipstick and started to apply it carefully to her soft, full mouth.

She was fine-boned, her movements light and fluid like those of a dancer. Who was she, where had she come from and why…why did she stay here, living like this, when quite plainly…?

Claudia reined her thoughts in. One of the first things she had learned was that it wasn't her role to judge or to question.

'You don't *have* to do this, Katriona,' Janice told her quietly. 'An hour from now, you could be trapped in a car with a john who's got a knife at your throat and who's refusing to pay you for what you've done. Even if he does, you've got to get back here without any of the pimps catching you. Why bother when you could have a prescription for methadone and—'

'Go into rehab? Forget it.'

'You're a fool, Katriona. One day, you're going to be like Lucy downstairs, too drugged out to bother closing your legs between punters, never mind getting dressed. Is that what you want?'

'I'll *never* be like Lucy,' Katriona denied fiercely, her green eyes flashing with fury as she rounded on Janice. 'Now, get out of here. Get out! And the next time,' she commanded as Janice shrugged and started to head for the door, 'next time…send her.'

Send *her*. Claudia blinked in astonishment as the other girl pointed towards her.

'I mean it,' Katriona stressed. 'She gets in…you don't. Understand?'

7

'You're looking awfully peaky, darling. Is everything all right?'

'Everything's fine, Mummy,' Claudia snapped, then regretted it as she saw the hurt expression on her mother's face. 'I'm sorry,' she apologised, placing her hand on Jean Fulshaw's arm in a gesture of remorse. 'I'm…I'm just a bit tired, that's all and…'

Mentally, she gave herself a small shake. The last thing she wanted was to start feeling sorry for herself or to start complaining to her mother that she was missing Garth.

The regiment was in Northern Ireland. Garth had managed a snatched and unsatisfactory twenty-four-hours' leave before his departure, and they had made love with a passionate intensity, which, while physically fulfilling, had somehow left her feeling emotional and weepy.

It hadn't gone down very well at work when she had asked for leave herself at such short notice. Eyes glistening with tears, she kissed her mother goodbye and watched as she climbed onto the train.

She had come up to London to spend the day with Claudia and do some shopping, but

Claudia simply hadn't been in the mood. The heavy cold she had had the previous month had left her feeling lethargic and run-down. It hadn't helped that one of the other probation officers had been transferred, leaving Claudia to take on most of his workload in addition to her own.

Janice might be right, she acknowledged wryly. Perhaps she really wasn't cut out to do the job.

'Don't take it home with you,' Janice had advised her, but Claudia was finding it increasingly difficult to put up the necessary emotional barrier to separate herself from the problems of her clients, especially Katriona. 'You're becoming too involved,' Janice had warned her and she was right. There was something about this particular girl, something compelling and haunting about the sheer, senseless waste and tragedy that her life had become.

'It doesn't *have* to be like this,' Claudia had counselled her, forgetting her professionalism in her longing to be able to do something to help change things for her before it was too late.

'It's already too late,' Janice had told her shortly when Claudia discussed the case with her, her emotions overcoming her awareness that her supervisor already thought that she was overly emotional for the job.

But how much of that assessment was the truth and how much was caused by a not unnatural sense of resentment because of the way Katriona had insisted that the only person she would speak with was Claudia?

'She's doing it because she knows you're new to the job,' Janice had warned her grimly, shortly after a case conference meeting, where it had been decided that in view of the rapport Claudia seemed to have established with Katriona, she be assigned as Katriona's permanent caseworker.

'Personally, I don't know why we are so accommodating with the girl,' she had sniffed, but of course she did. They all did.

Katriona was playing a very dangerous game. In return for a certain amount of leeway as regards her own activities, she was supplying the police with information on a large ring of drug suppliers who, like her, operated in the sprawling underworld the flats had become.

'You'll have to be careful,' Claudia had warned her when Katriona had talked derisively to her about how easy it was to get men to confide in her. 'If they find out…' But Katriona had simply laughed.

'They won't. To them I'm just another quick fuck. They seem to forget that while I've got my mouth wrapped round their cock, I might not be able to talk, but I can still listen, and anyway, what can they do?' She had shrugged. 'Nothing. I know too much. Not like you,' she had taunted Claudia. 'You know nothing. How old were you when you lost your virginity?' she had demanded.

Claudia had shaken her head but had still not quite been able to stop herself from blushing.

Katriona sometimes seemed more interested

in cross-questioning Claudia about her life than in talking about her own.

'Mummy and Daddy,' she had mimicked once. 'I'll bet they spoiled you rotten, didn't they? And I'll bet *he* does, too, doesn't he?' she had challenged as she grabbed hold of Claudia's hand and looked at her wedding ring, demanding, 'What's he like...is he any good in bed? God, why am I asking you that? If he is, you know what that means, don't you?' she had taunted. 'They don't get to know what turns a woman on by saving themselves for their little bridey wifey, you know.

'Has he ever used a pro? How do you know? Have you ever asked him?' she had asked as Claudia shook her head during one meeting, then had laughed when Claudia started to gather up her papers. 'Hit a nerve there, didn't I?' she had crowed. 'They *all* do it, you know,' she had added softly. 'No matter how respectable, how faithful, how loving they make out they are, they all do it. For all you know, he could be a regular client...one of *my* clients....'

She had paused, waiting, for even though Claudia had begun to get the measure of her and to know how much Katriona loved getting her off guard, she had still risen to the bait and returned coldly, 'I very much doubt it. Garth is in the army. He rarely comes to London and—'

'Oh, the *army*. Well, they're the worst of the lot,' Katriona had interrupted her, her mouth curving in a triumphant smile, her green cat's eyes glittering with the onset of the craving she still told herself she could control. 'How did you meet him?' she had asked casually, but Claudia had got herself back under control.

Katriona had a long, raw wound on her left arm that looked as though it had been caused by a knife. Even as she made that judgement, Claudia was aware of just how much she had learned already. Six months ago, she wouldn't have known what a knife wound looked like, never mind instantly recognise one.

'Lucy did it,' Katriona told her carelessly as she saw Claudia frowning at it.

'It looks nasty,' Claudia commented. 'Has anyone seen it?'

'Sure…every punter I've had since she did it two nights ago, and that must be, oh…I dunno, say…ten or maybe twenty. There was a group of them last night. Kids from some posh school, too shit scared to do it alone, so I said the others could watch while I showed one of them what it was all about. Christ, they were a real bunch of wankers—literally—but still, they paid well.'

Claudia said nothing. She was used to Katriona by now and knew how much she liked to shock her.

Firmly refusing to be sidetracked, she sat down. Katriona had steadfastly refused to give them any personal details about herself, and it was part of Claudia's job to do what she could to find out something—anything—about her background and her family.

'You must have parents, Katriona,' she began. 'They—'

'Must I?' Katriona interrupted her bitterly. 'Why? Because the rule book says so? Well, I've got news for you. Life isn't always played by the rules.'

'But you must have someone. A mother...a father...grandparents...'

'Grandparents.' Katriona gave a bitter yelp of laughter. 'Christ, if I had, they'd be ancient. My mother was forty-seven when she had me—I was a miracle baby. They thought they couldn't have children, you see. They'd been married twenty-six years when I arrived. Perhaps someone should have told them that they needed to have sex a bit sooner than they did.'

'They must have loved you very much,' Claudia suggested gently.

'Must they? I wouldn't know. My mother was still in shock from the trauma of the neighbours knowing that she'd slept with my father. She died...a heart attack, because having me had weakened her heart, you see. She was just too damned old, that was the truth of it.'

Although Claudia winced at the cruelty in Katriona's voice, she forced herself not to make any comment other than saying quietly, 'What about your father?'

'My father... Oh, he was a saint,' Katriona told her cynically. 'Everyone said so, and so it must be true, mustn't it? Can't think how they produced me, can you?'

'Is he still alive?' Claudia pressed her.

Katriona shrugged. She had injected herself just before Claudia's visit and the drug was already beginning to take effect. The last thing she wanted to do right now was to talk about her bloody parents.

'*I* don't know and I certainly don't *care*. Why should I? He never cared about me. His bloody school mattered more to him than I did.'

'His school?' Claudia questioned.

'He was a teacher. A housemaster,' Katriona emphasised mockingly, her accent changing, mirroring the clear, well-modulated tones of Claudia's own voice. 'He taught at a private school—for boys. They didn't take girls, so *I* had to go to the local village school, but he taught me at home, as well. They…my parents…had originally met when they were both up at Oxford, and although they couldn't afford to send me to a private school, he was determined that I would get a place at my mother's old college.'

'Which college was that?' Claudia asked her, guessing when Katriona made no response but simply closed her eyes and turned her head away, 'Lady Margaret Hall…Somerville?'

'Think you're bloody clever, don't you?' Katriona growled at her. 'What the hell does it matter *which* college it was? There was no way I was going there. If I had wanted to go to university, I'd have wanted it to be somewhere a hell of a lot more trendy than bloody Oxford. Essex…somewhere like that, but *he* would never have agreed to that. So far as he was concerned, it was Oxford or nothing. Even Cambridge wouldn't have been good enough.'

Claudia said nothing but she could hear the

bitterness and the anger beneath the seeming contempt in the other girl's voice.

'Did you like school, Katriona?' she asked.

'Like school?' Katriona yelped with laughter. 'Oh sure…I loved it. I loved sticking out like a sore thumb and being the target of the other kids because I was the one with the dad who taught at the big posh private school. Just like I loved having to spend every damned evening locked inside with him, listening to him ranting on about how important it was for me to have a good education. Well, I soon showed him that as far as I was concerned, there was far more to life than the classics and that when it came to what really mattered, what was really important, I could teach those upper-class idiots *he* was supposed to be educating some far more important facts of life than anything they'd ever learn from him. Not that he or the head saw it that way.'

She opened her eyes and gave Claudia a vulpine smile.

'So learning how to go down properly on a boy wasn't on the timetable. So what? I'll bet they got a hell of a lot more mileage out of what I taught them than they ever did from Pa's lessons and it made him realise that I was there.'

Claudia could see the anger and resentment in her eyes now, as well as hear it in her voice, and her tender heart ached for her. Reading between the lines of the sketchy tale Katriona had just drawn for her, Claudia suspected that her father, so much older than his daughter and plainly more used to the company of boys than girls, had perhaps in Katriona's eyes appeared to reject her after her mother's death and that she had decided if the only way she could gain his attention was by behaving 'badly' and breaking the rules, then that was what she would do.

'It's not too late, Katriona,' she had said softly. 'You could *still* go back. You could—'

'Of course it's too bloody late,' Katriona interrupted her furiously. 'My God, you make me sick, you're so stupid. And what makes you think I *want* to go back? What the hell is there for me to go back *to*? He's probably dead now anyway,' she added uncaringly, 'and if he's not, then he ought to be. Everyone over twenty-one should be dead…I certainly intend to be,' she added broodingly.

Claudia's heart missed a beat. She had already been warned by Janice that given her current lifestyle, Katriona was unlikely to live much longer, just as she had been warned about the danger of allowing herself to become too emotionally involved with any of her cases.

Later that evening working at home, dutifully trying to fill in the empty blanks in Katriona's case history with the fragmented bits of information she had been given earlier, Claudia put down her pen and stared tiredly into space. She had a bruise on her arm where a young boy had tried to steal her bag as she left the flats, and there had been an unpleasant few seconds in one of the stairwells when another addict had tried to hassle her for money. If she was honest with herself, she knew that she was finding the work depressing and exhausting and without the payback of feeling any satisfaction that she was actually doing anything positive.

Today had been a bad day, she acknowledged as she rubbed her aching forehead. Katriona in particular, despite the rapport she felt she had established with her, or perhaps because of it, seemed to delight in deliberately trying to get under her skin, her barbed remarks designed, or so it sometimes seemed to Claudia, not just to nettle her but to actually inflict damage on her. Katriona was a formidably intelligent young woman and Claudia had no doubts whatsoever that her father had not been overly ambitious in wanting her to go up to Oxford.

She knew what Janice was all too likely to say about the family background Katriona had supplied her with today; *she* would think that Katriona was likely to have made it up, that it was simply a clever fiction she had created around herself, but Claudia sensed that, for once, the girl had been telling the truth.

As she started to write down the gist of their interview, Claudia paused to nibble on her pen and to ponder on the probable details of her life that Katriona had not revealed to her. That she had been intensely jealous of her father's dedication to his job and the pupils he taught had been patently obvious—and natural. The tragic death of her mother must have traumatically affected them both. It was easy to see why a shy, scholarly man already middle-aged might have retreated from his wife's death and its unfortunate consequences. Being left the sole parent to a young daughter, he more than likely found solace in his work. As a result, Katriona had undoubtedly tried to make him aware of her presence, her needs, by becoming difficult and rebellious, the classic situation of a child deciding that attention gained through bad behaviour was better than no attention at all.

'So how old were you when you left home, Katriona?' Claudia had asked her casually, slipping in the question, but not apparently casually enough because Katriona had instantly been on guard, her response dagger sharp and instantaneous.

'I was fourteen,' she had replied, 'and I didn't leave…I was told to go.'

When she saw the expression on Claudia's face, her mouth curled into a derisive smile.

'You don't believe me. Well, it's true. I was given an ultimatum and so was my father. If he wanted to keep his job, then I had to go. My presence as a teenage girl was too disruptive to the boys for me to stay.' She gave a small shrug. 'Of course, my father *could* have chosen to live outside the school. I hated living there, anyway, but he liked the flat we had. The rooms were elegant and classically designed. Sure they were, but rooms with ten-foot-high ceilings take some heating and the school wouldn't install central heating in the staff's quarters. My bedroom windows had ice on them in the winter, we could only have a bath after the boys had had theirs, the water was always cold…' She gave a small shiver.

'It must have been hard for you,' Claudia had responded sympathetically. Katriona had made no response; the drug she had injected was clouding her mind, her ability to think. Claudia recognised the surly, mistrustful look entering her eye and knew that there was no point in questioning her any further.

Fourteen… She sighed now before recommencing her writing. A child still, but the streets of London and far too many other large cities were home to runaways of that age and much younger—a sad fact she had good cause to know.

'You shouldn't be working here,' Janice had told her acerbically yet again only the other week. 'You're more equipped for delivering meals on wheels in some pretty country village.'

'I'm fully qualified to do my job,' Claudia had felt bound to remind her stiffly.

'Academically, yes,' Janice had agreed, her upper lip curling, 'but emotionally…' She had shaken her head vigorously. 'No way, you're the sort who'll grit her teeth and pretend until the job gets too much for her and she cracks. Then we end up having to cope with her workload. You need to be tough to work in this environment. You need to understand what we're working with. Feeling sorry for them won't do it and the only way you *can* understand them is from living with them, from growing up alongside them—'

'Like you did?' Claudia had interrupted her.

'Like I did,' Janice had agreed, adding grimly,

'Face up to it, Claudia. There are some people who are never going to make it, who are born simply to die. There you see, I've shocked you, but it's the truth. They have no purpose, no future, no hope, nothing.'

Claudia hadn't been able to make any response, the pain of what Janice was saying hurting her too much.

It hurt now thinking about Katriona. She wasn't like that; like those whom Janice had described with such cruel accuracy. Katriona had the intelligence to make something of herself, of her life. If she would just agree to try a rehab programme, Claudia was sure she could be helped to see how much better her life could be.

'She doesn't want to see,' Janice had told her. 'And the harder you try to persuade her, the more she'll dig her heels in. Katriona's sole mission in life is to degrade herself just as much as she possibly can. It's her way of punishing whoever it was in her life who hurt her. It gets some of them that way. Be careful, Claudia,' she had warned her curtly. 'She'll hurt *you* if she can— whatever way she can. She needs to hurt others nearly as much as she needs to hurt herself.'

And Claudia had known that it was true. There had been several occasions when she had sensed a cruelty, a malevolence almost, about some of Katriona's comments to her, just as she had sensed the girl's angry determination to undermine and unsettle her, to denigrate and, if she could, destroy everything and everyone contradicting her own warped and destructive view on life.

But understanding why Katriona behaved the way she did did not always lessen the efficacy of her bitingly cruel tongue, Claudia acknowledged ruefully.

Claudia woke up, yawning and stretching, blinking in the dazzling glare of the oncoming headlights of other cars as Garth turned into their street.

They had spent the weekend—his first off since his tour of duty in Northern Ireland—with Garth's parents, and after two late nights and Garth's mother's justly famed cordon bleu cooking, Claudia had fallen asleep on the way home.

It had been an enjoyable weekend—she got on well with Garth's parents, who had never made any secret of the fact that they welcomed her as a daughter-in-law—but Garth had been slightly on edge, not specifically with her, or indeed with anyone. It had been more as though he had been having difficulty in gearing down to everyday civilian life after a high-tension existence with his regiment.

Not much mention had been made of his tour of duty at either of the two dinner parties his parents had given during their visit, but Claudia suspected that it would have been something that he and his father would have discussed when Garth had gone to join him in his study while Claudia helped his mother to prepare Sunday lunch.

An old school friend of Garth's father had been present at the Friday evening dinner party. He ran his own PR business, his clients in the main drawn from the world of politics and high finance. Claudia had heard him telling Garth quite seriously that if he were to leave the army he would certainly be interested in having Garth come to work for him.

'I don't know the first thing about public relations,' Garth had said, laughing.

'That's where you're wrong,' Nicholas Forbes had corrected him immediately. 'Through your work, you're promoting an image, and that in essence is what public relations work is all about. You're good with people. You know how to deal with them, how to work with them and bring out the best in them,' he had continued, and as she listened to him, Claudia had realised that he had judged Garth's character very shrewdly and accurately indeed.

She wondered if he knew through Garth's father that Garth was concerned about how much of a future he would actually have with the army now that he had a wife to consider.

'It isn't that I'm fiercely ambitious,' Garth had told his parents over lunch on Friday just after they had arrived and the four of them were seated around the comfortable kitchen table. 'But one day, hopefully, I will have a family to support.' He had smiled, giving Claudia a teasing glance, before adding more seriously, 'and besides, I don't want to be an absentee father.'

What Garth wasn't saying to his parents, but

what they had both agreed on, was that, unlike them, their own children were not going to be sent away to boarding school—an experience that neither of them had particularly enjoyed.

While Garth brought in their cases and the boxes of fresh fruit and vegetables Garth's mother had insisted on giving them from her own kitchen garden, Claudia went over to the sink to fill the kettle.

She heard Garth come in and close the door, and as she turned her head he came towards her, blocking her into the small space between the sink and his body. He wrapped his arms tightly around her and started to nuzzle the nape of her neck.

'Garth,' she protested, 'I was just going to make some tea.'

'I don't want tea...I want you,' Garth growled, tightening his hold on her, one hand covering her breast, the heat of his breath hot against her skin.

When Garth had arrived home on Wednesday, they had had a passionately sensual and sexual reunion; on Thursday night, too, they had made love, and on Friday morning Garth had woken her with the slow suckle of his mouth on her breast.

She had known instinctively that the urgency of his lovemaking and the intensity of his sexual desire for her were heightened by his recent tour of duty. Whenever he came home on leave, he was always hungry for physical contact with her;

eager to make love and to make up for the time they had been apart. But this time, there had been a new sense of urgency, an edge not of aggression towards her but of some tautly controlled male emotion.

Lying in bed next to him at his parents', profoundly thankful for the size of their house and the fact that their bedroom was the full length of the house away from his parents' room, Claudia had suddenly been acutely aware of how very fragile human life was. All the time Garth had been in Belfast, she had steadfastly refused to allow herself to dwell on the fears that she knew must be experienced by everyone for the safety of someone they loved when that someone was in a dangerous and hostile environment, telling herself that to give in to her fears, even subconsciously, might somehow or other weaken Garth and make him more vulnerable. But the first night he had been home, she had woken constantly in the night, reaching out to touch him just to reassure herself that he was actually there beside her and safe.

She had not even objected when he had insisted on making love to her at his parents' home, something that normally made her feel acutely self-conscious and unable to completely relax. But her urge to be close to him, to be held by him, to be a part of him, had been so strong that it had overwhelmed her usual inhibitions.

'Garth,' she protested again, but already she could feel her body starting to respond to his touch, tiny shivers of delicious sensation quivering across her skin where his mouth was caressing it.

'Mmm…' was the only response he made to her half-hearted protest. Against her body as he pressed closer to her she could feel the hard throb of his erection.

The hand caressing her breast slipped inside her top, pushing away her bra while the other hand tugged at her skirt.

'Garth, no,' she told him breathlessly. 'We can't, not here.…'

'Oh, yes, we can,' he told her thickly in response, his hand already touching her body, caressing her sex, his own reacting to the hot, wet feel of her just as she was reacting to the hard male pressure of him.

The musky aroused male scent of his body was making her feel dizzy just as he enveloped her. She could feel the hardness of his thigh pressing against her leg. She could hear the urgency in his voice as he started to move rhythmically against her.

'Lean forward,' she heard him instruct her. A fierce thrill of shocked excitement raced through her.

She had never been particularly adventurous in bed and, compared with what one heard and read, her sex drive seemed nowhere near as high or as demanding as that of other women of her age, but suddenly, with Garth caressing her with his hand at the same time as he started to penetrate her with quick, fiercely hungry thrusts, to her own bemusement she found herself grinding her own body back against his, panting with a mixture of urgency and excitement as she started to quiver from head to foot with the onset of a need for him that was almost as intense and immediate as his for her.

When his thrusts became slower and more deliberate, she moaned in taut feminine frustration, which elicited a hot, savage groan of excitement from Garth as he moved faster and deeper within her body, responding to the message of her demanding and wholly female body language.

When it came, her orgasm was so swift and so intense that for a few seconds Claudia actually felt as though she might pass out. When Garth withdrew from her, she was trembling so much that he instinctively wrapped his arms protectively around her, rocking her gently as he soothed her back down to earth.

'Do you know what we're going to do now?' he whispered lovingly to her as he scooped her up in his arms. When Claudia shook her head, he told her huskily, 'We're going to go to bed and I'm going to make love to you all over again, only this time…this time, it's going to last all night.'

'Garth…' Claudia began to protest and then stopped. She didn't even have the energy left to tell him they should rest never mind make love a second time.

Only somehow or other she had found the energy and they did make love again, and it was only in the early hours of the morning, when she got up to go to the bathroom, that she suddenly realised what she had done or rather what she had not done.

Her packet of oral contraceptive pills lay reproachfully on the vanity unit where she had left them by accident when she was packing to go to Garth's parents.

Numbly, she stared at them. That was three pills she had missed taking. Three nights…three days when they had made love without using contraception. Her heart sank and then rallied. She had only missed three days. Surely she couldn't…surely that didn't…

In the morning when she told Garth—before she would allow him to make love to her—he didn't seem anywhere near as concerned as she had expected.

'So you might be pregnant. We *are* married,' he reminded her wryly, 'and we *were* planning on having a family at some stage.'

'*Some* stage, yes,' Claudia agreed, 'but not yet, not here, not while I'm still working. We can't bring a baby up here in this flat, Garth,' she told him, shaking her head and grimacing. 'And we certainly can't afford to move somewhere else, not in London.'

'No,' he agreed 'but would it really be so bad?'

'They'll be furious at work,' Claudia told him. 'I know that Janice doesn't really think I'm up to the job as it is. She's never really approved of me.'

'I know how much being able to work means to you,' Garth responded, 'but…' He paused and then put his arms around her, tucking her head under his chin so that she could hear the rumble of his voice in his chest and smell the early-morning man smell of him, something she had missed desperately the first few days after he returned to the regiment following his leave. Now, instinctively, she drew it deeply into her lungs to savour and treasure it for the time when she would be alone. 'Are you really happy here…living and working in London?'

Claudia opened her mouth to tell him that of course she was, but instead, she found herself shaking her head, her eyes filling with tears as she admitted tiredly, 'No…not really. Perhaps Janice *is* right after all. Perhaps I'm simply not equipped to deal with the kind of problems I'm having to face. Perhaps all I'm fit for doing is delivering meals on wheels and opening village fêtes.'

'Don't be silly,' Garth reassured her gently. 'There's just as much poverty and hardship in the country as there is in a city. It's just that it's a different *kind* of poverty and a different way of life.'

Three weeks after Garth's leave had ended, Claudia sat up in bed and promptly felt so acutely nauseous that she knew, even before the routine doctor's test had confirmed it, that she was pregnant. Even so, she waited until she had that confirmation before telling Garth.

'It's bad news, I'm afraid,' she told him as calmly as she could, the telephone receiver sticky in her hand as she tried to blink away her tears. 'I'm pregnant, Garth.'

As she listened to him asking if she was absolutely sure, Claudia guessed that he had to be as dismayed by the news as she was herself for all his reassuring comments before he went back off leave. It wasn't that she didn't want a child—a family—she did, they both did, but not yet, not until their lives and their marriage were more sturdily established.

After she had said her goodbyes to Garth and replaced the receiver, she squeezed her eyes tightly closed and fought to suppress her tears. It isn't that I don't want you, she told her baby silently. It's just that this is too soon. I'm not ready. *We're* not ready.

Why, oh why hadn't she remembered to take those wretched pills? Tiredly, she looked round their small cramped flat. It was completely impossible for them to bring up a baby here—even if the landlord would allow it, but she already knew he would not. And then there was her job. Janice had remarked earlier on her pallor and noticeable lethargy. The work she was doing was both physically and emotionally demanding, their department too busy to have any room to carry someone who wasn't up to working at optimum output.

There would be those, she knew, Janice among them, who no matter what they said publicly would privately believe that she was using her unexpected pregnancy as a cop-out, a way to save face, which would allow her to leave a job she simply wasn't up to.

But she *was* up to it, she defended herself fiercely. It was just that as yet she hadn't mastered the art of detaching herself enough emotionally from the people she was dealing with.

'You're too involved,' Janice had warned her again only the other evening when she found Claudia folding some old blankets into the boot of her car. Having coaxed them out of her own and Garth's mother, Claudia intended to give them to the growing group of homeless vagrants who took shelter every evening under the disused railway arches that Claudia passed on her way home. 'They won't thank you for playing Lady Bountiful,' Janice had warned her once she had cross-questioned Claudia on what she was doing.

'I don't *want* their thanks,' Claudia had returned quietly, ignoring the older woman's taunt.

Tiredly, Claudia pushed away the keyboard on which she had just been finishing up a report. The clock on the wall showed that it was just gone six o'clock. Most of the other staff had already left, although it wasn't unusual for any of them to work into the evening. Claudia was so exhausted it almost made her feel sick. Even the effort of pushing her chair back and standing up made her grit her teeth. Why on earth should carrying a baby, so small as yet that it scarcely qualified for the term, so small, in fact, that she, its mother, had actually lost weight rather than gained it, demand such an intense concentration of energy that it left her as physically depleted as though she had climbed Everest?

Wryly, she made her way back to the spot where she had parked her small car and unlocked it. Ten minutes later as she let herself into the hallway of the flat, she looked at the stairs in dejection and then slowly started to climb them.

By the time she had reached the flat, she felt sick and dizzy. As she put down the shopping she had collected during her lunch hour, she opened her bag for her key. Suddenly, the flat door opened and Garth was standing there.

'Garth.' She blinked at him stupidly. 'What are you doing here?'

'I live here,' he told her cheerfully. Then with a grin, he reached out and plucked her off the floor, swinging her up into his arms. 'I managed to wangle a twenty-four-hour pass,' he explained. 'You sounded so fed up on the phone that I— Hey…what on earth are those for?' he demanded gently as she started to cry.

'I'm sorry…I don't know…' Claudia sobbed, then added between hiccuping tears, 'Yes, I do. I'm frightened, Garth. I'm not ready for this. We didn't plan—'

She didn't get any further because he was holding her tight, kissing her forehead and then her mouth before telling her with loving firmness, 'Now you listen to me. Everything's going to be fine. We may not have *planned* for this to happen quite so soon, but now that it has…' He paused and when Claudia looked uncertainly into his eyes, he told her softly, 'I love you so much, Clo...even more than ever now if that's possible. I love you both,' he said passionately, placing one hand possessively on her stomach, then adding teasingly, 'and if it turns out to be a boy, I think we'll call him Hector.'

'Hector? No...never,' Claudia objected, outraged, asserting determinedly, 'Anyway, he, it...is going to be a girl.' Her laughter faded quickly, though, as she shook her head and protested, 'You really shouldn't have come home.' She knew how difficult it was for him to get extra leave, but Garth stopped her.

'I *wanted* to be here with you, with you both, and anyway...let's have a cup of tea and then we can talk,' he suggested. 'You go and sit down. I'll make it...you look whacked.'

Claudia tried to smile but it was a distinctly wobbly attempt.

Five minutes later as they sat cuddled up together on their small sofa, Garth told her quietly, 'I've decided to leave the army just as soon as it can be arranged.'

'Oh, Garth,' Claudia protested. 'I know we've been talking about it, but not yet. You—'

'All right, yes, perhaps I will be leaving sooner than I'd planned,' Garth agreed, 'but that doesn't matter. I'm going to give Nick Forbes a ring and see if he was genuine about that offer of a job. I think on balance that he was.'

'Oh, Garth.'

'Look, this baby is as much my responsibility as yours, probably more,' Garth told her ruefully, thinking about the weekend the baby had been conceived. The tour of Northern Ireland had been even more stressful than he had expected and the release of tension had caused a sexual urgency to burgeon within him, had sparked such a need to be alive so that perhaps in some ways it was inevitable that the creation of a new life should be the result.

There had been such a fear of death on that tour that it would have been extraordinary if they had *not* been affected by it and by the sense of having escaped from underneath its weighty, oppressive shadow with the need to celebrate life.

He could understand now why those who had completed several tours there said they got to a state where they felt they were involved in a macabre game of Russian roulette, wondering with each fresh tour if this would be the one from which their return would be in a wooden box.

But he made no mention of any of this to Claudia. They had, of course, talked about the fact that he was a serving soldier. She knew the risks—she was, after all, a soldier's daughter. But he could see quite clearly how vulnerable the pregnancy had already made her—had heard it in her voice when she had rung him with the news. His first instinct was to protect her and the new life they had created together, and so far as he was concerned the best place, the only place, for him now was at her side.

He would leave the army and hopefully get a job with his father's old school friend; they would buy a house in the country but within commuting distance of the city. The future, if not rosy, certainly looked reasonably bright. In his arms, Claudia started to relax.

8

'You've changed. There's something different about you. What is it?' Claudia sucked in her breath sharply as Katriona fired the fierce questions at her.

Surprisingly for someone with the extent of the drug habit that Katriona possessed, she could be very intuitive as Claudia was quickly learning.

'Nothing…' Claudia began, only to instinctively place her hand protectively across her belly as the youth who had been lying in the corner of the room on a piece of filthy sacking got to his feet and started to lurch towards her.

'Leave off, Oz,' Katriona told him. 'She's my probation officer not a supplier.'

To Claudia's relief, the youth turned away from her, stumbling towards the stairs instead, pausing to retch nauseously in the doorway as he did so.

'He took a bad trip last night,' Katriona told her emotionlessly, shrugging her shoulders dismissively as he clattered down the stairs. 'He won't be around much longer.' Graphically, she drew a line across her throat and then laughed when she saw Claudia's expression. 'I suppose you think the same thing about me, don't you?

Don't you?' she demanded, her earlier good humour giving way to sullen anger.

Her lightning changes of mood were as much part of her personality as her drug habit, Claudia observed, responding to her quietly. 'Katriona—'

'You're pregnant, aren't you…aren't you?' Katriona suddenly demanded wildly, ignoring Claudia's attempt to talk objectively to her. 'How does he like that, your fine army husband? I bet he's not too pleased. They never are—'

'As a matter of fact, Garth is delighted,' Claudia interrupted her sharply, then realised her mistake. She could see from Katriona's triumphant expression that she knew she had got under Claudia's professional guard.

'Garth,' the girl mimicked mockingly. 'So *Garth's* delighted, is he? Well, aren't you the lucky one. *I* got pregnant once. The father wasn't delighted. He told me to get rid of it.' She heard the betraying sound Claudia made and laughed.

'There wasn't any need in the end. I lost it, didn't I? Just as well. Not that the likes of you would ever know anything about that. Planned it all beforehand, had you? What did you say to him? Come on, darling Garth, please fuck me now so that I can get pregnant and then I won't have to go and see that dreadful Katriona any longer. Of course, your baby will have everything, won't it? A delighted mummy and daddy…everything of the best. I expect Mummy is getting the christening robe down from the attic already, isn't she? The same one that you wore when you were christened, the same one she wore...'

Claudia saw the bitter resentment clouding Katriona's eyes as she mocked her. The girl's anger and jealousy were so intense Claudia could almost feel and taste them. For the first time in Katriona's presence, she felt a sharp thrill of fear—not for herself but for the baby, and for the first time since she had discovered she was pregnant, she felt the deep stirrings of real maternal love, the maternal instinct to protect her unborn child. For the first time, she realised how much she *did* want her baby. *Their* baby, hers and Garth's.

'Have you thought any more about this rehab programme?' she asked Katriona firmly, ignoring the girl's taunts.

She wasn't three months pregnant yet, but just as soon as she was, she intended officially to tell them at work she would be leaving.

Garth had approached Nick Forbes, who confirmed that he meant every word he had said about wanting to employ him; and he had even mentioned a salary that far exceeded anything Garth had hoped for.

'With that, we'll be able to afford to buy something pretty decent as long as we look outside London,' Garth had told Claudia enthusiastically.

Both sets of parents had been given the news that hopefully they were to become grandparents and they had responded with natural excitement and enthusiasm. They were an extremely fortunate young couple as Claudia was the first to acknowledge.

Garth was going to be a wonderful father. His reaction to her unplanned pregnancy was showing her a side of him that made her love him all the more deeply—and allowed her to show her love for him all the more uninhibitedly.

'Being pregnant suits you,' he had told her one night after they made love. 'It makes you very sexy.'

'You don't think we might have harmed the baby, do you?' Claudia had asked him in some alarm, the darkness hiding her blushes as she acknowledged that her response to him had been more passionate and intense, more womanly, as though her pregnancy somehow conferred on her a new and more sultry adult status.

'No way,' Garth had reassured her, adding softly, 'After all, that's how he or she got there in the first place, isn't it?'

Cupping the back of her head with his hand, he very slowly drew her down towards him until she could feel the warmth of his breath against her skin.

'Have I told you lately how much I love you and how very sexy you are like this?' he asked her in a whisper as his free hand stroked the curves of her body.

'I'm going to get fat,' Claudia protested.

'You're going to get sexy. You *are* sexy,' Garth corrected her.

'It's fashionable to be thin,' Claudia reminded him. 'All the models—'

'All the models are bags of bones,' Garth told her extravagantly. 'They can't hold a candle to you. Being pregnant suits you.' As he bent his head to kiss her, Claudia relaxed into his embrace.

During her lunch hour earlier in the week, she had been tempted into a store specialising in baby things. Garth had already insisted that he wanted an old-fashioned, easy-to-steer, as he put it, traditional coach-built pram.

'For when I take him out on a Sunday morning while you're preparing lunch,' he had told her teasingly.

Claudia had laughed back. Now that she was over the initial shock of her pregnancy, she was as thrilled at the prospect of becoming a mother as Garth was a father. It was, after all, what she had always wanted. Having children, a family, for her was a very important part of what being married was all about and she could now understand and accept far more reasonably the words of one of her tutors that she had taken as criticism. 'Your maternal streak is very strong,' he had cautioned her, 'and you'll have to guard against letting it take control and lead you into making incorrect assessments of situations. 'Mothers tend to be notoriously blind to the faults of their offspring.'

'I'm due to see the CO soon,' Garth told her. Hearing the tension in his voice, Claudia raised her head and looked anxiously at him.

'Are you sure this is what you want to do, leave the regiment?' she asked him. 'I know I said that I didn't want our children to be army brats like I was, but...'

'No, I feel exactly the same as you do. If I'm honest, one of the main reasons I went into the army was because I didn't really have any stronger idea of what I wanted to do. After going through public school and then university, I suspect that, psychologically, it felt safer opting for a career that echoed the same familiar, organised type of routine.'

Gravely, Claudia nodded her head. 'It does tend to make you feel slightly institutionalised, our kind of education,' she admitted.

'Institutionalised!' Garth gave her a wry look. 'Oh, thanks. Once I've spoken to the CO, though, we're going to have to get busy thinking about where we're going to live.'

'Somewhere in the country,' Claudia suggested promptly.

'I'll be working in London,' he reminded her, 'but, yes, I agree. And preferably somewhere with a bit of land, close enough for both sets of parents to visit, but not too close.'

'No, not too close,' Claudia concurred. 'I'll start making enquiries with a few estate agents, shall I?'

'Mmm...' Garth agreed, nuzzling the delicate and so sensually responsive spot just behind her ear. 'But remember to tell them we want plenty of bedrooms.'

'For when we have people to stay? Whom are you planning to invite, the whole regiment?' Claudia teased him.

'No, not for guests,' Garth returned before warning her huskily, 'You don't think we're going to stop at this one, do you? Not now I know how easy it is—and how enjoyable. Do you know…you actually felt different the night this—' his hand covered her stomach '—happened?'

'Garth,' Claudia protested, 'I forgot to take my pill for three nights and—'

'No,' Garth interrupted, shaking his head. 'I know exactly *when* it was—it was the evening we came back from my parents, when I…when we—'

'You were very deep inside me that time,' Claudia broke in, her voice as husky with emotion as his.

'Very deep,' Garth agreed, adding as he drew her fully into his arms, 'God, but we're lucky.'

Contentedly, Claudia snuggled up against him. She couldn't imagine being any happier than she was right now, but instinctively she knew that she would be, once their baby was born. A feeling of such intense excitement and joy welled up inside her that it made her wriggle slightly against Garth, an expression of sheer bliss illuminating her face.

'Now, what brought that on?' Garth asked her. He moved against her and she felt the hardness of his arousal. 'This…?' he added hopefully.

'No, not that,' Claudia answered truthfully. 'I was thinking about the baby. Oh, Garth, I'm so happy…we're so lucky…'

'Mmm...' Garth agreed, reaching for her hand and placing it firmly against his body.

'Mmm...I see...'

Having come to the end of his speech informing the colonel that he intended to leave the regiment, Garth watched as his commanding officer stood up and went to stand in front of the window, hands clasped behind his back.

A tall, spare man in his fifties, the colonel came from a long line of military men, but even he was not completely immune to the cultural changes taking place in the current decade. His own son, ex-Eton and destined to follow him into the regiment, had decided that he preferred to travel to India and sit at the feet of some guru. There had been arguments about it, of course, but nothing could persuade the boy to change his mind. The boy, in his father's opinion, looked more like a girl with his long hair and peculiar clothes, and the colonel wasn't alone. Only the previous week he had been with a fellow Etonian whose own son had been due to follow him into the Guards; instead, the boy had joined a pop group.

'The regiment will be sorry to lose you,' he told Garth, turning to face him and adding, 'and so shall I.'

Silently, Garth expelled his pent-up breath. It was no secret in the regiment that the CO had been a bit sticky recently. Word had it that the disappointment he had suffered over his son had put a distinctly sharp edge to his always somewhat choleric temper. But he was a fair man, honest and just, and Garth liked and respected him.

'I'd like to leave before the baby arrives,' Garth requested. The regiment was due to be home based for the following six months, which would allow him to take sufficient leave to sort out his and Claudia's house move and it made sense to Garth that he would have at least a couple of months to settle into his new professional life before their son or daughter arrived, and it was for that reason as he told the colonel that he had hoped to quit the regiment in three months' time.

'I don't see any reason why not. You're coming to the end of your term with us and we can't force you into signing on for a further period of time,' the colonel remarked.

It was a matter of honour for Garth, both as an individual and as a soldier aware of his rank, not to leave when the regiment was about to be posted overseas or sent into the field. He was only glad that the regiment was not due for another tour of duty in Northern Ireland for some time—not so much for the danger that this entailed, at least not for himself. No, it was Claudia he was thinking of. She had dealt calmly and practically with his recent tour of duty in Belfast, but even so he had sensed her anxiety and concern and he knew how much greater that would be now that she was carrying their child.

After she was over the first shock of discovering her pregnancy, he could see how much her forthcoming role as a mother thrilled and delighted her. It wasn't just her body that had matured, ripened with the conception of their child. Claudia herself had grown, too. Some women seemed by nature more maternal, more nurturing and caring, more suited perhaps to be mothers than others and Claudia was most definitely one of them.

Even now, Garth sensed that their child, once it had arrived, would automatically lay claim to Claudia's loyalty and love—and she would bestow these unstintingly—but he didn't see any reason to feel threatened or dismayed by the idea. Why should he? He, too, shared Claudia's joy, enjoyed the glow of fulfilment that prospective motherhood had brought her.

Claudia had never felt happier. She hadn't told them officially at work yet that she would be handing in her notice, but she suspected that they must know. Not even Katriona's acid sniping had the power to affect her any more. She had even suggested to the girl that since she seemed to have nothing but criticism for the way Claudia was handling her case, she might prefer to be dealt with by someone else, but Katriona, who seemed to have developed a love-hate relationship with her, flatly refused, flying off the handle and accusing Claudia of wanting to walk out on her and not having time for her any more now that she was pregnant.

The time would come, of course, when Claudia would have to hand over the case to someone else, but at the back of Claudia's mind was the knowledge that despite her ferocity, despite the fact that Claudia knew that Katriona deliberately tried to needle and upset her, the girl was very vulnerable. Claudia didn't want to be yet another person who had turned her back on her, and besides…

Furiously though she might deny it, Katriona was becoming increasingly dependent on drugs—and increasingly at risk physically.

'She'll be dead within a year,' Janice had remarked brutally the last time she had accompanied Claudia on a visit to the squat. 'You mark my words. I've seen it happen with her type before. For a long time, they seem to be able to withstand the abuse they're subjecting their bodies to, and then suddenly, they're gone.'

Claudia's footsteps quickened as she hurried down the street. She had a lunch appointment with one of the estate agents in the city who also had branches in the country.

A happy smile curled her mouth. Garth had warned her that they wouldn't be able to afford anything grand, but something grand wasn't what she wanted. What she wanted was a house that would be a proper home, a house with a large, comfortable kitchen and a big garden for their children to play in. Their children. Blissfully, she closed her eyes. She was just so… so…happy.

Even her morning sickness brought its own peculiar sense of pleasure, reaffirming as it did the reality of her pregnancy.

What she felt was impossible to describe or explain. What she felt was a sense of…of rightness, of completeness, of fulfilment. What she knew was that the prospect of motherhood made her feel that she had suddenly discovered the true purpose of her life. She loved Garth, of course, but instinctively she knew that the love she would have for their children would be the strongest and most powerful emotion she would ever know.

Bleakly, Garth stared out across the silent barracks yard. It was a good hour since they had heard the news, a shock that still hadn't fully sunk in. The enduring conflict in Northern Ireland had claimed many lives, both Catholic and Protestant, and now another tragedy had occurred.

A coachload of British soldiers on their way to their depot had been ambushed on an isolated Northern Irish road. Out of the fifty-odd men travelling in the coach, there had been only eight survivors, and all of them so badly maimed that even if they survived…

Impossible not to suffer that churning stab of dread to the stomach coupled with a guilty relief that it was not oneself lying dead on that country road or, even worse, lying on a hospital bed with what was left of one's shattered and destroyed body. It would take much more of a miracle than modern medicine could provide to piece back together a body whose limbs had been blown off.

He hadn't known personally any member of that other regiment but that didn't matter. They might have their regimental rivalries and jealousies, but underneath them, they were all army. They were all vulnerable; it could have been any of them.

'They'll have to bring back the rest of the regiment now,' one of the other officers had commented to Garth when the news had broken. 'They can't leave them out there after this. It would be bad for morale. Heaven help whoever they send out to take their place. I hope to God it isn't us. Anything like this makes the men damned jittery and that's when…'

He didn't say any more. He didn't need to. Garth was aware of the psychology of good morale as any other responsible and intelligent officer.

'You don't think we *will* be sent out in replacement, do you?' he asked instead, frowning at the prospect.

'Hard to say. We've got the training and the experience, but it isn't that long since we completed our last tour of duty.'

Garth frowned again, recalling their conversation. In a matter of weeks he would be leaving the regiment, his intention being to view some of the houses Claudia had weeded out of the possibilities sent to her by the estate agents and then spend some time getting to know the ropes of his new job before the birth of their baby.

Claudia was now four months pregnant but her stomach was not yet beginning to show. Garth's frown changed to a smile as he remembered how the last time he had been on leave she had proudly showed him the maternity clothes she had bought. He hoped they weren't being sent out to Northern Ireland. If they were, he would feel honour bound to go.

'But...but you said that you weren't due to do another tour in Northern Ireland,' Claudia faltered as they sat side by side on their small sofa.

When Garth had telephoned to say he was coming home unexpectedly, her first thought was that now he could come with her to see the pram she was thinking of ordering; the very last thing on her mind was that he would have the kind of news for her that he had just given her.

'We weren't,' he agreed quietly. 'But there's been a change of plan.' No need to remind her of the month-old tragedy that was now, in media terms at least, stale news, but Claudia wasn't an army daughter for nothing.

'It's because of the bombing, isn't it?' she guessed immediately. 'They're sending you out because they've had to recall that regiment.'

'Yes,' Garth replied, his tone sombre.

'Oh, Garth, but surely you don't need to go. You've only got a few weeks left and—'

'You know better than that, Clo,' Garth reminded her. 'I can't let the men down, and if I don't go...'

'Yes, I know,' she conceded heavily.

Northern Ireland. Claudia shivered with foreboding. Every army wife dreaded hearing the news that her husband's regiment had been posted there, but normally Claudia would have tried her best to keep her fears to herself. This time, though, it was different. This time... She forced herself not to break down completely and beg Garth not to go, remind him that it wasn't just her he had to consider now.

But Garth it seemed had read her mind. 'I know what you must be thinking,' he told her gently, 'and don't think *I* haven't thought it, too, but this is something I have to do, Clo.'

Numbly, she nodded her reluctant agreement, swallowing hard before asking him, 'When... when do you leave?'

'The end of next week.'

Claudia closed her eyes.

That night after they had made love, instead of turning over to lie on her side as she normally did, she remained curled up against Garth, clinging to him even in her sleep, afraid to let him go.

'Look, darling, why don't you come to us for the weekend?' Claudia's mother suggested when her daughter telephoned her to tell her the news. 'We could do some shopping together for the baby.'

Claudia agreed, and Garth, when she told him about the invitation, was pleased that she would have something to help take her mind off worrying about him.

Garth's regiment was scheduled to leave for Northern Ireland on Friday afternoon. On Friday morning, Claudia went to check on Katriona, but her anxiety over Garth made it hard for her to concentrate fully on the girl, a fact that Katriona very quickly picked up on.

At first, she accused Claudia of not paying any attention to her and then when that didn't provoke Claudia's normal concerned response, she demanded tauntingly, 'What is it? Not had a row with darling, wonderful Garth, have we?'

'Nothing's happened,' Claudia denied, 'and we have not had a row.'

'Oh, coming home this weekend, is he?' Katriona mocked her.

'No, he isn't,' Claudia returned shortly.

'Oh, poor you, you'll be all on your own,' Katriona mocked her.

'No, as a matter of fact, I shan't. I'm going to see my parents,' Claudia told her.

What time was it? Would Garth have left yet, or would she just have time to ring him before he did? If she could only manage to get away from Katriona… What time was it anyway? She glanced at her wrist and then remembered that she wasn't wearing her watch. She had put it in her handbag because the strap had broken. Unfastening her bag, she reached inside, unaware of the furiously resentful and bitter expression in Katriona's eyes as she realised that Claudia wasn't really listening to her.

Smug bitch…who did she think she was anyway? What made her think she was so special…so wonderful?

A scuffle broke out in the corridor outside Katriona's room, and while Claudia's attention was distracted, Katriona reached forward and deftly removed the keys she could see gleaming in Claudia's handbag. By the time Claudia

looked back, Katriona had the keys tucked safely
away out of sight. It gave her a sense of triumph
and power to have taken them and gleefully she
imagined Claudia's reaction when she discovered they were gone.

Served her right. Katriona fingered the keys
she had tucked beneath her skirt. What did the
flat she shared with her precious Garth look like?
Katriona already knew where it was; she had
sneaked a look at Claudia's driving licence one
day when Claudia's attention had been distracted and it had been easy enough for her to
memorise it. And now she had the keys, and
Claudia didn't even know.

An hour before Garth's regiment was due to
leave, one of the men was found hanging in his
room. He had taken his own life rather than face
the fear of what the next few months might hold.

It was impossible to keep it a secret, of course,
and just as impossible to allow the regiment to
go. Rearrangements were hastily made to find a
substitute regiment to send out in Garth's regiment's place.

'Look, why don't you go home and see your
wife?' Garth's commanding officer suggested.
'There's nothing any of us can do here now.
There'll have to be an enquiry, naturally. Not
that we need one to tell us that the poor sod was
so shit scared of suffering the same fate as the
men he would be replacing, that he chose to take
his own life rather than let some bomber do it for
him.'

Numbly, Garth did as he suggested. He hadn't wanted this particular assignment, but to be reprieved from going by something like this...

As he drove towards London, he tried to imagine what the young squaddie must have gone through in those last hours before he had decided to take his own life. *Why* hadn't any of them realised...guessed...? Garth could picture the boy now. Tow-headed, tall, his body still possessing the angularity of youth. He had been a quiet lad, almost inarticulate, and the others had ribbed him a bit because he had a stammer. Well, they wouldn't be ribbing him any longer.

Furiously, Garth punched the car horn when another driver cut in front of him. Suddenly, he couldn't wait to get home to Claudia. It was only when he parked the car outside the flat that he remembered that Claudia wouldn't be there.

Grim-faced, he unlocked the door to the flat, and without even bothering to take off his coat, he opened the cupboard and removed the bottle of whisky his father had given him the last time they visited.

Garth had never been a heavy drinker, but right now he felt the need for a good stiff drink...for *several* good stiff drinks. He was half-way down the bottle before it struck him that he ought to have something to eat, but Claudia, good housewife that she was, had carefully cleaned out the fridge before she left.

The whisky had begun to take effect, and although he found a tin of baked beans, Garth could only stare owlishly at it while he wondered vaguely where the tin-opener was kept.

In the end, it seemed easier to simply pour himself another drink. That poor little sod. Garth put his hand to his own neck and rubbed it as though he could actually feel the rope tightening round his own flesh, choking the life out of him.

He was getting very drunk, he recognised. Perhaps he ought to go to bed. He was, after all, soon to be a father. Unlike the lad who had done away with himself this morning. He would never be a father, but he had had a father. How had he felt when they had broken the news to him? How would *he* feel if anyone ever had to tell him that his son, his very own child, had committed suicide? Garth paused in the act of undressing to pour himself another drink.

He had been the first officer on the scene, summoned there by the private who had found the body. He had seen death before, but this had been different.

Garth filled up another glass before dragging off the rest of his clothes, which he left lying where they fell before crawling into bed and spilling some of his whisky on the bedclothes as he did so. God, but he wished that Claudia was here with him. That poor little sod.

His face felt damp, but it was only when he raised his hand to touch his skin that he realised that he was crying.

Gloatingly, Katriona fingered Claudia's keys. Had she missed them yet? Had she guessed where they were? Katriona doubted it; she had been too busy thinking about her damn bloody husband and her bloody baby to notice what Katriona was doing. Bloody, bloody baby. For a moment, Katriona was tempted to hurl the keys through the open window of her room, but then she stopped herself, gripping them tightly as she brooded on Claudia's shortcomings.

She was the one Claudia was supposed to be concentrating on. She was the one who needed help...who needed *her*. That Claudia thought she was so clever, so secure in her precious little world. Bitch. Katriona hated her...hated her.

The drug she had injected earlier was starting to wear off. It wore off frighteningly quickly these days, or at least it would have been frightening if Katriona was the type of person to allow herself to be frightened, which she wasn't. She wasn't frightened of anything or anyone. Not the punters who paid her for their inept use of her body; not the pimps who tried to threaten her and make her work for them; not even the dealers who supplied her with drugs.

And if she wasn't afraid of them, she most certainly wasn't afraid of someone like 'Miss Smarty-pants.' It was pathetic, really, the way she doted on that husband of hers, the way she believed in him. All men were shits, Katriona knew that. Given half a chance, no, *less* than half a chance, he'd be just like all the rest, led by his balls and not his brains.

Katriona fingered the keys again. Her dealer had recently put up the cost of supply; he knew

how desperate she was for her fix now. He was
trying to trick her, to trap her into giving in to the
pimp who was persuading her to work for him,
telling her that she needed his protection, that *he*
could guarantee her an income for her habit, that
if she worked for him she would never need to
worry again about finding her own punters.
Balls, she didn't worry about finding them *now*.
Why should she? She would have to go out
working tonight. She frowned as she studied
Claudia's keys, remembering that Claudia had
said she was going to be away for the weekend.
Which meant that the flat would be
empty…which meant…

Unsteadily, Katriona got to her feet.

'Where are you going?' one of the other girls
yelled out after her as she staggered down the
stairs. 'It's too early yet to go out looking for
business.'

'Mind your own,' Katriona snarled viciously at
her as she opened the flat door and blinked in the
sharp, clear, late-afternoon daylight.

By the time Katriona had made her torturous
way to Claudia and Garth's flat, it had already
gone dark, the air crisp with the scent of autumn,
haunting and sharply nostalgic, but Katriona
wasn't aware of the acrid smell of wood smoke
and burning leaves that hung on the evening air.
A wide, triumphant grin curled her mouth as she
found the house she was looking for.

Luckily, the lobby was empty when she
walked in. The craving for her next fix, which

had been nothing more than a background irritation when she set out, had now become a savage, sharp-toothed, drilling pain.

When she tried to insert Claudia's key into the door lock, her hand was shaking so much it took her several attempts to do so but eventually she succeeded. She turned the handle and the door swung open. Marching aggressively into the small hallway, she almost stumbled over the kitbag that Garth had dropped there on his way in.

Once she had found the light switch and discovered what the obstacle was, she stared at it warily for several seconds, straining her ears for any sound from within the flat. Hearing nothing, she bent down and quickly started to rifle through the bag, discarding Garth's neatly rolled and folded clothes as she did so, then sitting back on her heels and grimacing in disgust when she didn't discover any money or anything else of value she could sell.

There was a mirror in the hallway set over a small shelf, both wedding presents from one of Garth's relatives, and Katriona paused to peek into it, making a series of gargoyle-like, simpering faces at her reflection as she pretended to ape the way she imagined Claudia would check her own appearance.

Claudia. Bitch. She deserved this. She had no right to go off and leave Katriona on her own. She had no right to have a bloody baby.

Automatically, Katriona started to rub and then scratch at her arms, which were already itching, her skin crawling from the effects of withdrawal.

Angrily, she made her way into the sitting room. She needed money and Claudia was the sort of silly bitch who would have some hidden away somewhere, probably in her knicker drawer. She was that sort, Katriona decided savagely.

The sitting room was empty and Katriona scowled as she studied the clock on the mantelpiece above the fireplace. Too heavy and awkward to carry, she decided in disgust, just like the other pieces of silver and the old-fashioned china figurines that decorated the highly polished sofa table and filled the pretty mahogany cabinet standing against the wall behind it.

The figures were Dresden, eighteenth century and highly saleable, and the silver had been handed down through four generations of both Garth's and Claudia's families, but it was money that Katriona wanted...money.

Grimacing in disgust, she ignored the kitchen in favour of the bedroom. She might just as well have gone out onto the street; at least by now she'd have had a couple of punters and twenty pounds or so to show for it.

She pushed open the bedroom door and then rocked back on her heels, her body stiffening in shock as she saw Garth sprawled out completely naked across the bed, the virtually empty bottle of whisky and glass at his side.

Instinct told her to leave, but overriding this instinct was a sharply savage surge of dangerous excitement. Here was Claudia's husband, Mr Perfect...the father of the child she was carrying. The man who was all the things that all the men who had passed through Katriona's life were not.

Stealthily, she approached the bed. She knew a dead-drunk man when she saw one; after all, she had seen enough of them. There was no way he was going to wake up this side of tomorrow morning, at least not without a considerable amount of help. A triumphant grin split Katriona's face, suddenly making her look much younger, as young, in fact, as she actually was.

She reached for Garth's hand and gripped his fingers. Nothing, no response. She lifted his arm and then let it drop. Still nothing. Interestedly, she studied his body. Not bad. He had good long legs, a well-muscled torso, a flat stomach and... Without the slightest trace of self-consciousness, she moved even closer to the bed and studied his sex, even reaching out and prodding it ungently.

Hmm...not the largest man she had ever seen, but he could certainly claim to be reasonably well-endowed—and much more so than the majority of men with whom Katriona had had to deal. No, perhaps Miss Sly Boots Claudia wasn't as prissy as she liked to make out after all. That is, if her precious Garth knew what to do with it and if he wasn't just the shove-it-in, move-it-up-and-down, take-it-out type and—even more unlikely, she decided unkindly—if Claudia herself knew how to take advantage of what nature had given him, which she doubted. She was definitely the 'lie there and think of England' type.

Katriona could just imagine her reaction if she walked in now. How shocked and disgusted she would be when she saw her precious husband sprawled stark bollock naked across their bed, very obviously drunk. And how much more shocked she would be if she were to walk in and find Katriona herself straddled across him, riding that interestingly sized cock, while he begged for more and told her he was having a better time fucking her than fucking his wife. They all did. After all, that was why they paid her for sex when most of them could have had it for free at home.

Experimentally, Katriona climbed onto the bed. If she turned her head, she could see her reflection in the mirror and anyone coming in now would have a perfectly clear view of her backside as she rode up and down on Garth's prick. Her grin widened as she imagined Claudia's reaction again. *She* wouldn't be so calm, so distant, so sure of herself and in control then, would she? *No*, she, Katriona, would be the one in control, the one making *her* dependent on her goodwill.

Almost absently, Katriona started to remove her clothes, although, unlike Garth, she didn't scatter them all over the room but folded them neatly on the floor instead. Then she glanced towards the neat dressing-table and saw a single small vial of scent. On impulse, she climbed off the bed and went to pick it up, then dabbed it generously on her body, especially her breasts and just above her sex.

And then still smiling, she climbed back onto the bed. Only this time when she straddled Garth and reached for him, instead of simply touching his penis briefly, she squeezed it between her fingers. In his drunken sleep, Garth jerked and frowned, mumbling something but not waking up.

Katriona pinched him much harder a second time. With a roar of protest, Garth awakened and tried to sit up, but Katriona was too quick for him, leaning forward over him so that his face became entangled in the thick length of her hair, her body pressed tight against him as she commanded huskily, 'Put it in me, Garth, put it in now.'

Still drunk and totally confused, Garth tried to respond to the warning message his brain was sending him, but it was impossible for him to clear the fog of alcohol and sleep clouding his thought processes.

Above him, Katriona reached down and took him in her hand, firmly massaging him to erect thickness at the same time as she pushed her breasts towards his mouth and commanded fiercely, 'Suck.'

Instinctively, Garth opened his mouth. Somewhere at the back of his mind, a sharp, shrill alarm bell sounded but he couldn't hear it, couldn't hang on to the brief recognition that this breast, this dark pointed nipple did not belong to Claudia, that Claudia would never do what this girl was doing…never command, demand, as she was doing.

But how, after all, could it not be Claudia? Claudia was his wife. This was their home, their bedroom, their bed. Still, even if the last thing he felt like now was sex, his body…

Reluctantly, sluggishly, Garth's body responded to Katriona's expert ministrations. *She* was the one who was the aggressor, he the passive recipient of her attentions. *She* was the one who held him rigid while she slid onto the hard shaft she had brought into existence, holding him with her muscles as she growled triumphantly deep in her throat.

What do you think of him now, your wonderful husband? she crowed mentally to Claudia as she pumped vigorously up and down on Garth, half-smothering him, making sure that her hair and the pillow were making it impossible for him to actually see her while she rode him as exultantly as any Valkyrie.

Technically, it wasn't possible for a woman to rape a man, at least not in the act of normal sexual intercourse, and if Claudia were to walk in now, she would never believe that Garth hadn't instigated the apparently passionate sex that was taking place between them.

'Yes, come on, fuck me,' Katriona purred. 'Fuck me really hard, really, really hard.'

Garth was vaguely aware of her verbal demands but it was to the message that his body was giving him that he was really responding, answering the primal, primitive call that was as ancient as the human race. Gripping Katriona's wrist, he started to thrust up into her, ignoring the pain in his head and the distant awareness that something wasn't right, that she didn't feel right, that she didn't sound right…that she just *wasn't* right.

Katriona felt him grow more rigid just before he released himself inside her with an explosive surge.

Smiling to herself, she let him slide away from her. When would Claudia be coming home? In the morning…just in time to discover her… Katriona, snuggled up in bed with her husband….

Still smiling, Katriona reached for the bedclothes and lay down beside Garth.

9

—→←—

'You're sure you're feeling well enough to drive back to London on your own? You could leave your car and Daddy—'

'I'm fine,' Claudia assured her mother. 'It's just this wretched morning sickness.'

'I was the same,' her mother admitted, adding comfortingly, 'but it should stop soon.'

'I hope so,' Claudia returned. She was well into her pregnancy now but the weight she had lost along with her appetite meant that her pregnancy didn't show very much yet and she certainly looked far from the bloomingly healthy picture a pregnant woman was supposed to present.

She already had a short list of houses to see, although with Garth in Northern Ireland he wouldn't be able to go with her as they had planned.

Garth... A sharp tremor of anxiety tensed her already queasy stomach. What was he doing now? Was he safe? Was he...?

It was almost lunch-time before she finally got in her car and set off for London, but it wasn't until she stopped to fill the tank with petrol that she realised she hadn't got her flat keys.

'Damn,' she swore as she quickly tipped out the entire contents of her handbag to go carefully through them. She tried to remember when she had last seen her keys but couldn't. Another facet of her pregnancy along with her nausea was her increasing forgetfulness.

Well, she would just have to contact the landlord—he had a spare set. Perhaps she had left her keys behind at her parents'. She would have to ring them when she got home to find out.

It was the noise that woke Garth, his brain registering it as alien and therefore potentially dangerous even through the agonizing pounding of the headache that felt like two cavemen bludgeoning one another with stone clubs inside his skull.

He opened his eyes.

It was the soft hiss of his indrawn breath that alerted Katriona to the fact that he was awake. Crouching on the floor beside the bed as she went through his pockets, she rifled through the wallet she had found, quickly pulling out the notes and stuffing them into her pocket at the same time as she got to her feet and turned to run towards the door.

Garth was fast but Katriona was faster and she had the advantage of being fully dressed and alert.

As she raced down the stairs heading for the front door and freedom, Garth cursed; he knew that it was impossible for him to pursue her completely nude.

Who *was* she and, more importantly, how the devil had she got into the flat?

Grumpily, he picked up his discarded and now empty wallet. The area they were living in wasn't exactly up-market and he had noticed the gangs of youths loitering on the pavement; the girls in their suspiciously short, tight outfits who hung around the corner of the street watching the men driving slowly past them. It was just as well that he and Claudia were planning to move. London, in his opinion, was no place to bring up a baby. Babies, children, needed fresh air, space and freedom, the kind of country childhood that both he and Claudia had enjoyed.

There was no point in his going back to bed now. He turned and studied the bedroom floor and his scattered clothing. The room, the whole flat, stank of whisky and stale air. As he went to open one of the windows, he was frowning. The girl who had gone through his wallet must have got into the flat somehow, but how? God, but his head ached, his memories of the previous evening blurred and irritatingly incomplete. He could remember getting home and having that first drink, but after that... Garth shook his head. There were odd shards of something there, a woman...her hair...her voice... His frown deepened as he fought to concentrate on them, but they were too vague...too elusive...more dream shadows than reality.

How *had* that damn girl got in? He went to

check the lock, but as he had already seen, it hadn't been forced.

He would have to have a word with the landlord, check if any of the other tenants had had anything stolen from the other flats, but before he did that he ought to get their flat straightened before Claudia returned from her parents'.

Claudia was thinking about Garth as she turned into the street, but as she drew level with the house and saw Garth's car parked outside, the unexpectedness of the sight caused her to stall her own car before parking it clumsily and racing upstairs to their flat. Knocking impatiently on the door, she called out, 'Garth. Garth, are you in there?'

A shower, several mugs of black coffee and some headache tablets had made Garth feel distinctly more his normal self even if they hadn't restored his memory of the previous evening and the night's lost hours.

'Garth, I saw your car…you shouldn't be here…are you all right…are you…?'

'I'm fine,' Garth reassured her as he let her in, adding in concern, 'but you don't look too good.'

'I was thinking about you all the way here,' Claudia said as she followed him inside, shivering slightly. 'I was worrying about you…but what are you doing here? You're supposed to be in Northern Ireland.'

'I know. It was cancelled.'

Something in the tone of his voice warned Claudia. She scanned his face anxiously before saying uncertainly, 'Something *is* wrong. Are you…what…?'

'Nothing's wrong with me,' Garth assured her, then told her quickly what had happened, his voice and face grim.

'Oh, Garth, no. Oh, no, that poor boy. His family, his parents…'

'They had to cancel the tour, of course. There was no way of keeping it a secret. A thing like that affects the men's morale. There'd have been talk about the tour being jinxed, that kind of thing.'

Claudia looked shocked, her hand going to her mouth in distress.

'I had to tell his parents.'

'Oh, Garth…'

Instinctively, Claudia wrapped her arms around him, and as he held her close and breathed in the familiar sweet, fresh scent of her, Garth closed his eyes against the hard acid burn of the moisture stinging his eyes.

'The CO told me to come home. I'd forgotten that you wouldn't be here.'

'Oh, Garth,' Claudia reproached herself, 'and you were all on your own. What did you…?'

She broke off, giving him a rueful look as he gestured towards the empty whisky bottle he had just been about to throw out.

'Stupid, I know,' he agreed when he saw the look on her face. 'But I can promise you I'm paying for it this morning. Today I've got the mother and father of all headaches. How about you, though?'

'I'm fine. It's just this awful sickness.' She made a face. 'It's supposed to stop at twelve weeks and it's still with me now! Oh, Garth, I nearly forgot,' she added. 'Have you seen my keys anywhere? It was only when I was driving back I realised I hadn't got them.'

'No. No, I haven't,' Garth responded. 'Could you have left them at your parents'?'

'I might have done. I'll ring them later to check.'

'I think you should ring them now,' Garth told her. 'When I woke up this morning, there was someone here going though my wallet. The lock hasn't been forced and—'

'Someone...someone broke into the flat,' Claudia concluded. 'Oh, Garth, I... But do you really think they could have used my keys?'

'We won't know until we check with your parents,' Garth gently pointed out to her, 'but it isn't exactly inconceivable, is it, given your work, that someone might have taken your keys?'

'No. No, it isn't,' Claudia agreed, shivering a little as she thought about the dismal, yawning canyons that were the corridors and stairwells in the tower blocks she visited with their fetid smells of urine and rubbish and their ever present gangs of youths.

What would have happened if *she* had been the one to be woken up by some intruder going through their things? It didn't bear thinking about.

As though he had guessed what was going through her mind, Garth hugged her tightly, saying gruffly, 'The sooner the three of us find ourselves a proper home, the better.'

As Claudia smiled up at him, Garth's hold on her tightened.

'It's two o'clock in the afternoon,' Claudia protested as he bent his head to kiss her.

'So?' Garth teased back, adding wickedly, 'Isn't a woman in your delicate condition supposed to rest in the afternoon?'

'That was in our mothers' day,' Claudia responded indignantly, but Garth noticed that she made no attempt to move away from him and he noticed, too, how warm and soft her body felt, how familiar.

How familiar... Somewhere, a warning bell went off but it rang so deep within his subconscious mind that all he could hear of it was a very faint echo that faded almost as soon as he tried to grasp it.

'Garth, do you really think someone might have stolen my keys?' Claudia mumbled against his mouth.

'Well, it's a distinct possibility, isn't it?' he returned. 'I'll get a safety chain and bolt to fit on the door before I go back to barracks,' he promised her as he bent to pick her up and carry her through into the bedroom.

He had changed the bedding that reeked of the whisky he must have spilled on it and taken it down to their local launderette to wash. Guessing the question that Claudia was going to ask him as she saw the fresh bedlinen, he bent over and slowly started to kiss her.

Now that she was carrying their child, their lovemaking was different—quieter, gentler, less intensely passionate perhaps, but to him somehow deeper and richer, as though their mutual awareness of the life they had created bonded them at a new, more mature, less carefree level.

'I'm getting to be almost afraid to do this in case I hurt you,' Garth whispered to her as he slowly started to penetrate her.

'I know, but the doctor *said* it was all right,' Claudia reassured him.

Her own sex drive had diminished with her pregnancy, her breasts felt sore and tender, and her constant nausea left her feeling almost permanently tired. But as though in compensation, her desire to be close to Garth, to be held by him, to feel close to him both physically and emotionally, had increased. She loved the feeling of protection and safety it gave her to be held close to his body, to be wrapped in his arms, to know that he was there for both of them, her and their baby.

'I was so afraid about your going away this time,' she told him in a whisper while he moved carefully inside her. 'You won't still have to go, will you?'

'I doubt it. Now that I know this tour has been cancelled, I intend to bring my leaving date forward to what it was originally supposed to be. Mmm…you feel good. I'm not hurting you, am I?'

Claudia shook her head, closing her eyes and letting her thoughts drift, accelerate, as her body quickened to the rhythm of Garth's.

Their lovemaking was tender and leisurely, Garth's orgasm not as fiercely intense as she was accustomed to on their first time in bed after they had been apart.

'How long have you got at home?' she asked him a little later as she lay beside him, her body curled towards his.

'Only forty-eight hours,' Garth replied. 'Mmm...' Garth reached out and placed his hand over her belly. 'You know, I sometimes can't quite believe it,' he told her huskily.

'No, sometimes I can't, either,' Claudia agreed.

'You...you aren't sorry, are you?' she questioned him. 'You *are* pleased?'

'Of course I'm pleased,' Garth answered gruffly, reaching out for her and rocking her in his arms as he held her tight. 'Of course I'm pleased.'

10

➤◄

Kicking open the kitchen door, Estelle put down her supermarket carriers of food and went to switch on the answering machine.

Blade was sulking with her. She gave a small shrug—so, let him sulk. She was familiar enough with his moods to know that ultimately he would get in touch with her.

She was halfway back to the kitchen when she heard the familiar male voice on the tape. For a moment, she tensed and then very deliberately closed the door between herself and the answering machine, leaving her father's voice to speak into the silence of the empty room.

Her father! Rather the man who had fathered her. Well, he could keep his pretence of wanting to get in touch with her, of wanting to see her. What use did she have for him now?

Three months—*that* was the length of time he had stayed around for her after her birth, three months before he had had enough of being a father to her. He hadn't wanted her then and *she* certainly didn't want him now.

It filled her with angry contempt to see the way people like Tara carried on about *their* parents, their precious mummies and daddies. Savagely, she mimicked an upper-class accent under her breath as she mouthed the words. And what made her even more contemptuous was to see the way that Garth so obviously adored his daughter.

In her opinion, parents were a necessary evil that one had to put up with until one could break free of them. Not that *she* had had too many problems in that direction. Her mother had a hedonistic, selfish approach to life, which meant that being a hands-on mother had never been a role that held any appeal for her.

Estelle could remember how appalled Lorraine had been when Blade's school threatened to expel him.

'But that means we shall have to have *both* of them here with us,' she had protested to Ethian.

They had been in their bedroom at the time and Estelle—six years old—had been listening outside the bedroom door.

'He hasn't been expelled *yet*,' Ethian had calmed her, 'and even if he is, well, I expect we'll be able to find another school to take him.'

'I'd like to send Estelle away to school,' Estelle heard her mother telling him. 'But, of course, if I do, her father will no doubt insist on paying her fees direct and cutting my maintenance.'

'Does he know that you've moved her to a state school?' Estelle's new stepfather asked Lorraine.

'No, of course not. He doesn't have the least idea just how expensive she is to keep. I can hardly bear to think of the money he must waste on that wretched house he's bought for Sophie, never mind the money he's undoubtedly settled on *their* son. Why on earth couldn't he have done something like that for Estelle?'

'She's a girl,' Ethian answered dispassionately. '*She* hardly warrants that kind of investment.'

So now she knew the reason her father had wanted nothing to do with her. He had gone away when she was a baby because she was only a girl.

Thoughtfully, she had made her way back to her own bedroom. She was used to listening to her mother's complaints about her father's financial meanness towards them.

Her mother liked wearing pretty clothes and going to all the best parties; she liked summers in Tuscany and winters in Barbados. And Estelle had learned while very young that her mother deeply resented whatever or whoever prevented her from doing what she enjoyed.

There was nothing Lorraine enjoyed more than accompanying her husband to the large number of corporate 'dos' his work required him to attend.

A pretty, vain, completely self-centred woman, she divided the rest of her time between shopping and visiting beauticians and hairdressers.

Estelle knew perfectly well that if she were to dial the number of the apartment in the exclusive block that her mother had persuaded Ethian to buy the previous year, she would be unlikely to get a response from anything other than the answering machine and that even if she did leave her a message, her mother would probably not bother to ring back.

'You're an adult now, a woman,' she had told Estelle on the day of her eighteenth birthday. 'And I really do think, darling, that it's time for you to look around for somewhere of your own to live.'

Estelle had known immediately what her mother had meant. They were both women and her mother had no intention of sharing anything she considered to be hers with another woman, not even her.

'You'll have your father's allowance and I'll speak to Ethian. I'm sure he'll want to do something to help you,' her mother had assured her.

Estelle had been living in her cramped little flat for less than six months when Ethian had stopped paying the allowance he had promised to make her. She still had the money she received from her father, of course, but she wasn't able to live on that, and the pittance she earned working in an exclusive Bond Street shop didn't even pay for the clothes she bought there at cost.

It had been one of the girls she worked with who had suggested that she might know of a way Estelle could improve her finances. It wouldn't be so different from what her mother did anyway.

Yes, her mother might be married to Ethian, but it had never been any secret to Estelle that Lorraine used his sexual hunger for her to get from him what she wanted in terms of clothes, money, holidays.

The only difference between them was that *she*, Estelle, didn't have to restrict herself to one man.

'Has Estelle rung back yet?' Sophie Frensham asked her husband John.

Estelle's father shook his head. 'I'll leave it a couple of days and then try again.' Correctly interpreting the look on his face, Sophie pushed aside the fruit she had been preparing to make jam with and, wiping her hands, walked across the kitchen and put her arms lovingly around him.

The kitchen, like the rest of the house, was huge and old-fashioned. When John had inherited the place from his father ten years ago, he had promised her that just as soon as he could afford it, she could start work on modernising the whole place, but while John might be wealthy in terms of land and assets, he was unfortunately cash poor.

Farming was no way for a sane man to try to make a living, he was fond of saying, but despite that, Sophie knew how proud he was of the fact that Ian, their son, was determined to follow in his father's footsteps.

She had known John since childhood. Her grandfather had been Lord Lieutenant of the County, and while John's family were not tenants of her grandfather, John, like all the other local children, had been invited up to the hall for the biannual parties her grandparents gave for their tenants and neighbours.

Although they were of a similar age, as teenagers they had gone their separate ways to follow their separate interests. She had worked abroad for a while, learning and then teaching French, while John, like many of his peers, had turned his back on tradition and the role in life expected of him, and instead of making his life here at the farm he would one day inherit, he had gone instead to London, which had then been a Mecca for young people. London in the seventies—she had heard about it, read about it, but still found it difficult to envisage John, the John she knew and loved, being a part of that reportedly wild and exuberant scene.

Her parents had been a little concerned when she had first announced that she wanted to marry him.

'He's a divorced man with a child,' her mother had pointed out quietly, but Sophie had refused to be swayed, and her faith in him had been more than justified, more than repaid.

At the end of the month, their daughter Rebecca would be celebrating her twenty-first birthday.

Sophie's brother, who had inherited from their grandfather, had offered the ballroom at the hall for the event, and she knew how much it would mean to John to have his elder daughter Estelle there. Privately, she had her doubts about the kind of life Estelle was living—Sophie had a woman's instinct about her stepdaughter, which warned her that her beloved John could be very shocked and hurt by the way his daughter lived her life—but she loved him too much to want to voice such thoughts to him. She didn't want to disillusion him and she just hoped that Estelle herself wouldn't do so, either!

'She's my daughter, my first child, yet she's a stranger to me,' he gruffly told her now. 'And that's *my* fault. I should have tried harder, done more. I was so damn glad to get out of that marriage that I never even gave a thought to ensuring that I had proper access to Estelle.'

'Things were different in those days,' Sophie tried to comfort him. 'Everyone believed then that a child was better off left with its mother, and you did try,' she reminded him, remembering all the useless attempts they had made to persuade his ex-wife to allow Estelle to come to them during school holidays. She had never refused point-blank, but what she had done was quite simply make it impossible for them to have her other than for the odd short visit.

And then there was the matter of the very generous allowance that John had paid his elder daughter right up until her twenty-first birthday, a far more generous allowance than either of his children from his second marriage had ever received.

While Ian, their son, had been at agricultural college, he had had to work in his spare time to help finance his education, as had Rebecca. New agricultural policies, coupled with the crippling effects of things like BSE, the usually fatal cattle disease, had dramatically changed the way John farmed their land, and every bit of money they managed to accumulate had to be put back into the farm. But Sophie had reminded herself every time she felt herself starting to resent the financial strain that John's elder child made on their resources of just how very much more fortunate her children were in that *they* had the loving presence of their father in their lives on a day-to-day basis.

John had admitted to her that he had never taken very much interest in Estelle as a baby.

'The whole thing, Lorraine's pregnancy and Estelle's birth, was a total mistake, something that just wasn't meant to happen. Lorraine swore right through the first few months that she intended to have her pregnancy terminated. But I…I couldn't let her do that,' he had confessed grimly.

'We fought like cat and dog over it. We should never really have married. The whole thing was a disaster right from the start. God alone knows what I thought I was doing, and then, of course, when Lorraine realised that I was serious about our moving back down here to the farm, that was it. There was no way she was going to leave London.

'In fact…' He stopped. What was the point in going over it all again? Sophie had, after all, heard the story of his destructive and thankfully brief marriage often enough.

Silently, Sophie watched him. She could guess what he was thinking, how much he hoped that

Estelle would get in touch with them and how much he wanted her to be there with them when they celebrated Rebecca's coming of age, to be a part of them.

Sophie wasn't quite sure what had alerted her to the truth about Estelle—a certain sixth sense perhaps, an awareness, a horrible dark knowing that she had tried desperately to avoid until its darkness had been innocently confirmed by a friend who mentioned that she had bumped into Estelle in London and that she had been accompanying a man known to them both.

The man in question was nearly thirty years Estelle's senior, very wealthy and very, very married. Sophie's friend had assumed that their being together was completely innocent and the result of his having been introduced to Estelle over the previous Christmas when Estelle had totally unexpectedly turned up on her father's doorstep, but Sophie had known otherwise. She could never tell John because she knew how guilty he already felt about her.

'I should have sued for custody,' he had said forcefully one summer when Estelle had been eleven.

She had just spent a week with them, disdaining the activities and company of their own children, shutting herself away in her room for most of her visit and running up a huge phone bill.

'She ought to have been running around outside with the others…and not…' He had paused, shaking his head. 'She's not like a child. She's more of a miniature adult. I feel so guilty,

Sophie,' he had said often, 'so helpless. I ought to have done more, tried harder.'

Would it have made any difference if he had, if Estelle had been brought up surrounded by love and security as their own children had? If *she* had been subjected to the loving, caring discipline they had exercised with Ian and Rebecca, if *she* had known as they had known, that she was loved and wanted?

As he saw the sympathetic look on her face, John knew that there was nothing that Sophie could say to change how he felt. His guilt went too deep.

Watching Sophie measuring out the sugar to put with the fruit in preparation to boil up the jam, John silently thanked whatever beneficent presence in his life had arranged for Sophie to love him. She was totally different from his first wife, so totally different in every possible way.

He had met Lorraine during the early seventies while he was living in London. Originally from a small working-class town in the north of England, she had been in London for just under two years when she and John had first met at a party thrown by a friend of a friend John had met at college.

His family, especially his father, had been filled with disapproval when John had announced that instead of following family tradition by going to a local college, he intended instead to study at the London School of Economics.

'That's not a university. It's a breeding ground

for drop-outs and lefties,' his father had growled
furiously, but John hadn't been prepared to
change his mind. At eighteen, nearly nineteen,
what he thought of as the narrowness of his parents' lives, the constraint and dullness of the life
he himself would be expected to live, had filled
him with a fierce determination to escape, to live,
and it had been in this reckless mood that he had
met Lorraine.

Eighteen months his senior, she had just broken up with her previous boyfriend, a forty-year-
old recording studio executive who had, he later
discovered, balked at her efforts to get him to the
altar. Lorraine might have been part of the London 'scene' and everything that it encompassed,
but she still was a hard-headed, shrewd north-
erner—sex before marriage was all very well just
as long as it ultimately led to marriage.

Lorraine had seen her grandmother, her
mother and her aunts live gruellingly hard lives
that had worn them out by the time they were in
their forties. She could see her friends from
school starting the same inevitable progression,
getting themselves a lad, falling pregnant by
him, getting married quickly and shamefacedly,
renting a small terraced house if they were lucky
enough to have a lad who could afford such lux-
ury, or moving in with his or their own mam and
dad if he couldn't, their lives virtually over before they had begun, at least in Lorraine's eyes.

That wasn't going to happen to her. So very
deliberately, she had packed her bags and taken
herself off to London, getting herself a job in a

shop to start with, in one of the multitude of new boutiques that were springing up all over the capital.

It was an age of crumbling barriers, of a new interaction between the classes. Northern accents were something to be worn proudly, but even so, Lorraine quietly and secretly learned to smooth out the rawness of hers. She quickly came to realise, too, that her passport to the kind of money and comfortable life she wanted would have to be a man.

And she had openly told John when their marriage was in its final throes that initially he had seemed the ideal candidate. Well-connected, and so she had mistakenly thought then, comfortably wealthy, and even more importantly, not as yet tarnished by the cynicism that had begun to dull the glow of London's gilded youth. Lorraine had quickly set about capitalising on his obvious infatuation with her, while he was still naïve enough to believe she shared his feelings, still naïve enough to adore and worship her.

Less than three months after they had met, they were married. John's family had not been pleased and John could still remember Lorraine's reaction to them when he had taken her home so that he could show off his new bride.

'Ugh... My God, how could *anyone* live here in all this mud?' she had demanded disparagingly when she had first seen the farm—and in his father's hearing. When his mother had offered to lend her a horse so that they could go out riding, she had shuddered in disgust and exclaimed, 'Ride a horse? Certainly not. They smell.'

No, she had not endeared herself to his family, nor had she realised at that point that, apart from his grant, he was totally dependent on his father.

'What do you mean your father's stopped your allowance?' she had demanded of him angrily after their return to London. 'What does your father have to do with it? It's your money.'

'No, no, it isn't,' he had denied quietly, going on to explain his true financial situation to her. He had money in trust, it was true, but he would not have access to it until he was thirty, and then because it was family money, it had already been tacitly agreed that most of it would go into the farm.

'Go into the farm? No, no way at all!' Lorraine had declared furiously.

Ten weeks later, after his parents had made it clear how they felt about his marriage, he and Lorraine were summoned home.

'In view of the fact that you and your wife are expecting a child, I've decided to reinstate your allowance,' his father told him curtly. 'I'm still not at all happy about the situation and I still believe that you've behaved recklessly and without proper consideration. You've always known that...' He had stopped and shaken his head before adding tersely, 'I'm not going to say any more. Lorraine is, after all, your wife and soon to be the mother of your child, even if I...'

John could remember even now the sense of shock and disorientation he had felt while listening to him. As soon as he could, he had escaped from his father's study and gone in search of his wife. She had been sitting upstairs in their bedroom.

Going over to her, he demanded, 'Why didn't you tell *me* that you're pregnant?'

'I was waiting to make sure,' she told him coolly.

'You didn't tell *me*, but you told my parents?' he continued angrily.

'Your mother's offered me your old pram,' Lorraine told him before bursting out angrily, 'My God, you'd think that at the very least your parents would offer to equip the nursery. After all, it isn't as though they can't afford it. All they need to do is sell one of their damned fields.'

John had listened to her in disbelief. The scales had well and truly fallen from his eyes in the few short weeks of their marriage, and now with her blatantly selfish comment about the field, she had shown him, *underlined* for him, if it had needed underlining, just how vast the gulf between them actually was, vast and unbridgeable.

That had been the moment when he knew that their marriage was over. It was a mistake he should never have made, and to his eternal shame, the last thing, the last person, he had thought about as he contemplated the trap he had so stupidly set for himself was the child that he and Lorraine had conceived.

On the way back to London, Lorraine had questioned him ceaselessly about his trust fund, complaining that she had heard of umpteen people who had managed to obtain access to theirs.

'I can't,' he had protested, 'not without the agreement of the trustees.'

'Then *I* can't have this baby,' Lorraine had told him savagely.

It had taken several minutes for the threat to sink in properly, but once it had, John knew that she meant exactly what she was saying.

Her determination to get access to his trust fund money became a war she waged with merciless aggression over the following weeks, and the day she showed him the appointment card from the abortion clinic, he knew that she had won.

John knew that he would never forget the shame and humiliation, the sense of having let the side down, the *family* down, he had experienced when he had gone to his father and told him, *begged* him, to approach the trustees on his behalf. He knew, too, that he would never forget the look of sadness in his father's eyes as he listened to what he had to say.

At his father's insistence, half the money from his trust fund was used to buy a house. The other half went into their joint bank account, which Lorraine proceeded to empty while they were waiting for their divorce.

What he could never forget was that there had been a moment, a heartbeat of time, when he had actually wished that Lorraine *had* simply gone ahead with the termination of her pregnancy. The baby she was carrying might be his child, but he had felt no sense of having fathered it, no pride or joy, no love, just an immense sense of doom of being burdened by something he didn't want and hadn't planned to have.

Once during her childhood, when he had tried to talk to Estelle, she had turned to him and told him coolly, 'It's too late to pretend that you care about me now. Mother has told me everything. I know you wanted her to have an abortion. I know that you didn't want me....'

And he had felt too heartsick to tell her the truth, too afraid of what it might do to her, to tell her that her *mother* had been the one who had threatened *him* with the abortion. Neither had he ever been able to bring himself to tell her that Lorraine had, in his view at least, deliberately conceived so that she could use his child as a means of manipulating and controlling not just him but his parents, as well.

He might have been the one who had paid financially for his mistake in marrying Lorraine, but he had never been able to totally rid himself of the suspicion that it had been Estelle, his daughter, his child, who had paid the greater price in emotional and psychological terms.

Lorraine's second husband was shrewd with money, as mean and greedy as Lorraine was herself. More than once on the few brief occasions when they had been obliged to meet, John had had to listen to him boasting about the 'perks' that went with his high-powered job.

He was, Sophie had suggested dryly, the kind of man who despite earning a six-figure annual salary nevertheless experienced an almost orgas-mic-like thrill at the thought of using his firm's stationery to save on buying his own.

'They're two of a kind,' she had told John ob-servantly after one particularly trying incident involving Estelle's school fees, before adding lovingly, 'and so are we.'

At least Ethian had been able to provide Lorraine with the kind of lifestyle she had always craved, John acknowledged. Ethian's company regularly sponsored charity events, polo matches, balls, corporate days to the Goodwood races and the Chelsea Flower Show and many other activities on the social calendar. And if what he had heard on the grapevine was true, Lorraine invariably appeared at these occasions wearing glamorous clothes and revelling in play-ing the part of the executive wife.

'She always looks so glamorous and elegant,' Sophie had commented ruefully the previous Christmas when a friend had shown her a copy of a *Country Life* feature with photographs of a ball Lorraine had attended.

'Maybe, but inwardly she's still undoubtedly the same cold-hearted, greedy, self-centred woman she's always been,' John had responded before grasping Sophie's arms and telling her softly, 'I thank God every day of my life that I've been lucky enough to find you, my Sophie. *You* are *all* the things that she isn't, that she never could be. All the things any man could ever want in a woman.'

He looked at the phone. He'd give it another

couple of hours and then he'd try Estelle's number again. Nothing could ever alter the fact that he hadn't been the father he should have been to her when she had been young. It had taken the birth of his and Sophie's first child, Ian, to wipe out the bitterness and anger, the sense of entrapment and betrayal he had felt at Estelle's conception, and to show him what being a parent, a father, was really all about. He had tried to make it up to her, had tried and was still trying.

She was his first-born child, this daughter of his, but she was Lorraine's child, as well, and deep in his heart of hearts, he knew that was something he could never forget, that it was a barrier between them that had never truly been breached.

11

→ ←

'What's brought that look to your face?' Janice asked Claudia when she saw the way the younger woman frowned as she suddenly pushed away her desk chair and got to her feet. 'And don't tell me it's the thought of leaving this and us,' she added bluntly.

Claudia gave her a forced smile. She had been feeling uncomfortable all day, not in pain exactly, just...just... As though just to contradict and spite her, a jagged pain splintered through her body, causing her to gasp and try to catch her breath. She clung to the back of her chair for support.

She was five months pregnant—another few weeks and she would be stopping work. Garth would soon be leaving the army and they had agreed that he would not take up his new job until after she had had the baby.

Rather unexpectedly, Garth's father had been elevated through the parliamentary ranks and their frantic new lifestyle meant that his parents were going to be out of the country for most of the next twelve months.

'Why don't you move in here?' Garth's father had suggested when Garth and Claudia had told him and his wife about the problems they were having finding somewhere suitable to live, but neither of them had wanted to do that.

'It's a kind thought, but we really need to find somewhere of our own,' Garth had explained to his father.

Claudia gave another gasp as a second sharp pain ripped through her body.

'Claudia...?' she heard Janice demanding anxiously and then more ominously muttering under her breath, 'Oh my God, someone ring for an ambulance. Quickly. Now! *Now!*' But Claudia was beyond listening, beyond comprehending anything other than the pain, the *agony* threatening to tear her body apart.

She stayed conscious all the way through the siren screaming its frantic, wailing message from the office to the hospital. She was still conscious when they rushed her from the delivery room into emergency surgery. And she was conscious long enough to see how much blood she was losing and for her own horror and panic to seize hold of her—long enough to want to suspend her awareness of the searing pain that was savaging her body.

But she was not conscious when the surgeon pronounced her baby dead, nor was she conscious when he made the decision to remove her womb.

'It's either that or watch her bleed to death,' he declared bluntly.

By the time they managed to locate Garth, it was all over. He reached the hospital just as they were wheeling an inert and still-anaesthetized Claudia back to the ward.

'What's wrong? What's happened? Claudia…?' he protested as the nurse shook her head and placed her hand on his arm.

'Sister wants to have a word with you, Mr Wallace,' she advised him gently.

Garth didn't bother to correct her, to tell her that officially, at least, he wasn't a Mister but a Captain. After all, what did such niceties matter when Claudia, *his* Claudia, was lying on that hospital trolley, her face so drained and pale, her body so still that he might have been looking at a corpse? So still…and so *flat*.

'Sit down, please, Captain Wallace,' Sister instructed rather than invited him. She was in her fifties, efficient and brisk with the experience and weight of a lifetime of breaking bad news to patients' relatives behind her, but that never made it any easier.

'Claudia, my wife…what…?' Garth questioned, refusing her offer of a seat and ignoring the brief firming of her mouth that suggested he should listen rather than talk.

'Your wife, Mrs Wallace, is rather poorly at the moment,' she told him directly. 'She's lost a good deal of blood and, of course, the trauma of the operation causes the body to go into shock and—'

'Operation? What operation?' Garth demanded, his own face losing colour. All he had been told was that Claudia had been rushed into hospital with what her colleagues feared might be a potential miscarriage. 'My wife's expecting a baby and...'

Her very stillness and her silence warned him of what the sister was going to say next, but even that warning was not enough to fully prepare him for it.

'I'm afraid that your wife has lost her baby. He was stillborn. It happens sometimes.'

It was like having a land-mine go off unexpectedly beneath your feet—only worse, much worse. The pain, the confusion, the awful, sickening fear while you waited to assess the damage, waited in the eerie silence for the sound to begin, the cacophony of men crying, *screaming* in panic and in fear.

'Claudia has lost the baby.' Garth heard himself say the words without knowing why he had said them. After all, the woman had spoken plainly enough.

'Yes. I'm afraid so....' There was another small pause and Garth felt his body tense in response as a sharp tingle of prescient alarm jangled down his spine.

'What is it...what's wrong...?' he demanded tersely. 'What...?'

'Your wife was bleeding very badly. Mr Knowles tried to stem it while he transfused her, but...' The neat, short-nailed, scrubbed hands that she had folded in front of her suddenly twitched betrayingly as Garth waited. 'I'm afraid it was no use. In the end, Mr Knowles had no option other than to remove her womb.'

'Remove her womb,' Garth repeated. He felt

like a diver who had gone down too deep, like a
swimmer trying to fight against a relentless tide;
his body grew heavy and lethargic, his thinking
slow and dull.

'Yes. I'm afraid so,' the sister acknowledged.
'It was either that or…' She stopped and then
told him quietly, 'There was a risk that without
surgery she could have bled to death. It does
happen—fortunately infrequently—'

'But not infrequently enough,' Garth interrupted her savagely. 'Oh, my God… Does Claudia know?' he demanded. 'Has she…?'

'She was conscious—just—when…when the
stillbirth occurred,' she told him. 'But she was
anaesthetized for the actual operation, of course.'

Garth closed his eyes. 'How long…how long
before I can see her…talk to her…?'

'Not until morning. She should be out of the
anaesthetic before then, but I'd advise—'

'I want to be with her. I want to be there when
she comes round. I want to see her now,' Garth
interrupted peremptorily.

'I really don't think…' Sister began, but Garth
refused to listen.

'I want to see the surgeon,' he insisted and the
sister sighed under her breath. If there was one
thing she disliked on her wards, it was someone
making a fuss, and this man looked as though he
knew how to make a fuss to very good purpose,
knew how to and was fully prepared to do so.

'Your wife has been put in a small side ward,'
she told him severely. 'As I've already told you,
she really is rather poorly.'

What she wasn't going to reveal was that she had already detailed one of her nurses to position Claudia's bed so that she herself could keep a watchful eye on her through the night—even though officially tonight was her night off. She hadn't liked the look of her as they wheeled her into the ward, and the last thing she wanted right now was an angry, worried young husband pacing her ward and disturbing all the other patients.

Quickly, she made up her mind.

'Very well, then, you may stay in the side ward with your wife, Captain, but only, *only* for so long as you remember that this is *my* ward, and on it my word is law. As you are a military man, I hope you understand me when I tell you that on *this* ward *I* am the officer in charge and the *commanding* officer, and that I expect instant obedience to my orders and instructions.'

She was only a little over five feet in height, but as he looked at her, Garth was conscious of not just her determination but her strength, as well, and oddly, in the midst of all the anguish and shock he was experiencing, he felt a small flash of relief that she was there; that Claudia was in her hands.

The side ward was virtually bare, furnished only with the high-sided hospital bed on which Claudia lay motionless, her chest barely rising and falling with her breathing, and a hard, uncomfortable-looking chair.

There was a drip attached to Claudia's arm

and pristine sheets covered her inert body, pristine…and flat.

Garth felt his eyes sting sharply with tears. He was stillborn, the sister had said. He… That meant that he and Claudia would have had…*should* have had a son.

Now his tears were hot, burning his eyes, burning his skin. His son. His child. His… Gone before he had even had a chance to see him, know him. Deep down inside his body, a new pain flared, a blazing, fierce dark sorrow that he knew would never leave him. His arms ached to hold the small life that should have been. He saw the sister hovering in the doorway.

'The baby, my son,' he choked. 'Where…can I…?'

It was normally the woman, the mother, who asked this question and it caught Sister a little off guard that Garth should do so and Sister did not like being caught off guard and unprepared.

He's in the mortuary, she had been about to say but just in time caught herself up.

Stillborn, pre-term foetuses were not normally considered to be 'babies', but St Chad's was a world leader in the field of obstetrics and very forward thinking. The research they had done there among mothers who had suffered stillborn births had shown that there was a very clear need for such women to know something of the children they had lost. No one with the experience that the maternity staff at St Chad's had could doubt or deny that even such early stillborns as Claudia's were quite distinctly recognisable as 'babies', their bodies and limbs fully formed—if minute. Sister had seen herself the comfort that their mothers derived from seeing and even holding these heartbreakingly tiny, lifeless forms, and so the policy at St Chad's, unlike other hospitals, was not for the stillborns to be quickly and silently disposed of, but for them and their parents to receive rather more gentle and compassionate treatment.

And so instead of giving Garth the stark truth, she caught herself and told him, 'I don't have any spare staff at the moment, but in the morning if you wish to see him…'

'To *see* him?' Garth stared at her.

'Some mothers find it easier to…to accept their loss once they have seen their…their child,' she told him quietly.

Garth swallowed. *Was* that what he wanted? Did he…ought he…?

Breaking into his quandary, Claudia coughed. Frowning, the sister shooed him out of the way as she bustled towards the bed.

It was two o'clock in the morning—the death hour—just as his own eyelids were starting to grow heavy and ache, he saw Claudia's begin to flutter into warning wakefulness. She moved in the bed and then opened her eyes and stared at Garth, her gaze unfocused, her face waxy pale in the low night-light from the main ward outside, her eyes bruised with the starkness of her pain. Two o'clock in the morning—the death hour. Her initial keening mourning cry rapidly escalated to rapid-fire, short hysterical screams that brought two nurses running to her side. Sister walked, but she still got to Claudia first, firmly taking hold of her wrist while she checked her pulse. She obscured Garth's view of the bed while she gave her two nurses low-voiced instructions.

'What's that? What are you doing?' Garth demanded as one of them scurried off to return with a hypodermic.

'Tranquilliser,' the staff nurse told Garth hardily. 'Mr Knowles left instructions for us to administer it—if necessary.'

Garth had been about to protest that Claudia was only just coming round, but it was too late; Sister was already inserting the needle into Claudia's vein.

'She still doesn't know that Mr Knowles has had to operate on her,' the sister told Garth once Claudia had sunk back into unconsciousness. 'She isn't strong enough yet to be told. Her body needs time to recuperate from the blood she's lost and from the operation, and in her present state…'

As she was talking, Garth had got up from the chair to walk over to Claudia's bed. He looked down into her frighteningly shrunken and pale face.

'I want to see him,' he told the sister abruptly. 'I want to see the…my son.'

She had been expecting it and this time she was prepared. So, too, was the pathetically small scrap of humanity waiting for Garth in the quiet, simple 'parents' room', where parents were taken to be with their stillborn child.

The room was painted in soft water-colours to look as though the sun was coming up through mist. It was furnished with a deep, comfortable sofa on which two people might sit comfortably side by side, their bodies touching, and its interior could be discreetly monitored from behind a small screen set into the wall just in case things should get out of hand.

The babies were placed in a traditional crib draped in fine white voile.

Garth's heart missed a beat as he walked into the room. The young nurse who had escorted him quietly disappeared, gently closing the door behind her. Garth hesitated just inside the room, unable to move, unable to do anything other than stare at the draped crib.

Almost, almost, he could see it move, hear that sharp, high-pitched cry of the newborn, and perhaps, if he concentrated enough, he would do. Perhaps...

Grimly, Garth gritted his teeth and walked towards the crib. The baby lay inside it, dressed in white, his eyes closed.

Garth wasn't sure what he had expected but it wasn't this...not this tiny but perfect little face and body. Very gently, he reached out and touched one cold little hand with the tip of his finger. His hand was longer than the whole of the child, his finger longer and broader than its arm. Garth closed his eyes and for a moment the nurse watching on the other side of the small screen thought he was going to turn round and walk away, but then Garth bent and very carefully lifted the small body from the crib.

The nurse looked away. Some things were too private for anyone else to witness. Some sorrows, some griefs, were too intense to be borne.

Very slowly, Garth lifted the lifeless body of his son towards his face. He was so tiny, so fragile, so... He was, he discovered, holding his breath, afraid that somehow in his clumsiness he might inadvertently hurt...

Numbly, Garth swallowed. The small body actually felt almost warm, almost what? he asked himself bitterly. Almost alive?

'I'm sorry,' he heard himself telling him. 'I'm sorry...I'm so sorry.' It hurt more than he could say that they would never know one another, never share the joy and despair of being father and son; that this, *these* moments now would be all he would have of him, that for this, his child, there would be, could be, no memories, no knowledge, no awareness of how much he had been loved and wanted.

As he kissed the cold forehead and placed him gently back in the crib, Garth remembered how he had teased Claudia for talking to the baby as though he could actually hear and understand what she was saying. Perhaps...perhaps he had known of their love. Garth certainly hoped so. As he stood up, he felt a surge of fiercely protective father love sweep over him, a desire to prevent anyone else from touching, hurting, doing *anything* to the small lifeless body. Why had this had to happen? *Why* hadn't anyone been able to do something to save him? Why hadn't *he* been able to do something?

'We'll always remember you,' he told his son softly, 'and so will your brothers and sisters.'

As he left the room, the nurse watching saw a single tear slide down his face as he gave the baby a final lingering look.

But it wasn't until he was back on the ward that the full reality of what had happened hit him. We'll always remember you and so will your brothers and sisters, he had told him. But of course, there would be no brothers and sisters, no child or children. Not now, not ever.

It was Claudia's screams that woke Garth up. He had fallen asleep in the chair just after dawn had broken. Claudia had awakened shortly afterwards, fully conscious this time and all too aware of what the ominous flatness of her stomach meant.

Garth went with her when they put her in a wheelchair and took her to see the baby. When he lifted him out of the crib to give him to her, she held him so tightly that Garth almost winced and had to stop himself—ridiculously—from protesting that she might hurt him.

It was the nurse—more experienced by far than Garth—who recognised what was going to happen and who discreetly alerted the sister so that when Claudia refused to allow anyone to remove the baby from her arms, the sister was there within seconds and deftly administering the second dose of tranquilliser as she had done the first. Even so, they had to wait until Claudia was unconscious before they could prise her hands away from her child.

In the end, it was almost a week before Claudia was well enough to be told about the removal of her womb.

'You're very lucky to be alive,' the surgeon informed her.

'Lucky...lucky...'

Garth winced as he heard the sound of her uncontrolled and uncontrollable weeping.

No one was to be told about her hysterectomy, Claudia insisted to Garth. No one at all, and because he was so concerned for her, Garth agreed. So far as even their parents knew, Claudia had suffered a miscarriage.

'It's awful, darling, I know,' her mother had tried to comfort her once Claudia was allowed home from hospital, 'and I know you don't want to hear this right now, but one day there will be other babies and...'

Over Claudia's bent head as the tears poured down her cheeks, her mother gave Garth an apologetic look. She had suggested that perhaps Claudia might like to go back with them to recuperate for a while, but the doctor had already told Garth bluntly that the best possible thing for Claudia would be to encourage her to get back to work just as soon as she was physically capable.

'No point in allowing her to brood,' he had

told Garth man to man, 'and that's what's bound to happen, given the situation.'

'Yes,' Garth had agreed bleakly.

There was no talk now of continuing with their search for a new home, or of his taking time off to be at home before getting on with his new job, but Claudia was still not well enough to be left alone or to go back to work. She alternated between clinging tightly to Garth, refusing almost to allow him out of her sight and telling him that their marriage might as well be over; that for all she cared he might as well leave. After all, what was the point in their staying married when so far as she was concerned at least, the very purpose for which it was ordained no longer existed?

'Thousands of women, couples, can't have children, Clo,' Garth had told her gently. 'We could adopt....'

'Adopt...adopt what...who...? I want my *own* child...*our* own child,' Claudia had screamed at him.

They hadn't had sex since her return home despite the fact that her own doctor and the surgeon had pronounced her well enough. At the merest hint of any sexual advance from him, Claudia simply froze. What was the point in having sex, Claudia had demanded passionately, when she was no longer a proper woman, no longer able to conceive?

Plenty, Garth had been tempted to respond pithily, more than plenty as his body was urgently reminding him. His desire for her was not dependent on any ability to conceive—unlike hers for him, or so it seemed—but whenever he tried to talk to her about the subject, Claudia refused to listen.

'Sex, sex, that's all *you* ever think about,' she stormed at him when he pointed out to her very gently, or so he had thought, that it was now some little while since she had left hospital and that although they were still sharing a bed—they had to since the flat only had the one bed after all—sharing it *was* all they were doing, with Claudia putting just as much distance between them as she possibly could.

This was his last leave before he formally left the regiment, a few weeks after he'd originally intended to leave, but the timing was, for obvious tragic reasons, not so critical now. He had come home full of good intentions; he would take Claudia out for dinner somewhere special, and perhaps after a good meal and a few glasses of wine, she might relax enough for them to be able to talk—really talk—together as they had once done.

But it hadn't worked. Claudia had been tense all evening, and now that they had returned to the flat, she was angry and defensive as she faced Garth across the small sitting room.

'Claudia, that's not true,' he protested.

But she refused to allow him to continue, interrupting him to demand hotly, 'Isn't it? Isn't that why you took me out for dinner, so that you could get me "in the mood"?'

'Claudia, making love, being intimate—'

'Having sex,' she corrected him bitterly.

'Very well, then,' he agreed curtly. '"Having sex", if you must, is an important part of marriage. When you and I got married, we—'

'*I* didn't get married to have sex. I got married to have babies, children, a family,' Claudia told him fiercely. 'Without that…without them…*sex* to me means nothing.'

Dumbstruck, Garth looked at her.

Was what she was saying the truth? Had the intimacy between them, the sex, the loving he had thought they shared for their mutual pleasure never been anything more than a mere means to an end? Once, he would have laughed at the very idea, his body, his mind, his emotions, warmed by the memory of her responsiveness to him, but it had been a long time since Claudia had reacted to him with anything other than bitterness and rage.

Her claim that she had never desired him for himself as a man hurt as much as if he had been kicked in the stomach, leaving him grappling with the sharpness of the pain and the humiliation of having been caught out by the unexpectedness of the blow. Her words had damaged his male pride, made him feel less of a man, and he acted instinctively, crossing the floor and taking hold of her by the upper arms, denying, 'That's not true.'

'Let go of me, Garth.' Angrily, Claudia tried to prise his fingers away from her arm. 'You're hurting me.'

Bleakly, Garth focused on her. 'And do you

think that you're not doing the same to me?' he challenged her, but Claudia refused to listen.

'Sex, sex, sex. I'm sick of hearing you complain about it. If you want it so badly, why don't you go and find someone else, someone who's a proper woman…a woman…'

She broke off, her voice suspended by the tears that were suddenly pouring down her face. Instantly, Garth's anger retreated, melted by the fierce surge of protective love that swept over him.

'I never said that,' he contradicted her gently. 'You *are* a proper woman, my woman, the only woman I could ever want.'

'Oh, Garth.'

Suddenly, she was the Claudia he remembered, the Claudia…his Claudia, who suddenly felt all softness and warmth in his arms, all woman. With a husky groan, Garth tightened his hold on her, but this time she made no objection, her mouth opening eagerly beneath his kiss.

It was impossible for him to be as restrained and gentle as he had planned, impossible to hold a tight curb on his emotions, on the needs, both physical and emotional, that were swamping him, but gloriously, wonderfully, Claudia seemed to be just as eager for him as he was for her, clinging to him, kissing him back with a fervency, a passion that made his heart race.

She was the one now who was the aggressor; she was the one tugging his shirt free of his jeans and pulling impatiently at the buttons.

They made love quickly, passionately, desperately almost, there and then in the sitting room. Garth responded to Claudia's fierce exhortations and demands by turning her around and bending her over the low arm of the sofa so that he could enter her from behind, his hands free to caress her body, his fingers stroking her nipples and then moving lower, parting the outer lips of her sex and finding the tight, hard nub of her clitoris and caressing it with the same rhythmic pressure with which he was moving within the welcoming warmth of her body.

But even in the intensity of his passion, his drive for physical release, a part of Garth remained aware of her body's potential fragility, and just before he exploded into orgasm, Garth acknowledged that their lives were never going to be the same, that quite simply they could not go back to being the people they had been. For the rest of their lives now, there would be a part of him that felt extra protective towards Claudia, extra aware of her vulnerability. A vulnerability that he knew she had hidden from everyone else—her parents, her colleagues and even her new doctor. She had decided none of them was to be made aware that it wasn't only the child she had been carrying that she had lost and she had fiercely resisted all his attempts to persuade her to tell them.

His fingers still caressing her clitoris, Garth felt her body explode into orgasmic shudders of release, but when he turned her around he knew that the tears on her face were not merely tears of sexual satisfaction.

'Oh, Garth, I don't know if I can bear it,' Claudia cried against his chest as he folded her protectively into his arms.

As he tried to comfort her, his gaze fell on an open file she had been reading, the girl's face staring up defiantly at him from the photograph attached to it. His stomach muscles tensed in sharp recognition.

'Who's this?' he asked Claudia as he released her to bend over and pick up the file.

'Katriona Spencer,' Claudia told him, taking the file from him and closing it. 'I'm very worried about her. She's disappeared, left the squat, and no one there seems to know where she's gone. Why did you ask?' she added. The privileged aspect of her work meant that Garth rarely asked her any questions about the clients—he was very sensitive and acute over such matters and Claudia was grateful to him for the fact that unlike some of her colleagues' spouses he had never shown any resentment over the fact that there were certain things about her work that she was not free to discuss with him. But then, of course, his training in the army meant that he was well aware of the importance of confidentiality. And there were, after all, certain things about his own work that naturally he could not discuss with her.

'No reason,' Garth denied in response to her question, shaking his head.

How could he tell Claudia that he had recognised the girl in the photograph as being the same one he had woken up to find going through his clothes? She had quite obviously 'acquired' Claudia's house keys. His frown deepened. He wasn't quite sure why he felt reluctant to tell Claudia about his discovery other than perhaps because, male-like, he didn't want to cause any upset. They had, after all, changed the locks and fitted a safety chain on the outer door, and besides, with any luck, they would soon be moving anyway.

Dismissing Katriona from his thoughts, he pulled Claudia back into his arms and whispered teasingly to her, 'That was very nice for an apéritif. Now how about something a little bit more...sustaining for our main course?' As he spoke, he was gently urging her in the direction of the bedroom.

'Garth, we said we'd spend the rest of the evening going through those new details the agent sent,' Claudia reminded him.

'Mmm...I know. But there's nothing to stop us going through them in bed, is there?'

Claudia laughed. 'You know quite well that that isn't what you've got in mind at all,' she reproved him.

Garth didn't bother to deny it. Instead, he gave her a wicked smile as he picked her up bodily and carried her towards their bed. This was more like it. This was more like the *real* Claudia...*his* Claudia.

The letter was waiting for him when he returned to camp. It was marked 'strictly private and confidential' and had been placed discreetly on his desk.

Frowning slightly, he opened it. When he saw the contents, his face lost colour.

There was a plain sheet of paper on which someone had written in large uneven capitals, 'Congratulations', and then as he lifted the sheet to see what was pinned behind it, he caught his breath.

It was a simple and very brief typed letter confirming that its recipient was pregnant.

At first, he thought it was the very worst kind of bad joke—a cruelly bad joke, the kind that would surely destroy Claudia if she ever got to hear about it. But then he realised that if it was a joke, it was being played on him by life... fate...and not some boneheaded rookies out to put one over on an officer, because the letter *wasn't* addressed to *Claudia*. And the letter had been sent by a Katriona Wallace—a woman using his surname.

Garth swallowed and stared at the top left-hand corner of the letter again.

'Katriona Wallace, Flat 12, Stanway House, Victoria Street.'

Katriona. Katriona Spencer.

Claudia's client, the girl who had stolen her house keys, the girl who had broken into the flat, the girl he had caught going through his wallet...Katriona. The girl, who it now seemed was trying to claim that *he* was the father of the child she was carrying, which was, of course, impossible. He had never been near the girl. He had never touched her. He had always had a strong suspicion that some of the people Claudia had to deal with came very close to being pretty psychotic. Now he had proof of it.

What on earth had made her pick on *him* for the role of father to her child? Surely not the fortunately small amount of money she had taken from his wallet.

So what then? Had her choice been a deliberate act of spitefulness or merely a motiveless act of pointless boredom? She must have got his address from his wallet but she hadn't actually taken his ID papers, which meant that she must have memorised it.

Congratulations. His face contorting, he screwed up both papers and hurled them into the waste-paper basket. Then on some impulse he couldn't define, he got them out again, smoothed them flat and reread them before searching in his desk drawer for a box of matches. Very deliberately, he proceeded to rip them into small pieces before burning them.

The girl was obviously just trying it on. She had to be. There was no way *he* could *possibly* be the father of her child. No way at all.

'Any luck with the agents?' Garth forced himself to sound bright and cheerful as he waited for Claudia's response, picturing her standing by the telephone they had recently had installed in the flat as she answered his call. He had hoped to get home for the weekend but there were one or two matters he had to tie up at HQ before he took his final leave of the army.

'Nothing we'd be interested in,' Claudia responded. 'All that seem to be around at the moment are rambling country rectories, not the sort of thing we'd want at all.'

'But that's…'

Just in time, Garth stopped himself.

As they were never going to have a family, there was no point in looking at family houses, Claudia had told him. Since she had now decided to stay on at work and since he, too, would be working in London, they would be much better off with a modern London apartment rather than buying some ridiculously oversize country house.

Garth didn't agree with her. The last thing he wanted was a soulless city apartment. He had been looking forward to spending his weekends and his free time in some sleepy little country town, preferably one with a decent stretch of fishable river close to it and certainly one with a good golf course, but he had learned over the past few months to tread warily around Claudia and not say or do anything that would bring on one of the deep, dark moods of despair that were caused by anything reminding her of what had happened.

To Garth, she had become heartbreakingly and very worryingly frail in recent weeks, both in appearance and manner, but she stubbornly resisted all his attempts to discuss his concern for her with him. She was perfectly all right, she insisted. But, of course, they both knew that she wasn't. And Garth had taken to telephoning her every day when he was away from her just to make sure.

Just to make sure of what? It was a question he didn't want to ask himself, never mind answer.

'I'm going to see what sounds like an ideal place in a new block with views over the river,' Claudia told him brightly—overbrightly, Garth recognised. 'It will be perfect for us—almost within walking distance of where your office will be.'

'Claudia, I didn't think—' Garth began, but she refused to let him finish.

'I must go, Garth,' she broke in abruptly. 'I've got a conference meeting in half an hour.'

Garth's meeting finished earlier than he had anticipated. With a free afternoon and evening ahead of him, his first instinct was to go home to Claudia, but a couple of miles from the flat, he got caught up in a traffic jam caused by some roadworks he had forgotten about, leaving him no alternative but to sit and wait. On some impulse he refused to name, he reached into the glove compartment and withdrew the *A to Z* road map he kept there and thumbed through it.

As he had suspected, Stanway House in Victoria Street had to be a sixties tower block built by one of the city councils.

There was a side-street several yards away and after a very creative interpretation of the traffic laws, he was able to turn into it and follow the labyrinth of narrow backstreets into which it led, eventually coming out half an hour later onto the main road that ran past the block of flats.

Wisely, he parked his car far enough away not to be at any risk from vandals and, having re-checked the *A to Z*, started to make his way on foot towards the flats.

The smell that reached him as he climbed up the first set of stairs made him wrinkle his nose unappreciatively, but when the group of youths clustered together in the shadowed overhang started to make jeering comments about his appearance, all it took to silence them was one quick, steady look.

'Fucking copper pig,' he heard one of the youths muttering as he started up the next set of stairs.

'Naw,' one of his companions denied. 'He's no pig. He hasn't got the look. He's army. Look at his hair.'

Ruefully, Garth applauded the youth's visual astuteness—pity he wasn't putting it to better use. Claudia had already teased him about the fact that once he was formally 'out', he would have to adopt a more trendy hairstyle, but Garth suspected that he would feel uncomfortable with the foppishly long hair currently favoured by so many members of his own sex after years of sporting a short army back and sides.

Number 12 was on the third landing, a no man's land of boarded-up windows and barred doors. The flats were quite plainly being emptied, hopefully getting readied for demolition, Garth reflected.

They were more like a nest of rat holes than a good environment for human beings to thrive in.

Number 12 looked no better than the rest. The only difference was that someone had removed the boarding evidently meant to keep unwanted house hunters out, a someone who did not intend to be put off by any would-be attempts to remove them if the graffiti scrawled across the doors and windows were anything to go by, Garth decided as he briefly read the colloquial message to the effect that uninvited visitors would not be welcome.

Ignoring it, he rapped sharply on the door. When no one opened it, he paused for a second, studied it thoughtfully, then reflecting briefly on the wisdom of his uncitizen-like behaviour, he leaned forward and, putting his shoulder to the door, gave it extremely professional if somewhat illegal encouragement to open of its own accord.

He was just about to make a second attempt when he heard sounds of movement behind the door and an irritable female voice calling out, 'For God's sake, if you're that desperate...' and then the door was being unbolted and pulled open.

As Garth stepped into the gloomy, dank darkness of the unlit hallway, his first thought was that she was far prettier than he remembered; in fact, so pretty that the shock of it jolted through him as though he had gripped hold of an electrical cable. That she had recognised him as immediately as he had done her was equally evident.

'Well, hello there, Daddy,' she spat viciously at him, giving him a wide and totally unwelcoming smile. 'Come to check it out for yourself, have you? Well, go ahead…here he is.'

Still smiling mockingly at him, she patted her round belly, the only part of her that was round, the taut mound of her pregnancy somehow grotesque against the shocking thinness and gauntness of the rest of her body.

'It isn't true,' Garth denied flatly. 'It can't be.'

'Can't it?' she taunted him. 'Then why are you here? What's wrong…frightened your little wifey will find out? What will she say? I wonder. She won't be pleased, will she? Not that she's got anything to boast about. She couldn't manage to hold on to hers, could she? Mine's going to be a big, fine, strong baby.' She patted her belly again and laughed. 'She wasn't even really showing, was she? Call herself a woman. I bet she didn't give you as good a time in bed as I did. I bet she's never even given you a proper blow job, has she, never mind if you had to go down on her? I bet it felt good, didn't it, getting a real taste of pussy juice, from the way you were licking away at it?'

'Stop it,' Garth warned her. 'Stop that right now. You're making it up. I've never been to bed with you. I—'

'No. Want me to tell you some more about what you did…what you said? Want me to describe the mole you've got right here?'

As she accurately touched the place on his inner thigh where he had a small, flat, oval mole, Garth winced and not just because of the fact that she was touching him.

'Not got much to say for yourself now, have you?' Katriona gloated. 'You were begging me for it,' she told him. 'Begging me…you couldn't wait to get it…couldn't wait to have me. You told me that you'd never had a fuck like it, that you'd never had a woman like me. You said it was a hundred, a thousand, times better than it had ever been with her. Do you want me to tell you how many times you had me?' she asked him softly, watching mercilessly as his colour came and went. 'For a man who had drunk as much whisky as you had, you did pretty well, but then I suppose you have to be tough in the army.'

As she was speaking, she was reaching out as though to caress his body. Instinctively, Garth stepped back from her.

What she was saying was some grotesque perversion of the truth. It had to be. It couldn't possibly be true. *He* couldn't possibly have made love to her…had *sex* with her, and yet as his brain was forging the furious panic-stricken denials, deep down inside a part of him was already recognising that somewhere in what she was saying there lay a vicious, poisoned shard of truth. He couldn't remember saying or doing the things she had said, but there was something not so much a memory as a shocked sense of awareness.

'What? Nothing to say?'

Swallowing hard, Garth tried to compose himself. No matter what he might feel towards her, if she was speaking the truth, then this wretched creature *was* carrying his child and if *that* was the case, no matter how unpalatable, how appalling he found the prospect, he had a moral obligation towards that child.

That child…*his* child. Oh, my God, what was he going to do? How the hell was he going to tell Claudia?

'We need to talk,' he announced curtly, starting to move farther into the hallway, but Katriona immediately blocked his way.

'Talk? What about?'

'About the fact that you're carrying my child. Arrangements will have to be made.' Wearily, Garth pushed his hand into his hair. Never in a thousand years had he ever envisaged himself being in this sort of situation, at least not once he had left his youthful wild-oats-sowing excesses behind him. It made him feel sick to think…to contrast *this* with the loving hopes he and Claudia had shared; the excitement and pleasure with which *they* had been looking forward to the arrival of *their* child.

'Arrangements. The only arrangement I'll be making is when to get rid of it,' he heard Katriona telling him ruthlessly.

'Get rid of it? No, you can't—'

'Who says not?' she demanded scornfully. 'This is *my* baby…*mine*, and I can do what the hell I want with it and there's not a fucking thing you can do to stop me.'

As he saw the way her eyes were glittering,

Garth recognised that there was no point in trying to reason with her. He was no stranger to the sight of someone on drugs. It happened. Even in the army.

'It might not even be yours,' Katriona was saying now. '*You* aren't the only man I've ever fucked, you know.'

Garth could well believe it. His stomach churned nauseously as he looked away from her, praying that she wouldn't guess how much he hoped the child she was carrying was *not* his, or rather how much he hoped that *she* was not going to be the mother of a child he had fathered, and not just because of what that knowledge would do to Claudia if she ever found out about it.

'What did you come round here for anyway?' Katriona challenged. 'Another chance to get a taste of what you don't get at home? I don't come cheaply. I don't *come* cheaply. Get it?'

She laughed wildly at her own joke, the humour dying from her face to be replaced by a sour look of dislike as she stared at Garth.

'Think you're so good, don't you? Too good for someone like me. Well, that wasn't the way it was the night you gave me this.' Eyes flashing, she jabbed downwards at her stomach. '*I* was the one you wanted then, not her, your precious Claudia. Claudia. My God, even her bloody name's precious, but I'm the one who's having your baby, not her.'

'You just said you didn't know if it *was* my child,' Garth reminded her grimly.

She shot him a sideways look. 'Yes, I did, didn't I?'

'If it *is* my child, then I have a right to—'

'You have no rights over me. No rights. No man does. No man *ever* will,' Katriona denied angrily. 'If this turns out to be a man child, then God help him,' she told him. 'I hate men…hate them. I'd have him castrated at birth. All men should have their balls cut off the moment they're born…'

Garth tried to hold on to his self-control as he listened to her drug-crazed ravings.

'I just want to help you,' he began when she eventually fell silent.

Was the child she was carrying his? Did she even know? Would he ever know if it was… If it was what?

'Now what are you going to do?' Katriona was demanding softly, watching him. 'Pay me to go away somewhere and keep quiet, to disappear…?'

Garth looked away from her. That thought had crossed his mind, but he knew that if he had voiced it, it would have been to open himself to even more verbal ridicule from her, to make himself and through him, Claudia, even more vulnerable. Because this was what all this was about, he guessed intuitively. It wasn't so much *him* the wretched girl wanted to get at but Claudia. He could sense it, feel it, *smell* it almost, as he listened to the hostility, the resentment and the jealousy in her voice whenever she mentioned his wife.

'I suppose she's trying desperately to get pregnant again, but I've beaten her to it,' she boasted triumphantly, confirming his suspicions. '*I'm* the one who's going to have your baby first. Just think,' she added cooingly, 'my baby and hers will be blood relations.'

'If you are carrying my child, then certain arrangements will have to be made,' Garth persisted determinedly. He knew he would *never* forget the sick feeling that filled him as he recognised that, through him, Claudia was now vulnerable to the malice of this malevolent harpy, this…this creature, who looked at him with eyes as old and as knowing as time.

Thank God she didn't know the whole true story; thank God she had no idea that for Claudia there could never be another child.

'Don't you want to feel it…touch it?' she asked slyly now, thrusting her small taut stomach towards him.

Nervously, Garth looked away, his emotions contorted by the vicelike grip of his pain as he compared the obvious blooming health of her pregnancy with the pale wanness that had been Claudia's.

It was all so bloody unfair. You only had to look at this wretched being to know she could never be half the mother that Claudia would have been.

'Been struck dumb have you?' Katriona taunted. Sullenly, she added, 'If you want me to get rid of it, you're going to have to pay me. It won't be cheap. I should have done it before…I meant to…I shouldn't have let it go on so long.'

She was talking more to herself than to him, Garth recognised. He also recognised that beneath his instinctive rejection of her suggestion ran an ugly thread of relief. Why not give her some money…why not…?

He closed his eyes as he felt the sweat break out on his forehead. For Claudia's sake, for everyone's sake, it would be the best thing, the sensible thing to do. For everyone's sake…including the child's…his child's… 'I don't have any money on me—' he began.

'But you can get it,' Katriona interrupted him swiftly. Her supplier was getting impatient for her to pay him what she owed. She hadn't been able to work much recently. She hadn't been feeling well enough. She felt sick a lot. 'Bring it here tomorrow,' she snapped at him, 'and make sure you do. Otherwise…otherwise Claudia could find out what her precious husband has been up to.'

Half an hour after Garth had gone, Katriona opened the door to the man she was sharing the squat with.

'Come on, we've got to get out of here,' he told her tersely. 'We're leaving.'

'I can't,' Katriona objected. 'I've got a john coming round tomorrow…he owes me.'

'Let him,' he retorted forcefully. 'We're leaving.' Even as he spoke, he was looking shiftily over his shoulder. 'I'm in big trouble, girl, and you're going to be in it with me. I owe some bad men some big money. There's some guys I know. They're on the road...travellers...we can join up with them.'

Katriona frowned and nibbled on her bottom lip. She and her companion had been 'friends' but not lovers on and off for several years. She knew he was heavily involved in the drug scene both as a pusher and a user and she knew what he meant when he talked about bad men with big money. It wouldn't mean anything to them that she wasn't him if they broke in here and found that he had gone and *she* was here. If they were out for revenge...for punishment... Set against what she had to lose, the money she could expect to gain from Garth was nothing.

'Are you coming or not?'

'I'm coming,' she agreed.

12

'Katriona's turned up.'

Garth's head jerked back in an involuntary re-action to Claudia's casual announcement. They were eating a late supper, both of them having been working late.

'Katriona?' Garth questioned dry-mouthed, hating himself for the pretence he was enacting, the carefully tailored tone in his voice that suggested he couldn't really remember who 'Katriona' was when, of course, he could. Of *course*.

For over a month after she had accused him of fathering her child, he had tried unsuccessfully to find her, but that had been over six months ago. He had told himself in relief that the whole thing had been a try-on, an attempt to get money out of him, and that it was impossible for him to have been responsible for her pregnancy and that he had been a complete idiot to ever let her panic him into believing that he could be. But he had still not said anything to Claudia.

'Mmm… Remember…she was one of my cases? Apparently, she's been on the road travelling. She just turned up at one of the squats. She was there the other day when I went round to see someone else. She'd been asking for me, or so one of the other girls said. They tell so many lies it's sometimes hard to know when they're telling the truth.'

'So she's back?'

'Mmm-hmm, and not alone. She's had a baby.'

'A baby...?' Garth abruptly put down his fork, his appetite lost.

'It seems she gave birth while she was on the road. The baby's a girl, a pretty little thing. Of course, Katriona is refusing to say who the father is—if she knows. I don't think she's feeding her properly—she can barely look after herself, never mind a baby. One of the other girls in the squat seems to be helping out with the baby to some extent. The baby's such a darling, Garth. I just wish...' Quick tears filled Claudia's eyes and she looked down at her plate.

Outwardly, she might seem to have come to terms with her miscarriage and to be getting on with her life, but no one else knew, no one else saw as Garth did, the nights when she woke both herself and him with the sound of her heart-rending grief. Then Garth would hold her and comfort her and eventually she would grow calm. But there were other times, times when the anger and the pain were so great that she turned them on Garth as well as herself, screaming at him that he should leave her and go find a woman who could be a proper woman, who could give him children as she no longer could.

Garth said nothing of any of this to their parents. So far as they were concerned, the two of them were simply biding their time before trying for another baby.

His own father had even congratulated them quite recently on their foresight in waiting until Garth had established himself in his new career before taking on the additional responsibility of a child.

Not that they saw much of his parents lately. His father's work took him abroad a great deal, and increasingly, Claudia tended to shun family gatherings or indeed any events that might either bring her into contact with children or remind her of what she had lost.

He had had to turn down so many invitations from his colleagues at work that he was beginning to feel quite uncomfortable.

Claudia's heavy work schedule had been given as the excuse, and it was true that she was working longer and longer hours. But both of them were working increasingly long hours—because neither of them could face the reality of what their empty flat actually meant. They had deferred thinking about making a move until they both felt they could put more enthusiasm into it.

'There's something I need to talk to you about,' he told her now as he tried to dismiss the memories Claudia's words had raised. It made him feel edgy and uncomfortable to realise that Katriona was in contact with Claudia, even though with the breathing space that time had given him, he was convinced that Katriona had simply wanted to panic him into giving her money. So what if she had identified that mole on his inner thigh. He had been so out of it with the whisky he had drunk that she could have been in the flat for any length of time before he had woken up, certainly long enough for her to have pushed back the bedclothes and... And what? Looked at his naked body? Just looked, or had she...had *they*...?

'Garth, you said you wanted to talk to me about something,' Claudia reminded him, adding tiredly, 'I hope it isn't going to take too long. I've got some case notes to write up and I want to go in early in the morning.'

She looked as well as sounded tired, Garth acknowledged. She was working far too hard, using her work like a tourniquet pulled tight over a gaping wound, but all it was doing was stemming the loss of blood. It wasn't doing anything to promote any real healing and the moment it was removed...

'Garth,' Claudia prompted him irritably.

'Oh, yes. Nick Forbes is thinking of retiring. His wife isn't very well, as you know, and her doctors have advised that she needs to live in a warmer climate. Since Nick is the agency, without him...'

He paused as he saw the way Claudia was frowning.

'What are you trying to say?' she demanded. 'Is Nick trying to get rid of you? Does he—'

'No, nothing like that. Far from it,' he reassured her hastily. 'In fact, what he's suggesting is that I set up on my own. I've already got a good portfolio of my own clients. He's been offered a very good financial deal by one of the other agencies and of course there's no way I could ever be in a position to buy him out.'

'Set up on your own, but—'

'It makes sense,' Garth interrupted her. 'I had a word with Dad about it over the phone.'

'You spoke to him before saying anything to *me*?' Claudia protested angrily.

Garth gave a small sigh. 'You've been pretty tied up with your work recently,' Garth reminded her tactfully.

'It will be very risky—setting up on your own,' Claudia commented, her expression reflecting her concern.

'Yes, but Nick seems to think I can make it work. More and more blue-chip companies are turning to PR agencies these days to handle certain aspects of their business for them. It's all about presenting the right image to the public, showing their human face, not being seen as unapproachable institutions.'

As she listened to Garth's increasingly enthusiastic explanation of what he planned—what he *wanted* to do—Claudia had to close her eyes against a sharp stab of envy.

Garth loved his work in a way that she did not love hers. Her relationship with what she did was more of dependence and resentment. She *needed* to work to stop herself thinking about…about the past, but there were so many things about her job that she disliked, so many times when she was aware of the fact that she could not give each case the time she could see it needed. And it wasn't really an 'it'. Each case represented a human being, a person whose needs she knew she simply did not have the time to meet. No matter how many courses she went on, how much she absorbed about the ways to best reach each individual, what was the *point* when she simply did not have the time to put that learning into practice?

On her latest course, there had been people who were in private practice, and listening to them had been a revelation. Seeing how much sense of achievement they derived from following a case through, from being actively part of an improvement in the life of their client, had reminded her of just why *she* had been drawn to her work in the first place, something that tended to get overlooked in the sheer volume of work with which they were confronted. And now suddenly and unexpectedly she felt a sharp stab of envy for Garth. *He* had so much to look forward to...a new career...a new life...and most probably a new woman, a wife who could provide him with the family that she could not.

Claudia closed her eyes tightly, but it was no use; the tears still burned their destructive path from behind her eyelids and down her face.

'Clo, please *don't*, *please* don't,' Garth soothed her gently as he came round the table to lift her out of her seat and take hold of her.

'It's so unfair, Garth. *Everything's* so unfair,' Claudia protested. 'Even someone like Katriona...a drug addict who'll be lucky if she lives another year, can produce a healthy baby…a baby she doesn't even want, never mind love. But I can't,' she cried bitterly. 'You ought to leave me, find someone else…I'm no use to you, I can't…'

Garth suppressed the emotions threatening to rise inside him. It was pointless reminding Claudia that they had been through all this before, pointless and cruel.

'I don't *want* anyone else,' he told her. 'I only want you.'

And as she looked into his eyes, Claudia saw that it was true now, but would it always be so?

'We've got each other,' Garth assured her softly, 'and that's all we need.'

Only it wasn't, not for her, Claudia acknowledged, lying awake beside him in bed later that night. Much as she loved him, it wasn't enough. She ached, yearned, *needed* to have a child, to be a mother. Just looking at Katriona's baby earlier on today had awakened all the feelings she had been trying so hard to suppress. When Katriona had casually dumped the baby on the filthy, thin blanket on the floor of the squat beside her while she turned to squabble with the girl who had just come in, Claudia hadn't been able to resist picking the baby up and holding her.

She had smelled of stale milk, urine and vomit, but that hadn't meant a thing to Claudia. She had been overwhelmed with such a surge of fiercely protective love for her that she had momentarily forgotten that anyone else existed. The urge to hold the baby close to her, to nourish and protect her, to love her, had been so strong that she had instinctively found her hand going to her blouse to unfasten the buttons before she realised what she was doing.

And as though she, too, shared the same need to be close, to love, the baby, so quiet and wide-eyed in Claudia's arms as she focused silently on her, had started to cry in protest when Katriona suddenly turned round and snatched her back.

'Give her to me,' she had demanded aggressively. 'She's mine.'

'If you haven't already done so, you'll need to register her birth,' Claudia had reminded Katriona with a Herculean effort to detach herself and remain professional. She would need to tell the local health visitor about the baby as she was obviously a child at risk. Possibly suffering effects from Katriona's drug addiction.

'I'll…do it when I'm ready,' Katriona told her sullenly. They had had this discussion before.

Claudia knew better than to ask Katriona any questions about her little girl's father. To do so would inevitably provoke a stream of invective and anger, and apart from her personal dislike of being under that kind of attack from a professional point of view, for Katriona's own sake, the last thing Claudia wanted was to put herself in a position where Katriona might refuse to have anything further to do with her.

For Katriona's sake, or for her baby's?

Deliberately, Claudia looked away when the infant made pathetic little mewling noises and pushed her face hungrily against Katriona's breast.

'Not there, you little rat,' she heard Katriona screeching angrily. 'Here, have this,' she added more practically as she reached for what Claudia guessed was a cold and certainly very un-hygienic-looking half-full bottle of milk. Then she shoved it into the baby's mouth without any apparent concern for whether the child could suck on it properly or not.

'No prizes for guessing what you're thinking,' she told Claudia sneeringly with one of those flashes of sharp intuitiveness that still managed to surface past the drugs dulling her brain. One of the things that depressed Claudia most about Katriona's situation was the fact that the girl was obviously very, very intelligent.

'If she'd been yours, she'd have been breast-fed. Well, she's not yours, although...' She stopped and then suddenly smiled, giving Claudia a mocking, taunting look that made the tiny hairs prickle at the back of her neck. So knowing and secretive and yet at the same time almost sadistically triumphant was the look she could see in Katriona's eyes.

Her heart started to thump heavily, her chest tightened, and the familiar sensations of fear, panic and bitter resentment gripped her by the throat. Surely Katriona couldn't have guessed the truth that she could never, ever have a child; surely she couldn't *know* of the sense of helpless longing and envy, of isolating pain and desolation, she experienced every time she saw another woman with her child. How could she know? No one knew, apart from herself and Garth.

'Here...take her.' The abruptness with which Katriona thrust the baby at her took Claudia off guard. Automatically, she held out her arms to take hold of the small bundle, instinctively and deftly positioning her comfortably against her own body as she picked up the bottle.

But the baby wasn't interested in the milk—didn't need or want its questionable comfort now she was back in Claudia's arms—or so it seemed. She nestled happily there as though *Claudia* was her mother and not Katriona, opening her eyes to gaze up unblinkingly into Claudia's face with a grave intentness that made Claudia catch her breath as she was swamped by a responsive rush of fiercely protective and yearning mother love.

It was like falling instantly and compulsively in love, Claudia recognised. The feeling was so intense, so strong, so sure, that as she gazed into the baby's dark green eyes, Claudia felt as though she had stepped through a special door into a private place, a special world where only the two of them existed.

'Reminds you of someone does she?'

Katriona's taunting question and sharp voice brought her back to reality. 'She looks very like you,' Claudia told her diplomatically, even though in reality she could see no resemblance between the baby and her mother.

'Think so?' Katriona gave her one of her cruel, catlike smiles. 'Me, I think she looks more like her dad. What's wrong?' she challenged Claudia. 'Surprised I know who the father is? Oh, I know all right. She's got a very special daddy, this one has. *She* wasn't fathered by some scummy punter. No, he didn't have to pay me for sex.' She gave Claudia a sidelong, mocking look and asked her softly, 'Want me to tell you about it?'

Katriona had tried to goad her before, but never quite so specifically as this. There was no reason why she shouldn't talk sexually explicitly to her, Claudia acknowledged, but for some reason she knew that she was already recoiling from the idea, unwilling to have Katriona confiding the details of her baby's conception to her.

'He was good. He was *very* good,' Katriona told her smugly without waiting for Claudia to make any response. 'He even went down on me. He said that he wanted me to be really wet and ready before he had me. He said that he was tired of having sex with a woman who didn't know how to enjoy herself, how to enjoy him; a woman who didn't know how to pleasure him properly. I pleasured him properly all right, so properly that he gave me her,' she added, nodding in the direction of the baby Claudia was still holding.

The self-satisfied, purring tone of Katriona's voice jarred Claudia's nerves like the rasp of metal on glass, her distaste so intense that she almost physically shrank from her. The temptation to forget professionalism and to demand acerbically of Katriona just why this apparently so doting male was no longer on the scene was one she only just managed to resist. And as she fought it back, she felt herself break out in a cold sweat. Too many times recently, she had experienced this frightening sensation of being close to the edge of a precipice, of being one step away from total loss of self-control. As though she could sense her distress, the baby started to cry. Instantly, Claudia forgot her own problems, holding the infant close, soothing her.

'Look at her,' Katriona taunted, watching as the baby nuzzled close to Claudia's breast in the same seeking way she had earlier to Katriona's own. 'You won't find anything there,' she told the baby derisively. Her expression turning sulky again, she reached out and snatched the child back from Claudia. 'She's mine,' she declared fiercely. 'Mine—and she's going to stay mine, even if... Good job you're a girl,' she addressed the baby grimly as her body started to give in to the pull of the drug she had injected before Claudia's arrival. 'Let's hope you grow up pretty. That way we can get you earning your own living. There's plenty of men around who like 'em young,' she added unemotionally to Claudia, ignoring her sudden indrawn breath of shock. 'The younger the better, it turns 'em on.'

Claudia knew better than to protest or to plead with Katriona that for her daughter's sake, if not for her own, she ought to at least try to change her current way of life.

Common sense told Claudia that it was already too late. The Katriona who had returned from the months spent 'travelling' looked almost a decade older than the girl Claudia had last seen. She was thinner, frailer, harder, her ultimate fate already showing in her eyes, and knowing Katriona as she did, Claudia suspected that the girl herself knew it. Even so…she had to try.

'Katriona,' she began quietly, 'you—'

'I'm what?' Katriona provoked her grimly, her body taut with defiance as she silently dared Claudia to say what she was thinking.

'You know where I am if you need me,' Claudia said simply, resisting the urge to take up the dare, then getting up to go.

She had reached the door when Katriona stopped her, calling out to her. Slowly, Claudia turned round.

'Give me your telephone number,' Katriona demanded tersely.

Claudia frowned. 'You already have it. The office—'

'No, not the office, at home. Give it to me.' It was strictly against all the rules, but instead of refusing, Claudia found herself hesitating, then urged by some instinct she could neither define nor ignore, she quickly scribbled her number down on a piece of paper she tore from her diary and gave it to Katriona.

Back at her desk later, she broke another rule. When she was writing up her case notes, she made no mention of the fact that Katriona had asked for her telephone number and no mention of the fact that she had given it to her.

13

'Look, are you sure you'll be all right?'

'Garth, I'll be fine,' Claudia assured him, trying to force the irritation out of her voice and put a smile on her face as he stood watching her, overnight bag at his feet, one hand already poised to open the door onto a new life for both of them, or onto freedom for him. From her?

Tensely, Claudia swallowed. Garth had sworn over and over again that he loved her. But there were still images like now, when she could only see—what? who?—a stranger, a man dressed in his business suit, his mind already on the meetings that lay ahead of him, looking frighteningly unfamiliar, not her Garth at all.

'I can cancel these meetings, stay here with you, if you—'

'I *want* you to go,' Claudia insisted even though both of them knew it wasn't the truth. She had been having one of her periods of feeling extremely depressed and the knowledge that Garth's business meetings were going to keep him away for two nights—normally something she would have taken in her stride—had caused her to feel even worse.

Why, oh why didn't Garth simply go? Didn't

he know how tempted she was to beg him to stay? Every second he delayed, that temptation grew worse.

'Just go, Garth,' she finally snapped at him. 'I'll be fine.'

With Garth gone, she wandered around the flat, picking things up and putting them down. She supposed she ought to make herself something to eat but the idea simply didn't appeal.

Although she had tried to hide it from him in bed, she could feel Garth carefully measuring the shrinking width of her waist with the span of his hands. He was constantly urging her to eat more, bringing home tempting boxes of chocolates, which she took to work and gave to the others.

It wasn't food her body, her emotions, her whole being, craved; it was a baby. Confirmation of her womanhood, fulfilment of the very reason that nature had made her.

A baby...

Claudia was asleep when the phone rang. As she stretched out her hand for the receiver, she saw the time on the alarm clock and frowned, tensing her body as sleep receded, driven away by the surge of adrenalin-fuelled anxiety that filled her as she registered the fact that it was gone one o'clock in the morning.

Her first thought was that something had happened to Garth. Either that or one or other of their parents. Telephone calls at one a.m. could only herald bad news, and at first she found it hard to make any sense of the unfamiliar and very slurred female voice at the other end of the line. 'I'm sorry, I don't—' she began.

But the girl cut her off, swearing volubly, then telling her frantically, 'It's Kat...she said to ring. She's bad...she wants you to come.'

'Cat...?' But it was too late. The girl had hung up, leaving Claudia grasping for answers.

Cat...Kat...Katriona. It had to be her. Suddenly, Claudia was up and out of bed, pulling on her clothes, mentally running through all the possible things the phone call might mean. Grabbing her bag and car keys, she headed for the door.

For some people, one a.m. was not particularly late, and this was, after all, London, whose streets were far from empty. Yet somehow, despite their busyness, Claudia was filled with a sense of alienation and deep foreboding. The fact that the squat was in an area that no one would think of visiting at night never even crossed her mind as she parked her car and got out, throwing a darkly challenging glare at the gang of youths watching. A little to her own surprise, they shuffled off, leaving her free to hurry towards the block of flats.

Someone, somewhere, was having a party, the music so loud the building almost shook with the violent force of it, and as she passed one flat, Claudia could hear the sounds of arguing coming from inside it, followed by a crash of shattering china.

Grimly, she hurried on. Without being fanciful, she suddenly had the feeling that she wasn't making her swift journey to Katriona's side on her own; she could almost hear the threatening beat of his wings as she sensed the ominous presence of death's winged messenger at her heels.

The squat unexpectedly was in complete darkness, causing her to come to an abrupt halt. For some reason, she had expected it to be ablaze with light, filled with noise and people, but instead it was totally silent. As she raised her hand to bang on the door, someone opened it and a girl she vaguely remembered from a previous visit stretched out a skinny, clawlike hand to drag her in.

'She's upstairs…waiting,' she whispered to Claudia, who recognised from her voice that she was the girl who had rung her.

Claudia demanded, 'What's wrong…is she—'

'She's a goner,' the girl replied brutally. 'She's been into a bad scene. Took some spooked heroin.' She shrugged.

'Have you called a doctor…an ambulance?' Claudia asked her, hurrying towards the stairs.

'No use,' the girl said. 'Wouldn't rush to come anyway, not to the likes of us, and besides, that wasn't what she wanted.'

'Go and ring for an ambulance now,' Claudia instructed her. 'Tell them it's an emergency. Do it,' she commanded. 'Now!'

Shrugging, the girl headed for the door, telling her, 'It won't do any good. It's too late!' But Claudia wasn't listening; she was heading for the stairs instead.

Like the rest of the flat, Katriona's room was

virtually in darkness but the illumination provided by the single flickering candle propped up
in a corner and supported by its own wax was
more than enough to show Claudia that the girl
had spoken the truth. Katriona was indeed dying.

Unbelievably, though, she was still conscious.
Not only conscious but calmly aware of what
was happening, Claudia recognised as she saw
the girl's eyes flicker in mocking acknowledge-
ment of the shock Claudia knew was visible in
her own face.

'You came. I knew you would....'

The voice was a whisper, barely as loud as the
whistling sound she made trying to draw air into
her lungs.

'Don't talk,' Claudia urged, kneeling on the
floor beside her and reaching out to take hold of
her cold hand. 'The doctor will be here soon.'

Katriona gave the ghost of a laugh.

'Not soon enough. Oh, don't look so shocked,'
she mocked Claudia. 'After all, isn't this what
you've been warning me would happen? You
should be pleased. At last you're being proved
right.'

'Katriona...don't try to talk. The doctor—'

'Can't do a damn thing. I'm not stupid. It's too
late. I owed the dealer. I couldn't pay.' She gave
a small shrug. 'I begged him for one last fix. He
took me literally, gave me a bad mix.' She smiled,
a mere shadow of a smile, her eyes shockingly
alive in the drawn, already waxen pallor of her
face.

Suddenly, from a dark corner of the room, Claudia heard a thin protesting cry.

The baby… Instinctively, she started to reach for her, but Katriona immediately stopped her, demanding, 'Give her to me.'

Automatically, Claudia did so, but if she was looking for some indication that in the last moments of her life Katriona was going to show some sign of mother love for her child, she was wrong.

'God but she stinks,' Katriona protested, her voice suddenly stronger and harsher, more familiar… 'Here, you take her,' she commanded, then thrust the baby towards Claudia.

The baby's cry that had grown stronger as Katriona held her suddenly, miraculously, magically almost, stilled as Claudia cradled her. Was it possible that that actually was a smile of recognition the baby was giving her? *Was* she imagining it or was she really reaching out with her tiny hands to clutch her? Claudia wondered.

Katriona was momentarily forgotten as the intensity of emotion she had experienced the first time she had held her came rushing back, if anything even more strongly.

'Still not pregnant, are you?' Katriona demanded.

Unable to take her eyes off the baby, Claudia shook her head.

'Something's wrong, isn't it?' she heard Katriona insisting. 'It must be, otherwise you'd be carrying another by now. You can't have any more, can you?' Claudia was too caught off guard for pretence, her shocked gaze focused on Katriona's triumphant expression, the skin of her face drawn tightly back against her skull—a death-mask.

'Poor Claudia, so desperate to become a mother. Aren't you afraid you might lose him if you can't give him a child, your wonderful Garth?'

As though sensing Claudia's distress, the baby started to cry again, a nervous, frightened sound. Then, automatically seeking the warmth and protection of Claudia's body, she squirmed closer to her. Claudia held her tight, soothing her as she shook her head at Katriona.

'Don't be frightened of her,' she pleaded. 'Katriona...take her.'

'No, I don't want her,' Katriona rasped weakly as Claudia tried to hand her daughter to her. Turning her head away, she told Claudia in a petulant, hoarse whisper, 'I never wanted her...I never meant to have her, but I left it too late. She'd have been better off with you as her mother, not me....'

Closing her eyes, she stopped speaking, her strength fading so quickly that Claudia felt she could almost see it draining out of her. Where was the doctor...that girl...?

'I want you to take her...to keep her...to be her mother. I want you to be her parents...you and your Garth. It's only right that she...' Katriona closed her eyes again, her breathing ragged and painful.

Take her! *Take* Katriona's baby...bring her up

as her own. She couldn't. It was impossible, *illegal*…it was… The baby had stopped crying. Claudia looked down at her.

'Do it,' she heard Katriona commanding her fiercely. 'You *know* you want to. She could be yours after all. She needs a proper mother…a real father. What will happen to her if you don't? A foster home, passed from pillar to post, rejected and unwanted. But *you* want her, don't you, Claudia? You want her so badly, it hurts. I can feel how much it hurts. Take her, take her now…now while there's no one here.…'

Helplessly, Claudia closed her eyes, wishing she could get away from the insidious and dangerous whisper of Katriona's voice but knowing that she had to stay; that she couldn't leave the girl, not while…

Outside, she could hear the sharp, fearsome clamour of an ambulance siren and her knotted stomach muscles started to relax. She replaced the baby in the grubby nest of blankets that was her bed and returned to Katriona's side.

'You'll be feeling much better soon,' she told her, trying to project an air of professionalism. 'The doctor—'

'The doctor…' Katriona laughed weakly. 'Oh, my God, no doctor on earth can stop what's happening to me now,' she whispered to Claudia in a voice that sounded like the rustle of dead leaves. 'I'm dying, Claudia…*dying*. Do you want me to tell you who her father is?' she demanded abruptly. 'Are you afraid of taking her because your Garth might not approve…because her *father* might be some drop-out druggie like her mother? He wasn't, Claudia. You'd be surprised if I told you who he actually was....' She started to laugh again.

The siren had stopped now and Claudia held her breath, praying that the ambulance crew would arrive in time. Not in time to save Katriona—that was impossible. Each breath she drew was forecasting her last and Claudia could almost see her heart straining beneath the thin wall of her chest. No. In time to save *her* from committing the crime of giving in to Katriona's tempting whispers. It would be easy enough. Katriona hadn't yet registered her baby's birth, and in the kind of environment that Katriona lived in, it was the easiest thing in the world for a baby to disappear. Any one of the peripatetic individuals who shared the squat might take it into their heads to take the child with them. No one would know; no one would ask any—

'Take her,' Katriona mouthed. 'Take her. Take her, Claudia.'

The door burst open as the ambulance crew arrived. Claudia got to her feet. 'I'm her probation officer,' she began. 'She's—'

'Dead or as near as damn it,' the paramedic who had knelt on the floor beside Katriona declared grimly, adding in disgust, 'Bloody young fool. Why the hell do they do it? Get her on the stretcher,' he commanded the two men with him. Then frowning, he suddenly said in a different voice, 'No, don't bother...there's no point.' He turned towards Claudia. 'She's gone, I'm afraid,' he told her.

'No, she can't be,' Claudia protested even though she knew he was telling the truth. 'She...'

But the man was ignoring her, giving a string of instructions to the men with him.

The squat, normally busy with people, had become strangely silent; even the baby wasn't making any noise.

The baby... Claudia looked into the dark corner of the room where she had carefully placed her.

Later she swore to herself that she had fully intended to warn them that the baby was there; that she had had no intention of doing anything else. But before she could open her mouth, the paramedic's radio started to crackle.

Frowning, he took the message, then turned to Claudia and told her, 'We've got another emergency to go to. Car accident down by Vauxhall Bridge. Sounds bad. There's nothing more we can do here. The authorities are following close behind us and they'll want to check out the death before the body is taken away. What did you say her name was?'

Automatically, Claudia gave it to him, watching as he quickly scribbled it down before sidestepping Katriona's motionless body and hurrying towards the door.

'Do I...shall I stay?' she began.

But he was already through the door.

Silently, Claudia glanced at Katriona's body. There was nothing left of the spirit, the presence, the life, that had once inhabited it; it was simply an empty shell.

Even so...

Claudia closed her eyes, and on some impulse she couldn't even begin to explain, she slowly recited the Lord's Prayer and then as much of the Twenty-third Psalm as she could remember, her voice growing stronger as she trembled over the familiar words.

How Katriona would have laughed if she could have heard her. But she couldn't simply walk away from her. Turn her back...*leave* her.

A movement in the corner of the room caught her eye. Her heart started to thump crazily. Slowly, she left Katriona and walked over to the baby. She had only intended to pick her up, that was all.

She had never meant to take her away, to leave the house with her, to carry her concealed within the fold of her coat to protect her from the cold, out to her waiting car.

The street was empty. Claudia unlocked her car door and got in very carefully, placing the baby still wrapped in her coat on the back seat. As she drove off, she glanced at her watch. A quarter past two. Wasn't two o'clock the time when the heart, the body, was at its weakest and death most likely?

'*Take* her,' Katriona had commanded. '*Take* her.'

In the back of the car, the baby was gurgling softly. Slowly, Claudia drove home, expecting with every yard to be overtaken by a police car, sirens screaming, and to be accused of stealing Katriona's baby. But the night remained silent, the roads bare of anything more threatening than the odd taxi.

The communal hallway to the flats was empty. Anyway, only the bottom flat was currently occupied—by an elderly couple presently away visiting their grandson in Brighton.

Calmly, Claudia carried the baby, *her* baby now, upstairs to their own flat, carefully unlocking the door and then equally carefully bolting and locking it again. The baby, *her* baby, was making happy, contented noises, her dark green eyes fixed on Claudia's face.

'You must be hungry, my darling,' Claudia murmured tenderly, 'but I don't know what I'm going to give you, or how, though you certainly need a bath. A nice, warm, lovely bath to make you all clean and pretty.' She hummed softly as she started to remove the soiled clothes in which the little girl was dressed, her mind racing as she made plans.

First thing in the morning, she would find a chemist, not a local one or a small one, no, a large distant one where an anonymous woman buying baby things would not be noticed. Or perhaps she would make several small purchases from a variety of stores—the amount of things that any normal mother would buy. She would have to take her with her, of course. She couldn't possibly leave her here alone in the flat, wouldn't *want* to leave her anywhere, be parted from her for even a heartbeat of time.

'Don't you worry, my little precious,' she crooned as she filled her washing-up bowl with warm water and placed it in the bath as a make-shift baby bath before carefully sponging her down and then lifting her into it.

She was so tiny, so perfect, so heartbreakingly fragile with her little ribs showing through her skin. Claudia's heart started to beat anxiously fast. The baby must be hungry. All she could give her tonight was some warm milk, after she sterilised the bottle she had found in the filthy blanket used to wrap her in.

Talking lovingly to her all the time she was bathing her, Claudia stopped every now and again to smile into her dark green eyes and tell her how much she loved her, her baby... hers now.

The telephone was ringing when Claudia returned from her shopping expedition. She had left the wheels of the pram she had bought for her in the car, carrying her new daughter upstairs in the canvas body of it and leaving her securely strapped into it while she went back down again for the rest of her shopping.

Breathlessly, she picked up the receiver, then tensed as she heard Janice's irritated voice.

'Claudia, are you all right? This is the third time I've rung.'

'Er...'

'If you aren't well enough to come into work, you might let us know.'

Work!

Claudia blinked. She had completely forgotten about it and of course she couldn't go back now. Not with her new baby to look after.

Quickly, she made up her mind.

'I was going to ring you, Janice,' she fibbed. 'But I just haven't had time. Garth and I have been having a talk and we've decided that since he's going into business on his own, it would be best if I gave up my job—'

'Gave up your job? But you'll have to give a month's notice. You—'

'I can't,' Claudia interrupted her calmly. 'I'm sorry, Janice, but I've got to go,' she said as she saw that Tara, as she had decided to call her baby, was beginning to wake up. She would be hungry, ready for her bottle and the nourishing baby formula that Claudia had bought for her this morning. Not as good as breast milk, of course, but far, far better than Katriona's half-hearted feeding routine.

'Claudia…wait…' Janice protested. 'There's something I've got to tell you. It's about Katriona.'

Katriona!

Claudia's fingers gripped the receiver, her body tensing. Was Janice going to say something about the baby…had she guessed?

'She's…she's dead, I'm afraid. The police reported it to us this morning. Apparently, someone alerted the authorities last night that she'd overdosed, but by the time the paramedics got there, it was too late. I thought you'd want to know. After all, she was one of your clients.'

'Er…yes…yes, thank you.' Claudia's brain was in a whirl. If the police had reported Katriona's death to the office, then that meant that no one knew of *her* presence there in the flat, obviously assuming that the ambulance had been sent for by the girl who had made the telephone call. 'Who…?' Claudia began.

But almost as though she had guessed what she was about to ask, Janice continued, 'The squat was empty by the time the police got there, not unpredictably. Claudia…about your job—'

'I don't want to discuss it, Janice,' Claudia interrupted her firmly, her mind racing as she replaced the receiver.

Janice had said nothing about Katriona's baby. Perhaps she didn't even *know*. Claudia had conscientiously mentioned her in her last report, and alerted the health visitor to there being a child at risk in the squat but by the time they got round to making enquiries, it would be too late. Tara would safely be hers. But just to make sure, this afternoon she would go and register her birth. She and Garth would definitely have to move now. There was no way she wanted to bring up a baby, *her* baby, in this flat. No, she needed fresh air, country air, a large airy nursery, a big garden. Smiling at Tara, she bent down to lift her out of the carry-cot, holding her gently against her shoulder as she went to get the bottle of formula she had prepared.

It was odd how some things came so naturally, so instinctively, Claudia acknowledged as she settled herself in a chair and gave the baby her bottle.

Tara sucked eagerly, almost greedily at first, but Claudia didn't let her rush. 'Gently,' she told her, 'We don't want you getting wind, do we, my darling baby. No, we don't.'

After she had finished feeding her, Claudia put the bottle to one side and cuddled her until she had fallen asleep in her arms, just for the pleasure of holding her.

She would have to ring the office to find out when Katriona's funeral was being held. This was a debt she had to pay the poor girl.

Tara snuggled deeper into her arms. Smiling tenderly, Claudia kissed her soft, downy head. She smelled clean and fresh, of baby powder and milk and baby skin, and she loved her as much, as intensely, as deeply, as though she had grown in her own womb, Claudia acknowledged. This was *her* baby. Hers and no one was ever going to take her away.

'You're mine now, my precious. Mine,' Claudia whispered to the sleeping baby as she picked her up and carried her over to the carry-cot. 'You're safe with me. I'm your mother now and I love you so much.' When Garth came home they would have to go and buy her a proper cot.

Garth... A tiny shadow of doubt and confusion darkened Claudia's shining happiness but she quickly dismissed it. Garth would understand. He *had* to understand, but when he rang later that night to tell her that his return was going to be delayed, Claudia was glad.

'Oh, Garth, by the way,' she added before he hung up, 'I've changed my mind about living in town. I've decided you were right. We ought to look for somewhere in the country, and I've decided to give in my notice at work, as well. You were right about that, too. Work *is* getting me down.'

Claudia sounded different, or rather Claudia had sounded more like her old self, Garth acknowledged after their call had ended. So why, instead of feeling pleased and relieved, did he feel distinctly disturbed?

Claudia was the only mourner at Katriona's funeral. Ignoring Janice's disapproval, she had arranged everything, paying for the grave and her headstone in the churchyard of the small Dorset village where she had been brought up and where her parents were buried. After it was all over, she stood at the graveside, Tara, dressed in new clothes and wrapped in a warm blanket, in her arms. Together they shared the stark silence of the morning and the bleakness of the newly turned earth.

'She's mine now, Katriona. I shall love her forever, for both of us,' Claudia told the dead girl in a silent whisper.

Pulling the hood of her jacket up over her head, she hurried back to her car, pausing to turn round to make sure that no one had seen her.

When Garth returned later that afternoon, the first thing he noticed about the flat was the smell—sweet and fresh, invoking memories of his childhood. The second thing he noticed was the fact that Claudia was smiling as she came to greet him. The third was the sudden and totally unexpected sound of a baby crying.

Dropping his overnight bag, he started to frown as he demanded, 'What's that?'

'Not what... who,' Claudia corrected him before adding simply, 'It's a baby, Garth...our baby.'

'Our baby...? What...Claudia...?' he began uneasily, but she was already turning away from him, hurrying into the bedroom and returning with a baby who had miraculously stopped crying and was now beaming happily up at her as she soothed her. 'Claudia,' he demanded, 'What—'

'She's mine, Garth,' Claudia declared fiercely. 'Mine, and no one's going to take her away from me. We'll have to move, of course, and it's just as well that both sets of parents are away. We'll have to tell them that we kept the pregnancy a secret because we were afraid I might lose her and that she arrived prematurely. She's so tiny that she could easily be a premature baby. Of course, when we register with a new doctor, I'll have to pretend that my medical records are missing. I'll make up a doctor's name and—'

'Claudia...Claudia...what's going on?' Garth interrupted her, telling her starkly, 'This baby *isn't* ours. She—'

'She is now. Her mother gave her to me, told me to take her. I had to take her, Garth. If I hadn't, heaven knows what would have happened to her. This way, she'll get all the love she needs. No one could ever love her more than me. Don't you think she's beautiful? She's even got my colouring, although her eyes are more like yours than mine. Katriona had dark hair, too, of course.'

Katriona... Garth's heart gave a shocked lurch. 'This baby is Katriona's...?'

'Was. Katriona's dead,' Claudia told him, her voice automatically dropping as she pulled the blanket round Tara's ears as though wanting to protect her from what she was about to say. 'She overdosed. She sent for me, told me she wanted me to take the baby. She *wanted* me to have her, Garth, she told me. She was so desperate for me to have her that she even tried to tell me who the father was. She claimed that he was someone special.'

'She told you the name of the baby's father?' Garth's body went still, his throat suddenly so dry that his voice sounded cracked and harsh.

'No, she tried to, but it was too late, and besides, it doesn't matter. I don't care *who* he was. *You're* her father now. I'm her mother and you're her father. I've called her Tara. It suits her, don't you think? And do you know, she's so clever, I think she knows her name already. She watches everything I do. She's going to be clever. Oh, yes, you are, my darling, you're going to be a very clever girl indeed,' Claudia cooed, ignoring Garth's attempts to question her as she added, 'It's time for her feed, Garth. She's so hungry, poor little thing, but she can't have too much food all at once as it might make her poorly.'

Helplessly, Garth watched as Claudia bustled about the tiny kitchen, heating milk and making up formula, the baby relaxed and happy against her shoulder, the pair of them looking for all the world as though they had been together since the moment of her birth. Looking for all the world as though they *were* mother and daughter. But this child was not theirs...not—Garth swallowed hard—not theirs perhaps, but she could well be his. *His*.

'Claudia, this isn't right,' he told her harshly. 'This baby *isn't* yours, ours. We *cannot* keep her. You *must* know that.' He tried to be gentle, make her understand, but Claudia rounded on him like a tigress.

'She *is* mine, Garth, and no one is going to make me give her up,' she retorted fiercely.

'Claudia, please, I *know* you've been through a bad time and I can understand that this baby—'

'Tara, her name's Tara,' Claudia interrupted him. 'Say it, Garth,' she urged him. '*Say* it. She likes hearing it.'

'This...Tara isn't ours, Claudia, and she must be handed over to the authorities. They're probably already searching for her, her family.'

'She *has* no family,' Claudia countered. 'Only us. The authorities will in all probability assume that one of Katriona's druggy friends has taken her. She *needs* us, Garth. She needs someone to look after her and love her. Do you know what would happen to her if we handed her over to the authorities? She'd be found foster parents and then she'd be passed on to someone else—'

'She'd be adopted by parents who loved and wanted her, Claudia,' Garth corrected her sternly.

'She doesn't *need* any other parents. She's got us. Don't try to make me give her up, Garth,' she warned him. 'Because I won't. If *you* don't want us, then we'll go away and make a life somewhere for ourselves.' Her mouth firmed aggressively. 'I'm not giving her up. She's mine.'

There was no reasoning with her, Garth recognised. She was like a tigress protecting her cub and anyone who tried to take the baby away from her would be asking for trouble.

'We can't do this,' he protested again, but he could see from her face that Claudia wasn't prepared to listen.

'We can,' she insisted. 'I've already told you, Garth, we must...'

At that moment, the baby turned her head and looked at him, her dark green eyes serious and thoughtful as though she knew what he was thinking, as though she was judging him, reminding him that *he* could be *her* father; that it was his own flesh and blood he might be rejecting; that, in fact, he owed it to her to go along with Claudia's determination to keep her...*his* child...*his* daughter, flesh of *his* flesh. But what if she wasn't? What if...? Could he take that risk? Could he live with himself if he turned his back on her? Might he not spend the rest of his life wondering, weighed down by a burden of guilt and regret?

But if they kept her, wasn't she going to be a constant reminder of an incident he would much rather be able to forget, an incident he had already, if he was honest, almost forgotten, telling himself that Katriona had lied to him when she claimed that he had fathered her child?

'We can't do this, Claudia,' he repeated, but he already knew that the battle was lost and that, rightly or wrongly, Tara was now theirs.

And what amazed him more than anything else was not Claudia's very evident and very fierce maternal love for the child, but the logic and determination with which she was planning to carry through her deception of being Tara's birth mother. It was as though all the dark despair of the past few months had been wiped away, restoring Claudia to her old self. No, not her *old* self. The Claudia now confronting him was a mature, powerful Claudia. Watching her was like seeing someone who had stepped out of the shadows and into the brilliance of sunshine.

'Why don't you hold her for a moment?' Claudia suggested softly, as seductive and determined as Eve. The mantle of motherhood, fiercely protective and all-powerful, now sat as easily on her shoulders, had settled as easily around her, as a cloud of lightest thistledown, no weight at all, no burden at all to a woman like Claudia for whom motherhood was the whole reason for her being.

Reluctantly, he took her. She lay in his arms,

frighteningly fragile and vulnerable, a scrap of human flesh who surely had nothing to do with him, had no claim upon him, and then she opened her eyes and looked unblinkingly into his, and Garth was lost.

He could actually feel the tug on his heart-strings as though she had physically gripped and yanked them. All his arguments, all his logic, all his objections to what Claudia was suggesting, vanished like mist in the heat of the sun. Whether she was his child or not no longer even mattered. To turn her away, to ignore that look of trust and contentment mingled with confident curiosity in those unbelievably green eyes, was something he simply could not do.

'You see?' he heard Claudia whispering triumphantly at his side as she put out a hand and gently touched the baby's face, watching as she turned her face from him to her and started to smile. 'She *wants* to be with us. She *needs* us. You should have seen her when I brought her home, Garth,' she burst out passionately. 'She was so thin, so…'

Claudia took a shaky breath. It still filled her eyes with angry tears to think of the way her precious girl had been neglected, her little bottom red and raw with weeping sores from lying too long in urine-soaked rags, her cries for attention sharp and thin with fear and hunger. But all that was past now. She was safe now. Safe, wanted, loved. Oh, so very much loved.

'Give her back to me,' she commanded Garth. Silently, he did so, finding it oddly disconcerting to have his arms feel so empty without the slight weight of the baby.

'She's ours now,' Claudia told him passionately. 'No one will ever know. I've registered her birth and named us as her parents and I've changed doctors. I told the new doctor that she was born while you were stationed abroad. It's a busy surgery. He won't check and soon we'll be moving away anyway because I want Tara to grow up in the country.'

There was nothing Garth could do and he knew it. He could only marvel at the speed and tactical expertise with which Claudia had mounted her campaign—and won her victory.

Tara was theirs, but was she *his*?

14

Raising her head from its comfortable position on Ryland's knee, Tara reached for the TV remote control and switched off the set. They had just been watching a hired video to accompany the take-away Chinese meal Ryland had ordered for them while they spent an evening in celebrating the anniversary of their first date.

'Mmm…just think,' Tara commented, stretching luxuriously before resuming her supine position across his body. 'This time next month we'll be in Boston.'

'Mmm…I don't know about that,' Ryland teased her, sliding his hand to her hair and letting it slip through his fingers.

He loved her hair, so thick and silky and shiny. It felt so strong and healthy, so full of life, just like Tara herself. That was one of the first things that had attracted him to her, that glowing look of happiness and well-being that practically vibrated from her body. He didn't think he had ever met a happier or better adjusted person than his Tara; the warmth of her personality, her relaxed self-confidence, her air of being totally at ease with herself and with her world had struck him immediately.

'*You* haven't got your visa yet and I don't know that they'd waive restrictions to let someone like you in,' he said as she sat up swiftly, the indignant look in her eyes fading as she realised he was deliberately teasing her.

'Oh, you,' she said, pouting at him, her mouth looking so deliciously full and sexy that Ryland just had to lean over and kiss her. 'Mmm…you still taste of chow mein.' Tara laughed softly as she kissed him back. 'Do you remember the first time I stayed over here with you?' she asked him.

'What do you think? Of *course* I do.'

'You didn't have any condoms and we had to go out and buy some—'

'I was expecting you to bring them,' Ryland fibbed, straight-faced.

His parents would adore her, he knew that already. His mother would take her to heart like another daughter and his father would be entranced by her. Not once in his life could Ryland ever remember a situation where he had been seriously at odds with his parents nor them with him. *They* would know just as he had known how right Tara was for him.

Where his aunt was concerned, though, the situation was perhaps slightly more complicated. Ryland didn't need to be told how important it was to her that he married and produced children.

After her husband's death, she had poured into the business all the loving and cherishing, all the hopes for the future, she would more normally have given to Margot and ultimately the grandchildren Margot would give her. Grandchildren who would be her natural successors in the business and the natural inheritors of the huge fortune she herself had inherited from her own extremely wealthy family and brought into the marriage, just as Ryland would be his father's.

But there would be no grandchildren for her. That had been made clear by Margot's defiant and bitter announcement that she would never be able to have children. Having been barred from having Lloyd's by the law of the land, she had now barred herself from having any other man's by the law of life.

'I've had a sterilisation,' she had told her mother flatly, adding with the intensity that was so much a part of her personality, 'I *can't* have the child of a man whom I don't love, and the *only* man I shall ever love is Lloyd.'

'How do you think your family, your aunt, will react to me?' Tara tuned into his thoughts.

Ryland forced himself to smile reassuringly at her. 'My aunt will be fine. Everything will be fine,' he told her determinedly, reaching for her.

He was keeping something from her, withholding something vital, Tara knew instinctively. She was getting the same feeling she could remember getting as a young girl when she had known something was wrong between her parents. In the beginning, prior to their divorce, they had tried to pretend that everything was all right in order to protect her, but she had *known* that it wasn't.

Ultimately, of course, they had told her the truth—they simply weren't the kind of parents who would ever deliberately lie to her—but their initial refusal to allow her to know what was happening had left her with a subconscious fear of having anyone close to her not be completely honest with her.

'There's something you're not telling me,' she challenged him immediately and quietly.

Ryland just managed to prevent himself from taking a sudden indrawn breath of self-betrayal.

'My family will love you,' he insisted, knowing it to be the truth, but even though she could hear the conviction and the veracity in his voice, Tara still felt that there was something he wasn't sharing with her.

What? A boyhood romance with a local girl, a girl whose background, whose familiarity, might make her seem more appropriate marriage material in his family's eyes? She knew him too well to suspect him of having had any serious relationship he had not told her about.

But she wanted to silence that sharp, anxiety-inducing inner voice that was gnawing away destructively at her happiness, but Ryland patently had other ideas.

'Ryland,' she protested as he leaned forward and started to nuzzle her throat, slipping his hand inside her blouse as he did so.

Ryland didn't want Tara to probe any further into his family background. He still had to figure out a way to explain to her that instead of becoming the wife of a reasonably well-paid young executive in a family business of which one day he would ultimately take charge, he was, in fact, being groomed for the role of heading a hugely profitable enterprise—one that, backed by astute past investment, meant that his and his aunt's personal fortune consisted of assets worth many millions of dollars. Add to that the money he would one day—hopefully a long, long way in the future—inherit from his aunt.

His stable, loving family background and his own keen brain might have taught him the danger of allowing people into his life simply because they were impressed by or envious of the wealth that would one day be his, but they had done nothing to prepare him for falling in love with a woman who knew nothing about the strictures that modern society could impose on the wealthy and who, he suspected, would enjoy them even less.

Boston wasn't Hollywood, but it didn't have to be. All over the world, even in Britain, wealthy men were finding that in order to protect their families, they had to provide them with the kind of security that would provoke an outcry from the human rights people.

Being shut away behind high fences and followed by their personal bodyguards certainly didn't make for the kind of life he wanted for his kids, or necessarily the kind of life they would have to have, but he doubted that they would be able to have the same kind of freedom Tara had enjoyed as a child, and instinctively he knew that Tara *would* want her children's childhoods to follow the same pattern as her own.

'But of course I want my children to have both their parents living with them,' she had told Ryland seriously when they had been talking on the subject.

When she had just finished telling him about her own childhood forays into the countryside with a gang of other kids to catch tiddlers and pick fruit, how could he tell her that such simple pleasures might never be able to be enjoyed by their own children? As the sons and daughters of a very, very wealthy man, for their own protection they would have to play behind the secure walls of their own home.

Perhaps he *should* have been more open and honest with her right from the start, Ryland acknowledged now, but in the early days of their relationship, he hadn't told her because, quite simply, he hadn't wanted to risk scaring her off. Some women might run a mile *towards* a man with money, other women run a mile away, and Tara quite definitely belonged to the latter category.

Well, with any luck, it would be a good ten years or so before his aunt finally retired. She was sixty now, but as she had said on the occasion of her sixtieth birthday the previous year, she certainly had no intention of stepping down from control of the business as yet.

Hopefully, by the time she did, Tara would have had time to accustom herself to the reality

of what his family's financial background entailed, Ryland decided, reminding her lovingly,
'We *were* meant to be celebrating our anniversary,' before he started to deliberately tease the
delicate spot just beneath her ear with his lips.

Impossible to persist with their conversation
when such delicious little thrills of pleasure were
running so distractingly down her body, and her
breast was already swelling appreciatively beneath the determined caress of his fingers.

'Mmm...' Closing her eyes, Tara told him
softly. 'Ry, you're so lucky.'

'Why, because *you* love me?' he teased her.

But Tara shook her head and told him seriously, 'No, because your parents are still together. I love both Mum and Dad to death, but
sometimes...' She paused and shook her head. 'It
would be the most wonderful thing in the world
for me if they got back together. It would make
everything perfect.'

'I *do* understand how you feel,' Ryland told her
gently, 'but they're two adults, Tara.'

'I hear what you're saying,' she said thoughtfully. 'It's just...I did try to get them back together once, but it didn't work.'

She had been fourteen at the time, missing
having her father at home, and suddenly with
her own burgeoning womanhood, very intensely
conscious of the attention her mother was attract-
ing from other men, aware of it and jealous of it
on her father's behalf.

There had been one man in particular, a client
of her mother's, a divorced man in his late

thirties. He had persuaded her mother to have dinner with him one night.

'I *have* to go, darling,' Claudia had told Tara apologetically. 'It's...it's business and Ashley is so busy, the only time we can discuss things is in the evening.'

'Then why can't you discuss it here in your study?' Tara had demanded sharply. 'Why do you have to go *out* and have dinner with him? I don't *want* you to go,' she had declared passionately, her eyes filling with quick tears.

'Oh, darling, please don't cry,' Claudia had begged her in consternation. 'What's wrong? Has something happened at school, someone upset you?'

'No, it's nothing like that,' Tara had told her truthfully before adding sternly, 'The other girls at school talk about what happens when...when women go out for dinner with men at night and I've seen it on television, as well. He just wants to get you into bed. Does Daddy know what you're planning to do?' Tara had challenged her.

Immediately, Claudia's embarrassment had turned to anger.

'What I do and whom I see has nothing whatsoever to do with your father. We're divorced, Tara, and we *both* have our own lives now. Your father has no right to comment on what I may or may not choose to do, just as *I* have no veto over the way he lives *his* life.'

'Daddy still has our photograph in his bedroom,' Tara had told her provokingly, 'and *he* doesn't take other ladies out for dinner.'

Her mother had compressed her lips and looked away from her.

The evening her mother was supposed to be going out for dinner, Tara had developed a sick stomach and her mother's date had to be cancelled.

A couple of weeks later while staying with her father, Tara had told him how afraid she was of her mother becoming involved with anyone else.

'I want the three of us to be together again,' she told her father passionately. 'I *hate* things the way they are.'

'Darling, you know that that isn't possible,' her father had remonstrated gently. 'Your mother has a right to live her own life, to see other people, go out on dates if she wants to. You know,' he had added quietly, 'I understand how you feel, we both do, but these things happen, and the fact that your mother and I don't live together any more doesn't in any way affect our love for you. We *both* love you very, very much, Tara, and I can promise you that *nothing* and *no one* will ever change that love.'

'I don't want Mum to meet someone else and get married to him. I don't want *either* of you to,' Tara had confessed, tears rolling down her face. '*You* are *my* father and mother and we should all be together. I *hate* things the way they are.'

'Oh, Tara…' her father had sighed, taking her in his arms to hold and console her.

'You could speak to Mum, say something to tell her…that… You could come back,' she had insisted, but her father had shaken his head.

'No, my darling, I'm afraid that I can't.'

Over the following months, Tara had tried relentlessly to get her parents back together again, but all to no avail. Now, as an adult, she could see with hindsight that they must have discussed what she was trying to do because they had remained steadfast, so immovable, so united in their calm determination to ensure that while she knew *she* was secure in their love, their marriage was irretrievably over.

Now, of course, she fully understood and accepted that they both had a right to live their own lives, but there was still a small idiotically idealistic and childish part of her that passionately longed to have them reunited.

As she had already told Ryland, once *they* were married, it would be forever. She would *never*, ever divorce him or allow him to divorce her, not once they had a family.

'I suppose you think I'm hideously old-fashioned,' she had challenged him on the subject.

'No. I agree with everything you're saying,' he had returned quietly. 'Our marriage *will* last, Tara, and it will be for life. How could it be otherwise when my love for you will last for eternity?'

He had spoken with such quiet conviction that all the doubts she had been harbouring about the thought of making such a huge emotional commitment had immediately been banished.

'We won't ever have any secrets from one another, will we, Ry?' she asked him now as she snuggled deeper into his arms. 'And we'll always tell each other the truth…everything. I don't want there ever to be anything about you that *I* don't know.'

'You mean like the fact that I turn into a were-wolf at full moon?' Ryland teased her, but although he was laughing, deep down inside he was guiltily aware of the fact that there were facts about himself that he *had* withheld from her. Facts that she had every right to know.

He *would* tell her before they left for Boston, he promised himself as he stroked the bare flesh of her hip. There was plenty of time yet for him to prepare her for the truth, and after all, marrying a millionaire *had* to have *some* advantages—one of which surely being that she could fly her mother out to visit them whenever she wished.

The year Estelle turned eleven, her mother had suddenly announced that she was to spend her summer holiday with her father.

'I don't want to,' Estelle had protested. 'The farm's miles from anywhere. There's nothing to do. I hate it. Why can't I stay here in London?'

'Ethian and I will be going away,' Lorraine told her coolly. 'You *can't* stay here.'

'Going away? Where?' Estelle challenged her sharply. 'You were away at Easter.'

'*That* was business,' her mother told her crisply.

'You went skiing,' Estelle reminded her.

'It was a business trip. I simply accompanied your stepfather, which is exactly what I shall be doing this time. He's been invited to join a group of other businessmen on someone's yacht.'

'Some business trip,' Estelle sneered.

'Estelle,' her mother warned, her eyes starting to harden, 'if you're going to be difficult about this…'

'You'll do what?' Estelle demanded. 'Leave me here on my own? That's illegal.'

'Estelle, I'm really getting quite out of patience with you,' Lorraine berated her. 'You're going to stay with your father and that's that.'

'You shouldn't have had me if you didn't want children,' Estelle threw angrily at her.

'No, you're quite right. I shouldn't have,' her mother retaliated evenly, 'and believe me, Estelle, increasingly I rather wish that I hadn't.'

Later that night, listening outside their bedroom door, Estelle had heard her mother complaining to her stepfather.

'Estelle's being dreadfully difficult about going to her father's. I think she's jealous of me, Ethian. She obviously resents the idea of my having any fun, and after all that I've sacrificed for her. John never wanted her.'

'Perhaps you should tell her that, make her realise how lucky she is,' Estelle had heard Ethian responding.

'I'm beginning to think you're right and that I should have sent her away to school.'

Estelle's visit to her father hadn't been a success. She had hated the farm and her stepbrother

Ian. Sophie's presence in her father's life she treated with cool disdain, and as for Rebecca— she loathed and detested her.

'You don't want me here,' she had accused her father after he had taken her to task for deliberately trying to upset Rebecca and Ian. 'You never wanted me....'

She hadn't known which of them she had resented more, her mother or her father. Neither of them loved her, and her father had compounded his lack of love for her by so obviously and generously giving his second family the love he had never felt for her.

It had caused her to feel a mixture of anger, bitterness and sharp resentment deep down inside to see the way he played with Rebecca, to see the love in his face, hear it in his voice when he was with her.

Ian, her stepbrother, she felt nothing but contempt for. The way he tried to placate her as though he actually felt sorry for her because he lived with their father made her despise him even more. Well, Ian could keep their father. He was the *last* person she wanted in her life, the very last.

When she grew up, she was going to find herself a rich man, richer than Ethian and much, much richer than her father and he would always, always put her first.

Estelle despised Ian and Sophie for trying to make friends with her. Why should either of them like her? She certainly didn't like them. She didn't like anyone, not really. People only pretended to like you because they wanted something from you. Her mother pretended to like her, to love her when she wanted to get her to do something like coming here so that she could go away and enjoy herself. Having children meant that you couldn't enjoy yourself.

Estelle was openly scornful of her father's very evident love for his second family and openly hostile towards his attempts to include her in their family activities.

She couldn't wait for the visit to end. At least in London she had the freedom to do what she wanted. Her mother was far too busy with her own life to interest herself over-much in Estelle's. Just so long as she kept out of her way, Estelle was pretty free to do as she pleased.

Determinedly ignoring all Sophie's warm overtures and her father's attempts to reach out to her, Estelle grimly sat out her visit in contemptuous loathing.

It pleased her to know that she was upsetting her stepmother by arguing with her father, the whole household, making them unhappy. Why shouldn't she? She hated them all, but most especially she hated her father. Oh, yes, she hated him.

But she was determined that, unlike Blade, she was not going to allow *her* father to send her away to boarding school.

Blade!

He alternately fascinated and antagonised her. Although her mother and Ethian had been married for almost four years, in all that time Blade had probably spent less than four months at home with them. Her mother and stepfather had refused to have him living with them full time.

'Having Estelle at home is bad enough,' Estelle had heard her mother complaining to Ethian. 'I'm not having Blade here, as well.' And so Blade had continued to do as he had done before his father's second marriage. He spent even some of his holidays at school.

'The only reason he married your mother is because he wants someone to have regular sex with,' Blade had told Estelle the previous Christmas—Christmas was the one time when her mother made an exception and had him at home with them. 'You *do* know what sex is, don't you?' he had demanded when Estelle made no response.

Of course she did. She had heard the sounds emanating from the room her mother shared with Ethian. She had seen people having sex on television, giggled about it with her school friends, and besides, her mother had had other men friends before meeting Ethian.

Blade hated *his* father as she did hers.

Their mutual distrust and hatred of the parents who controlled their world formed a strong bond between them and added to that there was something about Blade, something about the dark, brooding, deliciously frightening maleness of him that attracted Estelle.

He was so different from everyone else she knew—the girls at her all-girls' school; her mother, Ethian, her father and his family. Blade was…Blade was…dangerous…dangerous and exciting, but even more importantly, underneath they were the same kind of people. Estelle didn't know how she knew that fact; she just knew that she *did*.

15

━━▶ ◀━━

The noisy sound of a toddler indulging in a terrible two's tantrum with his mother outside her car window snapped Claudia out of her reverie, bringing her sharply from the past to the present. Her body felt stiff and cold and she was shocked to see that it was late in the afternoon.

How many hours had she spent sitting in the car reliving the past? Far too many.

And what had possessed her to do such a thing in the first place, to abandon her responsibilities and come here? Why ask herself a question to which she already knew the answer?

Guilt and pain had motivated her. Guilt and pain and fear. Not guilt because she had taken Tara—that was something she could never feel guilty about doing, she told herself fiercely. Holding Tara close to her own body as she carried her away from the squat, she had promised her that from her, Claudia, she would have every bit as much love as she would have received from her own mother. She had promised her, too, that she would love her just as dearly, just as closely, just as much as she would a child conceived within her own body. That to her, Tara was and always would be *hers*. No, it wasn't guilt for taking Tara that she felt but guilt because she had let Tara grow up in ignorance of the truth, not just to protect her daughter but to protect herself, as well.

'One day, you will have to tell her the truth— for her own sake,' Garth had warned her gently the first day Tara started school.

She had promised him that she would—when the time was right. Then before she could… before the time had been right, she had found out the truth about Tara's conception, had found out that Garth, her own husband, was Tara's father, and after that there was no way, no way at all, she could bring herself to tell Tara whose child she really was—no way she could even begin to admit to *herself* whose child she was.

At every point in Tara's life when the truth might have been discovered, Claudia had held her breath in dread, but to her relief no one had ever questioned anything and the lies she had told in order to register Tara's birth had never been exposed.

But all it would take for her deception to be revealed would be for someone to check at the hospital or at the surgery where Claudia had claimed a doctor had attended after Tara's unexpected early home birth.

When they initially moved to Ivy House, she had got away with claiming that their medical records had been lost. No one had ever questioned the fact that she had registered Tara's birth some weeks after it had actually taken place and Tara had a completed birth certificate naming Claudia and Garth Wallace as her parents.

Well, one part of that at least was true even if Claudia herself hadn't known it when she registered Garth and herself as Tara's father and mother.

But everyone knew how meticulous American embassies were about checking people out, and according to Tara, Ryland's aunt was even more particular.

Claudia could feel her heart starting to beat far too fast. Garth was right. She *couldn't* allow Tara to find out the truth from someone else, but how on earth was she going to tell her? And what would happen when she did? Would Tara understand or would she turn away from her, reject her, end up hating her? Tara loved her, she knew, but Claudia also knew how terrifyingly quickly love could turn to bitter hatred when the loved one was discovered to have lied and cheated, when one's trust in them was destroyed, when one's belief in them was shattered.

She would certainly never forget how she had felt the day she discovered that Garth *was* actually Tara's father.

It had been an ordinary enough day to begin with, apart from the fact that Claudia and Garth had had an appointment with the ear, nose and throat specialist at their local hospital to discuss the forthcoming removal of Tara's tonsils.

She had suffered very badly from throat infections ever since first starting school and their doctor had finally persuaded Claudia, much against her initial feelings, to seek the advice of a specialist.

Since Tara's birth, Claudia had been very wary of any contact with members of the medical profession, but only Garth knew that this sprang not so much from her memories of the baby she had lost, but her fear of anyone's questioning the supposed facts surrounding Tara's birth, and it was for this reason that Garth was taking time off work to accompany her to the hospital to see the specialist who had examined Tara the previous week and who now wished to discuss with them his belief that she would benefit from an operation to remove her tonsils.

The years since Tara's arrival and their move to Ivy House had passed so quickly that sometimes Claudia simply didn't know where they had gone. Garth's business had flourished and become extremely successful, involving his being away from home and working very long hours. But Claudia had been so involved and absorbed in motherhood and Tara's needs that there simply wasn't time for her to miss him.

Occasionally, she was guiltily aware that Garth was being pushed to the periphery of her life—a life that revolved almost totally around Tara and their home, but although Garth was inclined at times to make slightly acerbic comments about the fact that even on the rare occasion when they did have time to themselves, inevitably the sole topic of her conversation was Tara, deep down Claudia knew that he adored her just as much as she did herself.

And if their sex life had dwindled to the odd hurried, early-Sunday-morning coming together interspersed by the even less frequent, slightly more leisurely intimacy, well, she had concluded from what she heard from other women that she was not alone in finding it difficult to combine the roles of lover and mother, and fortunately Garth seemed to accept the situation.

It was a crisp autumn morning, and as they set off for the hospital, Claudia tried to relax and enjoy the novelty of being driven instead of being the driver.

'Remember the first time I took you out for a drive?' Garth reminisced as though he had picked up on her thoughts.

'Mmm...' Claudia returned. 'The car heater wouldn't work and—'

'I pulled off the road to check it,' Garth went on, adding wickedly, 'I never got the heater working, but I certainly enjoyed the way we eventually ended up keeping warm.'

'Garth,' Claudia reproved him, 'mind that cyclist.'

Garth gave her a wry look. Increasingly recently, Claudia had been stonewalling him whenever he brought up the subject of sex. Because she no longer wanted *sex* or because she no longer wanted *him*?

He understood how involved she was with Tara, how absorbed, how besotted, a less kind man might have said. And he knew, too, it was illogical of him to feel excluded and jealous, even resentful sometimes, of the way that Tara's needs always seemed to take precedence over his own, or rather the way that Claudia accorded Tara's more importance than she did his own. It was not so much that he was jealous of the time and attention Claudia gave to Tara but rather more that it hurt him to feel that Claudia preferred Tara's company to his; that he himself was somehow no longer of any real importance to her.

He understood, too, of course he did, that it just wasn't possible for them to share the same kind of uninhibited sex life they had enjoyed as a newly married couple living on their own, now that they had a soon-to-be-thirteen-year-old daughter running around everywhere—a very intelligent, aware, inquisitive daughter at that.

Worriedly, Claudia frowned, staring blindly out the window. She knew logically that there was nothing to fear from seeing the specialist; that everyone accepted that Tara was hers…their daughter. But she still felt apprehensive, her face clouding as Garth turned into the hospital car park.

When he saw her expression, Garth silently berated himself. Poor Clo. He ought to have been more sympathetic even if…even if what? Even if *he* felt that Tara ought to be told the truth or at least as much of it as she was capable of understanding.

Initially, Claudia had agreed with him, but recently he had noticed that she was becoming increasingly defensive whenever he brought it up.

'How can I tell her?' she had demanded the last time he tried to broach the subject. 'She's too young to understand. And anyway, what would I say…that I'm not your mother?'

'She'll have to know one day, Clo,' Garth had reminded her gently.

'She might not,' Claudia had denied stubbornly. 'Everyone believes that she's mine… ours,' she had hastily corrected herself. 'If anyone had been going to find out, they would have done so by now.'

Garth had sighed, not wanting to provoke an argument with her that he knew would upset her. Perhaps she was right. Perhaps Tara might never need to know. But what if she did…what if the truth were to come out by accident?

'One day I'll tell her,' Claudia had promised gruffly, 'when…when the time is right.'

'The appointment with the specialist shouldn't take too long. Do you fancy having lunch somewhere afterwards? There's that new Italian place. You always enjoy Italian food.'

'Oh, Garth, I can't,' Claudia had protested fretfully. 'I've got to get some material for the fancy-dress costume Tara wants to wear for her friend's birthday party, and anyway, it's my afternoon at the centre.'

Several times a month, Claudia gave her time and her expertise free to a local community centre, offering counselling services to those who needed them.

Garth knew that she enjoyed her work, but she had always stressed that she could only do it so long as it fitted in with Tara's routine.

'I *want* to be there for her, Garth,' she had protested when he once made the comment that she seemed to have precious little time for herself—and for him, he could have added but hadn't. 'It's not a sacrifice…it's what I *want* to do.'

The specialist had smiled warmly at them both when they were shown in to see him.

'It's a simple enough operation,' he assured them as he checked through Tara's file, 'and I would certainly strongly advise that you go ahead. The infections she's been having can be quite debilitating although unlikely to cause any permanent damage—at least to her health. We do find that children who are subject to these problems can fall behind with their school work and it's certainly a procedure that's better carried out now than when she's an adult. In fact, right now she's at the optimum age for it.

'The only problems we *could* have would be with her extremely rare blood grouping, but I can see from checking your records—' here he looked at Garth '—that you and she both have the same blood group.' With what he obviously intended to be humour, he added jovially, 'I know they say it's a wise child who knows its own father, but in Tara's case there could be no possible doubt.'

Claudia had glanced towards Garth, expecting to see him looking as astonished as she was herself, but instead and to her shock, she realised that he was looking instead highly uncomfortable and almost…almost guilty. She had known then immediately, instinctively, even if illogically, as she grappled with the shock not just of what she had seen in his face but of her own swift acceptance of it, that the specialist was right and that *Garth* was Tara's father. Even worse was the realisation that *he* must have always known it and kept that knowledge from her, and most painfully of all, that Tara, *her* child, was, in effect, not her child at all but Garth's.

She had managed to control herself enough to wait until they were back in the car before she hurled her accusations at him, the words almost choking her.

'Admit it, Garth,' she demanded, 'because I won't let it rest until I know the truth. *You* are Tara's father, aren't you?'

'There's a strong possibility that I could be,' Garth responded after a few seconds' silence, his mouth compressing as instead of looking at her, he stared straight ahead through the windscreen.

'A strong *possibility*? You *share* the same rare blood group. *You* must have—'

'I knew that there was a chance that Tara could be mine, yes,' he interrupted her grimly. 'But that was all. Believe me, Claudia, until today—'

'Until today you hoped that she *wasn't*?'

Garth said nothing. What could he say? That he had determinedly and firmly put what Katriona had said to him to one side, telling himself that so far as he was concerned, his love for Tara was not dependent on whether or not he had physically fathered her. If he had, then it was his responsibility and perhaps even his right to be her father, and if he hadn't, well, she was still his daughter and he still loved her.

Although he suspected Claudia would find it hard to understand, part of him simply hadn't wanted to find out. Not for a single heartbeat of time would he want to deny Tara's existence, but there was a part of him that desperately wanted to ignore that he might have had any part in it. It had seemed better, wiser, *safer*, to simply put to one side everything that Katriona had said to him, to remind himself whenever he did think about it that Katriona herself had had her own reasons, had not seemed very sure about Tara's paternity and he certainly had no real memories of ever having been intimate enough with the girl to have fathered her except that...except those odd, haunting memories of a woman who didn't feel or smell quite right, a woman who had *not* perhaps been Claudia.

'All these years you've known that Tara is *your* child. All these years you've deceived me, *lied* to me....'

Claudia started to cry with a mixture of shock and anger, but as Garth made to turn towards her and take her in his arms, she pushed him off and shrank back in her seat, spitting at him like a small, angry cat.

'Don't *touch* me,' she warned him. 'Don't you *ever* touch me again! You slept with Katriona. You had *sex* with her. Garth...why...why...?' Tears streamed down her face. 'How could you? How could you betray me like that...betray *us* like that? How often did you see her? How did you meet her? When...?'

'Claudia. It wasn't *like* you think,' Garth protested, adding, 'Look, let's go home where we can talk about this properly. I promise you that until today I had no proof that Tara *was* my child.'

'But you knew that she *could* be,' Claudia insisted.

Gripping the steering wheel, Garth admitted curtly, 'Yes. I knew there was a...*possibility* that she could be. Look, we can't talk here,' he told her. 'We need to wait until—'

'Until what?' Claudia challenged him furiously. 'Until *you've* had time to come up with more deceit? More lies...?'

'I have *never* lied to you, Claudia,' Garth retorted sharply.

'Yes, you have—by omission. You've already admitted that you knew that you *could* be Tara's father, but you never told me...never said anything. You let me walk in there today knowing—'

'Claudia, I did *not*. I had *no* idea that he... Look, please, Clo...I know what you must be thinking, but it isn't like...isn't like you think,' he finished lamely.

'Isn't it? How much of a fool do you think I am, Garth? I *know* that Katriona was Tara's birth mother. You've just admitted that *you're* her father. So far as I know, there is only one logical way that that can have happened, isn't there? *Isn't* there?' she stressed bitingly.

'Clo, please, if you'd just calm down for a moment,' Garth begged her urgently, 'I could—'

'You could what?' As he stopped the car at

some traffic-lights, Claudia saw her moment and seized it. She opened the door and sprang out, telling him, 'The only words I want to hear from you, Garth, are the ones we both know you aren't in a position to say.' And without giving him the chance to say anything more, she angrily slammed the car door shut, turned on her heel and walked sharply away.

Her pride kept her going as far as the first corner. Once round it, she could feel further hot tears starting to burn her eyes. Tears of shock, chagrin, rage and, most of all, anguished, agonizing pain.

All these years and she had never known, never guessed.

'Take her,' Katriona had urged Claudia as she lay dying, and now Claudia knew why. God, how Katriona must have laughed at her. How they both must have laughed at her, lying in bed together as they—

'Are you all right, love?'

The kind, motherly voice of the woman who stopped and put her hand on her arm brought Claudia to her senses. Swallowing hard, she nodded her head and lied, 'Yes…just something in my eye, that's all.'

Something in her eye! That gritty, saw-tooth, sharply destructive dart of betrayal and jealousy had lodged deep within her heart and was already beginning to poison her emotions.

It wasn't just Garth's *sexual* betrayal that hurt. Agonizing though that was, it was his other betrayal that was hurting her the most—the knowledge that he had known and kept secret from her all these years the fact that Tara was his daughter…his child…that she was, in truth, far more *his* than she was hers…that between *them* was a blood bond there never would be between her and her beloved daughter…that Garth legally had far more claim on her than she could ever have herself. She hated him for that and hated herself even more for having such a feeling.

Automatically, she started to make her way home, hoping that she wouldn't bump into anyone who knew her, her actions instinctive, her one goal to get home…to seek refuge where she knew she would be safe. Until she got there, until she was properly alone, she couldn't, dared not, examine her feelings too closely, and yet certain thoughts kept surfacing to torment her.

How often had Garth seen Katriona? Where had he seen her? Not that wretched squat, surely. The thought of Garth with Katriona in that filthy place…the thought of Garth with Katriona *anywhere* made her want to retch, to scream, to tear at her skin, her hair, to cry out aloud her anguish and sense of betrayal. But she knew that she could not do so, *must* not do so; for Tara's sake, she must try to behave as normally as possible.

Why had Garth gone to Katriona? What had been lacking in *their* own relationship, their marriage, for him to do so?

'Soldiers, army men. They're the worst,' Katriona had purred triumphantly. Had she known him even *then*? Had he, Garth, even *then*…? Tears burned her eyes like acid. Hastily, she blinked them away but it was impossible for her to stop torturing herself, to stop imagining the two of them together.

She already knew that Garth would not be home that evening. He had a business thing he was attending, a conference where he was due to make a speech, and as she let herself into Ivy House, she told herself fiercely that she was glad she wouldn't have to see him; that she didn't *want* to see him, not now, not *ever*. Not after what he had done.

How many times had it happened? How often had he made love…had sex with Katriona? Had he enjoyed it more than he had done with her? He must have done, mustn't he? He must have wanted her more than he had done her, his wife, otherwise he would never have…

And Katriona must have told him that Tara was his child…that she was carrying his baby while she, his wife, had been unable…

Claudia could feel the hysteria bubbling up inside her, the pain that could only be voided by screaming it into the silence of the empty house.

Suddenly, she was re-experiencing just as sharply and agonizingly as though it had only happened hours ago all the feelings she had experienced when she first realised that she would never be able to have her own child.

But Tara *was* her child…Tara was *hers*, her daughter. *She* had been the one to love her, to teach her, to mother her.

Tara… Soon it would be time to collect her from school, a ritual they both enjoyed even though Tara sometimes complained that she was old enough now to be allowed to walk home on her own. It was one of their special times together, that walk home from school, when Tara would tell her all about her day, chattering happily at her side, her hand tucked in Claudia's.

Tara. Her daughter. Katriona's child...Garth's child, but *her* daughter.

She was, she discovered, slowly rocking her hunched body backwards and forwards as she sat on her bed, their bed, hers and Garth's. Suddenly, overwhelmingly, she knew she was going to be sick. Had Garth taken her to their bed? Had he...?

She retched violently into the lavatory bowl and then leaned against the wall, shaking from head to foot.

Had Garth told Katriona that *she* could not have any children? Had he perhaps complained about her, bemoaned her inability to give him any children? Was that why...?

Stop it. Stop it, she urged herself as she flushed the lavatory and then started to run the cold water tap. She had to pull herself together for Tara's sake. Tara was the one who mattered, the only one who mattered to her now, she told herself dully. Her marriage to Garth was over. She knew that. How could it not be...?

How could he not have told her...warned her...? All these years when every time he looked at Tara, he must have been remembering Katriona. Perhaps *that* was why he hadn't told her—because he wanted to keep his memories of

Tara's mother sacred, his memories of her conception sacred. Had he loved Katriona...loved her perhaps more than he had ever loved her? He must have felt something for her. Was that why he loved Tara? Because she was her mother's child? Round and round her thoughts went, faster and faster, spinning out of control, dizzying her with their intensity and their immense capacity for causing her pain.

Tara... She had to go and collect Tara. The phone was ringing as she left the house. Numbly, she ignored it.

Cursing to himself, Garth hung up. If Claudia was there, then quite plainly she wasn't going to answer. If only he didn't have this *damned* speech to give this evening.

He needed time to talk to Claudia...to explain...to *make* her listen, but *how* could he talk to her with Tara there and...? On impulse, he quickly dialled the telephone number of Claudia's parents. As though surprised to hear his voice, his mother-in-law readily agreed to his request that she come to Ivy House to look after Tara for a few days while Garth took Claudia away for a surprise short break.

'I know it's short notice,' he apologised.

'Don't worry about it,' he was reassured. 'I think it's a wonderful idea. Where are you going to take her?'

'Er...it's a secret,' Garth told her, and after all, it wasn't untrue. As yet, he had no idea himself *where* he was going to take Claudia, only that it would have to be a place where they could be completely alone so they could get this whole sorry mess sorted out.

Too caught off guard to argue and still shell-shocked from her discovery, Claudia gave in numbly when Garth announced his plans. He had found a small country cottage to rent on the Welsh border not far from Hay-on-Wye. Claudia sat by his side in frozen silence all the way there. Not because she was deliberately trying to punish him by not speaking but simply because it was easier to remain silent than to unleash the pain she knew was waiting for her once she started to give voice to her feelings.

The weather had turned cold and wet, and Claudia's face had a pinched, bloodless look that made her suddenly look very much older. Even the way she moved was different, Garth acknowledged when they eventually reached their destination and Claudia got out of the car and walked slowly towards the cottage without waiting to see whether or not he was following her.

In the forty-eight hours since the truth had come out, he had cursed himself a thousand, no, a hundred thousand times for what he had done, and yet, if it had never happened, there would be no Tara. He could still put his hand on his heart and swear honestly that he had no idea how he had ever come to have sex with Katriona…and that it had certainly not been a premeditated or even a wanted act on his part.

The cottage had clearly been planned and furnished as a cosy retreat for two lovers. Downstairs there was an open fire; upstairs there was only one large bedroom accompanied by a good-sized bathroom complete with a huge Victorian bath and discreetly hung mirrors. Every room had candles temptingly on display, obviously intended to be used, and the whole ambience of the place was one of sensual intimacy.

He could almost see Claudia recoiling and he suspected that if he hadn't been on his way back into the cottage carrying the box of groceries he was fetching from the car and blocking the doorway, she would have turned and walked out.

'I don't think this is a good idea,' she told Garth bleakly as she watched him carry the groceries into the kitchen.

'We need to talk. We both agreed on that,' Garth reminded her.

To talk! How civilised he made it sound. *She* didn't want to talk. She wanted to rant and rave, to scream and howl, to beat her fists, her head, her whole self against the wall in an agony of self-denigration and loathing that she could ever have been so stupid as not to realise what had been happening.

'How did you meet her?' she asked him tonelessly. 'How often did you…?'

'I saw her twice,' Garth answered quietly. 'The first time was when I woke up to find her going through my clothes and pulling out the contents of my wallet. The second was…' He stopped and carefully bent down to put the milk and other fresh food in the fridge. 'The only other time was when I went to see her after she had contacted me to tell me about…about Tara.' He straightened up, then slammed the fridge door, ignoring Claudia's stony silence. 'Claudia, it *isn't* like you think,' he insisted emotionally. 'I don't even *remember* having sex with her. She—'

'You don't remember.' Claudia swallowed a splintering, savage barb of angry laughter. 'What was she like, Garth? Much, much better than me, of course. Did you talk about me, the pair of you, laugh about me?'

'Claudia, don't,' Garth groaned. 'You don't—'

'I don't what. I don't *understand*.' She laughed again, the sharp sound reminding Garth of something shattering, breaking. 'Of course I understand. I understand that *you* had sex with her. That *she* conceived *your* child. That you and she… Where did it happen, Garth? In our flat…in our *bed*?'

She could feel herself starting to shake violently from head to foot. The same nausea that had overwhelmed her before seized her again, but this time she managed to control it.

'Claudia, I *promise* you it just wasn't the way you're imagining it,' Garth declared huskily. It was vital she should understand what he could piece together of what had happened. How he had woken to find Katriona in the flat and how she must have taken advantage of him while he was the worse for drink. Even to his own ears his words sounded suspect. But he was struggling to explain clearly what was still, to him, just a vague memory, a hazy dream.

He could see that Claudia had taken in very little, if anything, of what he'd said. Was refusing, almost, to let his words touch her. 'I don't want you to say any more,' Claudia told him icily.

All that was turning over in her head was the brutally painful thought that Garth had taken Katriona into *their* home, their *bed*. He had made love to her in the same place where he had loved her, touched her, no doubt in exactly the same way as he had touched *her*, perhaps even told her that he loved her.

Claudia had thought that the pain of losing her unborn child and then all her hopes of any future children would be the worst pain she was ever going to be called upon to bear, but she realised now that she was wrong. That had been pain, but it had, even in all its searing agony, been a clean, sharp wound. This...*this* was something different. This was a slow-acting poison, a corrosive acid—a gangrene that was going to eat into her until she was totally destroyed, until all that she was was consumed in its slow death grip.

'I *know* how you must be feeling,' she heard Garth saying rawly to her.

'Do you?' she challenged him bitterly. 'How *can* you know, Garth? How could you do this to me, to *us*?' she demanded brokenly. 'No wonder you didn't object too much when I told you I was keeping Tara. I'll bet you had a really good laugh about that. Me, your wife, taking on your...your child by another woman...*loving her*...'

'Claudia. I didn't know then that Tara was mine. She could have been—'

'Anyone's. Any man's,' Claudia interrupted him, her voice cold once more. 'Yes. She *could*, couldn't she? But knowing that, you still... Did you love her, Garth?' she asked him bleakly.

'No.' His response was instant and immediate, but to his distress, instead of making her relent, his answer only seemed to increase her bitterness towards him.

'Then that makes you even more despicable,' she accused him quietly. 'If you had loved her, I could have understood, but to have done what you did without loving her... I can't stay married to you, Garth,' she told him emotionlessly, 'not after this. I couldn't bear to have you in the same room, never mind...' She broke off and turned away from him.

'You're overreacting,' Garth returned fiercely. He was beginning to get angry now. She hadn't even heard what he'd said or given herself a chance to work this through with him. She was ready to believe the worst of him without even thinking it through, almost as though...as though...

'This is exactly what you've been waiting for, isn't it?' he challenged her bitingly. 'An excuse to get me completely out of your life. After all, it isn't as though I've been allowed much of a role to play in it recently, have I? You don't want a husband, Claudia, and you certainly don't want a lover. In fact, you don't want a man at all. At least not this man. All *you* want is to be a mother. Well, you're not—'

'I'm not what? I'm not *Tara's* mother?' Claudia burst out.

Garth swallowed hard and stared at her. That *wasn't* what he had been going to say at all. Her eyes were red and swollen from crying, her face so pale she looked ill. In the eyes of the world, she might never have looked less physically appealing, but so far as he was concerned, he had never loved her more, never wanted to show her that love more, never wanted...

The cottage was small and all it took was a couple of strides to take him to her side, his arms going round her as he cradled her protectively against his body, murmuring over and over again, 'Clo...my love, my dearest love...'

'*Don't* call me that,' Claudia cried, tilting her head back to look up at him, but Garth was beyond recognising the fury and rejection in her voice. All he wanted to do was to cement the bond he still believed existed between them, to show her in the only way he knew that she was his woman, his only woman, that she always had been and always would be.

Bending his head, he lifted one hand to cup her face, the weight of his body pushing her back against the wall, the intensity of his passion catching her completely off guard as he started to kiss her almost frenziedly, using his mouth to smother any objection she tried to make as he kissed her over and over again.

Claudia felt so infuriated that she almost wanted to hit him—she, who had never been or wanted to be physically violent or aggressive in her entire life. She could feel the hot, hard weight of his body burning into her own and it shocked her how easily her own body responded to its familiarity despite everything that she had learned.

Angrily, she lashed out at him, striking a blow generated by the deepest, most primitive, most primeval source of her feminine emotions, *wanting* to hurt him, to damage him, to destroy him as he had done her by betraying her love.

She heard, felt, the shocked gasp of air leaving his lungs as her fists pummelled fiercely against his chest—a puerile, impossible attempt to wound him and an act that didn't even give her the satisfaction of emotional relief, she acknowledged as she felt the hot rush of acid tears stinging her eyes.

'I hate you Garth…I hate you.' She screamed the words at him and was still screaming them ten seconds later when he grabbed hold of both her wrists in one hand, scooped her up off the floor and across his body in a fireman's lift and carried her still pummelling and kicking towards the bed.

Afterwards, Garth swore both to her and to himself that all he had intended to do was to dump her on the bed and leave her there until he had calmed down, but as he did so, he saw her tear-streaked face and the compulsion to reach out and touch it swamped him, flooding him with remorse and anguish.

'Claudia, it wasn't the way you think,' he started to say, but Claudia had heard enough.

She raised her hand towards his face, intending to draw her nails savagely across it, to do anything...*anything* to silence those words, those lies, he was telling her.

'Claudia...no!' Garth exploded, reaching for her wrist, locking his hand with hers in a parody of the intimacy shared by a pair of lover's entwined hands. Enraged, Claudia leaned forward, closing the fractional distance between them, desperate to find an outlet for her emotions. Then, acting purely on instinct, she sank her teeth into his bottom lip.

Garth felt the sharp bite, the brief sting of pain, tasted the hot gush of blood that followed it, saw the shocked exultation in Claudia's eyes as she realised what she had done. And it was that, the sight of the look in her eyes, the knowledge that she had enjoyed hurting him that breached the fragile ramparts of his own battle-torn self-control.

He was nearly a foot taller than her and far, far heavier. Add to that his training as a soldier, and what surprised him was not how easily he overpowered her but how long she continued to fight him. What shocked him, though, was how physically arousing, how physically *erotic* it was to wrestle with her on the bed; to feel the soft warmth of her body beneath his; to know that above and beyond the anger they were both unleashing, there was for him in what was happening between them a very sharp and totally male awareness of the sexual heat being generated between them. It was a heat and urgency he had almost forgotten what it felt like to feel as he held her down beneath him and watched the way her body, her breasts, rose and fell with the exertion of her breathing. In his imagination, he was already removing her clothes, already laying bare the honey gold intimacy of her body to the touch of his hands and his mouth.

Lying pinned beneath Garth on the bed, Claudia saw the way he was looking at her and felt her body's response to that look—a look as old as the one Adam had given Eve, a look as old as the one Eve had tempted and taunted Adam into giving her. One shudder and then another went through her as she recognised that while her mind might loathe what was happening between them, physically and sexually her body was aroused by it.

She knew even before Garth had lifted his hand to push aside her clothes and reveal the hard-tipped fullness of her breasts just what he was going to do and how she was going to feel when he did. Not only was there anger, bitterness and contempt, there was desire, as well, in the hot, liquid, wrenching feeling that pulsed inside her.

As his hand curled round her naked breast and his mouth found hers, she could taste the warm salt shock of his blood on her own tongue. Behind her closed eyelids, black and red whorls of colour mingled violently together, reacting with her swirling emotions. Rage, pain, desire, need. They were all there and others, too, that she couldn't bear to acknowledge.

They made love quickly and fiercely, Claudia tearing at Garth's clothes as she would have liked to have been tearing at his flesh, ripping, shredding, hurting, raking his back with her fingernails as he thrust deeply into her, hating him for the way he was making her want him physically at the same time as she hated him so much emotionally, the dagger points of her nails shredding his skin and yet also driving him to thrust even deeper within her.

Their coming together was shattering and incredibly sensual. Claudia shocked herself with her own angry aggression that manifested itself in a need to make Garth reach orgasm deep inside her wave upon wave as though she was somehow subconsciously drawing from him all of his maleness, all of his 'seed', leaving him empty and drained, unable ever again to give to anyone else that which should only have been given to her, even though her body couldn't process it, couldn't use it…couldn't *grow* a new life with it. Her own orgasms were the most intense she had ever known, more of a pain than a pleasure, flooding her body with convulsive explosions so powerful that afterwards her body felt as light and empty as though she had been given a powerful emetic. But, as she discovered in the months that followed, if its purpose in her own subconscious had been to rid her of all her feelings for Garth, it had not worked, not by a long way.

To the outside world, their divorce was quiet and amicable.

'I can't live with you any more,' Claudia had told Garth distantly. 'I don't *want* you in my life, Garth.'

Garth had given in with a heavy heart. Despite all his attempts to reason with her, she had remained obdurate. She could not stay married to a man who had made the whole concept of their marriage a mockery and a sham.

Tara, it was agreed, would live with her mother, with Garth remaining very much a strong presence in her life.

'I can hardly refuse, can I?' Claudia had acknowledged at their final private meeting, giving him a bitter smile as she added painfully, 'After all, she *is* your daughter.'

'And yours,' Garth had insisted.

But Claudia had refused to look at him, and he had known that when she turned her face away from him, it was because she was crying. He had known, too, that any attempt on his part to go to her and comfort her, to reach out and hold her as he so much longed to do, to tell her how very, very much he loved her and always would, would achieve nothing and probably make her hate him even more.

16

As she drove through the London traffic, it was Tara who was in Claudia's thoughts. When she and Garth had broken the news to Tara that they were divorcing, her shock and tears, her pleading with them to stay together… Tara.

Had the circumstances been anything other than what they were, Claudia knew that she would have relented then and given in to Garth's pleas that they keep their marriage going. But how could she when every time she looked at him, every time he touched her, she could only see Katriona? Every time she saw him with Tara, she would be thinking of how and with whom her precious daughter had been conceived.

Gradually, Tara had come to accept the separation, and Claudia had stuck to her word that Tara could see as much of her father as she wished—had stuck to it despite the pain it caused her. Tara… Tara at fourteen…sixteen… eighteen—the age Katriona had been when…

And now her daughter was a girl no longer but a young woman, a young woman poised on the edge of her own adult life, a young woman whose life could be soured and spoiled as Claudia's own life had been by betrayal.

But not the betrayal of a woman by a man. No, the betrayal she would have to suffer would in its way be even worse—the betrayal of a child by her mother.

Once when Garth had been urging Claudia to tell Tara the truth, she had told him fiercely, 'I can't. How can I? I owe it to her to protect her—'

'It isn't Tara you're protecting,' Garth had cut in bitingly. 'It's *yourself*. Have you thought of what's going to happen, of how she's going to feel if she discovers it from someone else?'

'She won't *ever* discover it,' Claudia had insisted, but even then she had been afraid, aware how fragile the deception she had woven around Tara's birth actually was and how easily the real facts could be put together if someone was determined to discover the truth.

How would Tara feel if she had to face those facts alone in a strange country, if Ryland's aunt should discover the truth and confront her with it? How would *she* feel in Tara's shoes? What would her thoughts, her feelings, be towards the 'mother' who had made it possible for her to be put in that position by not warning her? By what yardstick would she judge the extent of that mother's love when she had put her own needs to be seen by her daughter in the best possible light above that daughter's need and right to be protected from anything and anyone in a position to harm her?

Tara would have every right to feel as betrayed by her as she had felt by Garth and to hate her with the intensity with which she had hated Garth.

Were her own feelings, her own needs, really more important to her than those of her child? Yes, *her* child, she told herself fiercely, because Tara *was* her child. *Her* love for her was that of a mother as surely as though she had been the one to give birth to her. Emotionally, Tara was to her flesh of her flesh, blood of her blood. She was the kind of mother who had always known instinctively when Tara was away from her if she was ill or unhappy, the bond between them so deep that in some senses it was almost psychic.

She couldn't let Tara go to America without knowing the truth, and as suddenly as though her vision had previously been clouded and hazy, now it was startlingly clear, its clarity almost a sharp, physical pain. How could she not have told Tara before? she accused herself. How could she have allowed her own fear of being rejected by her daughter to become more important than Tara's right to know the truth.

To the shock of the driver behind her, she abruptly swung the car round, cutting across a bus-only lane to turn left into the maze of narrow streets that, if memory served her, would take her to her destination.

With all the instincts of a homing pigeon, she knew there was only one place she wanted to be right now, only one person she wanted to see. Only one person could help her, could reinforce her decision and protect her from the danger of changing her mind, backing down, giving in to her fear.

Loving someone meant putting their needs above your own. True mother love was selfless, not selfish. True mother love.

Garth cursed when he found that he had a visitor. It had been a bad day made worse by the realisation as he drove away from Ivy House that despite all the years that he and Claudia had lived their separate lives, there was a part of him that had always recognised Claudia as his. His wife, his soul mate, his love. It would have been the easiest, the most natural thing in the world to have taken hold of her earlier and to have shown her.

To have shown her what? That he could still overpower her and force her to have sex with him? Oh, yeah, wonderful. What a hero that would make him.

He frowned as he flicked up the button on the door intercom and snapped a terse, 'Yes?'

'Garth, it's me…Claudia. We…I…need to talk to you. I…I've decided to tell Tara the truth…' Silence. 'Garth…Garth, are you there?'

'Yes…yes. Come up, Clo. No, wait there, I'll come down for you.'

He was acting like a wild kid, he chided himself as he practically ran down the flight of stairs that led to the entrance lobby, but he simply couldn't help it, couldn't restrain himself.

'Claudia…Clo…'

Lost in the unexpected warmth of the hug that

Garth gave her as he opened the door, Claudia was too taken aback to do a thing other than simply let him hold her and be glad that he was doing so, be *grateful* to him not just for his human warmth but for his instinctive and correct reading of her mood, her fragility and uncertainty, her vulnerability.

'I've been thinking all day about…about things,' she told him awkwardly as he released her and guided her towards the stairs. 'I went to the flat. It's all different round there now… private houses and—'

'Yes. I know.'

'You know.' Claudia stared at him as he opened the door to his apartment and ushered her inside.

'I…I drive down that way occasionally,' he told her. He wasn't going to tell her how often. When he felt particularly low he drove there and simply parked outside their old flat, remembering…wishing…

'I've been so…blind, Garth, so…so selfish. I thought I was doing the right thing protecting Tara, but today I suddenly realised… I don't know how I'm going to tell her,' she plunged on, unable to look directly at him, focusing instead on the view beyond the window. 'I just know that I have to…before someone else does. I'm so afraid, Garth,' she confessed, shocked not so much by her admission but the fact that she was making it to Garth, of all people. 'I'm so afraid that when she knows the truth, she won't… she'll—'

'She'll be shocked, yes,' Garth told her gently. 'But…Tara is *your* daughter, Clo, in all the ways that count. She's got your ability to reason and to judge only with compassion and kindness. She'll understand why you didn't tell her.'

'Will she? Will she understand that I was more selfishly concerned with my own feelings, my own fear of losing her love, than I was of her feelings? Oh, Garth…'

Suddenly, to her shock, she was shaking, trembling violently, so violently that it was impossible to conceal the intensity of her emotions. For the third time in the same day, she felt Garth's arms wrap round her, comforting her, soothing her.

'Come and sit down,' he urged, adding almost prosaically, 'Have you eaten? I was just about to make myself some supper.'

It wasn't true. He had eaten earlier in the day, but now it struck him that Claudia looked starved—not just for food, but starved in the emotional sense of being hungry for *every* kind of nourishment. Warmth, compassion, support… love.

'No…I'm not hungry,' Claudia started to deny, then stopped. What was she doing here? *Why* on earth had she come here to Garth? Garth, the very last person she should have allowed herself to turn to in her need to have someone help her, understand her.

'Yes…yes, I would like something, please,' she amended huskily, and she knew as she said the words that even if Garth wasn't aware of their importance, she was. For the first time since she had told him she wanted him out of her life, she was acknowledging that despite everything she knew she ought to feel, she did still need him.

Need him or…?

'Wait here,' Garth told her.

Claudia could hear him moving about in the kitchen as she stood in the living room, staring unseeingly out across the Thames. She had been in his apartment before, briefly. It was furnished comfortably in a very masculine fashion but it had, she suddenly recognised, an air of impermanence about it, a lack of personal touches, as though Garth had never truly adapted to it as his home.

It was obviously not a place ever lived in by a woman. Claudia smiled painfully to herself as she assessed her own reaction to that very female awareness. She didn't need to think about the presence of another woman in the life of her husband…her ex-husband, she reminded herself sharply. Hadn't it, after all, been her furious bitterness, her love-torn jealousy, at the thought of his intimacy with another woman, his betrayal of her and their love that had brought about the ending of their marriage in the first place?

She could smell food cooking in the kitchen and her heart suddenly jolted against her ribs as she recognised what he was cooking.

An omelette. The very first dish he had ever made her had been an omelette, which he had fed her as they sat together, and afterwards… afterwards…

An omelette's comfort food, she had murmured protestingly when he had produced it in response to her request for a romantic meal.

But Garth had been holding her foot in his hands at the time, gently stroking the flesh with his fingers while he slowly nibbled on her toes. She had very quickly lost interest in debating what did and did not constitute a romantic meal.

As she watched Garth walking towards her carefully carrying the tray with her supper on it, Claudia tried to remind herself that she was forty-five years old; that they had been apart for years and that he had betrayed her, but it was no use. She could hear the ominous crack in her voice, feel the tears threatening as she told him shakily, 'You've made me an omelette.' And then the food was forgotten. The only place she wanted to be, the only comfort she wanted, was the hard warmth of Garth's arms around her as she sobbed against his shoulder. 'Garth, I'm so afraid, so very, very afraid.'

'Hush, hush...come on. Come and sit down. Let's talk.'

'It's different for you,' Claudia told him almost half an hour later when she had finally felt she had herself under something approaching reasonable control. 'After all, you are her father.'

'Yes, and I'm sure she's going to be really impressed when she learns how I became her father.'

'I...the young these days have a different view of...fidelity. She might not—'

'That wasn't what I meant,' Garth interrupted

her grimly, explaining when Claudia frowned uncomprehendingly, 'I don't know *how* I came to father Tara, Claudia. As I tried to tell you before, I can't remember anything about it, or about…about her mother. All I *can* remember is half waking out of a drunken stupor and realising that…'

'That what?' Claudia pressed him.

'That there was someone…someone who didn't feel right. It's a memory so elusive that I can't even call it a memory. How on earth she managed to get…' He broke off, realising the infelicity of the remark he had been about to make.

But Claudia was older now and more worldly wise.

'You mean how you managed to have sex with her. But you took her to bed.'

'No,' Garth denied. 'I did *no* such thing. I went to bed, yes, and I woke up in bed to find an unknown young woman, who I later discovered was one of your clients, going through my clothes—a young woman who scarpered with the contents of my wallet too fast for me to be able to find out how she got in or why she was in our bedroom. It is possible for a woman to initiate sex with a man and—'

'Without his knowing anything about it?' Claudia interrupted him sharply. 'Garth…?'

'I was drunk,' Garth reminded her. 'That she obviously managed to get an automatic physical reaction from my body, I've never been able to deny—even though I personally can't remember a thing about it. But the *result*, Tara's conception, had nothing to do with me and it wasn't any more of *my* doing in any true sense than if I'd been a sperm donor. No, less, because a sperm donor is making a conscious decision to donate the seeds of life, whereas—'

'Do you think she did it deliberately, that she actually wanted...?' Claudia swallowed, feeling sick.

Now that she thought back, and she had deliberately blocked these thoughts since the divorce, she could remember Garth telling her about finding someone in the flat and her keys had also gone missing around that time. Could Katriona have deliberately planned...

'Who knows? I doubt that even *she* knew,' Garth told her softly. 'What I do know, though, is that *you* are the only woman I have ever loved or ever wanted, either emotionally or physically, the only woman I still want.'

Claudia swallowed—hard—and even then her voice, the only voice she could find, was still a very croaky and emotional whisper as she asked him, 'Garth, what are you saying? You and Katriona were *lovers*, you said.'

'No,' Garth contradicted her firmly, shaking his head. 'Katriona and I were *never* lovers. We had *sex*, yes, we *must* have had for Tara to have been conceived, even if *I* have no memory of it. But it was only the once, and for all that I knew of it, for all that I consciously contributed to it, I might as well have been completely comatose.'

'But you told me,' Claudia whispered painfully, 'you said that you'd been lovers.'

'No, Claudia,' Garth denied gently. '*You* said we were lovers. I tried to tell you how it really was but—you didn't seem to want to take it in.'

'You didn't try very hard to persuade me to listen,' Claudia defended herself huskily.

'Maybe not,' Garth agreed. 'Call it male pride if you like, but I was already feeling shut out, an unnecessary and unwanted distraction who was coming between you and Tara. It seemed to me that you were ready to seize on any excuse to end our marriage. I felt you didn't want to hear the truth.'

Claudia felt her eyes glaze with tears. She knew she couldn't wholly deny what Garth was saying even if now… Even if now what? Even if *now* she saw things differently, *felt* things differently? Even if now, right now, sitting here with him like this she felt…?

'I should have listened properly to you,' she admitted quietly. 'Perhaps if it had been anyone other than Katriona…'

'You'd been through a traumatic time,' Garth defended her. 'How traumatic perhaps neither of us truly appreciated then. You'd lost our child, your own child, and any chance of ever having another, and then Katriona… I've never said this to you before, Clo, but there've been so many times when I've watched you with Tara as she's been growing up and marvelled at the generosity of spirit that's enabled you to love her so totally and instinctively. In your shoes…' He shook his head.

'You'd have done what? Punished her for being Katriona's child…for the fact that *you* could not have children? No, you wouldn't, Garth,' she insisted. 'Not you.'

'And not you, either,' Garth reminded her.

Claudia bit her lip. 'She was so easy to love,' she told him thoughtfully. 'Right from the very first time I saw her…held her. Who knows?' She looked away from him. 'Perhaps subconsciously even then, a part of me somehow knew… recognised that she was your child. She's so like you in so many different ways.'

'That's funny,' Garth whispered softly. 'I think she's very like you.'

They both laughed and then Claudia's expression changed.

'*What* is she going to say when I tell her, Garth? *How* is she going to react…to feel?' She closed her eyes against the tears she could feel starting. 'I don't know if I can bear it. She's going to be so shocked. It will be like I'm taking away the whole of her past, everything she believes about herself. I've counselled adults who were adopted children…'

She swallowed hard, burying her head in her hands as she cried out in despair, '*Why* didn't I tell her years ago when she was young enough to simply accept that she wasn't mine? It wasn't just because I was afraid that she could be taken away from us…from me. I wasn't just afraid of losing her physically, but losing her emotionally as well. I was afraid that she would resent me for not being her *real* mother, for not being Katriona, for living when Katriona had died!'

'You are her real mother,' Garth told her fiercely, filling the glass of wine Claudia had been drinking as she ate her omelette, then pouring a fresh one for himself. 'Tara's an adult now, Clo. Of course she's going to be shocked and distressed, we both know that. And maybe even for a while she'll turn away from us—that, too, would be quite natural. But she's *your* child, remember, the child *you've* loved and taught. It's from you she gets her sturdiness of character, her strength and her ability to judge people and situations calmly and with compassion. It's from *you* that she's learned how to love generously and healthily.'

'I've made so many mistakes, Garth,' Claudia admitted, taking a deep gulp of her wine and refusing to be comforted. 'Look at the way I misjudged *you*. If I was counselling a woman in the same situation as you were in, would I blame her because some man had had sex with her without her permission? Would I reject her and turn away from her?'

'It's easy to be dispassionate when the person you're dealing with isn't someone close,' Garth reminded her.

'Yes,' Claudia admitted ruefully. 'I loved you so much that I couldn't stand the thought of you with someone else, anyone else, but especially Katriona.'

'Did you, Clo?' Garth asked. 'Perhaps if I'd felt more confident about that, about your love...'

'But you must have known how I felt,' Claudia protested.

'Once, yes. I thought I did. But after Tara came along, I often felt I was superfluous to requirements,' Garth explained wryly. 'I always seemed to be in the way, our sex life dwindled to next to nothing and—'

'I...I felt guilty and...and ashamed of the fact that I couldn't give you your own children,' Claudia whispered tremulously. 'I thought when you touched me...when we made love, that part of you must be thinking how purposeless it all was. Sometimes...after you'd come inside me, I used to cry, thinking of the waste, all that effort, all that energy, all those potential babies....'

'Is *that* what you thought, that making love was purposeless?' Garth asked her steadily.

'Sometimes,' Claudia admitted, 'but...but not always.'

Garth looked at her for a moment, then told her, 'When I took you to bed, Clo, when we made love, making babies was almost always the very last thing on my mind. What I wanted, what I loved, was *you*...holding *you*, hearing *you*, seeing *you*, feeling *you* respond to me, wanting me in the same way. And I'll tell you something else. Right now there's nothing I want more than to recapture those feelings. Right now the way I feel about you, the way I want you, has nothing, absolutely nothing, to do with any desire to procreate a new generation. It's your fault,' he murmured as she looked up at him, unable to conceal the expression in her eyes. 'It was all those memories you brought back when you talked about my coming inside you.'

'Garth,' Claudia protested, but it proved to be a very weak and ineffectual protest as she was the first to admit when he ignored it and instead simply removed the wineglass from her nervous fingers before cupping her face.

She didn't even try to move away when he looked searchingly into her eyes, keeping his own open as he gradually lowered his head, his mouth moving towards her own.

As his lips brushed rhythmically against hers, Claudia could feel her eyes starting to fill with tears of emotion. How *could* she have deliberately denied herself such tenderness? She could feel her mouth, her body, starting to soften and turn to liquid, to fill her with heavy, languorous heat.

'Garth.' Instinctively, she pressed herself closer to him.

As he heard her moan his name, felt her body react to his nearness, recognised all the little telltale signs that showed her responsiveness to him, Garth dropped his hands from her face and gathered her close, the touch of his mouth on hers becoming harder and more demanding, his teeth tugging on her bottom lip, his tongue savouring the melting sweetness of her mouth.

Claudia could feel herself starting to tremble violently as she clung to him. His kiss had been like a torch being applied to dry tinder and she was the one going up in flames. Had she been this ardent, this passionate, when they were younger? If so, she couldn't remember it, couldn't even begin to compare all these feelings that thundered down on her like the overpowering force of a sudden avalanche with the surely far tamer and less heated desire she had experienced in her youth.

Was it the years spent apart, the years of sexual drought that were causing this conflagration? And if so, why? Her celibacy had been self-imposed and deliberate; there had been men who, if she had shown the merest flicker of interest, would have been more than willing to love her. Luke, for instance, but what she had thought might develop between them was nothing compared to what she still felt for Garth. Sex had never really been a priority for her and yet here she was literally trembling from head to foot with need, aching with the raw, hot, urgent pulse of it, wanting Garth so much that she could quite easily, oh, so easily, have torn off his clothes.

Claudia gave a small gasp beneath the pressure of Garth's mouth and opened her eyes, shocked to discover what she was actually doing…that she had already removed Garth's tie and ripped open the top buttons of his shirt.

'Don't stop,' Garth begged her throatily.

Claudia licked her suddenly dry lips.

'Do it, Clo,' she heard Garth demanding hoarsely, his eyes burning hot with responsive ardour as he followed the movement of her tongue. 'Do it,' he repeated when she didn't move, taking hold of her hand, kissing her open palm and then slowly starting to convey it to his body before stopping and keeping his gaze fixed on hers, slowly, ever so slowly sucking on her fingers.

Garth's eyes were hot, so hot that Claudia felt she could burst into flame from their fierce heat. Burn up, melt, dissolve in the honey liquid flood of pleasure that was surging through her.

Her hands trembled so much as she unfastened the rest of his shirt that she felt she would never complete her task, but once it was done she gave a sharp, shuddering sigh when she saw his body. The hair on his head might just be starting to become flatteringly tinged with grey at the sides, but the soft curls of silky fine hair on his torso remained just as dark as they had always been, his nipples small and flat but staying sharply erect. Just like her own.

Claudia swallowed.

'Don't stop there,' Garth urged her.

Claudia looked down at his belt and then up at his face, her eyes betraying the fact that it wasn't just his belt she had noticed in that swift female glance.

'I never was much good at keeping my reaction to you a secret, was I?' Garth groaned, then added hoarsely, 'God, Clo, I want you so much…have wanted you so much and for so damned long that I don't know if I can…'

Now *he* was undressing *her* and with far more speed and skill than she had evinced, Claudia acknowledged, hesitantly aware that the last time he had seen her naked body, she had been a younger woman.

But she needn't have worried. Garth's reaction

as he exposed the soft, warm globes of her breasts made her catch her own breath in shocked delight.

No man could manufacture *that* kind of look, that kind of dazed and possessive appreciation and desire. She didn't really even need his words to confirm what she could see in his face, but it felt good to hear them anyway as he told her huskily, 'I'd forgotten just how...how perfect you are. How...how much a woman...my woman. Oh, God, Clo, I've missed you.'

And then he was burying his face against her breasts, caressing them with his fingers and then with his mouth.

It was almost like being young again, although Claudia knew that she could never have been as uninhibited then, as freely able to accept not just his desire for her, but even more importantly, hers for him; nor could she have been as truly accepting not just of his sexuality but of her own as well then as she was now. And she could certainly never remember glorying so openly, so eagerly, in the immediacy of a need that demanded instant and complete satisfaction, so much so, in fact, that in the end *she* was the one to tug Garth's trousers off, laughing at him while he groaned helplessly. But her laughter soon died when he reached for her, drawing her down against him, kissing her breasts again but this time lingering over the caress with deliberate sensuality, licking and then sucking her nipples in the way he had obviously remembered that she most liked.

Had he remembered, too, what else she liked?

She felt her stomach muscles start to contract while her body grew moist.

It seemed that he had, and as her fingers curled ecstatically into the still-thick springiness of his hair, Claudia looked down at the sight of him between her thighs and wondered how she could have lived so long without having him beside her.

It was like waking up from a bad dream and realising that it *had* merely been a dream; that *this* was reality, the hot, loving lap of Garth's tongue against her body, the aroused male scent of him, the feel of him, the…

She gave a small gasp as her body started to respond to the insistent pressure of his mouth against the hot, wet bud of her clitoris, wave after concentric wave of need building up inside her towards a crescendo that she knew would…

'Garth…Garth, not like this,' she protested. 'I want you inside me…I want…'

She was almost too late…almost.

All they had time for was the intimacy of Garth's body filling hers, an urgent, fierce thrust and then another before her sharp, high-pitched cry broke the silence like the waves of her pleasure breaking inside her.

'I don't want to move,' she confessed to Garth a few minutes later as she lay beneath him.

'I *daren't* move,' Garth admitted wryly, adding, 'but we'll have to…because…' As he looked down at her flushed face, he stopped to kiss her before adding lovingly, 'Because the next time I want to love you in the comfort of a bed.'

'The *next* time?' Claudia's heart jumped betrayingly but she said nothing, simply searching his face.

'This isn't a one-off thing, Claudia,' he warned her, reading her unspoken thoughts. 'Not for me and I hope not for you, either. It's not too late for us to start again.'

'To forget the past?' Claudia suggested shakily.

'No.' Garth shook his head. 'No, not to forget it, but to build on it, to *use* what we've learned from it, to make sure that *this* time nothing and *no one* comes between us or makes us want to part. I've never stopped loving you. Never. And I don't think that you've stopped loving me, either.'

Was he right? Claudia suspected that he could be. Above and beyond the sex they had just shared, there was something about being with him that felt so natural and right. So easy. She tried to imagine herself going home to Ivy House and back to her life without him, and she knew incontrovertibly, if unexpectedly, that it wasn't a prospect that pleased her. That right now, for *whatever* reason, she wanted to be with him. Because she needed his strength.

'Tara is going to need us both once she knows the truth,' Garth told her, once more reading her mind with such accuracy that she was silenced, 'and I think that you and I need each other, too. What do you say, Claudia? Shall we try again?'

'I...I don't know. I need time,' she had intended to say but instead, to her astonishment, she heard herself saying almost shyly, 'I...I'd like that, Garth. I'd...'

She didn't get any further. Despite his complaint earlier about his age and his aching muscles, he lithely sprang to his feet and immediately lifted Claudia up into his arms. 'Bed is the best place, the *only* place for this kind of discussion, the only place for you and me right now,' he whispered meaningfully as he carried her towards his bedroom door. And as she looked at him, he promised her, 'For tonight, there is no past, no pain, just our new beginning.'

A new beginning? Claudia opened her mouth to remonstrate with him and to make some mature, level-headed, adult response to his romantic and plainly fatuous statement, but then as she looked into his eyes, she changed her mind and heard herself whispering as adoringly and, no doubt, as idiotically as a young girl, newly, deeply, *drowningly*, in love for the first time, 'Oh, Garth, could we?'

It would be different tomorrow, of course; tomorrow she would need all her strength, all her maturity, all her *courage*, to face Tara and tell her what she had done. But tonight she badly needed this refuge, this anodyne, this peace, this *loving*, to help her to find that strength along with the wisdom to construct a bridge that would hopefully lead not just her but, even more importantly, Tara across the chasm that separated the

past from the future as well as the courage to
cross over it.

'I've never stopped loving you,' she heard
Garth saying passionately to her as he shoul-
dered open the bedroom door. 'I never have and
I never will.'

17

———►◄———

'Well, at least we know why my visa has still not arrived,' Tara told Ryland ruefully as she sat on the kitchen worktop munching a piece of toast while passing on to him the letter she had just been reading. 'There's been some sort of problem with their computer,' she informed him, 'and it's resulted in a huge backlog in dealing with visa requests.'

'Mmm...'

'I'm going round to see Dad later by the way. He left a message on the answering machine asking me to call. I wonder what he wants. He hasn't been in the office for the past couple of days. His secretary, said he'd rung in to tell her that something urgent had cropped up and that he didn't want to be disturbed—by anyone. I suppose it must be something to do with one of his clients. I tried to ring Ma yesterday, but I couldn't get hold of her. Maxine said she'd phoned in to say she was going away, but according to Maxine, she didn't say where or for how long, which isn't like her at all.'

The toast had almost all gone and she inspected the piece that was left with frowning scrutiny before licking off the marmalade and then grinning as she saw Ryland watching her youthful behaviour.

'Are you going to eat yours?' she asked him. 'I'm ravenous. Must be all the energy I used up last night,' she added, giving him a sideways grin.

Ryland shook his head. 'I'm not rising for that one,' he warned her dryly. 'I wasn't the one who insisted that we try some teenage magazine's sexual position of the month.'

'You said it was impossible,' Tara reminded him.

'And I was right—it was.'

'Not completely,' Tara responded mock-demurely. 'Your problem is that you're getting old. If you were supple—'

'If I was double-jointed, don't you mean?' Ryland interrupted her, 'and as for me getting old…I wasn't the one who complained that her knees hurt or that—'

'All right, all right. Well, you know I'm not that keen on going on top. It makes my stomach look huge, and besides—'

'Besides, you prefer to have me doing all the hard work,' Ryland teased her, opening his mouth for the piece of toast she was feeding him.

'No, I don't,' Tara argued back indignantly. 'It's just…well, you can call me romantic and foolish if you wish, but I just love the feeling of having you on top of me, all around me…inside me,' she murmured coyly. 'Mmm…especially inside me. Ry…when we stay with your family, they're not going to expect us to have separate rooms, are they?' she asked him.

'Probably…but it's all right. The house is pretty big, so I dare say we can manage something.'

'Mmm…I don't want just something,' Tara told him poutingly. 'I want everything. I hope you aren't going to want us to wait long after we get married to start a family. I've been feeling decidedly broody recently.'

Ryland pretended to look alarmed but he could see from her expression that she wasn't fooled. They had, after all, discussed the subject of children at great length, and both of them were agreed that they wanted what Tara called a proper family.

'At least three,' she had told him, 'and a couple of dogs…oh, and a decent-sized guest-room so that we can have people to stay and a granny suite for later when Ma gets older.'

'A granny suite. Have you told your mother about your plans for her? I hadn't realised her old age was quite so imminent,' Ryland had responded wryly.

Tara had giggled. 'No, of course I haven't. I'm going to miss her so much, Ry,' she had told him seriously. 'We've always been so close. Oh, not in that awful, cloying, possessive-mother-and-dependent-daughter sort of way. It's never been like that. It's just that she's always…well, it's just that she's always been there and somehow a little bit of me is almost frightened of what it's going to feel like when she isn't.'

Ryland had watched her. What she wasn't voicing but what he had already recognised was that Tara had grown up in an environment with a mother who had surrounded her with love, cushioned her with it, wrapped her protectively in it, used it to throw around her a magic cloak of security that showed in everything there was about Tara, from the tone of her voice to the tilt of her head. It showed that she had been nurtured and loved, that she had been given the intangible gifts of security, self-esteem, self-respect, self-confidence—gifts that he already knew she would ultimately pass on to their own children, gifts that *he* believed would make them rich beyond measure, gifts that were, in fact, priceless.

'It's going to be fun organising the wedding,' Tara commented now, her face clouding slightly as she complained, 'I just wish we were a larger family. There aren't any little nieces and nephews on my side to dress up as bridesmaids and page-boys.'

Now it was Ryland's turn to grin. 'You can borrow some of mine,' he promised her. 'I've got dozens, hoards, on my mother's side at least.'

Tara's expression was still sombre. 'I wish, too, that Mum and Dad were still together. Oh, I know they'll both be there being civilised about things.' She made a wry face. 'But I don't want them to be civilised, I want them to be the way they should be with one another. I want them to be…to be happy,' she announced, having struggled for the right words.

'I'm sure they are,' Ryland told her robustly,

adding in a more gentle but still-cautioning tone, 'They're old enough to make their own decisions about how they live their lives, Tara, and who with.'

'Yes, I know, but that's just *it*, isn't it? Neither of them *has* made any decision about…about living with someone else. I mean they might just as well still be married. They could *still* be married.'

'They hardly ever see one another,' Ryland reminded her.

'Dad still loves Ma. I'm sure of it. He's got photographs of her in his bedroom. They must have been taken shortly after I was born because she's holding me and—'

'It's probably because you're in the photo that he's kept them,' Ryland felt obliged to point out.

He already knew of Tara's conviction that her parents ought to be together. It was one of her favourite hobby-horses and one he felt sure that was shared by many other children of divorced parents, most of them adult enough and mature enough to know better.

'And Mum hasn't had anyone else,' Tara continued, warming to her theme. 'Not that she hasn't had the opportunity.'

'She's a very attractive woman,' Ryland agreed, then winced and exclaimed, 'Ouch' as Tara kicked him lightly. 'What was that for?' he demanded.

'You've said before how attractive you think she is. Just *how* attractive do you find my mother exactly?' Tara asked him ominously.

Ryland laughed, turning to tug her off the

worktop and into his arms. 'One hell of a lot...but nowhere near as much as I find her daughter,' he whispered teasingly as he started nibbling little kisses against Tara's neck.

'Mmm...I thought you had to go to work,' Tara reminded him.

'Yes, I do,' Ryland agreed regretfully.

'Well, Dad's asked me to go straight round to his apartment this morning instead of into the office. Heaven knows what he wants. A nice bonus would be rather useful right now,' she said, laughing.

Ryland smiled at her. He admired and respected the way that Tara's parents, both of them very comfortably situated financially, resisted the temptation to shower their quite obviously adored only child with life's luxuries.

Tara lived on the income she earned working for her father, and her salary was exactly the same as that earned by the other young graduates with the consultancy.

How was she going to react when he told her that economising wasn't going to be something she would need to do in the future—and more importantly, when was he going to tell her?

'Tara...' he began warily.

But she was already starting to tell him, 'I must go. I'm running late.' After kissing him lingeringly, Tara grabbed her jacket and purse and headed for the door, saying as she left, 'I'd better get going. It will take forever to get across London. Can you order Chinese for supper? I don't think we're going to have time to cook this evening.'

'What do you mean *we*?' Ryland teased her.

It was a standing joke between them that of the two of them he was the better cook.

After she had gone, he didn't know whether he felt pleased or sorry that he had not been able to admit the truth to her. There was still plenty of time, he comforted himself.

Half an hour after Tara had left, the phone rang just as Ryland himself was on the point of leaving. Frowning, he went to answer the call, the unexpectedness of hearing his father's voice deepening his frown.

'Son, you're going to have to get home,' he heard his father telling him heavily. 'We've already checked and there's a flight leaving Heathrow your time eleven o'clock. We've booked you a seat to New York with a connecting flight up to Boston. We'll pick you up at the airport.'

'Airport? Dad…'

'I can't explain now, son. Just get here.'

Ryland knew there had to be something very seriously wrong for his father to demand his immediate return home, and the heaviness he could hear in his voice sent a shiver of prescient doom shuddering down Ryland's spine.

'Dad, is Mom…are the girls…?'

'No. Your mom's fine and so are the girls. Look, I can't talk about it right now. Once you get here, you'll understand. And Ry...I think it's best if you come alone.'

Come alone! His father ended the call before Ryland could ask him any more questions. Just what the hell was going on? He could feel the adrenalin starting to churn through his veins as anxiety knotted his stomach. For his father to have booked him a flight home was alarming enough, but the tone of his father's voice had triggered off a primeval, gut-deep reaction in Ryland. Something was terribly wrong. Something was terribly wrong indeed.

Come alone, his father had told him.

He would have to ring the airport and check that they had him booked onto that flight. Pack a few necessities and get himself over to Heathrow before eleven. And he would, of course, have to let Tara know what was happening.

He checked their phone list and pressed the automatic number for her father's flat. The telephone started to ring at the other end. Ryland frowned when it became obvious that no one was going to answer it.

Obviously, the traffic had been even worse than Tara expected and she wasn't there yet. Presumably, her father wasn't there, either.

Frowning impatiently, Ryland replaced the receiver. He was going to have to leave Tara a note. He had no alternative, not if he was going to make that flight. But what could he say in it that would make any sense?

Shrugging, he went in search of paper and pen, then scribbled down quickly his number in

the States opposite the time he had written in the
top left-hand corner of the sheet of paper.

Call from Dad. He wants me back home.
Don't know why yet. Will ring a.s.a.p. Love
and kisses. Miss you, miss me, too.

'Garth, I feel that I just don't deserve this…to
be this happy,' Claudia confessed wonderingly.

She had just stepped out of the shower, shaking her head protestingly when Garth took the
towel from her and started to pat her dry.

They had spent almost three whole days together, days when, by mutual consent, they had
abdicated their normal responsibilities, including letting the answering machine take all their
messages, so they could talk and be together.
Dizzy with conversation and love, they had finally fallen asleep in one another's arms at night.
And during the day both of them had separately
and together wept over all the wasted years and
wasted emotions.

'Why didn't we *talk* to one another like this before?' Claudia had asked Garth woefully at one
point, her eyes full of tears after she had listened
to him telling her how distraught and disbelieving he had been when she had insisted that she
wanted a divorce.

'It isn't the talking that's important. It's the listening,' Garth had suggested. 'Maybe neither of
us had the maturity to do that then. Perhaps neither of us understood exactly what we were
throwing away.'

'I certainly didn't,' Claudia acknowledged, adding in a whisper, 'Oh, Garth, I've missed you so much…how much I'm only just beginning to realise. I feel like…like a river that's now suddenly restored and replenished after running dry. I don't deserve you…I don't deserve this, and I'm so afraid that… How do you think Tara is going to react?' she asked him painfully, adding, 'Listen to me, I'm the one who's the trained counsellor and I know—'

'It's always different when it's your own emotions that are involved,' Garth broke in to comfort her, cupping her face in his hands as he told her with soft honesty, 'It will take time, possibly more time than either of us wants, but I'm sure that eventually she'll be able to understand why we acted as we did, to know that—'

'I lied to her because I was afraid of losing her,' Claudia interrupted him bleakly.

'You didn't *lie*,' Garth corrected her gently.

'By omission I did. I withheld the truth from her, and Garth, I'm ashamed to say it, but a part of me still wants to go on doing just that.' As he looked steadily into her eyes, she shook her head, smiled shakily back at him. 'Oh, it's all right. I'm not looking for a last-minute reprieve. I couldn't *not* tell her. Not now. I feel as though these days we've spent together have been like…like a journey through the past and that I've brought back with me memories, images, a new awareness that can't just be neatly parcelled away and forgotten. Not this time.'

She closed her eyes.

'I keep trying to imagine how *I* would feel in Tara's shoes. How *I* would have felt if *my* parents had turned to me and told me that I wasn't their…that my mother wasn't…' She had to bite her lip to stop herself from crying.

'Oh, Garth, I'm so very, very afraid. Not just for myself, it isn't just a selfish fear. I'm afraid for Tara, afraid of what my selfishness could do to her. How it might damage her. When I took her from…from that place, I promised both her and Katriona that I would always love her and protect her.'

'And you have done,' Garth assured her warmly.

Claudia shook her head.

'No. No, I haven't. I have loved her, yes, but for my own needs. And out of my own needs, I've left her open to that very kind of pain and betrayal. Me, who should know just how much that hurts. Oh, Garth…'

'Stop torturing yourself,' Garth told her firmly as he wrapped the towel around her and took her in his arms, cradling her against his own body and gently comforting her. 'It's not going to be easy but have faith, Clo. Have faith in Tara even if you can't have faith in anything or anyone else.'

'Oh, Garth…'

'She'll be here soon,' he reminded her as he bent his head to kiss her. It was the firm, loving, tender kiss of a man for the woman to whom he has chosen to commit himself and his life, Claudia recognised as she returned it, giving her own female commitment to him.

18

'No. No, I don't believe you. It's…it's not true. It *can't* be true,' Tara protested wildly, shaking her head from side to side in denial of what she had just been told, panic and fear and pain sharpening her voice, lending it a pleading and almost begging quality that tore at Claudia's heart.

Fighting to suppress her own tears, she looked helplessly past Tara to Garth.

'Darling, it *is* true,' Garth affirmed, 'but it doesn't make any difference to us…to how we… You are still our daughter and—'

'*Your* daughter maybe,' Tara pronounced, ashen-faced, 'but not…'

As Claudia made to reach out to her, she stepped back, her whole body rigid with rejection and distrust.

'No. Don't. Don't touch me,' she cried out heatedly. 'I can't bear it. I just can't. How *could* you do such a thing?' she whispered in anguish. '*You*…who's always stressed to me the importance of trust, of being honest. I feel I don't know you. What kind of person *are* you? I don't know you at all. You're not—'

'Tara,' Garth interceded curtly, and immedi-

ately Tara stopped herself from saying what she
had been about to say. Who were they, these people, these strangers, who claimed to love her and
yet who had deliberately and remorselessly deceived her, kept from her truths that she and she
alone had the right to know?

They would tell her the facts, Garth and
Claudia had decided. Later she would need…
want…to ask them questions, but at first they
would simply give her the facts. Facts. A cold,
hard little word that embraced a whole world of
pain and emotion. Facts. How could facts trans-
late into what they were all feeling, what they
were all experiencing? How could facts relate to
twenty-three years of living, sharing, loving?
How could it suddenly turn those years, that loving, into nothing?

'Why have you never told me? Why have you
waited until now? If you *had* loved me, you *would*
have told me. If you *had* loved me—'

'I did love you, do love you,' Claudia protested passionately, desperate to hold her in her
arms, to heal and protect her as she had done so
many, many times in the years of her growing
up.

'No,' Tara shot back swiftly with all the mental
agility and cruelty that Claudia remembered so
vividly from Katriona. 'What you loved was the
idea of having a child…*any* child. That's what *you*
loved. If you had loved *me*, you would've said
something, not waited.'

'Tara, I *know* I should have told you, but please
try to understand. I was afraid.'

'*You* were afraid?' Tara gasped and then laughed bitterly. 'And as for me understanding you, can you understand how I feel? What it feels like to suddenly be told that the people, the *person* you thought closest to you, the *mother* you thought was yours, is really just a stranger. A stranger who picked you up and took you home, leaving your own mother to die in a—'

'Tara!' Garth thundered.

Claudia protested in a sick whisper, 'Tara, that simply isn't true. I—'

'Isn't? You said just now that my mother, my *real* mother,' she emphasised, 'told you to take me. Presumably, she was still alive when she said that, and since you did just that, she must have been alive when you left.'

Claudia bowed her head.

'Your *mother*,' Garth interrupted, stressing the word 'mother' as he looked at Claudia, 'was with Katriona when she died. Your *mother* arranged for her to have a proper burial. Your *mother*, for all the years of our marriage and I suspect even now, has always visited your...Katriona's grave three times a year, once on *her* birthday, once on the anniversary of her death and once on the anniversary of *your* birth.'

There was an infinitesimal pause during which Claudia brought herself to look pleadingly into Tara's eyes and just for a second, a millisecond of time, she thought she saw a softening, a small breach in the angry defence she had thrown up against her, but then it was gone and the wall was back in place as Tara derided bitterly, 'Oh, generous indeed. Where *is* she buried, or aren't I allowed to know?'

Wounded, Claudia closed her eyes, remembering.

It had taken a good deal of persuasion for her to get official permission for Katriona to be buried in the small village graveyard of the place where she had grown up, close to the graves of her parents, but she had managed to do it. She had planted rosemary there for remembrance and harebells to flower in the spring as wild and beautiful as Katriona had once been.

Understandingly, Garth watched his daughter. Her reaction was entirely natural and to be expected. He and Claudia had talked about the very real possibility that in her shock and pain she would initially reject them both.

'I know I *should* have told you before,' Claudia admitted in a low voice. 'You…Garth wanted me to, but I…' She swallowed, then looked directly at Tara. 'You're right, Tara. I *was* being selfish. I *was* afraid of losing you,' she told her simply, 'especially after I found out…after your father and I divorced. You were, after all, *his* child and—'

'You were afraid that if you told me the truth, I'd have wanted to live with him and not you,' Tara suggested. His child! She gave Garth a bitter look of dislike. '*Your* child maybe, but I was hardly fathered deliberately or with love, was I, "Father"?'

'How you were fathered is irrelevant to this discussion,' Garth told her, adding crisply, 'A person would have to be naïve, Tara, to believe that every child is conceived deliberately and in mutual love.'

'It's not irrelevant to me,' Tara informed him stonily, but Garth ignored the look she was giving him.

'What is surely more important,' he offered firmly, 'is that you were a much loved…a much wanted child.'

'By whom?' Tara demanded, her mouth twisting bitterly. 'Not by you, I'll bet. Did she *tell* you she was carrying me? Did she?'

'Claudia wanted you,' Garth overrode her. 'She loved you for yourself long before she knew *I* was your father. She loved you for *yourself*, Tara. Think…ask yourself how many people can say that? How many people know that they were loved and wanted, not because of the parental genes they may or may not have inherited, not because of any parental expectations for them, but simply for themselves.'

'In spite of my genetic make-up rather than because of it, you mean,' Tara sneered. 'I'm sorry, but I'm not convinced,' she announced, gesturing disdainfully towards Claudia, 'she wanted a baby to replace the one she'd lost, the one she knew she'd never have. I conveniently happened to be there. She loved *me* because she *had* to love me…because she had no choice. It was either *me* or nothing.'

Claudia gasped. 'Tara, that isn't true. I loved you the moment I saw you. There was a special bond between us.' She bit her lip. How could she tell this angry, contemptuous young woman who stood looking at her, hating her, rejecting her, just *how* special the bond was that formed between them virtually at first sight. How *could* she explain to her that the moment they had looked at one another, there had been love between them? It was a fact—another one of them—something so much a part of her that she couldn't express or explain it. She had just known when she looked at the infant Tara that she loved her and she had seen in this baby's eyes so full of natural wisdom that Tara had loved her, too. But she knew that it was pointless trying to explain that to Tara now, that Tara simply didn't want to listen…to hear…to know…

'Tell me again about my mother, my real mother,' Tara challenged them fiercely, ignoring Claudia's attempts to deny her accusation and to tell her about the deep emotional bond she felt had been forged between them the very first time that Claudia had held her in her arms.

'We've already explained to you that Katriona, your mother, was one of your mother's clients,' Garth told her quietly.

'One of your clients,' Tara mimicked, turning towards Claudia. The look of scorn on her face made Claudia react instinctively and take a step closer to her, but immediately Tara stepped back from her, stiffening her body, rejecting her.

Helplessly, Claudia exchanged looks with Garth. They had wondered how much they should tell her about her mother's history.

'She will have to know the truth,' Garth had advocated gently.

'But not all at once,' Claudia had pleaded with him.

'Let's wait and see how she reacts,' Garth had advised. 'How much she herself wants to know.'

Claudia had closed her eyes, trembling as he held her.

Tara was, by nature, courageous and determined. She would not shirk from demanding to know all the facts.

'Tara, Katriona was…' Garth began.

But Claudia shook her head, interrupting him to say huskily, 'No…I'll tell her. After all, I knew her better…better than you.'

And slowly she started to describe Katriona to her daughter, dwelling generously on all the things about her that she herself had felt drawn to—her intelligence, her independence, her keen sense of humour.

'You say she left home and came to London. Why?' Tara interrupted Claudia baldly.

'It…it was something that many young people did then,' Claudia explained hesitantly. 'London was the place to be. Katriona was just not the sort of person who… A small, enclosed community was too claustrophobic for her. She…'

Floundering badly, Claudia turned helplessly to Garth. It was one thing agreeing that they had to be totally honest with Tara in answering whatever questions she might ask about Katriona. Actually doing so was another.

Taking a deep breath, Claudia plunged on. 'So far as we could discover, Katriona came to

London having had a…a disagreement with her father. She—'

'She ran away from home, is that what you're saying?' Tara asked her sharply. Claudia swallowed hard, and as she noticed that slight, betraying gesture, Tara's eyes suddenly filled with fresh, angry tears. 'Oh God,' she gulped in a furious, tortured voice. 'I suppose I can guess the rest, can I? How old was she? Seventeen, eighteen…younger?' she flung out, shaking her head and waiting for Claudia to reply before continuing fiercely. 'You don't need to tell me any more. I can guess the rest. It's all so predictable and pathetic, isn't it? So—'

'Katriona was never pathetic,' Claudia interrupted her firmly. 'She—'

'She what? You've said she was one of your clients. Why? Or can I guess. Was it drugs?'

'She had a drug problem, yes,' Claudia agreed quietly. 'But—'

'A drug habit she financed by what? Prostitution?' Tara guessed, firing the question at Claudia.

Claudia's expression gave her away.

'Oh, you don't have to say anything,' Tara told Claudia tersely. 'I can see from your face that I'm right. So my mother was a drug addict *and* a prostitute. And what was my father?' she demanded with bitter contempt as she looked from Claudia to Garth. 'One of *her* clients?'

'No!'

The denial exploded from both Garth and Claudia at the same time.

'No? Is that why you divorced him? Because you discovered that he had a habit? A habit of using prostitutes?' Tara demanded of Claudia. 'Or was my conception some far-sighted social experiment…an innovative method or attempt at surrogacy? Perhaps you paid my mother to inseminate herself with my father's sperm?' she demanded with bitter cynicism. 'No, of course,' she answered her own question, 'that wasn't the way it was, was it? You paid her for the use of her body and she got pregnant. That must have been a shock for you. I'm surprised you didn't try to persuade her to have me aborted—'

'It wasn't like that, Tara,' Claudia interjected desperately. 'You must understand—'

'*I* must understand?' Tara gave a bitter, high-pitched, jarring laugh. 'My God, what kind of people *are* you? One of you, my father, uses a drug addict and a prostitute for sex and the other, my so-called mother, then steals the resultant by-product of that act. I don't know which of you I despise the most.'

'Tara,' Garth told her warningly, 'there's a lot that you don't know, a lot that—'

'So tell me.'

Claudia could see him giving her a quick, questioning look. She nodded her head. This was all so much worse than she had feared and she couldn't help wondering how she would have felt had she been standing in Tara's shoes.

She ached to be able to tell her how guilty she felt, how…how helpless in the face of Tara's justifiable anger and pain, how much she longed to be able to wipe them away, but instead she simply listened while Garth tersely explained the circumstances of Tara's conception, deliberately leaving out the fact that both of them had come to believe that Katriona, out of drug-induced jealousy or spite, had intentionally tried to conceive his child.

For a few seconds after he had finished speaking, the room was completely silent. Then Tara burst into a peal of wild, angry laughter, exclaiming contemptuously, scoffing, 'You really expect me to believe that? Oh, come on.'

'It's the truth,' Claudia told her quietly.

'The truth. What do you know about that? You are a liar and a thief. You had no right to do what you did,' she told Claudia. 'You took me, *stole* me from my dying mother, and then kept from me, *concealed* from me, the truth surrounding my own birth. You didn't just steal from my mother, you stole from me, as well, Claudia. You stole my right to my own past and I shall never, ever forgive you for that.'

Claudia bowed her head. That cold, deliberate 'Claudia' instead of Mum or Ma had hurt her more than anything else Tara had said. But she deserved to be hurt, didn't she? After all, Tara was being hurt. Tara was hurting. Tara was…

'I'm going now,' Tara informed them, 'and I *never* want to see *either* of you again. Not ever.'

As Claudia made a small involuntary protest, Garth took hold of her as though to physically restrain her from going to Tara, shaking his head as

Tara snatched up her bag and ran towards the door.

'Garth, we can't let her go like that,' Claudia protested miserably as they heard Tara opening the door and slamming it hard behind her. 'She needs—'

'She needs time on her own to come to terms with what we've told her,' Garth interrupted.

'None of this should have happened,' Claudia told him weepily, 'and it's all my fault that it has. You were right. I *should* have told her years ago when she was young enough to listen and accept. Oh, Garth, what have I done?'

'What you've done is be her mother,' Garth told her softly. 'The best mother any child could ever have, and ultimately Tara is going to recognise that.'

'Is she?' Claudia's mouth trembled. 'Right now, so far as she's concerned, Katriona is her mother and I'm just someone who stole her and…' She stopped speaking, her emotions overwhelming her, and she started to cry.

'Hush, hush, it's all right,' Garth comforted her tenderly. 'As you say, right now, Tara *is* angry—with *both* of us—but she's your daughter, our daughter, Clo and—'

'I can't forget the look on her face when she asked us about Katriona. Should we have told her so much, Garth? Couldn't we have…?'

'Couldn't we have what? Lied to her some more, pretended that Katriona wasn't what she was?'

'They weren't what she was,' Claudia protested. 'Drugs and prostitution were what she *did*…what she *was* was a young, vulnerable girl who felt rejected and unloved by her father. Oh, Garth. Garth, I'm so afraid for Tara. Where will she go…what will she…?'

'Tara isn't Katriona, Clo,' Garth reminded her. 'She's older for one thing, and for another…Tara knows that she is loved and wanted. She's also got Ryland, don't forget. Just give her time.'

'Perhaps we ought to ring Ryland and warn him,' Claudia suggested anxiously.

Garth frowned. 'No…I think we should let her tell him herself.'

'Garth, what if she never comes back, if she…?'

'She will,' Garth reassured her. 'Once she's had time to calm down and assess the situation, Tara will realise how much we love her.'

After she had left her father's apartment, Tara headed blindly and instinctively for her own flat and Ryland.

Despite the fact that it was a relatively warm day, she was literally shivering with shock and reaction, her mind, her emotions, still barely able to take in what she had just learned. It was impossible for her to analyse or assess her feelings, impossible almost for her to even begin to comprehend the enormity of what she had been told.

Impossible even to imagine that someone as close to her as her mother—no, *Claudia*—could have managed to keep something so important a secret from her for so long.

While she had been growing up, all those times when she cherished the closeness, the bond that she believed existed between them, no doubt Claudia had secretly been remembering that she was not really *her* child; that she was doing the charitable, the right thing, in giving a home…respectability to her husband's bastard baby…the baby *he* had fathered on one of life's losers, a junkie and a prostitute, a woman who sold her body to men for…

'No!' Almost screaming the word as the tears poured down her face, Tara clenched her fists, oblivious to the shocked and curious stares of other pedestrians.

All those years Claudia had claimed, pretended, to love her. How *could* she have loved her? Tara closed her eyes in pain. That was what hurt her the worst. Knowing that Claudia could not possibly have loved her in the way she had always believed. How could she? She wasn't her child.

'I loved you the moment I saw you,' Claudia had claimed. But of course, Tara knew better than to believe her.

'There was a special bond between us.'

What special bond? The fact that Garth, her husband, was her father? Some bond. And her mother, her real mother, how had she felt about the fact that she was pregnant? Had she felt anything at all or had the baby simply been an unwanted inconvenience?

'She wanted me to take you,' Claudia had said.

'She knew she was dying,' she had added gently. 'She wanted you to be safe, to be loved.'

Had she? Tara doubted it. How could she believe anything that Claudia and Garth told her now after what they had done, the way they had concealed the truth from her?

All those years and she had never guessed, never suspected. All those years when they had known and she had not. She hated them, despised them, and she never wanted to see them again. The sooner she and Ryland left for America, the happier she would be. There she could have a fresh start, put the past...

'Ry...Ry...' She was crying his name as she unlocked the door and hurried into the flat.

The smell of his shower gel still hung tantalisingly in the air. Eagerly, Tara hurried through the empty sitting room and into the bedroom. She came to an abrupt halt as it slowly began to dawn on her that the flat was empty.

Blinking back her tears, she returned dejectedly to the sitting room, then frowned when she saw the note he had left her. Her hand was trembling as she picked it up and started to read it. By the time she had put it down, her face was ashen, fresh tears welling up in her eyes.

Ryland wasn't here. He had gone...summoned home by his father.

He had left her a number to ring. Frantically, she started to dial it, then stopped and replaced the receiver.

Ryland had been summoned home by his family and that family included his aunt. Everything that Ryland had said to her about his aunt abruptly came back to her, including his own rueful admission that she had very strong views on the type of woman she wanted him to marry.

Numbly, she sat down. How would she feel when she discovered the truth about Ryland's prospective bride? How would his mother, his parents, feel? Did Tara really need to ask herself? Painfully, she swallowed the hard lump threatening to close her throat. She couldn't put Ryland in a position where he was forced to choose between them. She loved him too much for that, knew too well that if she allowed him to choose her, there would be a part of him that would always feel guilt at having to let his family down and she didn't want their marriage to be marred by guilt or regrets. She wanted it to be whole and healthy, perfect, but how could it be like that now? How could anything *ever* be the same again?

Her mother, a prostitute and a drug addict.

Helplessly, Tara started to rock herself to and fro, her arms hugging round her knees in a timeless gesture of self-comfort. But there was no escape from what she had learned as she mentally relived the recent meeting with her parents.

'Since you didn't see fit to tell me before, why have you decided to tell me now?' she had challenged Claudia, demanding bitterly at one point, 'Did you just suddenly decide you were bored with playing the role of loving mother, wanted a change, a different way of life? You wanted me out of your life, is that it?' she had accused wildly, watching as Claudia's eyes filled with tears.

Claudia had turned helplessly towards Garth before saying brokenly, 'I…I was afraid that there might be a problem with Ryland's aunt, that she might somehow discover the truth. Your visa—when it didn't come through immediately, I didn't want…I wanted you to be prepared.'

'It didn't come through because the computers were causing problems…not because they had discovered your lies,' she had told her coldly.

A part of her wished that they had left her in ignorance, that they had kept their secrets to themselves. But why should she expect Claudia to consider *her* feelings? It wasn't as though she really meant anything to her. She wasn't really *her* child…her daughter.

Clambering to her feet, Tara picked up the note Ryland had left her with his number in Boston and, before she could give in to the temptation to redial it, she tore the paper into pieces and threw it into the waste-paper basket.

She couldn't stay here. Not now. She didn't have the right. She wasn't the person to whom this flat had been home any more. She was someone different, a stranger who, as yet, she didn't even really know. The child of a stranger. She felt she had no home, no past, no future, no real identity.

Even the belongings around her, the clothes in the wardrobe, suddenly seemed alien to her. She was completely alone now. She had nothing…no one. Shaking her head to banish the tears she could feel threatening to flood her eyes, she stumbled towards the door of the flat. She had no clear idea of what she intended to do, only that everything that comprised what she had thought of as her life had suddenly been taken from her. Her belief in herself as a person had proved to be a fiction, a falsehood, a sham. She was not and never had been the person she had always believed. She was...nothing.

With her hand on the door handle, she stopped and turned around. Walking back towards the telephone, she pulled from her finger the ring Ryland had given her shortly after he had declared his love.

A single tear splashed down, but Tara didn't notice. With the removal of Ryland's ring, she was distancing herself from the Tara she had previously been. She was no longer that person. How could she be? And how could Ryland or anyone else, including herself, love or want the Tara she had become? The Tara who carried in her genes the blood of a stranger. What had she been like, her mother, the mother who had taken money from men in exchange for the use of her body?

Quickly, before she could change her mind, Tara headed back to the door, not daring to turn round and look at what she was leaving behind just in case she weakened and changed her mind.

'Have you thought any more about what I said?'

Estelle frowned as she looked into Blade's

sleep-softened face. He had turned up late the previous evening high on drugs, insisting on being let in and, for once, satisfying his sexual appetite had not been the focus of all his attention.

He had given her some garbled tale about being in trouble with 'the big man' as he called him, and Estelle's heart had sunk as she listened to him. That he both used and dealt in drugs was no secret to her. She had used them with him herself—harmless recreational stuff that had given an added edge to their sex. She could see nothing wrong in it just so long as you knew what you were doing—and what you were taking—but she had noticed recently that Blade was becoming increasingly involved in the drug scene.

Now he was pushing her again, demanding to know if she had found another girl yet that they could have sex with—someone classy enough to command a high price from the punters once he and she had trained and taught her.

'Straight three-in-a-bed stuff isn't what the kinds of guys I'm talking about are interested in,' he had told her when they had just discussed the subject. 'They've done all that. No, they want something special, something really hot.'

'Like what?' Estelle had asked him, intrigued but also, she surprised herself, irritated at the same time.

There were occasions, increasingly lately, when she felt not just irritated and, yes, bored by Blade's obsession with sex, but also almost actively repulsed by it—but she had learned to quickly dismiss such thoughts. They were too dangerous, too frightening. She had to stay loyal to Blade because without him she had nothing—*was* nothing!

'Oh, you know,' he had answered her. 'They want something…someone…exciting, original. Someone discreet and fresh. They don't live in this country and they want to take home with them some video souvenirs to remind them. They're willing to pay very well, very well indeed, but they're beginning to get impatient. You must know someone we could use. They don't want the usual stuff you can buy on the street. They don't want some jaded, overused hooker who's just going through the motions.'

'Well, if it's a virgin they're looking for…' she had begun dismissively, but he had shaken his head.

'No, not that. They want someone who understands, enjoys pain. You understand and enjoy pain, don't you?' he had whispered to her, his libido returning as the effect of the drugs he had taken started to wear off. '*You* understand and enjoy it very, very much.'

He had laughed as she started to evade him, playing the game she had played with him so many times before, her senses responding as they always did to the sharp thrill of fear that went through her as he overpowered her.

With Blade there was always this delicious edge of not quite being sure how far he would take things, how much he would frighten and hurt her, how much she dare trust him.

'You've been having someone else,' he had

told her once he secured her wrists to the bed head.

'No,' she had denied, flinching as he knelt astride her and tugged painfully on her hair before biting sharply into her breast.

'Don't lie to me,' he had warned her. 'I can smell him…taste him on your body. What did he do to you? Did he do this?'

She had cried out sharply as he tugged painfully on her nipple, using his teeth on the gold ring he had given her as a birthday present— along with the visit to the body piercer.

'What we need is someone new and… adventurous,' he had reminded her, continuing to arouse and tease her body. 'These men are close friends of the big man and they've expressed an interest in seeing an extra-special performance,' he added as he tugged sharply on her nipple ring.

'It won't be easy finding someone for that,' she warned him.

'You'll have to,' he insisted. 'These men are major league players and they're beginning to get impatient. There's no way I can disappoint them. Do you understand what I'm saying?'

She had understood all right. There had been an occasion in the past when she hadn't been able to supply him with what he wanted. She hadn't seen him for almost ten weeks. She shivered now, remembering how much she had missed him. How much she had ached for him. No other man ever came anywhere near as close to satisfying her sexually in the way that he could. No other man would.

'I'll do my best,' she promised him now. Her body ached all over from their sex session and the last thing she felt like was going to work. But it was her work that provided her with the opportunity to meet the kinds of men who were prepared to pay generously for the extracurricular activities she provided, and besides, it gave her a fierce *frisson* of pleasure to relate to Blade just what they had done to her, these men she had found for herself rather than men he had sent to her. After all, *she* didn't get paid for the ones she serviced for him and the money was extremely important to her, almost as important as the sex.

'Make sure you do,' he ordered, adding warningly, 'and remember, these guys want something with class, the kind of woman who looks and acts expensive. They won't be satisfied with some cheap tart.'

Someone classy and expensive—and where the hell was she supposed to find someone like that who'd be willing to do what his clients wanted? In the past, when she had found girls for him, she had done so by scouring the clubs where she had known she would find the kind of girl he was looking for. What Blade was demanding that she provide now was a completely different ball game and one she wasn't quite sure she wanted to get into.

Grimly, she finished getting ready for work.

As she removed her rings from her sore and swollen nipples, she flinched. Blade had been rough this time, even for him. She was going to set up an appointment later on this afternoon with one of the company's clients. If she didn't wear a bra, he would be able to see her swollen nipples quite clearly through the silk shirt she was planning to wear. She pursed her lips. He was only relatively small fry and she wasn't sure she wanted to waste her time dangling any bait in front of him. On the other hand, she still had the monthly payments to meet on her BMW, and Blade had probably emptied her purse of all her cash before he left.

She could tantalise him a bit without committing herself. It never did any harm to keep a bit of something in reserve. Soon it would be time for her to start looking around for a new job. She had suspected recently that Garth was on to her and he wasn't a man who would take too kindly to her using his business and his clients in the way she had been doing.

Pity, really. Had he been a different type, she could have quite enjoyed adding him to her client list and even offering him a specially reduced rate, but she had realised within weeks of joining the partnership that he was one man who was not open to the kind of sex she put on offer although that didn't stop her hoping she might find a way to change his mind.

He probably never does it any other way but the missionary position, she had decided witheringly when he had brushed off her first discreet attempt to interest him. But deep down inside that vital female part of her, she had known that while Garth might not be interested in the kind of sado-masochistic sex that Blade had taught her to enjoy, he was very definitely a man who knew how to arouse and satisfy a woman, albeit with rather more tender and gentler methods than she was accustomed to. Her father had been on the phone again but she had no intention of ringing him back. It pleased her to think of how he would feel—how he would react—if he discovered how she really lived. That would be something for him to tell his precious Rebecca about. Just for a second, her eyes gleamed with pleasure at the thought of procuring her for Blade, but she quickly dismissed the idea as unworkable. A pity, she would have loved to have seen her father's face if she had been able to involve her.

It was fortunate that the other girl she shared her small office with was away on leave, Tara acknowledged shakily as she started to open the drawers in her desk and remove her personal belongings. Beside her computer was the framed photograph she had had enlarged from the Christmas before last, showing her with her mother and both sets of grandparents. Her fingers trembled betrayingly as she reached for it, turning it face down as she rammed it into the nearly empty drawer and slammed it shut. It had no place in her new life. How could it?

Outside her half-open office door, it seemed

strange to see the normal activity of the office go on around her despite the traumatic change that had taken place in *her* life. There was no sign of her father. No doubt he was still with *her*... Claudia.

How ironic that after all the time she had spent, or rather, wasted, believing that her parents ought to be together, now that they quite obviously were, it meant so little to her.

As she opened another drawer, quick, helpless tears filled her eyes and splashed down onto the desk.

Estelle paused as she walked past the open door and saw Tara bent over her desk, tears running down her cheeks. Curious, she pushed it open even farther and walked into the office. After firmly closing it behind her, she went up to Tara and placed her hand comfortingly and restrainingly on her arm, asking her, 'Tara, what is it? What's wrong?'

The shock of realising that her distress had been witnessed by someone else robbed Tara of the ability to do anything other than shake her head in silent misery as the tears kept filling her eyes.

Using Tara's silence and obvious loss of composure to seize control of the situation, Estelle put her arms around her, holding her close, firmly ignoring all Tara's attempts to break free of her 'comforting' embrace. All her instincts told her that she might just have found the answer to her problems.

'Oh, you poor thing,' she murmured mock-tenderly, her sharp eyes quickly noting the fact that Tara wasn't wearing her customary ring.

Personally, had she been Tara, she would have insisted on being given something far more expensive and show-offable than the tiny heart-shaped diamond Tara had seemed so happy to wear.

'Come on, you have a good cry. Men! They're all the same.' As she had anticipated, this female empathising resulted in Tara's body heaving with fresh sobs.

Estelle smiled triumphantly to herself. It worked every time. Show a vulnerable over-emotional sister a bit of sympathy, and before you knew where you were, you had bonded for life. From the evidence in front of her, though, Tara was taking things a bit too far. Being reduced to tears by the loss of a man was one thing; being reduced to clearing out your office desk was quite another. To Estelle's experienced eye, Tara's office bore all the hallmarks of a woman who was on the point of running away.

Tara's next words confirmed her thoughts as she heard her hiccuping, 'Please let me go. I've got to get away...I've—'

'Of course you have,' Estelle soothed, her mind working quickly. 'Here, let me help you with all of this.'

Before Tara could either stop her or refuse, she had started to neatly stack all the small personal possessions Tara had removed from her desk.

'Look, let me help you out with these,' she suggested. 'You can't carry them all yourself.'

Before Tara could protest, she was opening the office door, her arms piled high with Tara's belongings as she martialled her protectively in front of her, keeping her from any close inspection by anyone in the outer office as she shepherded her towards the lift.

Tara's car was parked in the underground car park and listlessly she allowed Estelle to take the keys from her and open the boot.

'Look, where is it you were planning to go?' Estelle asked her, adding, when Tara made no response, 'I can't let you drive anywhere in this state. It would be on my conscience for ever. Look, I've got an idea. I'm due to break for lunch, so why don't we go somewhere quiet and…?'

Immediately, Tara shook her head. She and Estelle had never been particularly close; there had always been something about the other girl that made Tara feel slightly repelled by her, an air of sexuality and knowingness that, without understanding why, Tara had always found offputting. There had been rumours in the office about Estelle's supposedly slightly unorthodox sex life, but Tara had always firmly dismissed as envy and office gossip any suggestions she had heard that Estelle used her undoubted sex appeal to boost her more conventionally earned income.

'I'm not taking no for an answer,' Estelle told her firmly. 'There's no way I'm letting you go *anywhere* like this. Your father…'

Tara flinched, the colour fading from her face. The last thing she wanted was for any kind…any kind of contact at all with Garth.

'Yes...all right...I'll come with you,' she agreed.

When she saw the slightly nervous and very betraying look Tara gave over her shoulder, Estelle smiled cynically to herself before urging Tara into the passenger seat of her car, telling her determinedly, 'I'll drive. It'll be safer that way.'

Tara, who had been assuming that they would walk to wherever it was they were going to have lunch, simply couldn't find the energy to argue with her. She felt totally overwhelmed by the other girl's tenacity. All she really wanted to do was to get in her car and drive and keep on driving until she found somewhere no one knew her and where she knew no one, somewhere where she could start afresh, where she could be herself. The last thing she wanted or needed right now was some tedious lunch with a woman she barely knew, but to tell Estelle so would take too much effort, use more strength than she had left. It was easier, simpler, to just go along with her.

Leaning her head back, Tara closed her eyes and let Estelle manoeuvre her car out of its parking space.

As she watched Tara's eyes close, an idea was beginning to form inside Estelle's brain, an idea so challenging and dangerous that to think of it made her shudder deliciously inside with a mixture of fear and excitement.

'They want someone with class...style...' Blade had told her, and Tara had both of those and much, much more. Oh, she couldn't wait to see her face as she lay there spread-eagled, awaiting the entrance of her torturer. She wouldn't cry or scream, not at first, but that would only heighten the delicious anticipatory sexual pleasure of the onlookers who were there to watch her and often to pleasure themselves in orgiastic release at seeing her vulnerable naked body being subjected to the placement of the pretty but oh, so deceptive gold rings that the piercer would decorate her naked body with.

Those delicate gold rings weren't just there for ornament, not even for the teasing play of a lover; they could be used as a means of constraint and imprisonment threaded through with fine thin wires. Estelle started to smile and then to laugh. She had found Blade exactly what he had asked her for and more besides. She couldn't *wait* to see his face when he realised what she had brought him. It wasn't going to be easy, of course, but there were always drugs that could be used to soften and weaken a person's resistance and who knew better where to get them than Blade.

They were out of the car park now, Tara's eyes still closed. Estelle thought quickly. If she could pump her with enough to drink at lunch-time, it shouldn't be too much of a problem to get her to agree to go back to *her* flat, and once there…

To take her straight there now as she was tempted to do could be a bit tricky, though. No. Lunch first, and then…

In the seat beside her, Tara was too absorbed in her pain to pay much attention to what was going on around her.

Ryland... What would he think, what would he do when he came back and found her gone? He would contact her parents, of course, and then they would tell him. She swallowed hard. What would they tell him? That she wasn't fit to be his wife...to be the mother of his children...that she...

A hot tear ran down her face, followed by another.

Seeing these signs of her grief, Estelle gleefully laughed inwardly to herself. Stupid bitch. Well, she'd soon learn what real pain was all about. Very soon, no doubt, if Blade had anything to do with it. Some people might consider him to be warped but Estelle didn't. She knew what motivated and drove him. Pain. Pleasure. Call it what you would, it was the only sure thing in life. Far more sure and reliable than a lover's promises or a parent's—especially a parent's!

19

—▸◂—

His father was the first person Ryland saw as he came through the arrivals gate and he hurried to greet his son, embracing him fiercely when he reached him.

His father, Ryland recognised with a sudden sharp stab of concern, had aged in his absence. He looked greyer, shorter somehow, his body, his whole stance, now that of an older man. His face anxious and furrowed, he took Ryland by the arm and hurried him towards the exit.

'Pops, what is it, what's happened?' Ryland demanded.

Shaking his head, Jed advised him, 'Wait until we're in the car, son.'

The freeway was already busy with traffic as they pulled onto it, his father's concentration apparently given to his driving, leaving Ryland edgily irritated.

'Look, Dad…' he began. His body was starting to suffer the effects of the long journey, that and the shock of being summoned home so dramatically.

'I'm sorry, son,' Jed apologised, recognising his growing impatience, 'it's just…well, it's all been such a…such a shock.'

'What's been a shock?' Ryland demanded to know.

'There's been an accident on the island…a fire. By the time the fire department got out there—'

'A fire, but what…how…?'

His father shook his head. 'When we get home,' he replied sombrely.

'But who, who was there? Are they…?' Ryland stopped and swallowed, still unable to take in fully what his father was saying.

The small island off the New England coast that had come into the family with his aunt on her marriage to his uncle had been the scene of many happy family holidays for him while he was growing up. Even after her husband's death off its coast in heavy seas in his racing yacht, his aunt still continued to visit the island.

There was a tradition that the whole family spent Labour Day there, and this year he had hoped that he and Tara… He swallowed again.

'Margot was there…and…and Lloyd,' his father told him gruffly, going silent for a moment before adding quietly, 'and your aunt Martha was there, as well. It was the housekeeper's day off so at least Esme…'

'And Margot, Lloyd *and* Aunt Martha…?' Ryland started to question him but the words were sticking in his throat as though deep down inside he already knew the answer.

Jed's hands tightened on the wheel, then he told him thickly, 'All gone. The fire chief says it's more than likely that the smoke—'

'The smoke? But surely they *must* have known, had *some* warning…had time to get out?'

'I don't know, son. There is evidence that… The fire department and the police are still investigating. It seems likely that the fire started late at night and if they were all asleep…'

'I can't believe it,' Ryland whispered, his voice cracking. 'I just can't…'

'I know, son. I know,' his father consoled him. 'Let's wait until we get home to talk about it properly. Right now…'

'It's okay, Dad, I understand,' Ryland told him.

They were off the freeway now, taking the familiar road that led to the small New England town where Ryland had grown up. It seemed so ironic now that while he had been living in London, he had believed that the next time he made this trip it would have been with Tara at his side, his mood one of jubilation and excitement at the thought of introducing her to his family as his wife-to-be. He had pictured the smiling, happy faces of his parents, his siblings; he had visualised even his aunt's stern stiffness melting beneath the warmth of Tara's natural charm and loving nature. He had, he realised now, very much wanted his aunt to meet Tara and to see in her eyes the belief, the *conviction* that in Tara's hands and in the hands of the children she would give him, the future of the business and, more important by far, the future of the *family* would be safe.

Tara might not be happy when she knew

about the constraints that so much money would place upon her children but she had, beneath her outer softness, Ryland realised, a certain steely strength that was a combination of all of her mother's and her father's best characteristics, and he knew she would be steadfastly loyal, not just to him and their love, but to the concept believed wholeheartedly by his aunt that great wealth brought with it a responsibility to use such wealth wisely and for the benefit of mankind.

Tara. God, but he needed her desperately beside him right now. He needed her strength, her warmth, her compassion, but most of all he needed her love.

It was that time of the year when summer was beginning to end but fall had not yet properly begun, the green leaves of the trees listless and tired-looking, worn out, rather like his father, he acknowledged as he took a sideways glance at the older man.

The New England countryside never looked its best at this time of the year, Ryland considered. In these last days of summer, it always had an air of weary waiting and dullness before the burst of colour as the leaves turned in the fall. The pretty clapboard New England house that his great-great-grandfather had built for his bride and set in its own grounds overlooking the lake just outside the town looked as it always did around now, he noticed as his father swung the car into the drive and the house came into view—in need of a coat of paint. Painting it was something of a family tradition, a chore his father always carried out himself and one that ever since he could remember, Ryland had always got roped into helping him out with.

As a boy, his task was simply to stand at the bottom of the ladder, but the last summer he had spent at home, he had been the one to clean and paint the gutters while his father painted the lower portion. It struck him as he studied the house that his progression from the bottom of the ladder to the top was very much in line with the progression his aunt had been taking him through *vis-à-vis* his role in the business, but of course his aunt was now no longer around to guide and support him. Soberly, he focused on the house.

Even before his parents and the girls had moved into the family home—in the days when first his maternal grandparents and then after his grandmother's death when his grandfather had lived here alone—his father had still spent the last weeks of every summer repainting its large, rambling exterior.

It was a comfortable family house, if perhaps a little on the large side for modern-day living, but Ryland had already visualised, lying in bed beside Tara in her cramped London flat, the two of them buying a similar type of property close by that of his parents. He, too, would spend the last days of summer painting it with the help of his and Tara's sons and daughters—Tara would insist on that. Briefly, he smiled—just thinking about her warmed his heart and was almost as comforting as though he had been able to reach out and take hold of her hand.

His aunt had a large, grand house in Boston's Back Bay, but he knew even before they discussed it, that Tara, like him, would prefer the quieter environment of the New England town in which he had been brought up.

As his father stopped the car, Ryland could see his mother standing outside the house waiting for them, his sisters by her side, startlingly grown up now even though it was only just over twelve months since he had last seen them, their expressions betraying the sense of shock and disbelief he himself was experiencing.

'Oh, Ry, son, I'm so sorry you've had to come home to this,' his mother told him as she hugged him tightly. 'I hope your Tara will understand and forgive us for calling you home like this.'

Ryland hugged her back. His mother didn't need to explain to him that when his family met Tara, she didn't want that meeting to be overshadowed by the tragedy they were now having to face.

'Fortunately, your grandfather is away visiting an old friend,' his mother told him as he glanced automatically towards the path that led to the smaller adjacent house where his maternal grandfather lived. 'He thought a lot of Martha. They used to argue politics together and...' His mother's voice trailed away.

'Come on, let's get inside. Police Chief Amory has been on the telephone, Jed,' she told Ryland's father as the whole family headed for the house, arms wrapped comfortingly around one another in instinctive support. 'I told him that you'd gone to pick Ry up from the airport and that you'd call him back just as soon as you could. Why don't you take Ry into your study and tell him what's been happening while I go make both of you some hot coffee?'

Ryland's father waited until his mother had brought them both a large pot of coffee and quietly closed the door behind her before beginning to talk.

'I didn't want to start discussing this in the car, Ry, but it seems like the fire that killed... According to the evidence that's already been examined, it seems like it must have been started deliberately.'

'Deliberately?' Ryland stared at his father. 'Are you trying to say that this was the work of an arsonist...someone who...? But why...and how the hell did they get on the island in the first place?' Tiredly, Ryland ran his fingers through his hair. 'I guess because of her wealth, Aunt Martha could have been a target for... I know there was a time when Margot was a baby that kidnap threats were made against her.'

'This didn't have anything to do with Martha's wealth, Ry,' his father countered quietly. 'It's...'

Ryland waited as his father stopped speaking to pour them both a cup of coffee. His hand shook, Ryland noticed, and beneath his healthy tan his skin had a pinched grey tinge of shock and grief.

'It looks very much as though the fire was started by...by Margot.'

'Margot!' Ryland almost dropped the cup of coffee his father was handing him. 'But that's *impossible!*'

'It's no secret in the family how Margot felt about Lloyd,' his father started to explain painfully. 'Personally, I can't condone what...the relationship they shared, but I...I can't totally condemn them for it, either. I just thank God that I've never been in that position. I've loved your mother from the moment I set eyes on her. I know it was the same for your uncle and Martha. I guess as a family we're just kinda made that way.'

Ryland said nothing. Now was not the time to tell his father how instantly and completely he had fallen in love with Tara; that kind of father-and-son bonding and sharing was not something he wanted to be overshadowed by the horror of the black tragedy his father was beginning to reveal to him.

'How do any of us know how we would have reacted had we, like Margot, fallen in love with someone too close to us in blood? I guess we all like to think that we'd have seen the danger signs in time and removed ourselves from the situation, turned aside from it. Margot...' He paused and shook his head. 'Margot made Lloyd the centre and the focus of her whole life. He *was* her whole life.'

Ryland frowned. His father wasn't telling him anything he didn't know already.

'Lloyd felt the same way about her,' he reminded his father. 'Otherwise he wouldn't—'

'Lloyd loved her, yes,' his father hastened to agree. 'But his feelings were never as intense, as compulsive if you like, as Margot's, and I suspect that in many ways he continued with the relationship because he was afraid of what Margot might do if he didn't... I don't actually *know* that that was the case,' he stressed. 'I'm simply saying that with hindsight... Well, after it had been confirmed that Lloyd had perished in the fire with Margot and Martha, I got in touch with our UCLA office.' He stopped and shook his head.

'A couple of hours later, we had a telephone call from a...a college professor whose book Lloyd had been going to publish. She asked if she could fly down to see us.' He paused again and poured himself a second cup of coffee, then offered Ryland another one. Ryland shook his head.

'From what she had to tell us,' his father continued after taking a sip, 'it seems that she and Lloyd had become very close...close enough for them to be talking about having a future together. He'd told her about Margot, and it seems he'd also told her that he was going to tell Margot that...that the physical side of his relationship with her had to end.

'Lloyd and Jamie Friedland had only known one another a matter of weeks, from what Jamie told us—and I have no reason to doubt her. She isn't a girl but a very mature and intelligent woman—they both felt strongly enough about one another to believe… She told us that Lloyd had said he was in love with her, and I've no reason to suspect that that wasn't the truth.

'She also said he'd told her that he owed it to Margot and everything they'd been to one another to tell her what had happened and to spend a little time with her, helping her to come to terms with the change he wanted to make in their relationship.

'She did say that Lloyd had confessed to her that his feelings for Margot had changed over the years and that while he still loved her very much as his cousin, he no longer felt the same physical passion for her that she still felt for him.

'Additionally, according to Jamie, Margot had been deluging Lloyd with pleading phone calls begging him to return to the island and demanding to know what or who was delaying him. She also said that some of the calls had ended acrimoniously and that Margot had, on more than one occasion, threatened to take her own life if Lloyd did not return.

'She told me that she had begged Lloyd to be very careful about what he said to Margot and that she had even suggested he try to persuade her to see a trained counsellor.

'None of us is ever going to know exactly what happened or what Lloyd did or did not say to Margot. All we *do* know from the evidence that's been found is that someone, more than likely Margot herself, deliberately started the fire.

'From the forensic evidence and…and the autopsies, it's also pretty clear that both Margot and Lloyd had been drinking and that they were very heavily drugged with barbiturates. Margot had a prescription for sleeping pills. The police thought at first that their deaths might have been a mutual suicide pact—given the nature of their relationship that certainly could have been a…a possibility. I guess people had an inkling about what was going on between the pair of them and I guess, too, that out of sympathy, folks kinda turned a bit of a blind eye to it. Your aunt Martha was very well thought of in the area. She's done a lot of good there.

'The chief of police told me that when they interviewed her housekeeper, Esme, they had to as good as tell her that they knew about the relationship between Lloyd and Margot before she would open up to them about it.

'My reckoning is that knowing Lloyd was about to leave her, Margot spiked both their drinks with the sleeping pills, having previously gathered together everything she needed to start the fire.'

'But Aunt Martha…surely Margot didn't…?'

'I don't know, son,' his father told him sorrowfully, shaking his head. 'None of us will ever know. According to Esme, she had left a cold supper ready for Margot and Lloyd, who had gone out for a walk. Lloyd had arrived on the island only that morning and Esme told the police that he seemed on edge and anxious. Margot had driven down to the harbour to pick him up, but she said that when they came back to the house there was a lot of tension between them.

'It was Esme's day off and she was just about to leave the house—Lloyd and Margot had already set out for their walk—when the phone rang. When she took the call, it was Martha announcing that she had decided to come out to the island a couple of days ahead of the weekend but that Esme was to go ahead and take her time off. She told Esme to drive the Jeep down to the harbour and leave the keys in it for her, which was exactly what Esme did.'

'So Margot might not necessarily have known that her mother was in the house?'

'Possibly not. We know that she and Lloyd ate the supper Esme had prepared for them. Presumably, Lloyd had told her about Jamie and his plans for the future during their walk. Whether that was when Margot decided to do what she did, or whether she made that decision later, no one will ever know.

'All we do know is that at some stage she took a large can of kerosene from the generator room into her room. She emptied her closet and, we think, soaked her clothes and the room with the kerosene.

'We know that at some point she must have gone with Lloyd to his room, which is where they drank the barbiturate-laced wine. Perhaps she made a last-ditch attempt to persuade him to change his mind. Anyway, while they were there, Martha must have arrived but went straight to her own room without letting them know she was there.

'Having failed to convince Lloyd to change his

mind—and according to the police report, both Lloyd and Margot must have been feeling the effects of the wine and the barbiturates by that time—Margot left Lloyd to make her way back to her own bedroom. Once there...' He stopped and bowed his head. 'The police doctor said it would have been over very quickly. The smoke alone...'

'Oh, my God,' Ryland breathed, expelling the words on a long sigh. 'It doesn't bear thinking about. Do you think Margot actually knew what she was doing or...?'

'Who knows? She wasn't always easy to understand. It was as if there was a part of her nature that had just swung that little bit too far over the edge, made her just intense enough to be dangerous. I always felt very sorry for her, but I have to confess I felt more sorry for your aunt Martha.

'I'll never forget the look on her face when Margot told her that she'd never have children, that she'd been sterilized. We were all there. It was one Labour Day weekend and you kids were down on the beach. After Margot had run out in tears, Lloyd went after her to comfort her. Your mother and I were alone with Martha.

'"What have I done?"' she asked us. '"*Where* have I failed?" We tried to tell her that she wasn't to blame...that Margot was just...Margot.'

There was a long silence while the two men looked at one another.

'He's yet to confirm it officially to me, but from what the chief of police has told me privately— and as nothing can be proved, since none of us knows exactly what was in Margot's mind, whether she actually intended to kill herself and Lloyd or whether, in fact, she even knew consciously what she was setting in motion— Margot's death will be recorded as a suicide and Lloyd's and Martha's deaths as accidental.

'It was always your aunt Martha's wish that she be interred in the family crypt in Boston to be with your uncle.'

'And Lloyd and Margot?'

His father shook his head. 'Perhaps the kindest and best thing we could do would be to arrange for them to be buried with Aunt Martha—it is after all a *family* crypt and that way at least they could be together.'

'In death if not in life,' Ryland said quietly.

'Yes, your mother said the very same thing,' his father returned, then clearing his throat, he went on, 'I'm not sure yet how long it will be before we can go ahead and make the necessary arrangements. I've already been in touch with Martha's attorney. There'll be a formal reading of the will, but as you already know, you *are* Martha's heir. There are various charitable donations and gifts, of course, but as far as the bulk of her own private fortune is concerned and the shares she inherited from your uncle in the business, they go directly to you.'

'The girls?' Ryland began thinking of his sisters, but his father immediately hastened to explain.

'The girls will receive substantial bequests to be held in trust for them, but I'm afraid that the main burden of your aunt's assets and wealth falls on your shoulders, Ryland.' Placing a consoling arm around his son, he tried to comfort him. 'At least you'll have your Tara to share it with you.'

Ryland gave his father a bleak look.

'What is it?' his father asked in concern.

'Tara doesn't know yet, about…about the money. I…haven't told her. I…was going to but I was just waiting…' he began as he saw the worry in his father's eyes. 'I should have told her, I know,' he admitted. 'I guess I didn't want to risk spoiling things between us. She won't like it, Dad. Not for herself, but for our kids. She'll—'

'She'll like it even less that you haven't been up front with her,' his father warned him quietly.

'I know,' Ryland agreed sombrely.

It was too late now to regret that he hadn't found—*made*—the opportunity to discuss what lay in the future for him and Tara, the future that was now the present. He closed his eyes, flexing his tense shoulders.

He could almost feel the heavy weight of his aunt's millions pressing down on them already.

'I should have told her,' he admitted to his father. 'But I guess I was afraid of putting her off. I thought I'd have time to prepare her. I told myself there were years yet before Aunt Martha… Hell,' he swore under his breath as the full reality of what his aunt's death meant began to hit him. 'I *can't* tell her over the phone, and the business—'

'Yes, I was just about to come to that,' his father agreed. 'I hate to put more pressure on you, son, but right now we do need you here. The company's attorney needs to see you as well as your aunt's. I've set up meetings for tomorrow in Boston. And a formal company announcement will have to be made to the effect that you'll be taking over from your aunt.'

As his father continued to talk about the problems his aunt's death was causing in the day-to-day running of the company, Ryland felt his attention and his thoughts beginning to drift.

Tara. *Why* hadn't he looked into the future and foreseen that something might happen to his aunt? *Why* had he waited so long—left it so late?

20

————◄►————

Tara woke up abruptly, feeling totally disorientated. There was a sour tell-tale taste in her mouth and her head felt as though it was filled with a mass of gritty wire wool. She was lying on an unfamiliar sofa in an unfamiliar flat.

She tried to sit up and then stifled a small groan as the room swam giddily around her. The clock on the wall showed that it was half past four in the afternoon.

She had a vague memory of being in a restaurant with one of the girls from work who kept on insisting that she have another drink.

She tried to sit up again and this time she made it. From the room on the other side of the slightly open door, which opened off the small living room, she could hear quite plainly the sound of a couple having sex.

Grimacing to herself, she swung her feet to the floor. The events leading up to her inebriated agreement to return with Estelle to her flat were slowly beginning to come back to her now.

She shuddered. Heavens knows how many glasses of wine she had had to drink. Too many, that was for sure. It had certainly been a mistake to come back here with Estelle. She had never particularly liked the other girl and she had liked even less the gossip she heard about her at work.

During lunch, Estelle had talked quite openly about her sex life, even boasting about the men she had had, and Tara had gained the distinct impression that it had not been love or even lust that motivated her to be with them, but rather money.

'Oh, come on,' she had taunted when Tara grimaced over a particularly distasteful incident she was relating to her. 'Don't tell me that *you* haven't been tempted to try something like that.'

'Bondage isn't my scene,' Tara had responded quite truthfully.

Not *her* scene perhaps, but no doubt it had played an important part in her mother's, her *real* mother's, repertoire. All the time Estelle had been boasting about how easy it was to get men to pay for the use of her body, Tara had been writhing inwardly, wondering if it was because there was something inherent in her, something *she* had perhaps inherited from her birth mother that made Estelle aware…that made her talk to her so openly. Which was, no doubt, why she had gone on drinking even after she knew she had reached her limit, Tara acknowledged miserably.

'You should give it a try. You might even find you like it,' Estelle had goaded her.

'No, never…I couldn't. Tara had shuddered in genuine revulsion.

Listening to her even through her increasingly drunken dizziness, Tara abruptly had known deep within her soul and with unquestioning certainty that there could only be two reasons for *her* ever having sex, both of which were based on love—one being the love she might have for her sexual partner and the other being the love she had for whomever it was she was trying to protect by having sex with a man she did *not* love. To have sex for money as her mother had done was simply not an option she could ever envisage herself taking. There were, after all, other ways to earn money.

And with that knowledge had come the first small lifting of the black cloud of despair that engulfed her when she had learned the truth about her parentage.

She might be Katriona's *child*, but she was her *own* person. Katriona might have earned her living by selling her body, but Tara knew that *she* could not, *would* not, ever do the same.

Shakily, she got to her feet, picked up her bag, which was lying on the floor at her feet, her shoes and jacket, which were on a chair, then quietly tiptoed towards the door so as not to disturb the occupants of the bedroom.

As she stepped out into the street, she saw her car was parked outside the flat even though she had no knowledge of having driven it there, and she certainly didn't feel she was in any fit state to drive it anywhere now, she acknowledged. Out of the corner of her eye, she spotted a cruising taxi and immediately hailed it.

'Where to?' the cabbie asked her laconically as he stopped for her.

Just about to give him the address of her own flat, for no reason that she could think of, Tara heard herself saying instead, 'I want to get a train to Dorchester, but I'm not sure which station I need.'

'Dorchester. You'll want Waterloo, then, luv,' the cabbie told her, swinging the cab around in an illegal U-turn with a screech of tyres that made her aching head thud sickeningly.

Nervously, Tara sat back in her seat, her heart pounding and her stomach churning in a way that had nothing to do with the wine she had drunk earlier in the day.

'Your mother originally came from a small village close to Dorchester,' Claudia had told her quietly when she demanded this information. 'Her father, your grandfather, was a school-teacher at a public school there.'

Claudia had protested that she loved Tara for herself, but Tara felt that wasn't the truth. How could it be? If that had been, would Claudia have gone to such lengths to keep her true parentage a secret from her? If she hadn't been ashamed of who Tara's mother had been, then why had she said nothing?

'I love you,' Claudia had told her in tears and perhaps she had…but *only* as a second-best, a make-do-and-mend. How could *any* woman love another woman's child as much as she could love her own? How could a woman like Claudia love the child of a woman like Katriona?

No, Tara had convinced herself that Claudia loved her because she had had to. She just wasn't sure which of them had hurt her the most—her birth mother for being what she had been or Claudia for being someone she wasn't.

How was Ryland going to feel when she had to tell him? There was suddenly a frighteningly empty space in her life where the person she had always assumed herself to be had been but where now there was only a stranger. She was a stranger to herself, she admitted forlornly as the taxi pulled into the station.

Estelle grumbled mildly in complaint as Blade pushed her away and started to get off the bed.

'Come on,' he ordered her, 'I think it's time we went and woke up your little sleeping beauty, don't you?'

'She's going to need careful handling,' she warned him. 'She's not some homeless kid, Blade. She's got friends, family and—'

'Don't worry, by the time we've finished with her, complaining to her friends or her family is going to be the last thing on her mind, and just in case she does get awkward, I've brought something with me guaranteed to make her do as she's told.'

Estelle started to relax. Getting Tara drunk had been easier than she expected, and after making sure she was fast asleep, she had telephoned Blade to tell him what had happened.

'I'm coming right over,' he had told her with that purring note in his voice that told her he was pleased with her, 'and if she's as good as you're telling me, I'm going to be very pleased with you. Very pleased with you indeed.'

After getting off the bed, he pulled on his jeans and opened the bedroom door. Abruptly he tensed, slamming the door closed as he wheeled round to face her.

'What is it…what's wrong?' Estelle asked him uneasily, struggling into her dress.

'She's gone, you stupid bitch, *that's* what's wrong,' he shouted, cursing her as she opened the door to stare in disbelief at the empty living area.

'She can't have,' she protested, half-stammering. 'She was out cold, she—'

'Christ, but you're stupid,' she heard him saying, moving too fast for her to dodge the blow that caught her on the side of the head, sending her reeling back against the headboard. Her head exploded with pain, and as he hit her a second time, she bit through her tongue, the blood spurting into her mouth. She tried to scream, to fight back, but he held her down on the bed, imprisoning her.

It had been a long time since he last punished her like this. Violence did not arouse him sexually, but he knew how to hurt her and where, the pillow he was holding over her face silencing her screams.

'Stupid, stupid bitch,' he swore savagely at her as he hit her. 'You stupid, stupid bitch…'

'Just coffee, please,' Tara told the girl as she came round with the refreshment trolley. She felt completely sober now, but her stomach was churning too nervously for her to be able to eat.

The train was surprisingly full, but she had managed to find a seat at a table opposite a young woman in her early thirties who smiled warmly at her as she, too, merely ordered a coffee.

'Do you live in Dorchester?' Tara asked her. She was feeling slightly calmer now that she was over the shock of what she had done. It had been an impulsive decision to go to Dorchester and one she was already beginning to regret. What was she expecting to find? Not her mother, not even her grandfather; they were both long dead and...

'No, but my parents live there,' the other woman was answering with another smile. 'I'm going to collect my daughter. She's been staying with them. The first time she's stayed with them on her own and we've missed her horribly.'

The very way she had spoken about 'my daughter' had struck Tara like a blow. There had been so much love and pride in the words and it was politeness rather than any genuine interest that led her to ask, 'How old is she?'

'Eight. Would you like to see a photograph of her?' she volunteered.

Suppressing a faint sigh, Tara nodded her head. After all, what else did she have to do to pass the journey?

'She looks like you,' Tara offered when she had dutifully studied the snapshot she was handed of a pretty brown-haired little girl.

The other woman's smile broadened. 'Everyone says that,' she agreed, 'which is ironic, really, because Gemma is adopted.'

Tara's whole body went stiff, the colour draining from her face. Quickly, she picked up her coffee-cup, her hands trembling. This was taking coincidence too far and if she had any sense she'd end this conversation right here and now. She could almost see and feel the dark shadow of fate looming over her.

'I didn't find out until after we'd been married several years that I couldn't have children. I was devastated. We both were. We tried everything.' She paused and shook her head. 'Conceiving a child, my own child, became the most important thing in my whole life. Even, in some ways, more important than my husband in the end.

'Well, David gave me an ultimatum. He wanted a normal life, he told me, a life that wasn't totally focused on my getting pregnant. We'd put our names down for adoption early on when we knew I couldn't conceive, but we never really had any hopes of getting a baby.

'Then totally out of the blue, we got a call to say there was a baby for whom the agency thought we would make suitable parents. I couldn't believe it, and there are still some days when I have to pinch myself just to make sure that it's all true, that Gemma is ours. We've been so lucky, so blessed…'

The woman's eyes had started to fill with tears, and as she drained her now cold coffee, Tara blurted out, 'But it can't be the same as having your own child. You can't love her as much as though…'

The other woman was staring at her. 'Gemma *is* my own child,' she told her with quiet dignity. 'Yes, another woman carried her in her womb, but Gemma was six weeks old when she came to me. She was undernourished and underweight because she had not been feeding properly. Her mother, a teenage girl, already had two other toddlers by different fathers, and at first the paediatrician thought that Gemma might have suffered some small degree of brain damage during her birth because she was so slow to feed. The moment I held her and looked at her, though, I knew she just needed someone to love her properly.

'It's not something you can explain to someone who hasn't experienced it. People assume that you need to physically give birth to a child to love it, but that's not true. If it was, then there wouldn't *be* any abused or unloved children, would there?' she observed with a sad smile.

'Does she…does Gemma know she's adopted?' Tara asked her, dry-mouthed.

'Oh, yes, she knows that her mother simply wasn't able to look after her and that because she loved her, she wanted her to be with someone who could. We talk about it quite often. To tell you the truth,' she added, her face instantly softening, 'if anything, I love Gemma *more* because I didn't give birth to her. To me, to *us*, she is our most precious and wonderful gift and she knows that no matter what happens in her life, the bond of love I feel for her will never be broken. When she's old enough, if she feels she wants to seek out her birth parents, then that is her right, and David and I have both agreed that we would do everything we could to help her.'

'Aren't you afraid that she might—'

'Love them more than she does us?' the other woman supplied gently for her. 'Yes, of course I am, but at the end of the day, as any adoptive mother would tell you, what matters most is not that your child loves *you* but that *you* love him or her.'

'But you must feel concerned about...about what she might have inherited from her birth parents,' Tara persisted, her questions far more intense and personal than those she would normally have asked a stranger because they were due to her own very intense and personal feelings.

'No child is born good or bad,' the other woman told her positively. 'Gemma's birth parents were a couple of teenagers who had sex without any real thought of the consequences. Gemma's mother ran away from home to escape an abusive stepfather. She was pregnant with her first child at fifteen, had her second at sixteen and Gemma herself a year later. That doesn't make her bad. The only thing that makes it bad is the system, the *society* that failed to love and protect her.

'Gemma is her own special self and we love her because of her individuality. David, my husband, loves animals, and Gemma is like him in that. The pair of them are always bringing home injured creatures they find, but although neither David nor I have ever had any special talent for it, Gemma is becoming a very good rider. She has a *natural* ability, her riding school has told us—something she must have inherited through her parents.

'Having an adopted child is so very special in so many ways. Every day is an adventure full of new discoveries. You have no preconceptions and it's your responsibility to give your child the emotional nourishment to help them reach their full potential.

'Gemma knows how special she is to us and she will carry that knowledge with her wherever she goes in her life. Every adopted child *shares* that specialness.'

'But what would have happened if you'd gone on to have a child of your own?' Tara asked her forthrightly.

The other woman frowned and then responded gently, 'I don't think you understand. Gemma *is* my own. It is impossible, inconceivable, that I could love her any more than I already do.'

Her frown was deepening now and Tara could see that she was perhaps beginning to regret having spoken to her.

'I'm sorry,' she began to apologise. 'It's just that—'

Before she could finish her sentence and explain about her own past, the guard was announcing that they would shortly be arriving in

Dorchester and her travelling companion was already getting her things together and looking towards the window in eager anticipation.

Tara saw her again briefly after they had both left the train. She was holding out her arms to a small, pretty, dark-haired little girl who came flying down the platform to fling herself against her, crying out, 'Mummy... Mummy...'

Tears filled Tara's own eyes as she watched them. *Had* she perhaps been wrong to accuse Claudia of claiming that she loved her because she had had no other choice? Because it had been either her or nothing? But even if she had been wrong, Claudia had still hidden the true facts of her birth from her. Had she done it because she was ashamed and afraid of what she had done, of being found out and losing her, as she had claimed to Tara? Or because, as Tara believed, she was ashamed of who Tara really was and afraid that she would turn out to be like her biological mother?

The receptionist at the hotel Tara booked into was far too well trained to show any curiosity at her lack of luggage and vagueness about the length of her stay. But how could Tara answer that question when she didn't know the answer herself, when she still didn't even really know what she was doing here in Dorchester?

As she turned to walk away from the reception desk, she paused and turned back, saying, 'Excuse me, but I wonder, do you happen to know if there's a village locally that has a public school?'

The girl frowned. 'Well, there's Wheatly Park down the road, and Darlington, of course,' she informed Tara, 'but...'

Tara thanked her and turned away. It was going to be impossible trying to trace her unknown family without more detailed information. She had been an idiot to come rushing down here like this. There was a public telephone in the foyer. Determinedly, she headed for it, then picked up the receiver and dialled the number of her father's apartment, telling herself that Claudia might not even still be there, never mind be willing to answer her questions.

When she heard Claudia's voice on the other end of the line, she almost lost her courage and replaced the receiver. Instead, taking a deep breath, she said rustily, 'It's me, Tara....'

Standing in Garth's living room, Claudia wound the flex of the telephone receiver nervously round her fingers, her heart thumping frantically. When Tara had rushed out of the apartment, she had felt as anguished, albeit in a different way, as she had done when she learned that her baby was stillborn. The only difference was that *this* time the pain was even more acute, a searing agony that felt as though her heart was being ripped mercilessly out of her body.

'Leave her,' Garth had cautioned her. 'Give her time.' Now it seemed that he had been right.

'Tara darling...where are you...are you...?'

Tears choked her voice, preventing her from going on.

'I…need to know something,' she could hear Tara shakily demanding, her voice almost youthfully defiant, bringing back memories of a much younger Tara resolutely standing her ground as she enlisted Claudia's aid for whatever philanthropic project she had impulsively undertaken.

During the years Tara was growing up, their home had often become a sanctuary for whatever and whomever Tara was currently championing, be it animal or human.

'I need to know my mother's surname… and…where she came from,' Tara told her abruptly.

Claudia's heart sank. She felt instinctively that Tara was not ringing because, miraculously and no doubt on her part undeservedly, she had changed her mind, but simply because Claudia was the only point of contact she had with the woman who had given birth to her.

Silently, Claudia swallowed, blinking back her tears. Well, it wasn't as though she didn't deserve Tara's rejection and she had no one but herself to blame for what she was suffering. But Tara was also suffering, and that, too, was her fault, her responsibility.

'Your mother's name was Katriona Spencer,' she responded quietly. 'She was brought up in a village called Upton Villiers. It's near—'

'Dorchester, yes, I know,' Tara acknowledged curtly, her palm so wet with nervous sweat that she had to wipe it on her jeans before she could write down the information Claudia had given her.

'Tara darling, I know how upset you are,' Claudia sympathised, 'but please, darling, you must believe me. I love you so much, Tara, so very, very much,' she went on brokenly, 'and I can't bear to think that…that you would ever feel that I hadn't loved you. You were never in any way second-best to me and I have never thought of you as anything other than…than the most precious, wonderful thing that life could possibly have given me….'

Claudia's heartfelt words virtually echoed the words the woman on the train had used to describe *her* feelings for her adopted daughter. Tara had to fight hard to resist the overwhelming temptation to run home to London and to Claudia just as fast as she could, fling herself into her arms, knowing they would close safely and lovingly around her as her travelling companion's had around her much younger daughter. So overwhelming was it, actually, that she was just on the point of giving in to it when she reminded herself of the reality, of the fact that despite the love she claimed to have for her, Claudia had deliberately deceived her.

'I have to go,' she told her abruptly, then immediately replaced the receiver before she could change her mind.

As she heard Tara cut the connection, Claudia's eyes welled with tears. Garth had gone into the office, promising her that he would be back as soon as he could, and she wished desperately that he had been here when Tara had telephoned. He would have dealt with the situation so much better than her.

Garth!

It was amazing how easily and naturally she had slipped back into the role of being his, of how easily the years of their being apart had melted away, of how frighteningly quickly she had come to depend on him again.

No doubt her own life, her own affairs, her business, all needed her attention, but how could she concentrate on them…on anything, while all she could think about, all that really mattered, was Tara's happiness?

After she had ended the conversation with Claudia, Tara simply stood in a daze beside the telephone for several minutes, her hand clenched tightly over the piece of paper on which she had written the information Claudia had given her.

She needed a change of clothes, a map, a hire-car. It was already early evening.

The receptionist was able to suggest an out-of-town shopping mall that stayed open until late in the evening, and at Tara's request offered her a taxi to take her to it, promising to have the paperwork ready for her to complete on her return to enable her to rent a car.

Angrily, Estelle stiffened her body against Blade's grip. He was holding her too hard, hurting her too much, his hands locking round her throat as he shook her violently. Instinctively, she fought back, raking her nails down his arm and then gouging them into his face as he refused to let her go.

Her dress was twisted up around her body, but as he swore at her, removing one hand from her throat to reach out and grab hold of the hand she had raised to claw him, twisting it painfully behind her, Estelle recognised that this time his anger wasn't being fuelled by sexual desire.

'Bitch, stupid, useless bitch,' he swore at her, punctuating the words with a series of blows to the side of her head that left her reeling.

'Stop it,' she demanded thickly through her swelling mouth. 'Stop it, you're hurting me.'

'Good,' he snarled. 'I *want* to hurt you. You deserve to be hurt.'

As he raised his hand to hit her, Estelle managed to wriggle free, catching him off guard. She had never known him to act like this before, and suddenly she was afraid, overcome with a fear that had nothing whatsoever of the usual thrill of sexual excitement she had experienced along with such fear. That fear was hot and arousing, enticing; this one was cold and foreboding. After struggling off the bed, she made straight for the door of the flat, pausing only to snatch up her jacket as she did so.

Behind her, Blade was pursuing her, still cursing her. She could see Tara's car parked outside the flat where she had left it; the keys were still in her pocket. Acting instinctively, she ran to it, jumped in and started the engine, ignoring Blade's shouts for her to get out. Then racing dangerously away from the curb and into the traffic, she left him standing on the pavement, watching his face contort with savage fury.

Her heart was pounding with the adrenalin-fuelled instinct for flight.

She started to shiver and reached out to switch on the car's heating system. God, but she hated him sometimes. Hadn't she always done everything he asked? Given him everything he wanted? It wasn't her fault that he had got himself in so deep with the drugs scene.

If he needed to buy people off, pay them off, then that was his problem, not hers. Why the hell should she offer to help him out? What the hell had he ever done for her?

Narrowly missing a pedestrian crossing the road, she put her foot on the accelerator and cursed him. She had no idea where she was going, but the sensation of speed, of power, was giving her an outlet for her fear and making her feel that she was strong and in control. Deliberately, she aimed the car for the small gap she could see coming in the traffic ahead of her, laughing as she ignored the right of another driver to take it, her sense of urgency and excitement increased by the challenge of narrowly making it through the space. The sense of danger...

She could drive like this all day. It made her feel good and it made her feel even better remembering the way she had left Blade standing impotently behind her on the pavement. Let him wait. Let him curse. She wasn't going to go back until she was ready. And she wasn't ready yet...no, she wasn't ready yet.

21

'Tara rang,' Claudia quickly informed Garth the moment he walked into the apartment. 'But she wouldn't tell me where she was—it was a public phone somewhere. She wanted to know Katriona's surname and where she had come from, Garth. Garth…what is it?' she demanded anxiously when she saw his expression.

Garth sat down, reached out and took hold of both her hands. There was no easy way to tell her what he had to say or any way to keep the information from her, either.

'When Tara left here earlier, she went straight to the office and cleared her desk. I've checked her flat. There's no sign of her there, just a torn-up message from Ryland saying that he's been summoned home urgently by his father.'

'She's cleared her *desk*?' Claudia stared at him with huge, haunted eyes.

Oddly, contrary to what he might have expected, the trauma of what was happening had, instead of ageing her, somehow or other made her look endearingly youthful and vulnerable, like the Claudia he remembered from their shared younger days, a Claudia who needed and valued him and who had no qualms about show-ing it.

'She…perhaps she's followed Ryland to America,' she suggested eagerly. 'She could have phoned from the airport.'

Garth hated to disappoint her but he knew he had to. 'I doubt it,' he told her regretfully, shak-ing his head. 'I've phoned the main airports.'

Claudia bit her lip. 'Have you spoken to Ryland…asked him…?'

'Not yet. I thought I'd phone him from here. Did she say anything to you about…?'

'No,' she replied unhappily. 'She was only on the phone for a few minutes and she rang off be-fore I could really ask her anything. Oh, Garth…'

Garth held her as she wept.

'She just needs time,' he said, repeating what he had told her earlier, but then he'd been as-suming that Tara would spend that time safely with Ryland and that Ryland would help her come to terms with what she had learned.

The discovery that he was in Boston had dis-turbed Garth more than he wanted Claudia to guess. The thought of Tara dealing with the pain-ful discoveries the day had brought with Ryland was one thing; the thought of her having to deal with them alone was quite another.

'Her car's gone,' he told Claudia sombrely.

Silently, they looked at one another. Then Claudia asked him bitterly, 'What are you think-ing, Garth? That she's gone to look for her mother, her real mother?' She started to shake with harsh, racking sobs that tore at her throat and Garth's heart.

'Try not to worry,' he counselled her. 'Right now, Tara will be feeling antagonistic towards both of us, and no doubt she's also feeling rather afraid and alone, and curious, too, about Katriona—that's only natural. Give her time, Clo…give her time.'

'I know you're right,' Claudia agreed. 'I just wish…'

'It's eleven o'clock,' Garth said. 'Let's go to bed. If Tara does ring again, there's a phone in the bedroom.'

'Tomorrow I must go…go home,' she told him huskily.

'Yes, I know.' Very gently, he touched her neck, brushing her skin with tender lover's fingers. 'I'd like to go back with you, but under the circumstances—'

'No, you mustn't,' Claudia broke in quickly. 'Tara might ring and—'

Firmly, Garth took her in his arms. 'Perhaps this isn't the best of times to say this, but there's no way I'd want to change what's been happening between us, Clo. No way at all. It might be an arrogant thing for me to say but…you and I were meant to be together. We *fit* together, belong together, and I'm putting you on notice that from now on I want to be very much a part of your life.'

Lifting her head to look at him, Claudia declared simply and truthfully, 'You *are* my life, Garth, you and Tara. Oh, I know I've got my friends, the business, my charity work, a busy and fulfilling life, and I'd be lying if I pretended that they don't mean a lot to me, but *giving* love, *being* loved by those closest to me…

'I've missed you,' she admitted bravely, 'and although you may not understand this, it's actually because I loved you so much that I had to end our marriage once I knew you were Tara's father. You see, I simply couldn't live with the knowledge that, as I then thought, you'd betrayed me with another woman—any other woman, but most especially Tara's birth mother. I hated Katriona so much then. You were mine and I felt that she'd taken you from me. You don't know how many nights I've lain in bed torturing myself by imagining the two of you together, imagining you telling her how much more desirable, how much more sexy, how much more of a turn-on she was for you than me.'

Claudia could see from Garth's expression how much her admissions had stunned him.

'It was never anything like that,' he protested. 'I never—'

'I know that now,' Claudia assured him. 'But then…'

'Why didn't you *say* anything?' Garth groaned, drawing her closer. 'When you said you wanted a divorce, I thought it was because you were completely disgusted and revolted by me…that discovering I was Tara's father was simply the last nail in the coffin for our marriage. I'd felt for so long that you were irritated by me and tired of me…that I was simply someone who came between you and Tara, demanding your time and attention when you wanted to give them all to her. I thought discovering that I was Tara's father was simply giving you an excuse to end our marriage. I thought you wanted me to go.'

'I did,' Claudia agreed, 'and yes, I know there was a time when I was guilty of…of neglecting you and our relationship. I don't honestly know why. All I do know is that a good many other young women in their early thirties with young children come to me for counselling saying much the same thing. They complain they just don't have the time, the space, the *energy* to be both good mothers and loving wives. Perhaps it's because nature has designed us to put our children first when they are young. Young children need that love and protection from their mothers in order to survive, to flourish. But I never stopped loving you, Garth, and once you were gone—'

'Why didn't you *say* something…tell me…?'

'How could I? You seemed more than content with your new life. I even began to ask myself if you were relieved that I had asked you for a divorce, if I had simply pre-empted a step you yourself had been wanting to take. My pride wouldn't let me tell you how I really felt. In fact, it wasn't until I was sitting outside our old flat reliving the past that I finally admitted openly to myself what I had known deep down inside for years. I told myself I was coming to see you for Tara, but—'

'It doesn't matter *why* you came,' Garth whispered as he looked lovingly into her eyes. 'All that matters is that you did…that you're here and that we're together, now and for always. Come on, let's go to bed. We've got a lot of time to catch up on,' he reminded her wickedly.

'I wonder where Tara is now?' Claudia remarked sadly as she let him guide her towards the bedroom door.

Tara thanked the receptionist for her help and took the keys she was handed for the rental car she had organised for her.

It was just gone nine and still relatively light. Common sense urged her to wait until morning when she was properly rested after a night's sleep.

Hearing Claudia's voice over the phone had disturbed her more than she expected and she told herself it was crazy to feel concern for someone who had deceived her so heartlessly, and yet when she heard the tears in Claudia's voice, her instinct had been to try to comfort her.

In the taxi back from the hypermarket, she had studied the map she had bought, quickly finding the village where Claudia said Katriona had been brought up. It was less than twenty miles away, that was all, a relatively short drive.

Her hire-car was by coincidence the same make and colour as her own car. An omen? Maybe, but of what? What was she expecting to find? What did she *want* to find? Not Katriona. How could she? Katriona was dead, she reminded herself fiercely as she unlocked the car door and got in.

Though sturdily built, the car hadn't been designed to be driven recklessly round sharp bends at high speeds, especially not by a driver whose mind was not really on her driving.

By the time she realised she had misjudged the sharpness of the bend and her own speed, it was too late. The car was careering out of control, skidding at a frightening speed towards the line of mature trees that marked the edge of the road.

The elderly couple who lived several yards away from the bend heard the sound of the car hitting the tree when they opened their door to let their equally elderly dog out. They telephoned the police immediately, but as the grave-faced traffic officer informed them, even if they *had* gone out to the car there would have been nothing they could have done for its sole female occupant.

'She must have died instantly,' he told them. What he didn't tell them but what his accident report would was that she had not been wearing a seat-belt. Whether having done so at the speed she must have been driving would have made any difference was academic now. She had had nothing to identify her but he had radioed in the number plate of the car.

Since it was registered to an owner living in London, it would not fall to him to go and see them. London was Met territory and they were a relatively small country force.

* * *

Garth was just about to take Claudia a tray of tea and toast when the constable from the Met arrived, his grave expression at odds with his youth.

After Garth had let him in, he asked him formally, 'I wonder if you can tell me, sir, if you are still the owner of a vehicle registered J850 AYG?'

'Yes, that's my daughter's car,' Garth replied. The car was registered in Garth's name simply because the partnership paid a contribution towards the running costs of both of their cars since they used them for work.

The constable looked away from him and then back before clearing his throat and telling him, 'I'm afraid I have to tell you that the car has been involved in a…fatal accident. You say the car belongs to your daughter? The young woman who was driving had no identification on her, and in the circumstances, I'm afraid, I'm going to have to ask you to identify the body.'

'Garth, I heard the door…is it Tara?'

Claudia checked the doorway of the living room, the hope dying out of her eyes as she saw the policeman.

'Oh, I'm sorry,' she began, apologising and backing away, but then as though something in the fixed stances of both men alerted her, she suddenly froze in her tracks. Turning to Garth, she demanded, 'What is it…what's happened? It's Tara, isn't it? Something's happened to Tara.' As her voice started to rise, her whole body seemed to crumble, the blood draining from her face as she clutched the doorway.

'There's been an accident,' Garth was forced to tell her. 'I...I have—'

'Where is she? Which hospital?' Claudia demanded immediately of the policeman while he looked at Garth.

Going to her, Garth placed his hand on her arm, almost unable to form the words. 'She isn't... Tara is...'

As he watched her absorb and interpret his message, he could see in her eyes a reflection of the pain and disbelief he knew were in his own.

'You stay here,' he advised her gruffly. 'I'll go with the officer.'

'No...no...I'm coming, too,' Claudia told him fiercely, struggling to suppress the avalanche of emotions threatening her self-control.

Tara dead...? No! It couldn't be true. She would have known, *sensed*... But the grave expression on the face of the young policeman and the shocked anguish in Garth's eyes persuaded her that it was true.

She felt as though she had opened the bedroom door and walked into a nightmare. Tara dead... It wasn't possible.

'Where...?' she began to ask, dry-mouthed, as Garth guided her towards the door. 'How...?'

Garth touched her arm. 'Later' he whispered.

They sat silently side by side in the back of the police car, frozen into immobility by the sheer weight of their loss, feeling almost as though by not moving, by not breathing, they could somehow keep the news they had been brought from actually becoming reality.

The hospital morgue was at the end of a long, seemingly endless corridor. Their footsteps echoed hollowly as they slowly made their way to the door at the end. Garth couldn't help remembering the time so many years ago when he had looked upon the face of his stillborn child. Painful though that had been at the time, it had been nothing like this.

They both hesitated outside the door to the morgue, but the police constable pushed it open and stood back to allow them to pass.

The girl lay on a long table, the empty, body-length drawer open in the wall behind her making Garth shudder as he looked away from it. As a former army officer, he had seen death before, but this was different. This was his own flesh and blood.

Tears filled his eyes. He turned towards Claudia and to his shock heard her saying in a firm, clear voice, 'That isn't our daughter. That's not Tara.'

Garth shook his head. He had known, of course, how hard this would be for her, and for her to deny the facts was perhaps not unexpected. But to do so this positively, this determinedly... His tear-distorted glance swept over the dark head and the pale, lifeless arm that lay across the covered body.

'Clo...' he began beseechingly. 'Darling, I know—'

'It isn't Tara,' Claudia interrupted him, pulling

away. Before he could stop her, she walked
quickly towards the table and around it. 'It isn't
Tara, Garth,' she repeated more gently, her own
eyes filling with tears as she stood facing him
across the body, her gaze fixed on the face that he
still hadn't had the courage to identify. 'Come
and look,' she invited him as tenderly as if he
were a small child. 'I promise you it isn't her.'

Reluctantly, he did as she said, grasping the
hand she held out to him, feeling its warmth and
reassurance, too grateful for its comfort to question the fact that she was the one giving support
and he the one taking it.

'Look, darling. It isn't Tara,' Claudia repeated
once more, her expression turning sombre as she
confounded him completely by brushing her fingertips over the dead girl's face in a gesture of
loving comfort and then bending down to kiss
her cold cheek. 'Poor child. I don't know who she
is but I'm profoundly sad for her and her family.'

As he blinked away his tears, Garth forced
himself to look at the dead girl for the first time.
His expression must have given him away, he
realised, because immediately the constable was
asking him, 'Do you recognise her, sir?'

'Yes, yes, I do,' he confirmed, turning to
Claudia. 'It's Estelle. She works for us.' Garth
tried to gather together his scattered thoughts.
Estelle might not be his daughter, his child, but
she was someone's, some man's, a man who as
yet had no awareness, no knowledge, of his
daughter's fate; a man who, if he was any kind of
a father, would grieve terribly for her once he

learned the truth. And Garth felt that it behoved him as a man, as a fellow human being, to allow a few seconds of respect both for Estelle and for that unknown man even in the midst of his own dizzy relief that the body before him did not belong to his own precious Tara. 'You say she was driving my daughter's car,' he remarked, looking at the younger man. 'I don't know how…'

'Perhaps Tara lent it to her,' Claudia suggested.

It was a possibility, Garth acknowledged, but from what he had heard on the grapevine about Estelle, he suspected that the reality was more likely to be that the other girl had 'helped herself' to the car. Perhaps in her furious rush to clear her desk, Tara had forgotten her keys, or perhaps while rejecting her parents, she had also decided to reject the car that had been a birthday gift to her and simply left the keys on her desk where Estelle had found them.

'If you could tell me her full name,' the police constable suggested patiently.

Dazed, Garth did so. To have gone from being told that Tara was dead and then discovering that she was not—all within the space of an hour—had left him feeling in very much the same frame of mind as he recalled once feeling in Northern Ireland when a companion had been hit by a sniper's bullet, leaving him still standing. Relieved, and yet at the same time, both disbelieving and guilty.

As they walked back to the police car, Garth saw that Claudia was crying, the tears pouring silently down her face.

Hugging her, he told her, 'It's just the shock. I know how you feel.'

Claudia shook her head. 'No…I'm not crying for that. I'm crying for that poor girl in the morgue and for her mother,' she explained tearfully to him. 'When I saw her and I knew she wasn't Tara, Garth, I realised that the worst thing that could happen to me *isn't* losing Tara's love and trust—the *worst* thing that could happen would be if Tara had been that girl.

'Maybe Tara never will forgive me for what I've done, maybe I'll have to live the rest of my life without her, but at least I'll know that she's *living*, that she has her life.

'I *knew*, you know,' she told him then as they got into the waiting car. 'I knew even before I saw her. Tara's life couldn't end without my knowing something, without my *feeling* something. It just isn't possible.'

'Mother love?' Garth teased gently.

'For me, Tara is my child,' Claudia told him fiercely. 'My love for her is the love of a mother. She is a part of me in a way I simply can't explain. I knew it the moment when I held her as a baby and she looked straight into my eyes. I couldn't love her more if I had actually given birth to her, Garth.'

'I know that,' he assured her, 'and so deep down inside does Tara.'

The police had asked him to supply them with what details he could of Estelle, so after dropping Claudia off at the apartment and telling her that he would call her in the evening after she had returned to Ivy House, he went back to the police car.

Sophie saw the police car first, hesitating just those few vital seconds before calling out to John, who was in another room. Instinctively, she knew if not what the news was that somehow it was bad. As the car stopped, it seemed to be enveloped in an ominous stillness, a darkness.

The policeman broke the news as gently as he could, but Sophie could see in John's eyes how ill-prepared he was for the shock, his eyes blank, his mouth trembling slightly as he mouthed the words. 'No. Not Estelle...she can't be...it can't be...'

Immediately, Sophie reached out to grasp his hand and held it tightly.

Through his tears, John looked at her, his expression dazed. 'It shouldn't have come to this,' he told Sophie brokenly. 'She shouldn't have come to this. My poor Estelle...my poor, poor girl.'

Too late now to wish that they had tried harder, acted sooner, done something to repair their broken relationship with her, Sophie recognised, and knew as the thoughts formed that what she really meant was that it was too late now to save her.

'Rest in peace, Estelle.' She sent up a silent prayer to her stepdaughter. 'Be at peace now wherever you may be.'

* * *

Tara was already awake before she received her wake-up call. Halfway down the country road that led to her destination last night, she had abruptly changed her mind and turned round.

Because she had listened to the voice of good sense and reason advocating that her quest could best be accomplished in daylight or because she had suddenly become afraid of what she might actually find?

What was there that could possibly be worse to discover than what she already knew? Katriona, brought up by an elderly distant father, had run away when he had refused, failed to recognise, that her bad behaviour was an unspoken plea for him to give her the love and attention she craved. And having run away, she had turned to prostitution to finance the drug habit she had developed.

It was, after all, almost a drearily mundane story, a modern cliché almost too commonplace to merit more than a dismissive shrug from any outsider learning of it, but she wasn't an outsider. And then there was Ryland.

Ryland… How was he going to feel when she had to tell him what she had discovered? Ryland loved her, she knew that, and her reaction yesterday to the kind of life Katriona had lived made it more than plain to her, if she had needed any kind of confirmation, that her mother's way of life could never be for her.

From Claudia she had learned to feel compassion for others and to make allowances for their weaknesses and vulnerabilities, but she knew that no amount of hardship would persuade her to abandon the ideals she so fervently believed in.

Because, through her unstinting love, Claudia had given her what Katriona's parents had never been able to. Quite simply, she *knew* she was loved, Tara acknowledged. By her parents, by Ryland and, most importantly, by herself.

Very shortly she got out of bed. The sky beyond her bedroom window was a soft, clear blue, the sun shining warmly, no cloud on the horizon to disturb the promise of a perfect day. If she wished, she, too, could dismiss the clouds on *her* horizon by merely turning round and going home.

Like Claudia, if she wished, she could choose to carry the burden of her real parentage in secret. Nothing need be any different and Ryland need never be put in a position where he would feel honour bound to disclose it to the world, to his own family. The choice was hers, but she knew she simply didn't have that kind of strength, that she would never be able to keep her silence.

Tara left the hotel around mid-morning. She found the village easily enough, then parked her car and got out to walk its length. From her map, she had discovered the whereabouts of the school where her grandfather must have taught. It was a few miles outside the village, a large old house set in its own grounds, the headquarters of some multi-national organisation now apparently, the school having closed over a decade ago.

Tara tried to visualise her mother living in the village as a child, although Claudia had told her that she had actually lived at the school with her father. Had she made friends here in the village, been a happy, well-adjusted part of the community as Tara had been in her own home town? Or had she been an outsider, rejected by the other children, not really one of them?

The church was at the end of the village street, set back from the cottages and separated from them by a pretty stone-built rectory. It was the kind of church that brides dreamed of, small, its stone walls softened by time and its lych-gate crying out for artistic floral decorations.

Tara walked up to the church door, opened it and stepped inside. The church felt cold although light flooded in through the stained-glass window beyond the altar. Around the walls, other stained-glass panels bore the names of those who had donated them to the church.

Her mother had known this church, might perhaps have stood where she was standing now, Tara reminded herself, but instead of feeling the rush of emotion she had expected, all she actually felt was a rather detached sense of curiosity. The photograph Claudia had given her, which she had taken from Katriona's file, depicted a pretty, dark-haired young woman. Try as she might, though, Tara could not imagine her as flesh and blood, could not breathe warmth and life into her. And most tellingly of all, as her mind had formed the words 'my mother', the image flashing across her brain had not been of Katriona but of *Claudia*.

A graveyard lay beyond the church. Slowly, Tara made her way towards it, tensing as she saw the familiar back of the woman crouching on the grass beside one of the gravestones.

When she had left Garth's apartment, Claudia had not intended to drive down to Dorset, even though she suspected it might be where Tara had gone. She had no right, she realised, to be part of Tara's life now. Tara herself had made that more than plain to her, but Claudia had been irresistibly drawn towards the village and not just because of Tara.

The woman in the small florist's shop had smiled at her in recognition when she walked in. After all, she had been a regular visitor to the village for a good number of years, always taking care and time over the flowers she chose. Today, though, she had seemed more preoccupied than usual, less inclined to stop and talk, the shop owner noticed as Claudia paid for her flowers and left.

Unlike Tara, Claudia did not linger in the village or go inside the church but instead headed straight for Katriona's grave. It was in a far corner of the graveyard, protected from the wind by a yew hedge that separated it from the countryside beyond it and close to the graves of her parents.

The headstone was cream, decorated with

dancing, fat-cheeked cherubs, and had inscribed on it:

Katriona Spencer
Daughter of Robert and Patricia
Mother of Tara
Rest in Eternal Love

As Claudia arranged the flowers in the small vase at the foot of the stone, filling it first with the ice she had bought from the florist, the movements of her fingers deft and swift, she paused to brush her fingers over Katriona's name.

'I never meant to lie to her or deceive her, Kat,' she told her. 'But she's right. I *was* afraid of losing her, of losing her to you, just as I felt I had lost Garth. I always felt so dull and stupid compared with you. You had an air of excitement and I envied you that. Tara has that special magical quality, too. She would have been fascinated by you.

'She was wrong to say that she was second-best, though. Tara could never be that. *You* know how it was. That first time I held her, you said then that you could see how much I loved her and I did.

'She has been the most precious gift that life has ever given me. Loving her has been the easiest, the most natural thing I have ever done. All those years when I fussed and worried protectively over her, when she was growing up, you know what I mean. I told you, didn't I, that time when I thought she had pneumonia, and then again when she had to have her tonsils out.

'You laughed at me then. I knew you would. Just as you laughed when I worried about her teenage desire for independence.

'Let her grow up, you told me. She needs to have her freedom. All those years when I tried to protect her, and yet now *I'm* the one who has damaged and hurt her.

'I should have told her. I know that, and by not doing so, I've cheated you both. She's right. She had a *right* to know about you, to make you a part of her life, and I've denied her that right because I was jealous of you, jealous and afraid that she might love you more than she did me. I could almost hear you mocking, saying to me, "Yes, but *I* am her mother."'

'But she isn't. *You're* my mother.'

Claudia knocked over the vase of flowers as she stood up clumsily, her face flushing. 'Tara, I didn't know. How…?'

'I saw you here when I came out of the church,' Tara said. 'I've been listening to you.'

Claudia bit her lip and looked away. 'You have every reason to be angry with me—'

'Yes, I have,' Tara agreed, cutting her off. 'Every reason, and I *am* angry, but…' Now it was her turn to look away. 'I…I *do* understand and I'm sorry for what I said about your not loving me as much, about my being second-best. I know *that* isn't true.'

'Oh, darling,' Claudia told her shakily, 'if only you knew how much it isn't and never could be true.'

'What else have you told her about me?' Tara

asked Claudia, nodding in the direction of the headstone.

'Everything,' Claudia replied simply after a small pause. 'I told her when you started to walk, and how your first word was "pretty" but how I couldn't be upset that it wasn't "Mum" because you said it to me. I told her that she was the one who really deserved that description. She was, you know, Tara, she was the most...she was very like you,' she declared emotionally. 'But you have a different nature. Katriona was like a diamond, sharp, brilliant—'

'Hard,' Tara suggested wryly.

'You are more like an emerald, deeper, richer, full of warmth and light.'

'While you are like a pearl,' Tara returned softly. 'Warm, pure, lustrous, glowing with inner beauty. Did she deliberately try to conceive me with Dad?' Tara abruptly asked her, watching her.

Claudia took a deep breath. This time she wasn't going to lie. 'I'm not really sure. She was a creature of moods. I doubt that was in her mind when she broke into the flat, but when she found Garth there...'

'Do you mind talking about it?' Tara asked her.

'Not now.' Claudia shook her head. 'When I thought that Garth had been unfaithful to me with her, then, yes, I would have minded. I couldn't bear to think that, like you, he would have preferred her to me.'

'Why should I have done that?'

'She was your mother. I was just…a substitute.'

'But you told me yourself that love does not depend on genetics,' Tara reminded her. 'You said that when we looked at one another, you and I, woman and baby, we bonded with one another, loved one another. The way you described it, you made it sound like a two-way exchange.'

'Yes, it was,' Claudia agreed. 'You gave me this look, this old knowing look as if you just knew. It seemed you were *willing* me to pick you up and hold you and when I did—'

'Perhaps I knew instinctively that you would give me the mothering I needed,' Tara suggested.

'I've always liked to think so.' Claudia gave a small sigh. 'But that doesn't alter the fact that what I did was wrong. I never meant it to happen. I genuinely intended to hand you over to the authorities. Only you were there and…I couldn't help myself, and once I had taken you home… Tara, I can't ask or expect you to forgive me but what I do ask is that you at least try to accept that you truly, truly are loved by me as my most dearly loved child. I cannot believe that it would be possible for me to love a child from my own womb any more than I love you because, quite simply, it just isn't possible.'

'I do accept it,' Tara asserted gravely, and as she said the words, she knew she meant them.

Listening to Claudia as she talked to her mother, she had seen illuminatingly just how much she was truly loved.

'Did you come in your car?' she asked Claudia now.

'Yes, I did,' Claudia replied, giving her a puzzled look. 'Why?'

'Good. Can you give me a lift back to London? On the way you can explain just what you've been doing these past few days sharing a bedroom with a man,' she added mock-severely.

Smiling, Claudia took a step forward, then stopped, hanging back. Gravely, Tara watched her. Suddenly, feeling immeasurably moved, she closed the space between them, hugging Claudia as though she were the mother and Claudia the child.

'It's all right. Everything's going to be all right,' she reassured her quietly.

But as they walked back through the churchyard, Claudia noticed sadly that Tara was unconsciously putting a slight distance between them instead of holding on to her arm as she normally did. And she noticed, too, that Tara had not called her Ma as she always so affectionately had before.

22

'They're boarding my flight,' Ryland told his parents, turning to hug first his mother and then his father. 'I'll be back just as soon as I've spoken to Tara.'

His aunt's funeral had taken place and yesterday he had spent most of the day in meetings with various legal and financial advisers following the reading of her will and the confirmation that she had indeed left the bulk of her estate to him.

As he got on board the plane and settled in his seat a little guiltily, Ryland admitted that his thoughts were not on what he was leaving behind but on what or rather whom he was going back to. He had missed Tara like hell, all the more so because he had not been able to even reach her by phone. The discovery, via her mother's assistant, that Claudia was away for a few days had caused him to guess that Tara must have taken advantage of his absence to spend a few days with her mother.

If he was honest, he was occasionally just a little jealous of the closeness that Tara shared with Claudia. Not that he wasn't close with his own parents, but *he* wasn't an only child. Tara shared a special bond with Claudia that in no way was that of an overly possessive parent for a much loved child. Claudia, it was obvious, both expected and encouraged Tara's independence and Ryland knew that she liked him and welcomed their relationship. It was just that the two of them had something that was so damned special.

They would be able to return to England for frequent visits, though, and have Claudia over to stay with them whenever she wished.

Claudia. She was one sassy, independent lady with her own business to run and, from what he had observed, not much free time to fill. His own mother would like her and enjoy her company even though, in many ways, they were very different.

Tara... Ryland closed his eyes and settled down to while away the few remaining hours that separated him from her. How was she going to react to what he had to tell her?

It had been relatively late when Tara got to bed. Her parents had taken her out to dinner, her father insisting that he wanted her there as a witness when he formally proposed to her mother. She was pleased about the way things had turned out for them, of course, but it had been hard. As she watched them, she had been wondering bleakly how she was ever going to fill the empty space in *her* life where Ryland should have been.

She could accept now just how much Claudia loved her and even to some extent understand why she had done what she had done. Claudia, on her part, had suggested gently that she might want to join a support group of other adopted adults, where she could freely discuss her feelings of pain and betrayal, but Tara had refused, not wanting to add to Claudia's obvious guilt by telling her that very soon she was going to be called upon to deal with a pain potentially even more devastating than discovering that Claudia had not given birth to her.

She was certain that Claudia would blame herself, but she hoped that she would understand the reason why she had to end her relationship with Ryland. She simply couldn't bear to be the cause of a rift between Ryland and his family. His aunt and Ryland, too, belonged to the élite of Boston society—a society that she had heard attached great importance to family background. How would *they* feel about Ryland marrying her? Tara already knew the answer. That Ryland loved her, she didn't for one moment doubt, but sometimes love was just not enough.

She hadn't dared allow herself to ring him in Boston, frightened that if she did he might hear what she was feeling in her voice and demand to know what was wrong. When she told him, she wanted it to be in person. She wanted, if she was honest, to hold him, to be held by him one last time before she revealed the truth. She wanted...

She wanted Ryland, she admitted, closing her eyes on the pointless tears she knew she was going to shed.

* * *

It was gone three in the morning when Ryland let himself into Tara's flat. There had been a delay at Heathrow before they could land and then another with the luggage, but finally he was here—home.

Dropping his case and his jacket, he picked his way through the darkness of the sitting room and opened the bedroom door.

Tara was lying star fashion, arms and legs outstretched, across their bed, her eyelashes ridiculously long against her sleep-flushed skin, her hair curling wildly in glorious abandon around her head, one deliciously rounded breast exposed where the duvet had slipped away from her body.

Ryland discovered that his throat had suddenly gone dry in the flood of aching arousal that gripped him. He had noticed Tara's breasts the first time they met, noticed them and wondered...wished...

He started undressing without taking his eyes off her. He *couldn't* take his eyes off her; he was afraid if he did she might disappear, a mirage conjured up by his intense longing for her. One pink foot had escaped from under the duvet. Grinning to himself, he bent towards it. She hated his touching her feet, she always claimed. She was so sensitive, they were so ticklish, that even his breathing on them sent her into paroxysms of giggles.

Very, very carefully he kissed one pink digit. In her sleep, Tara's lips parted as she gave an almost soundless soft sigh, her mouth starting to curl upwards.

Smiling himself, Ryland cupped her foot and slowly started to suck on her toe.

'Mmm…' Ryland could feel the shiver of pleasure that curled her toes and tightened the muscles in her leg as she responded to the sensuality of his embrace. He stroked the bare skin with his fingertips and sucked a little harder.

'Ooooh…' Tara shot up in bed, her eyes wide open as she stared in disbelief at Ryland. 'Ry! Ry…oh, Ry, when did you get back?' she demanded, flinging herself into his arms, torn between tears and laughter.

'Just now,' he told her mock-complainingly. 'Why did you have to go and wake up? I was just beginning to enjoy myself.'

'No, you weren't, you fibber. You were trying to torment me,' Tara said, giggling.

'Mmm…talking of torment,' Ryland murmured in between the hotly passionate kisses they were sharing, 'have you *any* idea just how much I've missed you?'

'Missed me, have you?'

'Mmm…want to know how much?'

Their kisses were growing longer and deeper, the words that separated them shorter and more breathless until they weren't talking at all, the only sound to break the silence of their bedroom the heightened tension of their breathing and the soft sound of their mouths meeting and fusing.

Tara shivered in delight as Ryland cupped her face to kiss her more intently and then broke away to look into her eyes before kissing her again, watching her this time as she was watching him. Her eyes closed only when his hands started to lovingly stroke the full length of her body.

She loved it when Ryland made love to her like this, slowly and oh, so thoroughly, taking his time, making *her* wait, making them *both* wait.

She gave a small, soft groan as his hands cupped her breasts, his thumbs rubbing sensuously against her tight nipples, her stomach muscles already tensing in expectation and anticipation.

'Ry...Ry...I can't wait any longer,' she moaned as she reached out for him. 'I've missed you so much. I want you so badly...so very, very badly.'

Later, holding her tightly, watching the dawn break across the sky, Ryland took a deep breath. It couldn't be put off any longer.

'No, Ry, please let me speak first. There's something I *have* to tell you.'

The tension he could feel in her body even more than the anxious uncertainty he could hear in her voice alerted him immediately, causing his own stomach muscles to clench on a sharp sensation of doom.

Although he had firmly pushed such thoughts to one side, the fact that she had not rung him while he had been in Boston, coupled with his own inability to reach her, had caused him to feel uneasy and concerned, to worry that she had somehow already discovered the truth. Despite the fact that the lovemaking and intimacy they had just shared had been so intensely close and special that it had almost moved him to tears, he was suddenly conscious of Tara's distancing herself from him. Not so much physically—she was still lying close within his arms, her body resting against his—but emotionally. He could virtually feel her withdrawing herself from him.

'Tara...' he began, but she shook her head firmly.

'No, Ry, please don't say anything. Just *listen* to me,' she begged. 'This is going to be the hardest thing I have ever had to do, the hardest thing I have ever had to say, and I need you to listen and to...to understand.'

She had rehearsed this conversation over and over inside her head so many times these past few days, but she still stumbled over some of the words, still had to pause and hesitate, to search for what she wanted to say, all the while avoiding looking directly into Ryland's face, knowing that if she did, *once* she did...that if she should see the morning light illuminating his beloved face, she could never, would never...

Taking a deep breath, she began.

'Oh, God, Tara. I should have been here for you,' Ryland burst out, interrupting her at one point as she was telling him what she had learned. 'Please don't hate me too much for not being here. If I had known...'

'I don't hate you, Ry, I could *never* hate you,'

she assured him, her voice choked with tears as she mentally added to herself, but soon you'll hate me.

She could sense the different quality to his silence when she revealed just what kind of person her mother had been, but to her relief he made no attempt to interrupt her or say anything.

'For a little while, I really hated Claudia for what she had done, but...I think I understand her now. There was this woman on the train when I was going to Dorchester. It was so odd...fate, really, I suppose. She turned out to have adopted a little girl herself, and listening to her, I...' She stopped, hesitant. She was waiting, deliberately putting off the moment she was most dreading.

'I've done a lot of thinking while you've been away, Ry and...' Her head dipped down as she turned her face completely away from him. 'I...I can't marry you, not now...not after what I've learned. It wouldn't be fair to you. Oh, I know you'll say that it doesn't make any difference, that it's *me* you love and that I'm still the same person no matter who gave birth to me, and if there was just you and me to consider then it would be different, but there's not. There's your family and...and the business. I'm not the kind of woman they would want you to marry—to have in the family.'

'Tara, Tara. My God, don't you know that you...you are far, far more important to me than anything, anyone, else,' Ryland declared passionately.

Even though she couldn't bear to see his face, Tara could hear the anguish and the love in his voice.

'You are the woman I *love*, the *only* woman I will ever love, and I don't give a damn about anything or anyone else!'

'You say that now,' Tara countered, finally turning to face him, 'and I know you mean it, but I know, as well, how much your family means to you, and I can't stand the thought that one day you might come to regret marrying me. Your aunt—'

'My aunt's dead, Tara,' Ryland told her heavily. 'She was killed by her own daughter.'

He hadn't meant to tell her quite so abruptly and he could see from her expression just how much he had shocked her.

'*That* was why I had to go home so unexpectedly.' He quickly explained what had happened while Tara listened in loving concern and dismay.

'Oh, Ry, how awful for all of you,' she exclaimed.

'There's something else, something I should have told you weeks ago…months ago,' Ryland said slowly.

Tara could feel her heart starting to race with sick apprehension. Whatever he was about to disclose, she knew it must be serious. What was it? Had he been married before and never told her…had a previous serious relationship…a child…children…? Frantically, her mind raced.

'Ryland…' she began, but he shook his head.

'You've just told me about…about the circumstances of your birth, Tara, and I truly meant it when I said that they don't make the slightest difference to the way I feel. You are the one I love. *You*. And *you* are the same person you have always been to me. I love you for *yourself*, not because of your family background. You could have told me that your parents were criminals of the worst sort and it still wouldn't change my feelings, my love, for you,' he told her emotionally.

And as she looked into his eyes, Tara knew that he was speaking the truth. The knowledge that he loved her so profoundly, so deeply, so all-encompassingly, was like a cool, soothing balm being applied to a rough, sore place. She reached out to touch his face, but he caught hold of her hand, stopping her.

'No. You haven't heard everything I have to say yet,' he said roughly. 'When you were talking about Katriona, you said that what hurt more than anything else was that Claudia had deliberately concealed the truth about a very important part of your life from you.' He took a deep breath. 'There's a very important truth about myself that *I* have kept a secret from you, Tara. Not because… I *wanted* to tell you…fully *intended* to tell you, but…but I was so afraid that it would make you turn away from me, that I would lose you.'

'What is it…what are you talking about?' Tara asked him, her mouth dry and her heart pounding.

'We've talked about the fact that I would take over the family business when my aunt retired,' Ryland began quietly.

'Yes,' Tara agreed. 'You told me that when you said that you were over here to study the British publishing industry, but I don't see—'

'What I omitted to tell you was that in addition to inheriting my aunt's controlling share of the business, I also knew that ultimately I would inherit the bulk of her personal estate.'

When he saw that she was frowning at him in bewilderment, he explained quietly, 'My aunt was a very wealthy woman in her own right, Tara. She…she inherited a good deal of family money and she is…was… We're not talking here about a comfortable inheritance we could tuck away to give to our kids. We're talking…' He took another deep breath. 'My aunt's estate runs into many millions of dollars.'

'*Millions* of dollars?' Tara stared at him in disbelief before repeating shakily, 'Millions of dollars. You mean…is that why she, your family…? Is that why…she wouldn't have wanted you to marry me?' she asked uncertainly. 'Not—'

'The *money* had no bearing at all on her concern about whom I might ultimately marry,' Ryland interrupted her firmly. 'She simply wasn't like that. What worried her…well, she was worried because of Margot, because of Margot's compulsive and dangerous love for Lloyd. Margot's problems hit her very hard and hurt her very badly and I guess I've kinda grown up feeling that I owed it to her to try to make it up to her by—'

'Marrying someone she would have approved of,' Tara supplied quietly for him. 'She would *never* have approved of me, Ryland.'

'You're wrong,' he told her fiercely. 'She would have *loved* you.'

Tara looked away from him, her eyes full of tears. 'No…no, she wouldn't,' she argued, 'and you must have had doubts about…about *me* yourself. If you hadn't, you would have told me…about the money. Why didn't you, Ry? Did you think I might turn out to be a gold-digger, that I might—'

'No…don't be silly,' he protested quickly. 'Quite the opposite. You'd talked a lot about your childhood and about how much you wanted your own children, *our* children, to grow up the way you had done, so I knew… Tara, we live in a very dangerous world. Sometimes, in order to protect our children, we have to curtail the amount of freedom we are able to give them. When I was growing up, I was lucky. My parents are well off rather than rich, but for us, you and me, it will be different. My aunt was an exceedingly rich woman.'

'And now you are an exceedingly rich man.'

'Yes,' Ryland agreed sombrely. 'I wanted to tell you,' he assured her, 'but at the same time I wanted to protect you, to protect our love, to give it a chance to grow.'

Tara blinked away the tears she could feel threatening her, weakening her. 'What is it about me that makes people...you, my parents...feel that I *need* to be protected? Do you really see me as so weak...so naïve...so stupid that I can't be trusted to make my own judgements and my own decisions, to protect *myself*?'

'It isn't your vulnerability that motivates us,' Ryland told her huskily. 'It's our own fear...our fear of losing you,' he explained when she looked questioningly at him. 'We're the ones who are vulnerable because of our love for you. It's *our* awareness of the wonderful uniqueness of you, the irreplaceability of you, that makes us afraid of not being worthy of your love. *We* are afraid of not being good enough for *you*, Tara, not the other way around.'

As she listened to him, Tara could see that he meant every word he was saying.

'I was afraid of telling you the truth in case it drove you away from me,' Ryland admitted quietly.

'I was afraid to tell you the truth because I thought I might lose you,' her mother had said, and for both of them Tara had the same answer, she recognised now.

'How *could* you? How dare you even begin to think, to doubt that *my* love is any less strong and less enduring, any less whole and freely given, than yours?' she challenged Ryland chokily.

'I love *you...you*, the person, Ry...and I'll always love you. I don't care about the money, and right now I don't care too much, either, about the problems we might have to face in the future because of it.

'No, I don't want my children, our children, to grow up in a protective glass bubble that separates them from the rest of the human race—you were right about that—but neither do I want my children to be fathered by any man who isn't you. Somehow we'll find a way to give them some freedom, to let them learn and grow, to value themselves for who they are, not the money they will one day inherit.'

Her voice had grown stronger and more passionate with every word she spoke. Now flushed with emotion, Tara declared heatedly, 'End it all between us because of my background if you must, but *not* to protect me or because you think I'm not strong enough, that my love isn't strong enough to endure.'

'*End* it? Oh, my love, my dearest love, that's the *last* thing I want to do,' Ryland responded fervently, then he reached out to gather her into his arms and held her tightly in a rib-crushing, breath-stopping hug.

Tara raised her head, intending to speak to him, but discovered instead that what she was actually doing was kissing him.

'I love you so much,' he told her thickly as he kissed her back. 'So very, very much.' He kissed her again and one kiss led to another and then another.

'Try telling me *now* that you don't love me,' Ryland challenged her when he eventually held her still-dewy, relaxed body in his arms.

'You were the one who doubted *my* love...'

Tara started to remind him before checking herself and saying tentatively, 'The money…'

'Forget the money,' Ryland said fiercely. 'I'd rather give it all away than risk losing you, Tara, but I do have a responsibility to my family, the business, my aunt…'

'We could buy some land perhaps, a farm, with some of the money,' Tara suggested sleepily as she nestled closer to him.

He was right. She did find the thought of so much money hard to deal with, but her love for him was such that she knew that being with him was more important to her than any potential problems his wealth could cause.

'And we could stay there with our children. That way they could have *some* freedom and—' she lifted her head and looked at him '—we could give some of it to…to others…charities…?'

'Of course we could,' Ryland confirmed promptly, adding warningly, 'My aunt had several pet charities of her own and I think you'll find that you'll be approached by them to take her place on their fund-raising committees.'

'I thought perhaps one for…for women…girls who—'

'I thought you might be thinking along those lines,' Ryland anticipated her gently, 'and the answer is yes, of course. But first things first, and the first and most important thing we need to do now, at least as far as I'm concerned, is to get married just as soon as we can.'

'My mother will want me to have a traditional wedding,' Tara warned him.

'Yours and mine both,' Ryland agreed.

'The church in Dorset where she…Katriona is buried is very pretty,' Tara told him softly. 'I can't think of her as my mother—Claudia will *always* be that—but…but she *is* a part of me, of my past, my history.'

'We can be married wherever you wish,' Ryland assured her gently before taking her back in his arms and starting to kiss her with tender loving relish.

An hour later as they ate an impromptu meal off their laps, they went through the post that had accumulated during their absence.

'Uh-huh, looks like this one is for you,' Ryland told Tara, tossing her an envelope with an American embassy stamp on it.

'My visa,' Tara guessed before starting to laugh. 'I expect we'll have to reapply now that we're getting married, won't we? Just think, if *this* hadn't been delayed, Ma would probably never have told me about Katriona. She was so desperately afraid that the delay was because they were querying the registration of my birth. Apparently, she's always been worried that some day it *might* be questioned. At first I almost wished that I hadn't had to know, but I'm glad now. In some odd kind of way, it's brought us closer, made me see Ma as more vulnerable and put us more on a par—one adult woman to another adult woman—but please…no more secrets,' she told Ryland lovingly. 'Not one single one, not ever.'

'No more secrets,' Ryland agreed, closing his eyes in mute gratitude. There was no way he could ever condone what Margot had done. He knew *he* would never in a million lifetimes want to deprive Tara of the right to love someone else, or of life itself, but he knew, too, that it would take the heart and soul of *his* life out of him to lose her.

Thankfully, fate and Tara herself had spared him that.

Epilogue

As she left the doctor's surgery and walked
back to her car through the bright spring sunshine, Tara patted her stomach, her mouth curled
into a hugely triumphant little-girl grin.

She drove home carefully, mindful of the new
life she was now responsible for. She had known
about the baby already, of course, but having her
doctor's confirmation made it fully official.

As she let herself into the pretty New England
house she and Ryland had bought in the same
small town where his family lived, there was
only one thing on her mind, one person.

Eagerly, she picked up the telephone, her
mouth still curved in a wide, happy smile, then
quickly punched in the numbers.

When she heard the voice responding at the
other end of the line, she burst into immediate
excited speech, exclaiming, 'Guess what…I'm
pregnant! I wanted you to be the first to know.'
She started to laugh as she heard the other person's response. 'I couldn't wait to tell
you…Grandma!' she told Claudia, chuckling as
her mother replied enthusiastically. 'Not even Ry
knows officially yet. I wanted to be sure *you* were
the first to know,' she repeated softly, her own

eyes filling with emotional tears as she heard the huskiness in Claudia's voice. 'And I want you to be here for the birth,' she declared warmly.

In the background, she could hear her father demanding to know who was on the line and then he, too, came on, congratulating her and reminding her that it would only be a matter of days before they flew over to Boston to see them.

'I know that, but I couldn't wait that long,' she said simply. 'I wanted you to know now.'

She was still beaming five minutes later when she replaced the receiver.

The rift that had threatened to destroy the relationship between her and Claudia was completely healed now and, if anything, Tara felt closer to her mother than ever before. Her work with deprived youngsters through the charity she and Ryland had established in his aunt's name had given her a deeper insight into the problems that could afflict children when they were deprived of parental love, and she had now seen for herself what could happen when drug-addicted mothers, however much they might love their children, quite simply put the needs of their habit first.

Tara had settled easily and comfortably into the life of small-town New England. 'Why shouldn't I?' she had asked Ryland lovingly when he had commented on this fact. Her home was within herself, encompassed by the love they shared. She missed her family and friends, of course, especially Claudia, but in the eighteen months of their marriage, she and Ryland had travelled back to the UK for several visits and had had her parents over to visit with them, as indeed they were due back again at the end of the week.

She and Ryland had spent their first Christmas together as man and wife in Britain with her parents.

Garth and Claudia had remarried one another in a quiet ceremony three days before Christmas, and Claudia had been glowing with love and happiness as Garth slipped her old wedding ring back on her finger.

Quick tears momentarily filmed Tara's eyes as she remembered the day of her own wedding.

She and Claudia had been together in her bedroom. She had been standing in her wedding finery while Claudia fussed nervously around her.

'Ma, I still haven't thanked you for all of this,' she had told her, her gesture encompassing not just her dress but all the formidable organisation that had gone into making her wedding possible despite the short notice that Ryland's impatience had demanded. 'And I…I haven't told you, either, how much…how much I love you and how very, very glad I am that you are my mother.'

She had seen Claudia shaking her head and guessed instinctively what she was going to say. She turned to hug her fiercely, ignoring her protests that she might spoil her dress.

'Don't say it. You *are* my mother, the best mother anyone could ever have and the only mother I could ever want. You *are* my mother and, even more so, I am your child. You're the one who has nurtured me, loved me, taught me, shown me. You are my mother.'

Later in the day as she emerged from the church, she had overheard one of the onlookers who had gathered outside the gate telling her friend, 'Oh, look, there's her mother. They look so alike, don't they? You can tell immediately that they're mother and daughter.'

Instinctively, she had looked across at Claudia to share the moment with her, her eyes brimming with a tearful mixture of love and laughter; the same love and laughter she could see filling Claudia's own.

'So it's official, then?' Ryland asked, kissing Tara's still-flat stomach.

'Yes,' she confirmed. 'I rang Ma the moment I got back from the surgery. I wanted her to be the first to know. I want her to be here for the birth,' she warned him.

'Of course,' Ryland agreed tenderly. 'After all, she *is* your mother.'

'Yes,' Tara agreed. 'She *is*…she is!'

A random predator is terrorizing Southern California. After children start disappearing, it's up to the FBI's finest to stop a killer...

RANDOM ACTS

Criminal profiler **Laurel Madden** is at the top of her field. But Agent Madden has a dark side and even darker secrets—which is why she understands the criminal mind so well.

Claire Gillespie is a reporter assigned to cover the case. She has another more personal agenda: to rip away the veil of secrecy that surrounds and protects Madden. Claire has evidence that the FBI top agent committed murder—and got away with it...until now.

Dan Sprague is the veteran FBI agent who stands between the two determined women—torn by duty and loyalty to one woman and an intense attraction to the other....

From the bestselling author of *The Best of Enemies*...

TAYLOR SMITH

MIRA BOOKS

Available mid-September 1998 where books are sold.

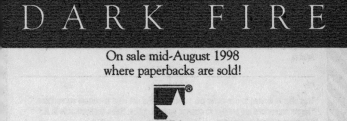

Take 2 of
"The Best of the Best™"
Novels FREE
Plus get a FREE surprise gift!

Watch for this upcoming title by
New York Times **bestselling sensation**

Cage Hendren was his twin Hal's opposite in every way.
Hal was dedicated to a worthy cause; Cage was the black
sheep of the family. Hal graciously allowed his fiancée,
Jenny, to help him with his work; Cage just loved her
with all his heart. When Hal died, Jenny was carrying
what she thought was his child. Now Cage had to trust
that the memory of his tender passion—rather than his
deception—would be enough to show her she'd been
with the wrong brother all along....

On sale mid-August 1998
where paperbacks are sold!

MIRA

MSB427

Her face was a mask
that hid the scars on her soul....

GIRL IN THE MIRROR

Years ago, Charlotte Godowski had become
Charlotte Godfrey at the hands of a brilliant cosmetic
surgeon. She had traded horrified stares for the
adulation of Hollywood, loneliness and mockery for
power, fame and love. She thought she was truly happy
and that her secret could be kept forever—until she
realized that as long as the swan still sees the ugliest of
ducklings in its reflection, so might
the world....

MARY ALICE MONROE

On sale mid-August 1998
where paperbacks are sold!

MIRA

MMAM451